from PROMISE *to* PERIL

A Family Saga

TRACKS OF OUR
TEARS TRILOGY

JAMES ALLEN

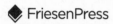

Suite 300 - 990 Fort St
Victoria, BC, V8V 3K2
Canada

www.friesenpress.com

ISBN
978-1-5255-8664-4 (Hardcover)
978-1-5255-8665-1 (Paperback)
978-1-5255-8666-8 (eBook)

1. FICTION, HISTORICAL, WORLD WAR II

Distributed to the trade by The Ingram Book Company

A Dedication

"Love does not consist in gazing at each other but in looking outward together in the same direction."

-Antoine de Saint Exupéry

In memory of my best friend in life to whom I will be forever grateful; for her spirited opinions and her total absence of fear for expressing them. Always faithful, forever supportive, she sustained me, she nourished me. She honoured me with her love in ways I can never fully understand or deserve. She was and always will be, my inspiration to have written this book and any others that follow. My darling wife for almost fifty years, I will miss you eternally Regina, until we meet again.

"When the golden sun is setting, and the road of life you've trod, may our names in gold, together, be written in the autograph of God."

-Regina Allen, December 1967

CHAPTER ONE

♂

IT WAS AN EVOLUTIONARY PERIOD IN HISTORY. THE Industrial Revolution had broken across the shores of Britain and flooded inexorably across Western Europe, changing among other things, the course of prosperity. In its wake, this "tsunami of capitalism" impacted the world for better and for worse.

At this time, Germany was comprised of numerous independent states—Prussia by far the most dominant among them. Politically and economically, there were major inefficiencies hindering the achievement of competitive advantage. Co-operative consolidation was required among these states to more efficiently meet the seemingly unattainable demands created by Germany's insatiable domestic appetite.

In response, a unified Prussia enacted tariffs on imports and removed existing tolls on domestic production within its provincial borders. These actions were critical to enabling Germany's industrial might to be unleashed. By so doing, Germany surpassed the production capacity of Great Britain in the late nineteenth century, primarily fueled by its people's limitless demands and boundless natural resources.

With successful industrialization came human suffering. This is a story of the constant struggle of humanity—people struggling not by premeditative choice, but by the condition and personal circumstances of the times in which they lived.

*****

Zeev Landesburg was raised as a young farm hand working on a small dairy farm in southwest Germany in the state of Baden-Württemberg. The rolling green pastures at the foot of the Bavarian Alps spread their glory to the open abundance of thousands of acres of rich grasslands. The air was ripe with the strong odor of nature providing the perfect balance of fresh breezes that caressed the open and expansive plains visibly rippling across the tall grasses. It was a most welcome daily cleansing that effectively carried the pungent stenches of urine and cow manure across the plains to diffuse inoffensively somewhere other than here.

It was the only life Zeev had known and it was difficult for him to imagine anything different, hence his subconscious acceptance of his natural pathway in life. In the not-so-distant past, he hadn't even considered he had other choices. As they did their best to carve out a modest living, he and his young wife Dahlia supplied the locals and themselves with a steady supply of fresh milk and a few other dairy products.

The advent of the milking machine however, immediately created a competitive advantage for this much more efficient milking method, enabling not only much greater quantities of production, but also a cleaner and purer product for human consumption. This unprecedented alternative inevitably changed the dairy industry completely, affecting thousands of small dairy farmers in a manner they had never imagined. Zeev was one of these so affected.

To bring matters to a head, he and Dahlia had just become the parents of their first and only son, Sigmund.

After another extraordinarily long and arduous day, which had become all too frequent, Zeev half dragged himself from the barn. He could smell the hot dinner beckoning him home. A few kerosene lamps dimly lighted his short walk to the farmhouse where Dahlia had his hot bath already waiting. Within a half hour he settled in for his dinner. He expected to be asleep within the hour.

Dahlia kissed his forehead as she did every night, and Zeev looked hungrily at his heaping plate of roasted chicken and potatoes. "You take such good care of me and the boy, sweetheart. I think I would die of starvation were it not for you. I would be too damned tired to prepare anything for myself."

It was the summer of 1872. Sigmund was a healthy baby boy of only three months of age. After his feeding, as was his habit, he continued to gnaw on his tiny, clenched fist, indicating he wanted more than his mother had already provided. Dahlia placed him lovingly in the handmade cradle fashioned by Zeev, while the young couple bowed their heads for the blessings that had been bestowed on them. Within seconds Zeev savored his first sumptuous mouthful and closed his eyes thankfully. He should have eaten hours ago, but when day's end was within reach, he continually pushed himself a little longer to get a better head start the following day. He quickly devoured every tasty morsel.

After their usual light banter and a well-deserved shot of vodka, the customary review of the day turned to more serious discussion.

"Day by day I'm coming to the reluctant conclusion that I can only work as hard and as long as is humanly possible, and the same can be said for you now that you have the boy to attend to. I can't seem to keep up with the bigger farms using these new-fangled milking machines everyone is talking about, no matter how hard I try. We can't afford to buy our own equipment, and I don't want to work a farm owned by someone else. It's an adjustment I don't think we can make. You can see our predicament too, Dahlia. I know you do."

"Yes, of course I do, but I didn't want to say it for fear of discouraging you. That's not something I would do to you Zeev. You always tell me that through tough times we must simply stay our course. That's precisely what I am doing."

"You know I'm not one to easily accept defeat but maybe this time, I was wrong."

"What is this all about, Zeev? It's the first time I've heard those words coming from your mouth. It's so unlike you to speak of these things."

"I must tell you I've been giving serious thought to selling the herd to some of the locals. We can fetch a pretty penny for these Ayrshires and the quality of the milk is in good demand. I wanted to discuss it with you first. It's a decision that will affect all three of us."

"But what would we do, Zeev? It's all we know; we've the boy to think about now too."

"He's the one I'm thinking about, Dahlia. This is no life for him. There must be something better in his future and it's not going to happen if we stay here busting our asses. Most of the villagers are thinking the same thing. The sooner we sell what we have, the better our price, and the sooner we settle somewhere in Berlin. Thousands of outsiders are resettling near to the city and the competition for jobs will be even tougher. My cousin has a decent job in an established machine shop there and they need reliable help. I think I should accept it, sweetheart, before someone else does."

Forced to adapt on the small farm, Zeev had become more than a farmer. He was a jack-of-all-trades with the gift of common sense and a natural adeptness with anything mechanical. In the weeks ahead, and backed by Dahlia's unflagging support, they apprehensively accepted the opportunity before them and prepared to leave the confines of the village for the burgeoning big city of Berlin.

Zeev had been correct about one thing; his herd consisted of prime dairy cattle and the auction fetched him top dollar. Other than a minimum of personal items, the auction also sold off the contents of the house and what remained of his once self-sufficient dairy and farming assets. Now he and Dahlia had their modest nest egg in hand to sustain them on their journey, until he could once again provide for the family's needs.

*****

The train route to Berlin was the most restful time the Landesburg family had ever experienced. It was transformative to take in the now prevalent rolling hills as they watched the final vestiges of the Bavarian Alps defining the distant borders of their familiar world. By nightfall the hills became shrouded in the darkness, leaving no visible frame of reference to be seen from the dimly lit interior of the railcar. It wasn't long after when Zeev also succumbed to his growing fatigue to join Dahlia and Sigmund in the depths and comfort of deep sleep.

By dawn's early light Zeev awoke to the sounds of screeching iron wheels as the train negotiated an almost imperceptible gradual turn to the northeast. Upon getting his bearings, he found Dahlia already tenderly nursing young Sigmund. "Good morning, sweetheart. I didn't intend to slip away that long, but I find the swaying of the train restful. Did you get much sleep yourself?"

"Oh, quite enough, Zeev. Once I start Sigmund's feedings I often drift in and out until he falls back to sleep. I'm a little drowsy but I'll be fine, sweetheart."

"Here, let me take him for a while. You must walk about a bit and get something to eat for yourself. I'll be just fine."

"Thank you dear. I'll see if I can get us both some coffee and pastry."

Once they shuffled about and Zeev had the baby securely rewrapped, his attention was drawn to the network of railway tracks stretching their way across flat, open land, as if stitching together the geographic diversity of central Germany. In no time there was sufficient light to enable him to discern the dingy, grey warehouses running adjacent to the tracks and the general suburban street traffic now reawakening to face another day. The scene overcame him with flashes of doubt and uncertainty. Compared to the beautiful open vistas he was accustomed to seeing and the scent of freshness in the air he'd once taken for granted, his first impressions of the outskirts of Berlin were not at all inspiring.

Within the next hour the train slowed perceptively when the density of taller buildings in the southwest corner of the city swallowed them whole and completely blocked the beams of early morning sunshine rising from the east. The streets were bustling with people coming from all directions as they funneled their way to the main streets of the city, crowding the sidewalks to the limits of their capacity. Zeev and Dahlia likely had similar uncertain impressions but were disinclined to share them with each other, being aware the option of turning back was not open for consideration. The only way was forward.

Within minutes of stopping, the blasting sounds of compressed steam were released from the engine. The porter assisted Zeev with the unloading of his family's limited possessions, seeing as Dahlia's hands were well occupied with the baby's care. They needed very little space on the vastness of the platform as hundreds of similar families scrambled to keep their belongings and their families huddled close together. Once inside the terminal, Zeev had no idea what to expect amidst this sea of humanity, the likes of which he had never experienced.

"Just stay as close to me as you can, sweetheart. I'll find a post or something to lean against to keep the crowds away from you. We don't know what to expect once we are all inside."

In true fashion Dahlia confidently suggested, "Don't worry about us, Zeev. None of our things really matter, as long as the baby is safe. I'll see to that!"

The most difficult moment was descending the forty-foot-deep steps leading down to the main terminal. No one among the crowd had so much as an empty hand to grasp the handrails. It was amazing no one stumbled because if they had, everyone would likely have rolled down the staircase to stop precariously on top of a small mountain of startled and injured travelers. It would have been a rude welcoming for these mostly rural farm laborers.

Fortunately, there was no such incident, and the priority was now solely focused upon locating Zeev's cousin Piotr, who had graciously offered to meet the family in view of the intimidating surroundings in which these newcomers would evidently find themselves.

Within fifteen minutes when the crowds had dissipated sufficiently, sure enough Zeev found his cousin. Piotr was clutching his cap in one hand while rubbing his head with the other, no doubt becoming exasperated with the exhausting strain and worry of trying to locate his cousin's familiar face and those of his family, whom Piotr had not yet met.

*****

Piotr was four years younger than Zeev and being unmarried, he only had a small room with a makeshift kitchen to offer for a few nights. It was adequate and must have been a terrible inconvenience, but he showed no remorse for having offered it to them. "I remember my first day in Berlin, so I know what you are probably feeling right now. Trust me, within a few days you will adjust. The money you will earn here is good, but you will work hard for it."

"We are used to that, Piotr, have no fear. But I must ask, are the streets always so busy with people? It's much worse than we imagined," Zeev asked.

"You and me came from small villages, where everyone knew everyone. Here, huh, despite so damned many people you won't know any of them. Within two weeks you won't even notice them, nor will they notice you. None of them give a shit about you or anyone else. The sooner you accept that the better."

Dahlia stayed mostly quiet, letting the men carry on with each other. She had nothing to contribute at this time and was learning a great deal from their rambling conversation.

"Tomorrow I will take you with me to the factory. You don't have anything to worry about, I promise you. Most of the workers are too stupid to say anything of value and the bosses there are fair, as long as you work hard and pretend you give a good god damn. We hardly ever see the big boss, but him and his foremen run a tight ship, Zeev. You are smarter than the others and you're used to hard work. It won't be long before the bosses take notice of you."

By next day, Zeev knew his cousin spoke the truth. Enroute to the factory, he was so immersed in conversation with Piotr, he really didn't seem aware of the thousands of strangers he was jostling with. He assumed Piotr would be just as correct about his new workplace; Piotr was.

Stottletter Iron Forging had been established over ten years prior and specialized in the design and manufacture of machine parts. Steel supplies came into the plant at one end and left out the other on heavy pallets loaded with iron-forged locomotive parts destined for a nearby, massive assembly factory known as the Borsig Company, owned by just one man, August Borsig.

Borsig's first locomotive had come off the line back in 1840, and with its innovative design he'd defied the very skeptical establishment by challenging a major, well-established, British locomotive manufacturer to a highly publicized race, in which he beat the British standard by ten minutes—a very significant accomplishment.

This event proved to his critics that for the first time, German engineering and manufacturing could compete with the British. This effectively meant it was no longer necessary to import foreign manufactured locomotives. In rapid order, Germany became an industrial colossus. Stottletter Iron Forging became a major supplier of the machine parts for Borsig, thereby ensuring its successful future as well.

In less than a year, Herr Stottletter noticed Zeev's potential. A key to Stottletter's success was his ability to adapt to changing business circumstances and he had a keen ability to sort out the laggers from the most dedicated hard workers. Catching the notice of his foremen, Zeev quickly acclimated to the continuous stresses involved in keeping the production lines up to speed, and that ever-so-uncommon asset, common sense. It was these assets that launched Zeev's career under Stottletter's trusted direction. In no time, Zeev was promoted to lead hand and was financially compensated to reflect his new responsibilities. It was the first indication that indeed his employer was a fair man.

Over the next few years, the sometimes-backbreaking work took its toll on many of the once-stalwart young laborers. This day would start out as an ordinary one, until Zeev was summoned to Stottletter's front office. Intrigued, he wiped the grease from his gnarled hands and quickly washed up before his meeting. The office was always kept in a state of pristine cleanliness. It was an obsession among top management.

Upon seeing Zeev enter the main office, Herr Stottletter turned to greet him and directed him to his private office while he concluded his prior discussion with one of his bookkeepers. "Be right with you Zeev. Go take a seat."

As Stottletter entered behind Zeev, he shouted, "Mable, please fetch a hot coffee for Zeev, would you?" He closed his door firmly behind him.

"Everyone well at home, Zeev? How's the boy doing in school?"

"Just fine sir, thanks for asking."

"Listen, as you may know, Gunter is having some physical difficulties with his bloody arthritis. It's becoming too painful for him working in the back. The old bugger's been with us since I first opened these doors and as you have already seen, I reward loyalty when it's due. This is one of those cases. I've decided to bring him into the office to finish his career with us."

"I'm sure he appreciates that, sir. I'm delighted you can do that for him. He's earned your respect. If I may ask, sir, how does that affect me? What can I do to help?"

"Always straightforward, Zeev. I like that about you. You can start by taking his place out back, as our newest foreman. He earned his spot, and by God you've earned yours, every goddamned day, Zeev! If I've ruffled any feathers back there, which I don't believe I have, you just come to me if you and your men can't work it out among yourselves. I'm grooming you for something more one day, Zeev, so consider this just another step forward. You OK with that?" he said as he slapped Zeev's arm with his usual display of affection.

"I am, Herr Stottletter. Of course, I am! Thank you for your confidence in me. I know you must have had other alternatives to replace Gunter, but I am delighted you chose me. I will not disappoint you, sir."

"Gunter is here to teach you the ropes, so to speak. It won't take long before you'll catch on, I'm sure of it. Congratulations, young man! And give my best regards to Dahlia, as always."

Soon thereafter, their relationship had extended well beyond the confines of the business. It became one of interdependence and personal support. In fact, over time Zeev and Dahlia solicited Herr Stottletter to become Sigmund's guardian, an honor he was eager to accept. Since Stottletter had no children of his own, Sigmund was taken under Stottletter's wing to such an extent as Dahlia and Zeev could never have conceived.

*****

It was a typical day, much as any other, when Herr Stottletter was overseeing the installation of a central-heating system that needed replacement before the oncoming cold winter season. It was a rare occasion for him to make an appearance in the shop, as he was usually preoccupied with office and other management matters. On this day, however, he was particularly intrigued to personally inspect the final installation of this state-of-the-art technology. He was a professional engineer and still enjoyed dabbling in more than paperwork.

"We don't often see you back here, boss. Can I help with anything?" questioned one of the shop foremen.

"No, not at all. Just snooping around this new heating system I heard so much about. To be honest with you, Francis, sometimes I just need to get the hell out of the office for a while. It's easy to get out of touch with my own staff, you know."

"Make yourself at home Boss. Careful you don't get dirty though. There's lots of dust and grease back here till this thing's properly cleaned up. As you can see, we had to remove part of the shop wall to get this beast in place, so just keep an eye out, OK?"

"Will do, Francis. Don't let me distract you."

Stottletter stood examining the installation through some left-over debris near to the removed portion of the shop wall. "You boys will have all this mess cleaned up before you head home tonight will you not?"

"No worries, sir. It will be done, sure as shit."

Suddenly, without warning, there was a loud bang, followed immediately by a screeching of steel on steel that could be heard by everyone throughout the warehouse. Before anyone could react, a high-speed flywheel exploded from its normally well-anchored moorings and sped through the opening in the wall. Instantly, Stottletter collapsed to the floor, losing blood before he had time to grab his severely gashed thigh. It happened so suddenly he had not yet even felt the excruciating pain. Within seconds he realized he had been seriously injured.

"Oh my God! Help me! Help me!" Stottletter screamed in terror.

Francis was the closest to him when he hollered "Holy shit! We need help over here, boys! Come quick! The boss is down!"

Unsure as to what to do, Francis just kneeled there, helplessly cradling Stottletter's head as he writhed in pain in the middle of a growing pool of blood on the concrete floor. Two or three others arrived and again were overwhelmed by the scene, totally unprepared as to what to do.

Zeev heard the commotion from the fabrication department on the far side of the warehouse and raced to the scene, along with several others. As he quickly assessed the horrific scene before him, he knew immediately Stottletter would bleed out in a matter of minutes without proper remedial action.

"Calm down boys! Call the hospital *now*! We need an ambulance in the next few minutes, or we will lose him. Somebody get lots of ice to pack his leg…quickly!"

Without hesitation, Zeev snapped his leather belt away from his waist and quickly rolled it around his left hand. "Someone get some blankets to keep him warm…he's already lost a lot of blood. We don't want him going into shock. And I need a leather punch from the shop right away! You! Hold fast to this and don't let go whatever you do. Ready? It's just blood, boys. We've all got it. Come on now, stay alert."

He unraveled his thick belt, pulling it very tightly as he carefully ensured it was not twisted and wound it securely around Stottletter's thigh above the gaping wound. "I need that punch! Where is it? Wilhelm, I can hear the siren. Go outside and get the medics in here pronto. Stop gawking and go now! We need every second. He's losing consciousness. Come on Dietrich, hold on."

Zeev refused to ease the pressure and held fast to his grip until the kid raced back with the leather punch. "You hold this very tight. Do not let it loosen. Do you understand?"

He grabbed the small punch press and quickly estimated where the new belt hole should fasten. Once completed, he locked the belt tightly, using it as a makeshift tourniquet. The loss of blood had been extensive, but the tourniquet would all but stop the blood flow. Next, he and Francis packed Stottletter's thigh in ice, and held it in place by wrapping a blanket tightly around the wound with the belt still holding in place.

The medics raced to the spot where Stottletter continued to lie. He had started shaking violently within the saturated bloody blankets due to the blood loss and dropping blood pressure. It was an ugly scene.

"Thank God you were here, Zeev. I didn't know what the hell to do. Well done, Zeev!"

Zeev knew the odds were very much against his friend's survival despite having done the best he could to save him. He was in God's hands now.

*****

Zeev's courageous effort to step forward in the absence of any viable alternative was the deciding factor that ultimately saved Stottletter's life, though sadly, his left leg had to be amputated well above the knee. His fighting spirit and pragmatic outlook on life eventually enabled him to return to work. His days of strolling through the shop however were over. "Enough of that bullshit!" he jokingly stated. "You are my eyes and ears now, Zeev."

Over the course of almost thirteen years of service, Sigmund's father had proven his reliability time after time, and this accomplishment distinguished him as a loyal and worthy junior partner for Stottletter. Due in no small part to his loyalty and dedication, the business would not have to be sold by the estate after the potentially fatal accident.

Following his recovery in 1885, an appreciative Stottletter made Zeev a one-third partner in Stottletter Iron. His reasoning was that without Zeev's heroic intervention, Stottletter couldn't take any ownership to his grave had he died on the concrete floor. In his mind, the least he could do in return was to provide well for the financial security of Zeev's family's future.

It was an appreciative and most generous gesture of his gratitude for the life he thought to have lost. Sigmund's father's actions had pulled this thriving business from the brink of a takeover that would have yielded pennies on the dollar to the Stottletter estate and little to nothing to the Landesburg family. The twists of life are such that kindness and dedication can ultimately be rewarded, perhaps in ways never intended. In this case, they surely were.

This was the single event, never anticipated nor predetermined, that would always remind Sigmund of the new course of life about to open for him. It was a defining moment of happenstance, now presented to him in this most formative time of his young life. As a consequence of one man's misfortune and another man's opportunity, a life of privilege awaited Sigmund, having been inevitably altered from its natural modest course.

Sigmund reveled in the opportunities before him, all of which were provided by his mother and father and his benefactor, Herr Stottletter. His grades had always been outstanding, a point of fact never in question. It was his intuitive inquisitiveness and thorough comprehension of matters far beyond his years, which were frequently manifested by the way he devoured books. This literary appetite and his natural adeptness at advanced mathematics were what distinguished him. Stottletter felt strongly he'd made a considerable and deserved investment in this young man, promising to yield possibilities of an outstanding future soon to be realized.

This enterprising young man would become the first member of his family to break the endless cycle of industrial labor his father and his ancestors had always known. Were it not for his father's unflagging dedication to his family and the generosity of his employer, the course of Sigmund's life would have remained inauspicious, perhaps even ordinary.

Sigmund strongly believed in the nobility of hard work, which could only be matched by that of his dear father, who was now approaching his mid-fifties. Superior intellect and steadfast work ethic would prove to be a magnificent combination.

*****

Admission to the Friedrich Wilhelm University in Berlin in 1889 offered many challenges for Sigmund, not only for academic achievement within this historic institution, but also for the maturity of his character and his social acceptance among his peers.

There were only 160,000 Jews living throughout Berlin, and for those fortunate enough to pursue higher education, each of them had no doubt experienced similar treatment from the students and faculty alike. They simply did not achieve the status and recognition other non-Jewish alumnae received. Although not blatantly discriminatory, there was an underlining current of animosity appearing reserved for the Jews and other ethnicities representing a relatively small minority of the student body.

To be certain, friendships still developed among these enterprising young men and women, despite the differences of ancestral beliefs. However, within a short time, Sigmund's effusive personality and superior intellect distinguished him as someone to be revered by his colleagues.

Young Sigmund could never be accused of conceit or egotism in any way. His proactive and self-confident approach to life was occasionally misinterpreted as arrogance, but for those who knew him, the genuine enthusiasm and deep consideration he had toward others in all manner of things, established him very naturally as an equal.

CHAPTER TWO

By the end of his freshman year in 1889, Sigmund had become increasingly popular among the academics and was one of the few who set the highest standards for both intellectual achievement and being unafraid of challenging the status quo. On the subjective matters of philosophy for example, he accepted little on face value, often questioning the merits of outdated concepts that had little relevance in the new world. His logical arguments stimulated his peers and his professors alike, in ways they found to be both refreshing and insightful.

In his second year, these leadership qualities were appreciated not only in the classrooms, but also among his athletic associates when it was announced he had made the active team roster. His first year on the football team he was only used sparingly, but he travelled with his teammates and worked out at every practice. His work ethic and budding physical prowess were unmistakable.

As a sophomore, when not surrounded by his academic colleagues, he quickly became the center of attention of his teammates. It was not uncommon to see him chide his buddies with jokes and good-natured ribbing, often at their expense. He also had the unique ability to display a self-deprecating sense of humor, serving to permit more latitude when teasing his close friends. This behavior demonstrated his natural proclivity to never allow himself to take life too seriously.

His aggressive, yet strategic play on the football pitch distinguished him as a fierce adversary. This young man was a long and lean athlete who frequently showcased his speed and agility inside the boundary of competitive play. Needless to say, these attributes made him a popular teammate among his peers. Sigmund deserved the general acclaim his chiseled features and robust personality had attracted. It would require something, or someone quite extraordinary, to intrude upon his well-established and self-imposed limitations of focused priorities.

It was the end of the summer season and the playoff rounds were well underway. In the finals, the season standings had pitted Wilhelm University against Goethe, out of Frankfurt. One hot and humid afternoon after a particularly strenuous practice, the team was visibly exhausted as they exited the football pitch, many of them still sucking air from stretching the limits of their stamina. Their coaches had driven them hard that day and reminded them to drink plenty of fluids after the game to avoid muscle cramping. They chose beer.

"Maybe if you hadn't been pounding down the ale till all hours of the night with the commoners, you wouldn't have so much lead in your ass this afternoon. I suppose a real man could have handled it though, right mate?"

"What the hell would you know about the life of a commoner, Your Highness?" Fritz retorted as he bumped Sigmund good-naturedly. "Your mother would never let you stay out late enough to ever understand real life, my boy!"

Sigmund affectionately extended his muscled arm around Fritz' broad shoulders exclaiming, "What say we hoist a few pints at the inn with some of the boys? It was hot as a bitch out there today. We've earned a few!"

"You buying, you cheap bastard? I'm in!"

"Me as well Sig. No game tomorrow, so what the hell!" Ignacio exclaimed. "I'll rustle up a few more of the boys. See you there in about an hour?"

The impromptu get together was enthusiastically arranged, and about a dozen of the young men soon assembled at the Library Bar at the Grand Hostel Hotel. They took up their usual tables, perfectly positioned to provide the best view of the usual array of young beauties, which always provoked flirtatious comments from their admiring heroes. It was a place where these adorable young women practiced their seductive gestures to the point of perfection; the newest ones learning from the seniors to elicit just the right degree of lasciviousness to seduce any one of these athletic catches.

As always, the girls had a few of the boys in play, and some of these relationships were already forged. The players knew who was spoken for and which of the girls were still eligible. They respected the unwritten guidelines for each other and did their best to avoid crossing the line. It was the strength of this brotherhood that reinforced their loyalty to each other, both on and off the field of play.

"We only have another five days before the final. Our strikers and wingmen look solid, but I still have concerns Heinrich's injury leaves us weak on the left side defensively. Any chance he'll be able to compete by Saturday, Nick?" Sigmund asked.

"The boy's a fighter, through and through. He's got great drive and spirit and is still in tremendous condition. Will his knee hold up to the strain of the game? That's the question. I'm betting he'll come through and steady the defense, same as he has all season. Coach seems to think so too."

"I agree. This is no time to have… to ha… I'll be damned!"

"To have what? What the hell is wrong with you Sig? Hey! I'm over here!" Nicholai waved his hands with exasperation.

Nick's animated gesture was enough to catch the interest of his teammates, who also saw what was happening. Undeterred by his teammates, Sigmund's attention remained fixated directly over Nicholai's left shoulder.

Nicholai turned around to see what could have possibly distracted his friend so visibly, and to no one's surprise there at the bar sat a new girl. This young beauty was indeed a vision. Her gorgeous, soft curls gathered about her shoulders as she stared right back at Sigmund. She wore a tight-fitting but stylish dress highlighting her stunningly long legs, leaving her sexy knee subtly exposed. She not only caught Sigmund's attention, she also demanded it. It was as if a spell had been cast over both.

With barely a heartbeat of hesitation, Nicholai stood up, shaking his head with incredulity, and walked directly to her seat at the bar. With a grin of confidence, he calmly addressed her. "Hello Miss. Please forgive my interruption. My name is Nick. I couldn't help but notice you appear to have placed my friend under your spell. Until now, I've never seen him at such a total loss for words."

Without shifting her gaze from Sigmund, she calmly and politely replied, "Hello Nick."

"Would you permit me to introduce you to each other?" as he extended his hand to hers, gently placing it on his arm to escort her to his own chair next to Sigmund.

Totally out of character, Sigmund fumbled and awkwardly stood up as she offered her hand to meet his. Neither one had broken eye contact.

"Hello, I don't believe we have met. My name is Marissa." It was all she had to say. He was mesmerized.

It only took minutes before Sigmund loosened up and became his usual silver tongued, twinkly eyed self. The boys were quite taken by Marissa too, and of course, her lovely companion Elisabeth, who had no difficulty teasingly asserting herself as Marissa's chaperone.

For Sigmund, he wasn't just taken with Marissa; he was completely smitten and totally entranced with her. Haltingly they slowly conversed in a manner that could only be described as dumbfounded. Neither could divert their eyes away from the other. For minutes they were totally oblivious of anyone else at their cluster of tables, with the only exception being Elisabeth.

Elisabeth was a vivacious young woman, who flirted relentlessly with a few of the team players, but never with Sigmund. He was already deemed an untouchable and although Elisabeth very much approved of what Marissa saw in him, she also knew when to withhold her usual sly humor and temporarily maintained her self-imposed strict limits.

After engaging herself with Nick and others to whom she was introduced, Elisabeth finally interceded to re-engage with the two love-stricken friends. "You know Sigmund, we have already been to some of your games this season and find them quite exciting."

Without turning his head, Sigmund responded as if to have finally realized the extent of his immediate infatuation. He continued his steady gaze saying, "You didn't tell me that, Marissa. Do you follow the game?"

"I wouldn't say I follow it, but I have very much enjoyed the few games I've seen."

Marissa was about to continue when Elisabeth interjected. "We mostly follow the players with the best asses in their tight shorts, although Marissa would never admit it!"

Sigmund and a few others choked on their beers, laughing as Elisabeth's directness was just being discovered.

"I see, so you're not really a sports fan, Marissa; you sound more like a *football fashionista*, if there is such a thing!" Sigmund teased.

She blushed at the suggestion but was quick to qualify the comment with a prompt rebuke. "It's true we weren't there just for the game, but our friends assured us there would be plenty to entertain us, if you know what I mean. They were correct in that regard!"

"Aha! The truth comes out! And here I was thinking you're such a perfect lady! Wait, that didn't come out the way I intended." He nervously corrected his attempt at teasing to reassure her. "You still are in my books Marissa. 'Perfect' is indeed the right word."

And so, the tone was set. There was attraction to be sure, Marissa was unlike anyone Sigmund had met before, but this beauty possessed a good sense of humor and quick wit, which was a rare combination he thoroughly enjoyed.

When the evening was sadly nearing its end, Sigmund and Marissa mutually agreed to see one another again...soon. It was a weekday, and everyone was facing another early start the next morning.

Sigmund and Nicholai escorted both ladies to the waiting carriage, as Nicholai gestured Elisabeth to the open side door. Sigmund was hesitant to release Marissa's hand from his secure grip. She made no effort to let go either. He pulled her closer to him and whispered in her ear, "I will never forget tonight. I cannot wait to see you again tomorrow."

He tenderly kissed the back of her hand as she softly responded, "I need more than that, Sigmund." She drew him closer to gently kiss his cheek, her gaze locked into his.

The gesture caused his knees to weaken and he felt emotionally drained. Never had he experienced such a captive and helpless feeling.

Marissa elegantly slid onto the bench beside Elisabeth. "Until tomorrow then!" she said with sultry enticement.

The moment the door closed, silence prevailed inside the carriage. Shockingly, neither friend appeared willing to discuss the events of the evening and sat mute...until a moment later when the horses were encouraged to lead on. Both women turned to face each other and exploded with laughter. "Well look at you, you sexy thing! No need to see what that young man wants. You got him Marissa! I'm proud of you!"

"He is quite adorable, isn't he? I'm so glad you approve, Lizzy. I don't know what I would do if you didn't."

"Like that would ever happen. You don't need any of my coaching. You did just fine!"

Neither Sigmund nor Marissa slept well that night. It was unmistakably destined there would be more such nights ahead of them.

*****

This beautiful young woman whom he barely even knew, totally preoccupied and essentially disrupted Sigmund's otherwise unwavering and focused approach, which he relied upon to give virtually all semblance of order to his life. He had consistently considered his ever-present responsibilities to be necessarily guided by his pragmatic and keen sense of obligation. Now his world was suddenly turned upside down. However, one thing of which he was certain was his firm belief his inner confusion would have no hope of clear resolution, unless and until he explored this relationship further. In so doing, he would surely come to know her better.

They had agreed to meet the following day shortly after class at a place on campus of Marissa's choice. Known to be a very suave man about campus, Sigmund was determined he would remain calm, cool, and collected. True to form, he arrived early. It was all he could do not to be there since early morning, such was his "calm demeanor". As soon as he rounded the library and approached the statue of Immanuel Kant, his heart commenced to pound and he drew deep breaths to ease his already quivering stomach.

Within minutes, Marissa appeared at the top of the steps to the main entrance. Her beaming smile instantly seduced him as she waved her hand to acknowledge him. Happily bouncing with enthusiasm, this vivacious beauty ran gingerly down the steps to eagerly take his hand and offered a brief but very satisfying hug of affection. "Hello again Siggy! My, my! You do look as handsome as I remember!"

Students were everywhere, but he saw only her. Incredibly, she was even lovelier than yesterday! How was this possible?

"As do you, Marissa! You are simply gorgeous this fine afternoon! Thanks for seeing me so soon. I hope I don't appear too eager?" he sheepishly enquired.

"Of course not. If you had not done so, I would have found it to be most unbearable. I couldn't sleep a wink last night just thinking about you!"

"Really? You are direct, aren't you! I feel the same way. It is something I've never truly experienced before but I am very much infatuated by you. Can we walk a little way? There's a park not far and I thought we could talk for a short while."

"Wonderful!" she said as she again took his hand, and within moments they resumed their conversation where they had left it the night before. There was no timidity or awkwardness between them. Marissa's relaxed and genuine manner dissolved Sigmund's initial anxieties, and by so doing made him certain he had found his new best friend. So much for being suave.

It had become late afternoon, but the September sun continued to shine, casting longer and longer shadows as it inevitably started to lose intensity behind the shelter of the trees.

"Can I interest you in a great meal? We've already been to the pub last night. Let me take you somewhere much more picturesque. I have just the place in mind."

"That sounds lovely, Sigmund, but I'm happy to go back to the pub too. It is not my intention to distract you from your teammates. I didn't notice anyone other than you last night, but I recognized the closeness you have with them. I know it's very early in our friendship, but I really enjoy being with you; however, I don't want to just start a whole new life with you. Please don't misunderstand me, though. I want us to share with each other the meaningful lives we already have, and that also means our friends and families too. Do you understand what I'm trying to say?"

"Thank you, sweetheart…uh, may I call you that?" he asked timidly.

"I would be disappointed if you didn't."

"It means a great deal for you to say such thoughtful things to me. My teammates are important to me, but for tonight I just want a quiet dinner overlooking the beautiful blue lake. Would that be alright?"

"Of course, my dear!" She hesitated very briefly and teased, "Oops, may I call you that?"

Marissa confidently placed her arm under his and she snuggled affectionately in his firm grasp as they happily giggled and made their way to the far side of the park. It was early in their relationship, but they were off to a good start. They fit together like a hand in a glove from that day forward.

Over dinner the two young ones shared the stories of their backgrounds, becoming more fully absorbed with each other. Nothing between them was forced or contrived. Neither was their genuine desire to learn more about each other.

Sigmund was neither bashful nor boastful when he conveyed the story of his parents' struggles before deciding to come to Berlin and that of his father's brave intervention which had ultimately saved Herr Stottletter from a tragic death.

"That's not the path I had anticipated to my acceptance by Friedrich Wilhelm, but I know how fortunate I have been to get here. My debt of gratitude extends to many people. I cannot imagine your story to be as fortuitous as mine."

"Perhaps not as fortuitous other than to say I was fortunate to have been born into an influential family. I am descended from the von Bismarck family; in fact, my grandmother is the Countess Marie Von Rantzau, the daughter of Otto von Bismarck."

"Really? That is incredible Marissa! I suppose we ordinary people read about your ancestors and hold them in such high esteem; we never think of them as people with living descendants. You must be one of the loveliest ones, Marissa. Of that I have no doubt. And what of your parents?"

"My father, whom I barely know, is an attaché serving as special secretary to the embassy in Vienna, where he now resides. At least ten months of the year my father is away tending to his duties. As for his responsibilities at home, they seem to be all but forgotten. All he ever wanted to be was a diplomat, so I suppose his dream was largely fulfilled. He's apparently rather good at what he does. My mother continues to live where I was born in Schleswig, not too far north of Hamburg. She is known as the countess of Hoyos, a woman of some note throughout the region. She is very active as a philanthropist and while her intentions are honorable, her impact is negligible, I'm embarrassed to say."

"That is not a story I could have imagined, Marissa. Forgive me but you sound embarrassed by your upbringing. You must understand no one chooses his or her parents. I'm sure you are loved dearly by them, but not everyone is best suited to be a parent."

"Siggy, I am new here at Friedrich Wilhelm. No one knows my heritage other than what had to be disclosed in the university records…and now you. I prefer to keep my background private, and I trust you to do your best to keep it that way."

"As you wish, Marissa. Whatever you ask of me, of course. May I ask why you chose to tell *me*?"

"I feel very fortunate to have met you, Siggy. I have never felt this way about anyone. I am innocent about the ways of this world, but not so much as to not recognize I have found in you an honorable and handsome young man I am eager to know better. It is important to me that I be open and honest with you, as you should be with me. That is all I ask of you."

"You honor me, Marissa, truly you do. I have difficulty controlling my focus since you came into my life. I haven't left your side and yet I find myself already thinking how long it will be until I see you again. Tell me, the team is booked with a heavy practice schedule the next few days. We have the big game against Goethe this weekend. I have an extra pair of tickets and they are hard to come by. They were intended for my parents, but they are committed to attending the synagogue the day of the match. Will you come to the game to cheer us on? Please?"

"I'd be delighted. May I bring Elisabeth too?"

"What a wonderful idea! Of course, you may!"

"Oh, my goodness! I must be off Siggy. We both have early starts tomorrow. You do provide such a wonderful distraction in my life, I must say. Do you realize it's almost midnight?"

"There's a carriage waiting outside. We'll be back in minutes. Oddly, I brought you here to enjoy the blue lakeside. The only blue the entire evening was what I beheld in your beautiful eyes."

"Oh Siggy! How do you come up with the lovely things you say?"

"Inspiration when I'm with you, my dear lady. Pure and simple."

CHAPTER THREE

♂

DESPITE GREAT DIFFICULTY, SIGMUND DID HIS BEST TO shift his focus away from Marissa to attending to his classes and the hectic regimen the team coaches had insisted upon in preparation for the championship match against the Frankfurt team. Home-field advantage was considerable for this game, as the travel distances had placed a strain on the visiting teams from the other divisions through-out the playoffs. Fortunately, Friedrich Wilhelm had earned the right. to host the final round, saving two days travel time to Frankfurt and back. It was an advantage they were determined not to squander.

The crowds were always predictably supportive this time of year, since the games had pitted only the best teams from each division against each other. Each match was a sudden-death event leaving no margin for error. Scholarship funding from corporate and personal benefactors each year was very much measured not by good efforts, but by winning results. The resulting pressure on the players and coaches to perform was notable on each contending team, but more so on the Wilhelm team, who once again were the odds-on favorites to win it all.

When the day was finally at hand, it was a sun-filled afternoon when players took the field for the pregame warm-up. As soon as they appeared, the mostly partisan crowd commenced to cheer and applaud. It was very much expected as the athletes waved apprecia-tively and quickly began the ritual routines to loosen up with the usual stretching of the legs and arms and twisting of their torsos. These finely conditioned athletes were serving notice they were ready to do battle.

As with many of his teammates, Sigmund maintained his single-mindedness as he and another forward alternated forty to fifty-foot shots on their agile goalkeeper, one from his left and the other from the right. Gradually, the pace and velocity of the shots increased, and the slicing spins demonstrated the profound curving motion of the ball as it exploded from the foot of these skilled marksmen.

Although Goethe was a worthy opponent, there was long history of animosity between the two rivals dating back more than a generation. For several players, their deep-seated rivalry was often based upon nothing more than that expressed by their fathers' generation. This year's crop of the few second and third generation players was highly motivated to exact revenge for previous crimes between the lines to defend the pride of their fathers, whose passions continued to be inflamed for transgressions that could never be forgiven by the passage of time. Such was the passion of most Europeans for the spectacle of the sport.

Occasionally, rematches such as this one found those who had old scores to settle. The sideline area near center field often provided interactions between protagonists to renew friendly rivalries, as well as bitter ones; designed to intimidate and provoke inappropriate responses from their opponents. These were moments typically charged with adrenalin and braggadocio, intended to adversely affect the self-confidence and focus of the key players. Disrupting their various coaches' game plans was a tactic, often enough to gain some immeasurable advantage. In matches such as these, it was regarded as the game within the game.

The same well-practiced routines applied for both teams, providing no apparent advantage based upon their pregame preparation. As other teammates rotated positions, Sigmund and his forwards completed several sets of wind sprints up and down the sidelines, being mindful to respect the Goethe side of the field. It was a sign of respect to honor the team boundaries, as each team traditionally kept within their respective half of the field.

The final sprint found Sigmund and Ignacio pacing each other one last time to find themselves within earshot of several beautiful and enthusiastic young ladies seated in the third row close to center field. Marissa was among them. Up to this point, Sigmund had remained totally focused on his game preparation, until his eyes met Marissa's. Her smile was disarming. She was sitting with Elisabeth and several other young ladies, who were scanning the field for a glimpse of their own heroes. Each was dressed in team colors, making it difficult to miss them.

After shouts of encouragement and support, Marissa harmlessly blew a kiss in Sigmund's direction. It was personal moment between them, which he immediately returned, not for a moment considering anyone else was watching. A broad-shouldered player wearing number 17 for Goethe was at the Wilhelm side of center, only a few feet from where Sigmund had expressed his affectionate gesture toward Marissa. This player was well known for his belligerence. It was he who had been yellow carded for clipping the star defender for Wilhelm late in the season. Today was Heinrich's first game since that injury almost four weeks ago.

"I vaguely remember that brunette from Frankfurt. She was a decent piece of ass that one! It wasn't her first time, but she knew what she liked!" he hollered out to his teammate who quickly chimed in, directing his remark at Sigmund.

"Hey, you're the Jew boy, aren't you? Is she with you now? That one gets around!"

The two laughingly bumped one another as they celebrated their insulting commentary. Sigmund was accustomed to harmless slurs against himself but not ones directed at someone he cared about so deeply. He was normally composed both on and off the field, but this went beyond a personal slight and he became enraged. He and Ignacio turned to glare at their antagonists and walked together authoritatively toward them with fists clenched. They did not have to cross the invisible centerline since the offenders had already done so. Neither raised his hands in a threatening manner, however, Sigmund did not stop until he surprisingly bumped his chest firmly into Number 17—the one with the big mouth, causing him to stagger backward about two feet.

Ignacio and the offending accomplice did not make any physical contact with each other but delivered their respective messages through a variety of profanities and very animated hand gestures not requiring translation. The partisan fans did not need to hear the verbal exchanges to understand the magnitude of the confrontation. They roared with delight at the prospects of fisticuffs and knew this incident had set the tone for the game ahead.

Marissa expressed her surprise at the emotional intensity of the game and what appeared to be a grudge between Sigmund and the other players from Goethe. "Whatever brought that about, I wonder? I've never seen anything quite like it before. It's not a side of Sigmund I am comfortable with. Emotions are already running high it seems."

Elisabeth understood the game better than most. Her brother Erik was in his second year on the team, a solid winger, not flashy but steady and reliable defensively. "It was just bad gamesmanship, Marissa. Goethe was just trying to get under Sigmund's skin about something. Get him upset enough to do something stupid and in so doing get himself thrown out of the game. He is the team captain, and I dare say he is also the only Jew on the team. He was the best target for that bully's abuse. I've seen him play before. What an asshole!"

The taunting continued and the escalating roar of the appreciative crowd became a feeding frenzy. Meanwhile players, coaches, and officials raced to the scene to restore some semblance of order before ejections became necessary. As it was, the incident resulted in two yellow cards issued against both Sigmund and Number 17 for Goethe. The ball had not yet been placed at center field by the referee.

When the whistle blew to kick the ball into play, it was readily apparent there would be carryover from the center-field incident. Players on both sides were chirping at one another and took every opportunity to make direct, punishing contact with their opponents. Any advancement of the ball for either team came at a painful cost. It was clear this would be a very physical contest.

The crisp passing was well executed and movement up both sides of the field seemed the best strategy to retain ball possession into the offensive zones, until the forwards were squeezed out of bounds by the steady defensemen. Neither team had any noticeable advantage with ball possession, certainly not in the front of the goal area.

Possession of the ball alternated back and forth as was anticipated. Every offensive surge by Wilhelm inspired supportive cheering, which would build and build, and quickly transform into collective groans of disappointment when the drive was broken up by a brilliant defensive maneuver by Goethe. The fast-paced first half was coming to an end and mostly featured a cautious and methodical style of play.

As they entered the final minute of the half, a brief lapse of judgment caused one of Wilhelm's defensive pairings to underestimate the positioning of the attacking striker, who found himself fifteen feet from the front side of the goal. As the perfect kick was launched from his winger from the opposite side of the field it arched only slightly, such was the force of the shot. The striker leapt to the full extent of his ability and struck the well-placed shot just over the out-stretched arm of the goalkeeper, who had anticipated the play well. A great defensive effort, but an even better offensive attack. Score one for Goethe.

When the half ended, the teams jogged off the field to the adoring and still boisterous fans. There was no feeling of despair in the air—none whatsoever. Shouts of encouragement permeated through the stands to the chants of *"Wilhelm! Wilhelm!"*

Although it was a cool afternoon, the players were dripping with perspiration as they gathered themselves along the benches about the locker room. As they rehydrated and toweled off, the coach motioned to them that he was about to begin.

"Well done out there today, boys. That's what we wanted defensively from all of you, forwards as well. You played them tight and other than one perfectly set-up shot, it was a dead even heat. The Goethe players performed well too; let's give them credit. Stick to the script like we have all season. We've all been here before. Sig, anything to add here?"

"Yeah Coach, thanks." Sigmund finished his cup of water and stood before his teammates. He continued, "You guys don't need me to inspire you by blowing smoke up your asses. We're doing what we do best. Our breaks will come if we just keep digging and play smart in our own end. Joseph, that was the perfect shot. Not many keepers could have stopped it but you almost did the impossible. Great effort, man!"

Coach Fuchs quietly separated Heinrich to step away from the rest of the team and placed his arm around his shoulders to ask, "You looked like your old self out there, how's the knee holding up?"

"I feel good, Coach—still a bit out of condition, but I feel strong for the second half. The knee was throbbing a bit before the half, but the trainers wrapped it in ice to calm it down. I'll stretch it out some more and be good to go. Don't worry about me, boss. I got this."

The equipment manager stuck his head in the locker room "Three minutes, boys! Go get 'em!"

The coach pulled Sigmund close to him. "Sig! Listen up. We wait till Goethe is already on the field before we enter, maybe just another thirty seconds or so. I want them to see we aren't panicking or overly pumped to play with desperation. It also won't hurt to let the crowd scream their lungs out when they see us coming."

Whether Coach Fuchs' strategy worked or not would never be known, but it served his players by instilling in them a calmer and more self-confident demeanor. It was a sign of team maturity.

The next quarter was as heated and physical as the first half and the denigration toward Sigmund showed no sign of abating, particularly from his archrival. The cat calling and derogation of his faith and his lady friend became more personally offensive. Number 17 knew he had touched a nerve with Sigmund, and he intended to work it to his team's advantage.

Sigmund shut it out as best he could and played on, driven harder by the accusatory insults.

About ten minutes into the final quarter, Number 17 appeared to become frustrated at his inability to disturb Sigmund's concentration by verbal slurs alone, and he decided to up his physical vendetta on the team captain. The officials overlooked a few highly questionable knockdowns and borderline tripping calls on both sides of the ball. They were intent about letting the players decide the outcome. They did not want a close game such as this elimination match to be decided by an offensive call that wasn't blatant.

Wilhelm started pressing Goethe with tighter coverage and their hard work was rewarded when Erik intercepted a risky clearing shot, and one-timed a perfect pass to put Sigmund behind the Goethe defenders. Sigmund was in the clear and bearing down on the net minder. His nemesis was right behind him, determined at any cost to prevent a clean shot. As Sigmund positioned himself to take the shot, Number 17 leapt forward, leading with his extended leg to kick Sigmund's planted leg out from under him. Sigmund crashed to the ground and rolled roughly onto the turf with his antagonist on top of him.

Sig was now at a distinct disadvantage. He was hurt and could not get up to defend himself from more shoving and pushing.

The hostile crowd booed relentlessly until the clear infraction was ultimately called. It was the second yellow card for 17 and the jeers of contempt rained down on him as he continued cursing at Sigmund for embellishing the infraction. Coach Fuchs and the trainer sped to the scene of the crime. It was critical Sigmund's physical condition was properly assessed to enable him to continue competing. This was no time for personal pride.

"Speak to me, Sig. Are you alright? Anything broken, Richard?"

Richard, the trainer, examined the captain's leg and ankle, as Sigmund addressed the coach's concerns. Two officials looked over their huddled formation while Sigmund grimaced in obvious pain to respond. "Hurts like a bitch but I don't think anything's broken. That bloody asshole! What do you think, Richard?"

"Let's go, gentlemen," the referee shouted. "Do we need a stretcher? We gotta get this game back in play. I can only give you another minute. If he comes out, you can sub anyone you want to take the free kick. It's your call."

"You're good, but you're gonna have one hell of a bruise, Sig," Richard advised.

"I can live with that. Help me to my feet, guys."

Within the minute, a very determined captain struggled to his feet amidst the roars of approval from the crowd and his teammates alike. The bruise had already begun to swell perceptively on his shin and the abrasions from the cleats on his mid-calf. "I'm good for the shot, Coach. I would never bullshit you. You know that, right?"

Sigmund used what few seconds remained to walk it off. It was bearable, but not for much longer. He knew when the swelling continued, the pain would become too much, and his calf would certainly need medical attention.

"I know this goalie well, and he knows my tendencies. I can beat him. I know it! Your call Coach, not mine."

Coach looked at Richard and saw his affirmative nod. "OK, go get him Sig! You earned the chance."

There is generally only a split second for any skilled goaltender to dive right, or dive left. It was a gamble either way on a clean shot. The din of the crowd noise was deafening as the referee placed the ball in position.

Sigmund blocked out the mayhem, hearing nothing, and he paused momentarily to gather himself. The tension was at its peak for those watching, but calmness prevailed in Sigmund's quiet poise. He had been here before.

He stood to the left of center as if to slice the ball into the left side of the net. The net minder stood anxiously in the center of the goal and bounced on his toes as Sigmund approached the ball.

The goaler dove immediately to his right side with both arms fully extended as Sigmund drove it hard to the middle of the net where the goaltender had been standing originally. The stadium exploded. Only at that instant did Sigmund allow the roar to creep back into his consciousness.

The game was tied when Sigmund was almost gang tackled by his teammates, who had raced to embrace their leader and carry him to the sidelines. Sigmund was done for the day.

He stayed on the bench with his knee and left calf wrapped in ice and elevated to reduce the throbbing. He had the best seat in the house. It was now up to his team to finish the job without him.

As often happens in high-level sports, when an injury hobbles a star player, teams respond with even stronger determination. In this case, it was the nature of the injury that brought out the best in them. With only minutes remaining, Wilhelm flooded the Goethe defensive zone, completely disrupting their attempts to mount an offensive. They were determined to end this in regulation time. Momentum was in their favor. Only one defenseman stayed back. It was Heinrich, who had played an exemplary game.

As soon as Goethe lost possession, they were scrambling on the defensive, and the raucous crowd were on their feet sensing a victory was at hand. The winger made a well-placed shot that was redirected on goal. The goaltender leapt to successfully deflect it, but the ball spun on a higher trajectory toward the right side of the net. Players from both sides converged beneath it as it seemed to hang in the air. Nicholai only had one chance to get a clear shot when he broke away only slightly to face toward his own end. Amazingly he leapt, and his momentum rolled his body fully backward to firmly drive the ball with his extended leg directly over his head to deposit it in the upper corner of the net. It was a miraculous shot!

It was the third straight championship for Wilhelm, but victory was sweeter every time. The team was jubilant, while Goethe was understandably dejected at only coming close. During the handshakes of congratulation only one player failed to appear: Number 17. Sigmund kept his poise and handled his crutches to maneuver the now-crowded field of play spilling over with hundreds of admiring fans.

In the melee, three Goethe players approached Sigmund with hands extended.

"Hell of a game, Sig! Amazing shot by Nick too! Give him my best. I'll buy him a beer next time I see him. Hope you're OK, man. There was no need for Sal's bullshit today. His actions didn't speak for all of us and I hope you can accept our apology on behalf of the team. And please, pass this on to your lady friend especially. His actions were totally unacceptable."

"I appreciate that, Karl. It means a lot coming from you."

Only a few seconds later, Marissa and Elisabeth managed to navigate their way to find Sigmund, who continued to remain surrounded. When he finally saw them, he pulled them both to his side and Marissa snuggled her head closely to his shoulder with one hand resting affectionately on his chest. "I'm so very proud of you Siggy. Congratulations, my darling." She planted a soft and slow kiss on his cheek. "I was so worried about you. How is your leg? I imagine you are still in a great deal of pain."

"Not so bad now, Marissa, but I have plenty of time to rest now that the season is over. Did you enjoy the game?"

"Other than being so concerned about you, I enjoyed every minute. Please, we can meet up later. Right now, you should enjoy the victory with your teammates. You were already a champion in my mind." She winked at him and kissed him passionately. It was the first time they shared such a display of affection publicly.

*****

Coach Fuchs had arranged for a team party at the university campus the following day. The players' families, many of the student body, and, of course, the press was well represented, as was the tradition for every championship celebration. It was a time to recognize the outstanding achievements of players and coaches and the financial support of the benefactors of Wilhelm University. More important than recognition, today the players were especially eager to have a good time together with as little regard as possible to strength, conditioning, and diet. It was an opportunity to cut loose.

Before the dignitaries and press departed from the public presentation, however, there was one particularly significant announcement the team had not expected.

"Before we get this party started," said Coach Fuchs, "there is one matter I am anxious to share with you young men. Professor Ulrich, I will leave this honor to you, sir."

"Thank you, Coach. Gentlemen, my heartiest congratulations to each one of you, and to your fine coaching staff. You performed brilliantly this year and are deserving of this championship. On behalf of our board members, we applaud your efforts and are proud of your achievements. This university has a longstanding tradition of setting the highest standards of performance in education and advanced learning. Your team effort yesterday also exemplifies our constant pursuit of physical and mental excellence, not just in the lecture halls but on the football fields across our nation!"

As he spoke, the throngs of football aficionados stomped, clapped, and cheered to encourage even more adulation from the stage.

"Many of you are aware negotiations have been ongoing in Stuttgart for almost two years now, to syndicate the best teams in the northern leagues with the best of the southern teams. The intent has been to finally establish a unified National German Football Association: the *Deutscher Fußball-Bund*. Various committees have worked tirelessly to achieve a functional merger of both associations.

"I am delighted to announce that on November 4th of this year, less than six weeks from this day, nineteen clubs have decided to formalize the German Rugby Football Union. The German Football Association will oversee this collaboration. Based upon many factors, none more significant than your championship victory of yesterday, I am delighted to confirm Friedrich Wilhelm University will be among them!"

The popping of champagne bottles, the pinging of wine glasses, and the chorus of German victory marches were all but drowned out by the cheers of jubilation from the excited participants.

"This official proclamation is the crowning glory of all our efforts. Sigmund!" said the coach. "I can't express how grateful I am to you for setting the standards of dedication for your teammates. I owe you all a debt of gratitude."

"Thank you, Coach! It was a team effort, top to bottom! May I introduce you to my sweetheart? Marissa, please say hello to Coach Fuchs. Coach, this is Marissa. She's a freshman this year at Wilhelm."

Marissa batted those beautiful blue eyes and flashed her embracing smile. "So wonderful to meet you. Sigmund speaks so highly of you and respects you a great deal."

"My, my," the coach replied. "You are most charming, Marissa. Welcome to Wilhelm. Were you at the game yesterday?"

"Yes. I wouldn't have missed it. I must say it was the most exciting match I've ever seen. The game captivated me. Now you can count me among your biggest fans!"

The players were all smiles as they milled about with one another, eagerly refilling their glasses and finding their way to the beer kegs. "Ladies, may we ply you with more alcohol? Beer suits me much better than champagne," Theo enthused as he hoisted a tall, cold ale. "Ahh, now that's the true taste of victory!"

"Follow me, my dear ladies and gentlemen…and I use that term loosely. I can smell the schnitzels and sauerkraut from here and I'm more than ready! Come Marissa. You must be hungry too!"

"I am a bit peckish; I must admit."

"We're right behind you, Sig. Lead on!" called Nick as he and Elisabeth joined their company arm in arm.

The food was excellent. There was no need for anything fancy today. With plates fully loaded, three or four young couples selected a table beside the riverbank and feasted; it was a great time had by all.

*****

In the following weeks, the lovers' fondness for one other continued to blossom and Marissa was enthusiastically welcomed into the sanctity of Sigmund's ever broadening circle of friends. She proved to be a more gracious and self-confident addition with every passing day. In no time she established her own companionships with the team members, as well as with those young ladies who were also considered worthy of similar recognition, Elisabeth among them.

Sigmund and Marissa's bond of affection was naturally becoming more open and did not escape the notice of their companions. Many, especially Nicholai, readily accepted Marissa with good-natured teasing, and she found comfort as she confirmed to herself that she could learn much more about Sigmund through the qualities and habits of his closest friendships. It wasn't about the words they spoke, but more about the way they lived their lives and interacted with others that reassured Marissa her attraction to Sigmund was well founded.

Nicholai and Elisabeth were well suited to each other as well and found comfort and budding romance in each other's company. Together, the foursome was often in the spotlight, both on campus and frequently when opportunity provided some off campus high jinx, usually initiated by Nick.

For Sigmund and Marissa, their close friendship evolved naturally, although not yet intimately. However, there comes a time in every adolescent life when sexual urges inevitably create confusion and personal conflicts, testing both the character and morality of the individual. This was such a time for Sigmund, and he was not alone. These matters were rarely addressed openly by anyone in these times and were usually confined to individual trial and error. Often addressing it consisted of advice sought from those peers feigning to be more experienced than they were with such matters. In the absence of suitable guidance, it is a wonder man nonetheless manages to survive.

Sigmund's family had consistently provided a stable and predictably conservative approach to life. Certainly, these awkward personal matters were better left unsaid between Sigmund and his parents. Sigmund thought it best to leave these life lessons to the wisdom of those very few significant others in his social circles with whom he was willing to confide such sensitive matters. He was wise enough to know it was also his relationships outside of the family whose influences helped to shape his pathway, providing direction and guidance, whether good or bad.

Based upon Sigmund's personal reflections, the direction of the road taken often depended upon strength of character established by his family upbringing and the moral compass already ingrained within him. This compass had years before established certain parameters enabling him to proceed through cycles of maturity of thought and in so doing, to eventually define who he would ultimately become. These factors were impenetrable cornerstones of Sigmund's life. As a man of science, he logically stayed within those frames of reference.

The dilemma was to control the physical urges and desires that were now confusing his objectivity. Could a resolution to his questions about romance be found in a logical and understandable solution? Sigmund had dated rarely and had not yet experienced a serious romantic relationship. Since Marissa had come into his life, she occupied his thoughts, his imagination, and his yearnings.

Shortly after the championship celebration, the twosome happily agreed to accept a dinner invitation from Sigmund's family. Whether it was premature or not was of no concern for either. Glowing with pride and mindful of his parents' traditional wishes, Sigmund was more excited about introducing Marissa than taking a game winning penalty kick in overtime. It was an ill-fitting comparison, but for a fervent young athlete, it spoke volumes about his state of mind.

The Landesburg family was equally enthused about the prospect of meeting Marissa. Although Sigmund had dated occasionally, there had been no one special warranting his parents' approval. This was the first time it had even been considered. His parents had noticed the dramatic impact this young woman was having on Sigmund. It was evident in his renewed energy, his exceptional good humor, and of course she was all he could talk about.

When the front door opened to welcome this lovely young creature, Sigmund's parents saw firsthand how magical she truly was.

"Mother, Father, I am so pleased to introduce you to my dear lady friend, Marissa."

"Hello Mr. and Mrs. Landesburg! How very wonderful to meet you. Sigmund has spoken so fondly of you." Her eyes sparkled and polite handshakes were immediately drawn closer, followed very naturally by warm hugs of genuine affection.

"Our Sigmund seldom exaggerates, and in your case especially so. You are so truly lovely, my dear. Welcome to our humble home," Herr Landesburg effused.

Once everyone was settled, tea and coffee were served, which almost became a distraction to the natural flow and comfort of their stimulating conversation. Marissa was entrancing and quickly demonstrated her engaging qualities, among them her genuine warmth of character. Sigmund remained mostly quiet, and the conversation flowed as it was intended. He was already quite self-assured, but even more so once his father gave him a wink and a smile of approval.

Dinner bore the fruit of Dahlia's labor and reflected the quality and care of its fastidious preparation. Mother was an outstanding cook and excelled that evening when her meal of choice featured some of her son's favorite home-cooked dishes. Time passed quickly but without haste. Nothing was pressured.

"Come Mother, let me help you tonight. The meal was extraordinary. It's the least I can do." The cleanup however was not only Sigmund's chance to assist his mother, but it also allowed an opportunity for his father to share precious moments with Marissa, moments used to simply validate his noticeable respect and admiration of her.

"Your father seems quite impressed by the young lady, as am I Sigmund. However did you meet such a charming beauty?"

"After practice one day, I was with Nick and the boys at the Hostel Bar where we go now and then. When I saw Marissa with her friend, she literally took my breath away, Mother. No one has had that effect on me, ever. Once Nick brought them to our table, I was literally dumbstruck. It wasn't my finest moment, I assure you. Only later did I learn she is a freshman at the university studying languages and mathematics."

"Well, she appears to have the same effect on your father! She is precious, Sigmund. Just treat her with respect and consideration and allow the Lord to guide you both."

When the evening concluded and his parents bid the couple goodnight, it was the first time the two young ones could share each other's company...unaccompanied. After assurance was given the young ones would not stay up too late and Zeev and Dahlia had retired for the evening, Sigmund and Marissa sat side by side on his parent's couch. It was his parents' way of saying they trusted them alone together, and that they were mature enough to use good judgment.

Thankfully, Sigmund's eagerly anticipated moment of truth was at hand. He and Marissa sat next to each other but for the first time, it was noticeable their conversation was no longer at ease, somehow becoming less natural. Responsively, Marissa snuggled more closely to his side and their speech became more teasing, ranging from Sigmund's feeble and slightly anxious attempts at humor, to Marissa becoming increasingly more coy and flirtatious.

Both stirred one another's passion as they were trembling with anticipation, eager to explore what was never spoken of before. It was the very cusp of a new beginning starting to follow its inevitable course. Marissa sensed their mutual awkwardness.

Sigmund's face was becoming more flushed, as Marissa apprehensively caressed him and drew him to her slightly parted lips. The moment lingered, as precious ones often do. Their kiss was classically elegant and was precisely what she had hoped it would be. Satisfying, respectful, and a small but appropriate taste of what was to come.

CHAPTER FOUR

IN NO TIME, MARISSA BECAME AN INTEGRAL PART OF family dinners, and was continually supportive in assisting Sigmund's mother with the necessary preparations. Her proactive role was genuinely comforting and fostered a close bond with Mother Dahlia, in particular.

The Sabbath meals were a new experience for Marissa, as she shared the lighting of the candles and the reciting of the Kiddush blessing before the meal. Sigmund did not regard himself as particularly devout to his Judaic upbringing; however, over time the traditions and spiritual aspects he had experienced as a child became more apparent and gradually restored his previously fading faith. Marissa's encouragement opened his eyes to more fully embrace his already established family customs.

Of note was that Herr Landesburg and his son also became closer than they had been in years, sharing the pleasure of each other's company much more frequently while the ladies were tasked with their newfound common pursuits. This bonding with his father was something most gratifying that Sigmund had not expected.

As with many budding romances, both Marissa and Sigmund became visibly closer to each other. Marissa was a year behind Sigmund, majoring in mathematics and languages. Despite their preoccupation with each other, neither of them ever compromised their academics, nor Sigmund's fervent dedication to his previous team responsibilities. In fact, they both continued to excel in their own individual pursuits, and with ever increasing aptitude. As they did so, they exuded a certain measurable inner glow when they were together.

Being a female attending this traditionally male populated institution, a rarity of note, exposed Marissa to some disparagement. Despite this, her relationship with the very popular Sigmund helped her already abounding confidence as she excelled in each endeavor befalling her. Every day Marissa proved to be a worthy and charming damsel, worthy of catching the eye and the heart of young Sigmund. What a formidable pair they made! She was a good match for him as she was equally popular and the envy of the female students, particularly when she and Sigmund fell openly in love.

Throughout the following years, Sigmund's focused excellence on attaining his medical degree was unmistakable. As the final semester was nearing completion Sigmund's stature reached new heights of distinction when he was named valedictorian. Although he never focused on nor strove to achieve such recognition, when it was officially announced, his friends and family were united in their admiration of him. They openly expressed their shared support that he was the best choice for this outstanding accomplishment.

It did not go unnoted by the university that Marissa was the great-granddaughter of Chancellor Otto von Bismarck, himself a former alumnus of Friedrich Wilhelm University. The legacy of the chancellor's many historic achievements in international politics was the very creation of the German Empire during his tenure as prime minister of Prussia.

Marissa's father, as always, was committed to his responsibilities in Vienna and was unable to personally attend Sigmund's recognition of distinction. However, both her mother the countess, and her grandfather, Count Herbert von Bismarck-Schönhausen, currently serving in the German House of Parliament, were most insistent about being present for the event. When it was learned the count himself, would be present at the graduation ceremony, military security teams unceremoniously sprang into action, virtually overrunning the campus. They were granted every request for the cooperation deemed necessary to ensure everyone's safety and security during the event.

This was not without precedent, as it was not uncommon for many dignitaries' sons and daughters to attend Friedrich Wilhelm University, and with each such graduation ceremony, it attracted more fame to the university, often resulting in significant financial bequests from wealthy benefactors. Amongst past alumnae were not only Otto von Bismarck himself, but also such notables as the world-renowned physicists Albert Einstein and Max Planck, and the founders of Marxist theory, Karl Marx and Friedrich Engels.

Sigmund and Marissa were the talk of the campus and significantly more so when Marissa's secretive ancestry was publicized, and their already popular status was now magnified. It was trend setting for others to be seen in their company. If there was a social event planned, and there were several, success was ensured so long as Sigmund and Marissa were on the guest lists. Among those students eagerly fawning over their favor, were no doubt many who silently sought their acceptance to establish themselves within their inner circle, invariably catching the eye of other mutual friends and associates.

The friendships and collaborations forged among the student body, whether during their research dissertations and completion of their theses, or due to Sigmund's high profile on the football pitch, inevitably served them well in their chosen fields of endeavor. Additionally, their qualified opinions were eagerly sought in the field of the arts and numerous philosophical pursuits.

Nonetheless, this young couple remained genuine and welcoming, but never naïve about the boundless limits of their new mantle of celebrity. As a popular and charismatic intellectual on the cusp of a successful medical career, one who evidently would select as his bride the most beautiful and much celebrated descendent of the former chancellor of the German Empire, Sigmund was naturally exempt from military service. Other selected graduates were equally privileged, but none for the strength of reasoning behind Sigmund's unique status.

Such was the first indication of their aristocratic celebrity and the advantages they would be afforded. In the years ahead, this new generation would make significant contributions to Germany's changing philosophical attitudes, which would enhance the development of numerous cultural achievements in the eyes of Eastern Europe. Many anticipated the impact of these expectations to be immeasurable.

Perhaps it was the frenetic but well-managed pace of life always seeming to demand more from this extraordinary young couple. Whatever the cause, their limited time together became sacred to them. It was as if they strove more than most to make every moment matter in what relatively little time they had together.

Despite the constant preoccupations of their lives, they seized every opportunity presenting itself for the chance to be alone. Their private moments had become most welcome for this couple, as indeed they always believed they would, but they were steadfast in their mutual agreement not to exceed certain boundaries before marriage. It was understood the consummation of the act of intimate love was sacred to Marissa and Sigmund, and it would be willingly deferred until after their vows of marriage.

On more than one occasion, their pledge of abstinence would be tested. As with many young lovers, lines may be drawn objectively and with clear consciousness, but can be easily obscured when obsessed by passion. Being together became their mutual addiction, never more so than one glorious afternoon when they both uncharacteristically skipped classes. Sigmund's parents were attending prayers at the synagogue, as was their custom a few days each week. Being the opportunist, he was determined to share some pent-up intimacy, to which Marissa was very receptive.

The normal stroll home was more briskly paced than usual, and steadily became more rapid as they approached the wrought-iron gate at the front of the house. As they ascended the steps to the doorway, Sigmund was already undoing the buttons of his shirt.

They had barely closed the door behind themselves when they became locked in an embrace. He savored the sweetness of her mouth and she tenderly slipped her hot tongue between his lips. Becoming visibly aroused, he was breathing more rapidly now and commenced groaning with longing for her. He gently wrapped his hand around her magnificent, slender neck, lovingly caressing and nibbling on her ear, licking her from here to there, all the while seeking her sensitive erogenous zones.

He swept her into his arms and carried her to his bedroom like a young bull charged with surging testosterone, driven by his lustful search for ultimate satiation. She felt his well-toned muscular body, taut with frenzy, as he enflamed her own desire. The two kissed each other repeatedly and he explored the glorious crevices of her superb, virginal body for the very first time. Her sumptuous, hardened nipples glistened in lovely contrast to her alabaster white breasts. It was a wonderful, passionate moment elevating their desires far beyond their full comprehension.

At the crucial moment of completely losing their senses, it was Marissa who eased Sigmund slowly back from the precipice of careless oblivion. She drew her mouth gently to his ear and softly whispered, "I love you! I will love you for always! Shhh…shhh. Just relax, knowing I am yours." With hushes of calmness trying to relax him, she tenderly stroked his hair with gentle caresses.

Sweetly she reassured him of her own constant desire for him and lovingly reminded him of their recent discussions about not crossing the invisible line of what was appropriate and what was not at this stage of their relationship. She pledged herself to him, as he did to her, both knowing the right time and place would come soon enough.

Subsequent romantic interludes were typically as alluring as their first such encounter. Their passion for each other could be instantly ignited by a subtle look, a sensitive touch, or a seductive personal gesture. Their familiarity was such that they read one another perfectly with the comfort of knowing each was always eager to please the other.

*****

About this time, Marissa graciously offered to regularly attend Hebrew Schule. She had been raised Roman Catholic and despite initial religious reservations from her family, they were also supportive of the bond of love becoming so palpable between the young couple. Sigmund's parents were particularly delighted to enjoy Marissa's company with the hope she would one day become their future daughter-in-law. As Sigmund was an only child, Marissa was a genuine gift from heaven above—the answer to Sigmund's parents' prayers.

Friday dinners provided the opportunity for Marissa to learn and to better understand the spiritual observances of the Jewish faith, to which she had become extremely receptive. Though her Catholicism would never be rejected, nor ever thought to be so required, she very much longed for the legitimization of their sanctified union within the synagogue, steeped in thousands of years of strong tradition.

Sigmund's mother was a woman of sensibility, and Sigmund was the sole focus of her devoted care. Her ever-present thoughtfulness and pampering nature toward Sigmund were reflected in her genuine adoration for Marissa. Because Marissa had no close bond with her own mother, due to other priorities too numerous to mention, it was as if Dahlia was the mother Marissa had always wanted. Marissa had no clear memories of the Countess since most of her young life had been shaped and parented by a boarding school for children with aristocratic roots. Other than a few photographs her father possessed, she had few happy recollections of family time as a child.

The loving relationship between Marissa and Mother Dahlia developed quite genuinely and led to the two of them passing more time together, especially when Sigmund's academic studies and his responsibilities as a teaching assistant had become more onerous. Marissa never wanted to appear to be too demanding of Sigmund's time in a way possibly interpreted as over-stepping. For this, she had truly earned the teammates' affection and respect. She stayed within her own undefined limits and was not at all unduly possessive or jealous and demanding of his attentions.

In fact, very much to the contrary, she was often regarded to be a fine example of what standards came to be expected of the other associates and teammates' girlfriends. Not all of them were as under-standing, but these women never seemed to take issue with Marissa, at least to her and Sigmund's knowledge.

Just prior to the upcoming Passover, Sigmund's mother had asked Marissa if they could shop together for some items she needed for the meal preparation. It was not anything requiring much time or effort, but this was more a matter of Mother getting to know Sigmund's charming young lady on a more personal level. Dahlia was also attempting to measure Marissa's interest and possible receptive-ness to the concept of embracing the Jewish faith she should not simply assume.

"It was so kind of you to ask me to join you, Mother Dahlia. This is an entirely new experience for me and I'm thankful for your kind offer."

"We enjoy your company Marissa, and each time we meet the affection and consideration you and Sigmund have for one another becomes increasingly apparent. This will be the first of many Passovers we hope to share with you, so I thought it would be best to help you understand how our customs have been shaped. It is a sacred time for many people of faith to remember and honor the traditions of their past."

"Sigmund has spoken with me about our different faiths and I am anxious to learn all I can. As you know, I was raised a Roman Catholic, but I reluctantly confess not a devout one. I admire and respect families of such spiritual faith, regardless of which one is followed. I believe it provides moral structure from within, giving direction and reassurance as we face the trials and tribulations a full life presents to us."

"Well-said, Marissa. Would that more people would have an open mind to the choices others have made throughout their lives."

"I would never stand in the way of Sigmund fulfilling his desire to remain a practicing Jew. And with your guidance I am willing to support his choices in wherever life takes him. I must confess I am falling in love with your son, Mother Dahlia. I am so very thankful to have him in my life."

The family was known to frequently extend invitations to accommodate Sigmund's teammates and other non-Jewish friends as well. Their hospitable generosity was neither dismissive nor disrespectful of anyone. That much was assured. Even Marissa knew Sigmund's only request of her was to honor his parents' wish that should they marry someday they would do so at the synagogue, whenever the time was considered appropriate. It was a request she happily embraced.

*****

It was a day tailored by Mother Nature, for anyone willing to seize the moment. While picnicking in Tiergarten Park, the young lovers had chosen to pass some quiet time together enjoying a rare moment of solitude. They found a lovely spot not too distant from the Grand Hostel Hotel, which dominated the far side of Tempelhofer Ufer, and provided a magnificent backdrop to the east side of the park.

The lush and expansive lawns always maintained to perfection, surrounded numerous abundantly overflowing beds of blue and purple dahlia blossoms, gloriously canopied by the cascading foliage of a mighty oak tree above. It was all too rare an occasion when they could both be together, without distraction or interruption. Fragrant scents of lavender bushes carried by the gentle breezes evoked a profound sense of serenity and pensive reflection.

Following some relaxing light banter, which was perfectly suitable for this glorious setting, in the back of her mind Marissa had been thinking carefully about broaching a topic Sigmund seemed to be avoiding. On the few occasions she had initiated such attempts in past weeks, what with his daily regimen of lectures, committee meetings, and writing his thesis, it was seemingly impossible to prearrange.

It was the matter of their future together, not romantically of course, but specifically pertaining to what wonderful options had been bestowed upon them: whether to accept a financially lucrative offer to apprentice in a highly renowned professor's private practice, or to humbly accept the equally humble salary offered to Sigmund to apprentice in the world-famous Charité Hospital. Graduation was fast approaching and sooner or later he would have to decide.

Thinking this was as good a time as any for such discussion, Marissa took it upon herself to bring it up directly. "Siggy, you know how very much I love you, and that I will always be so...but I'm of the thought we should both take pause to weigh the options before you. I am always here to support you; however, I hope you can trust me to also play an active part in your ultimate decision making."

"Take pause from what, my sweetheart? This sounds ominous. Are you certain you are not leaving me?" he laughed light heartedly.

"No silly, you know exactly what I mean. Sometimes I think people are too demanding of you, yet somehow you seem to thrive on the pressure. Even your father agrees with me on this."

"Your family, and especially your great-grandfather knew a thing or two about pressure. You, of all people, should understand both he and I are driven to succeed in all we do, whether in politics, medicine, or sports...whatever. Without constantly pushing himself to the very brink of exhaustion, I don't think Grandpa Otto would have ever survived. It's what gave his life meaning. From what I have read about him, it was all he ever knew, Marissa!"

"I know you are right, but I just don't want you to try and measure yourself against him. I am aware that for many he was an outstanding role model for success, but success comes in various forms...and... well, as Mother has often told me, he wasn't always a model husband or family man," she sighed. "Nor would I expect him to have been so, with all he accomplished. I guess I don't want to turn out like my great grandmother, bless her soul, as much as you know I respect what it must have been like for her. I just don't think I could make the sacrifices she had to make for the price of his fame and success. She was lost in history. Does that make me sound terribly awful?" She wrinkled her lovely nose and raised an eyebrow quizzically.

"Of course not. I would never think that of you. I see your point, but you very much knew what you were getting yourself in for when we fell in love...as did I, for that matter. We won't have the same regrets, I promise you, my darling." He snuggled closer and softly kissed the back of her long, graceful neck. She was always a vision of perfection, and he never hesitated to openly demonstrate his deep affection for her. He cherished Marissa very deeply and was never discouraged from doing so, even in the presence of onlookers.

"You always manage to change the topic of discussion to suit you best. Why do I love you so very, very much? You just drive me crazy!" She turned to face him and kissed him tenderly, pressing her soft, sweet lips against his. "But promise me we can work through our options. I know either road we take will work out well for us, but I just want to do everything we can to choose the very best for our family, and our future together. Would that be all right Siggy? Promise me?"

"As always, you are probably right."

"Probably?" she quipped.

"Definitely!" he confessed.

*****

When graduation day arrived, the awards hall was packed with alumnae, faculty, and many proudly dignified parents, friends, and families. It was a who's who of the social set, as these dignitaries of all disciplines were beautifully attired, and everyone was groomed to perfection. Philosophers of repute, theologians, revered medical minds, artistic elite, and of course military and political dignitaries were well represented. It would most certainly be a day of tribute and recognition for this next generation; they promised to one day be among the new pillars of German society.

As valedictorian, Sigmund fittingly addressed the alumnae before him and paid deserving acknowledgement to his father, as well as their benefactor, Herr Stottletter. Marissa was aware of his intention to specifically recognize the two towers of strength in his life.

Throughout his address, he frequently directed his tribute to these two guests of honor sitting adjacent to Marissa's mother and her uncle, Prince Nikolaus of the House of von Bismarck.

He never referred to his already well-known circumstances. Being Jewish had caused him to be frequently ostracized in his freshman and sophomore years.

Ridiculed by classmates in his early years, it was something to which he had long since grown accustomed, and he always persevered throughout those difficult times. Although he never referred to these challenges directly, his words had evident impact. He encouraged his privileged class of graduates to honor each other, to be thankful for the opportunities they had been given, and finally, to give back to others less fortunate than themselves, particularly in these turbulent times. To those in attendance, his inspirational message would always be remembered.

The highlight of this speech for Sigmund, however, was not as much how inspirational it was, although it would always be remembered as being so. Rather it was his decision on this day, to publicly do something that was quite unanticipated. It would be his public profession of heartfelt gratitude for Marissa's love and support. It was a last-minute opportunity to share the moment of recognition, not only for Sigmund and Marissa, but also in front of her family, as a sign of respect for her family heritage. Among these family members were her uncle, her mother, Countess Marie von Bismarck-Schönhausen and Marissa's first cousin, Countess Hannah von Bredlow, also the granddaughter of Otto von Bismarck.

"My fellow alumnae, faculty, family, and friends. This honor you have bestowed on me would not be complete without me requesting your indulgence for just a moment more. What I am about to do is quite unorthodox; however, that has never stopped me before." The gathering broke into laughter until Sigmund resumed. "Marissa, would you be so kind as to please join me at the podium?"

In disbelief, Marissa had no option other than to do as he requested of her. Knowing this was Sigmund's moment in the spotlight, she was reluctant to break from the tradition of this event. Inquisitively, but with her usual grace and aplomb, she elegantly walked to the stairs where he had graciously descended to offer his hand and escort her to the podium at his side.

"I understand this is highly irregular, and I thank all of you for your patience; however, I want to acknowledge to my dear Marissa, how very much she has meant to me since the day we met almost four years ago." Still holding her hand in his, he turned to face her and raised it close to his heart to say, "Marissa, my love for you has exceeded anything I could have hoped for. You have profoundly changed my life…and with each passing day, I love you more than the day before."

With that said, Sigmund chivalrously dropped to one knee, kissed her nubile young hand to declare pleadingly, "You mean more to me than life itself. My sweet Marissa, I cannot imagine the rest of my life without you by my side. Would you do me the distinct honor of becoming my dear wife?"

Marissa's eyes filled with emotion and her customary beautiful smile flashed across her perfect, glowing face. "Yes, my sweet, dearest Siggy! I love you, my darling! Yes! Of course, I will!"

His classmates had no idea he'd been intending such a proclamation and appeared suspended in time, many deeply moved with obvious emotion. In a warm embrace igniting the entire gathering, the raucous applause quickly gathered more momentum, and after several minutes finally crescendoed with wholehearted and enthusiastic acknowledgement. Mortarboards filled the air in celebration! It was a wonderful, poignant moment those in attendance would remember for years after.

For the first time in recent memory, Sigmund witnessed tears of pride in his father's glistening grey eyes. By contrast, von Bismarck displayed proud but uneasy anxiousness in his darkened and almost scornful black eyes.

Chapter Five

♂

October 1897 was as glorious a time as any in recorded history in the minds of Sigmund and his stunning bride to be, Marissa. Timing was essential, with the wedding ceremony set to begin at noon in Kreuzberg at The Neue Synagogue (New Synagogue), on the north side of the River Spree.

This sacred edifice, built between 1859 and 1866, was the very heart and soul of Judaism in Berlin, as it proudly welcomed more than eight hundred guests to mark the significance of the day. This event would surely reserve a place in the halls of tradition for this cornerstone of the Jewish faith within Germany, and throughout the world.

It would test the appropriate measure of the display of not only humility and deep tradition, but also the perfectly blended pomp and circumstance of those witness to such a sacred union. No one could ever deny the perfect balance of these definitive objectives, which were now unfolding in perfect harmony.

From the moment the wedding march began, an immediate silence fell over those in attendance. The bright sunshine fittingly shone through the massive skylight of the synagogue, as if God himself was providing glorious witness to this consecrated union. Sigmund was beaming, as were his parents seated in the front row. The slightest glance in their direction was cause to glisten the eyes of both sides of the exchange.

All eyes were turned to the rear of the synagogue when Marissa and her uncle approached the massive open doors for all to see the eagerly awaited procession. As anticipated, Marissa was the epitome of grace, elegance, and genuine loveliness. She had truly become a princess at that very moment. Her beautifully tasteful gown displayed its impressive and delicate train as it extended fully behind her gently gliding steps along the length of the center aisle. Through her impeccably and delicately designed veil, Marissa was genuinely glowing.

Behind her followed Elisabeth, the maid of honor who was escorted by Nicholai, the best man, and the remaining members of the bridal party. Everyone stepped in perfect unison to the steady pace of the organist in the upper balcony. The entire chamber was totally engulfed with the perfectly measured final crescendo of the processional march when Marissa arrived to face her betrothed, Sigmund. The magical moment stirred the soul, as was intended.

Marissa's frail but distinguished Uncle Nikolaus was at her side, proudly extending her delicate hand to Sigmund, and then graciously stepping back to be seated with Marissa's family. When Marissa's entrance began, Sigmund's eyes were solely reserved for his beautiful bride from that moment forward.

The ceremony was a heartfelt exchange between bride and groom, as it should be. There was none of the nervousness or hesitation often experienced by those sharing the nuptials accorded every newly wedded couple. Early in their romantic relationship this union had been unbreakably forged. The words of this day only served to formalize before Christ what had already been firmly established. It was a day of reaffirmation and joy.

With the placing of the ancestral wedding ring provided to Marissa by her great-grandmother Johanna, Sigmund truly honored her family heritage to the delight of the prince. Sigmund had upheld his promise to honor and respect not only his young bride, but also her historic family. The prince was genuinely moved.

The emergence of "this man and this woman" exiting the magnificent portals above the palatial staircase to the waiting throng below was an achievement due primarily to the fastidious efforts of Marissa, and their respectful and obliging friends and family. It was the culmination of a time for reflective pause from the harried pace of life often consuming their productive lives. This was truly a moment to savor.

Amidst the fanfare of the admiring crowd, many of whom were not even known personally to the bride and groom at this point, Sigmund proudly escorted Marissa to a horse-drawn carriage, which had been suitably adorned with white and red bouquets of fragrant, fresh-cut roses. The procession slowly followed the five carriages hired to carry the entire bridal party and immediate family dignitaries to nearby Tiergarten Park. The gazebo near the oak tree was prepared to host the entourage of photojournalists who had already set up their equipment to capture the event.

The Grand Hostel Hotel had been awarded the esteemed honor of hosting the marriage reception of the decade in all its wonderful glory. Located in historic Kreuzberg, it was Marissa's dream to host their special day here, just a short distance from their new home together on Cuvrystrasse.

It was a venue they had enjoyed on special occasions, often just in the company of each other. As such, they were well known among the hotel staff and indeed, many of the regular patrons of this fine centerpiece of German architecture. Their influence and social status, perhaps as a direct result of their frequent patronage at the hotel were evident, since they had hosted various social functions and numerous celebrations at the popular Library Bar.

That was a casual setting often enjoyed by the football team and various university luncheons hosted by Sigmund; however, this hotel also featured their personal fine dining restaurant of choice. Time was often of the essence to them, and they were always assured of prompt and expeditious service, but never at the expense of diminishing the quality and grandeur to which their eminence had become accustomed. Now the hotel was charged with the catering of a fine meal in the massive ballroom.

Beautiful floral centerpieces consistent with the colorful bouquets decorating the carriages adorned every table. No need for any conflicting décor not consistent with the purity of Marissa's bridal gown. Purity and sublime elegance need not be overstated. The fairy-tale was unfolding.

Once the bride and groom were seated and the welcoming aromas emanated from the kitchen, the guests were consumed by the setting, the company of family and friends, and the abundant joy of being part of such a memorable event. The guest list was a hotelier's wish list, featuring the very pinnacles of German society. The day did not disappoint.

"Siggy you have made all things possible in my life. To be seated beside you surrounded by so many of our family and friends makes my life seem surreal. I am so proud to be your loving wife and I will cherish you always."

"We are both so fortunate, my beauty. I never want to be apart from you. You are the essence of my life." Sigmund lifted his champagne glass and toasted his bride. "To love, Marissa. Be mine forever, as I shall be yours."

The reception line had been extensive and despite best efforts, there was simply insufficient time to enter discussions beyond a heartfelt welcome. Sigmund was determined to remedy that circumstance as best as time would allow and specifically sought out a few such guests he was most insistent on personally engaging for some individual discussion. Nicholai's parents were among those few.

"Herr Fahrner, just the man I am looking for! Madame Fahrner, how wonderful to meet you. We had so little time to speak earlier. You honor us by being here today. I trust you had a pleasant journey?" Sigmund enquired.

"Very much so. I don't get to Berlin often, and certainly not with my own lovely bride on my arm."

Madame clutched Herr Fahrner's arm more closely to her. "He never fails to make me smile, Sigmund. I wish you and Marissa as much happiness as we have found together."

Marissa was masterful at engaging people in conversation, and today was no exception. "Nicholai has been such a big part of Sigmund's life; I feel as though I now have a brother. He watches out for me constantly."

"Sounds a bit like the fox guarding the henhouse!" Herr Fahrner quipped.

"I suppose I deserved that one, Father!" Nicholai responded.

Sigmund embraced his teammate, placing his arm affectionately around his shoulders. "We tease the hell out of each other, but I can honestly say his game-winning shot was among the best efforts I've ever seen. He accepted my offer to be my best man; however, I didn't imagine he thought I meant on the football field as well!"

The group broke into rounds of lighthearted laughter until Fahrner Sr. engaged Marissa with his gentlemanly discourse. "Marissa you are most charming and a lovely sight to behold! Good fortune has shined upon both of you. We had the pleasure of speaking with both your families during dinner, and Herr Stottletter as well. They are very fine people indeed and sing their praises to the two of you. The accolades are well deserved, of that I have no doubt. You have both done your families proud."

After Marissa and Sigmund adeptly broke away, more mixing and social banter followed, with numerous guests intent on offering their best wishes personally. There were simply too many to count.

Finally, Marissa found her family in the confusing crowd and the couple excused themselves appropriately to make their way to the Countess and other relatives to whom she was conversing.

"I thought you might have forgotten us, my sweetheart. There are so many guests and so little time in which to meet them all, I suppose. Congratulations to you both! You make a wonderful couple together. Sigmund, welcome to our family, such as it is." The Countess turned slightly to address them and embraced Sigmund to kiss both his cheeks. It was apparent she had perhaps enjoyed a few too many cocktails. Her manner, while courteous, was bitingly sarcastic as well.

Sigmund deflected tactfully to the prince stating, "Sir we are indeed honored to have you here today, and to have you play such an important role in the ceremony. We had so little time to speak at the graduation ceremony and for fear of having inadvertently offended you, I was moved by your kind acceptance to present me the hand of your wonderful niece. I shall remember the moment forever, sir."

"No Sigmund. The honor is all mine. I will admit I had some initial reservations about your proposal of marriage, but I must say it takes a strong man to profess his love so publicly and so eloquently. I admire your candid and respectful manner and your gracious acceptance in honoring the memory of our mother and father. Those qualities will take you far, my young friend. You are a tribute to your parents for their fine upbringing."

This was the day Marissa had anticipated since the moment of their auspicious and very public announcement of betrothal. It was the unfolding of her dream, and Mother Nature continued to co-operate fully in its glorious splendor on this grand autumn day.

CHAPTER SIX

♂

OVER THE ENSUING TWO YEARS, SIGMUND'S NEW medical practice continued to expand. His innate sensitivities to the welfare of his patients were always foremost in his mind. He attended to their physical and mental well-being with the professionalism of a practitioner of many more years of experience, and never once yielded to the fatigue and exhaustion of long hours that could understandably have compromised his standards of care.

His marriage to Marissa continued as if it was a period of extended honeymoon and for them, this was their customary state of mind. Their love was deep and genuine but always demonstrated respect and mutual gratitude for one another. Sex was frequent and spectacular and was usually initiated by Sigmund's profoundly constant romanticism. He strove to be more impulsive and frequently found ways to thread humor and a touch of danger to their lovemaking.

One such day, on a rare and beautiful weekday, they both made an extraordinary exception and set a few hours aside to visit the lake together for some personal time. The lakeside was a secluded and often quiet place, which lovers were known to frequent from time to time, though not necessarily in the middle of a workday. A small rowboat had been arranged and was left tied to a little wharf, as Sigmund had requested. He and Marissa shared a small basket of food, which Sigmund carefully placed in the middle of the boat. Marissa was glowing under her white silk kerchief when Sigmund used the oar to push away from shore.

It was serenely peaceful, and they were just speaking softly and affectionately with each other, accompanied by the gently rustling leaves infused with the scent of the lavender bushes overhanging the shoreline. Tiergarten Park was one such refuge that Sigmund had always wanted to explore, but he'd never made it a priority to take such initiative, until today.

"I have an admission to make, Marissa. Do you fully realize even after two years of marriage, I continue to obsess over you, particularly the past several weeks? Truly, I do. You make me feel more alive than I have ever felt before."

"As do you for me, Siggy. You took me by surprise with this idea of yours. I used to come here with my father when I was just a child, but somehow, we allowed time to pass and haven't returned for years. Thank you for this moment. I know I shall cherish the memory with you always." She sipped her wine while he continued his slow and steady pace following closely to the shoreline. It was a weekday, so the adjacent parkland was mostly vacant up to and beyond the crest of a rising hillside.

Sigmund continued, "Before I met you, I thought I was already somewhat of a man of the world, and I believed I would always be in control of myself and my emotions…but I was wrong. Even as we speak, I have an overwhelming, and quite uncontrollable urge to throw the basket overboard and make passionate love to you, right here in the boat! I've never felt like this, Marissa, not with anyone. Look! Just look what have you done to me!" he said as he gestured to his pants bulging with his eager manhood.

"Really Siggy! What's wrong with you? I want you too but please cover yourself. This is embarrassing! People will see you!" she exclaimed as she nervously checked the adjacent shoreline turning her head from side to side.

"Tell me! Who's going to see us? The park is empty, and we are the only boat on the water!"

"Are you actually expecting me to make love to you right here and now?…You can be *soo* nasty!" she purred so softly and sultry. Her seductive response only served to encourage him more.

"Yes, I suppose I am. And yes, I want us to!"

Sigmund saw no anticipated reluctance from Marissa, and he eagerly rowed the small craft close to the shore under the cover of a magnificent willow tree, which served to provide some modest degree of natural privacy.

Marissa laughed with nervous astonishment and carefully balanced herself as she rose from her seat and stumbled over him to kiss him passionately. In so doing, she almost upset the wobbling craft. Uncharacteristically, she placed her hand on his crotch and squeezed with her trembling hand. Sigmund groaned with pleasure, shouting, "Oh my dear God Almighty!" Overcome by her unexpected co-operation, he nestled more closely toward her, and they wrapped themselves in each other's embrace, kissing, tasting, and lusting for each other awkwardly on their knees.

Marissa's chest was pounding. Shaking with desire, she slowly and carefully fumbled with the clasps of her blouse, while Sigmund simply ripped his shirt open, buttons popping into the boat and into the water. In the blink of an eye, he released his suspenders to drop his pants. The very sight of her delicate and shapely white breasts engorged him with overwhelming desire as he licked, kissed, and suckled them into his mouth. He returned to her lovingly open mouth and expertly, with his surgeon's hand, caressed her succulent breasts to stimulate her already hardened nipples. This was a taste of sheer heaven!

Moments later, it was simply too much to bear. Impulsively but always sensitively, he set her firm, perfect bottom gently on top of the closed lid of their picnic basket, and leaned her back, all the while supporting and protecting the back of her shoulders from touching the bottom of the boat, which was now rollicking on the water's edge. Bracing her now with one strong hand, and with deliberate slowness, he slid the other ever so gently above her knees. Her skin was warm and silk-like as he masterfully caressed her gradually welcoming thighs.

They kissed intimately while he lovingly fondled her already receptive love spot, now wet with her warm pleasure. She trembled uncontrollably and panted with short rapid breaths of delight. The moments seemed to hover as she took him deep within her, while he very slowly and deliberately thrust himself repeatedly to the sounds of her sensual moaning into his ear, so close he could feel her hot breath against his cheek.

Sigmund tried to resist, but the impulsiveness of the moment combined with the wonderful adrenalin rush he could no longer control, caused him to explode within her. She groaned loudly with complete ecstasy and squeezed him between her legs as if to prolong the moment for a few incredible seconds more. He remained motionless to savor their mutual magic until Marissa finally released her lover from her firm leg grasp.

Their impetuous lovemaking had exhausted them both and left them panting for air. Sigmund collapsed into the stern of the boat, totally spent. His head was spinning dizzily. In a moment or two, he struggled to regain his composure and catch his depleted breath. He languished longingly as he absorbed the amazing and unforgettable view of his darling lover, who had herself collapsed into the fetal position on the floor of their tiny love-craft, revealing for the first time the crumpled picnic basket and its crushed edibles, now flattened beyond recognition.

He started to laugh loudly and very much out of control, when Marissa finally regained her own composure to gaze at her man. He shook with laughter as he pointed to the basket behind her. They both broke into rounds of joyful delight with absolutely no awareness of anyone or anything as they both slowly allowed thin slivers of reality to gradually filter into their obsessive and lustful preoccupation with each other.

Sigmund eventually regained his composure sufficiently to cast his view toward the shoreline. There he saw an elderly couple leisurely walking their dog, simply staring at the passionate loving encounter, which had apparently entertained them with such mesmerizing interest. Their mouths were agape when Sigmund quickly pulled his sweetheart to her knees and held her protectively from their view.

When Marissa realized someone was watching, she hastily moved to protect her modesty, causing the couple to shift weight unexpectedly and lose their already precarious balance in the swaying boat. The young passengers struggled and lost control of the craft, which flipped and tossed them overboard with their arms and legs flailing uncontrollably. The water totally engulfed them, providing some much-needed discretion. Their laughter continued with a certain devil-may-care attitude as they savored this silly but memorable event.

How much the passersby had witnessed, the young lovers would never know. Awkwardly and almost reluctantly, but definitely admiringly, the elderly couple withdrew and mercifully faded from view, but not before the man turned to look back one more time and doff his cap, smiling appreciatively as a congratulatory gesture to young Sigmund.

It is amazing how satisfying impulsive sex can be, and how very indifferent to rational and prudent good judgment young lovers become at such a focused moment, until the first few seconds after the passion subsides and reality re-establishes itself. It is a moment we should all cherish and preserve in our memories as our love deepens over time and eventually loses the stark impulse of young, unbridled passion. These are the wondrous moments of life that should never be allowed to fade, nor become irrevocably lost.

Marissa and Sigmund's subsequent scrambling began amidst a flood of giggling and panic. How could they have done such a thing? What were they thinking? What did their private audience think of them?...What would Elisabeth say?...Oh my God, what would they wear...back to the car?....What did it matter? It was gloriously and splendidly wonderful!!

*****

Less than a year later, as Sigmund's practice continued to grow, so too did his family, when he and Marissa were blessed with the healthy and much anticipated arrival of Annabelle Marissa Johanna Landesburg. By their calculation, it was likely the day on the river's edge when Annabelle was conceived! This tiny princess was an enduring tribute to all the deepest expressions true love could possibly create.

Annabelle was more than they had ever hoped or imagined, and her arrival signified the sanctity of their union in ways they truly believed were entirely unique to their passion and devotion to one another. Marissa often wondered, *Was young parenthood always like this?* Their perception of this beautiful creation was for them all-consuming, engorging them with sustained and lustful passion for each other as well as thankfulness beyond anything they had ever anticipated. Annabelle was their unique creation of nature. She represented the absolute purity of their eternal love for each other.

On their wedding day, when Sigmund had slipped her great-grandmother's diamond ring onto Marissa's delicate extended finger, the unending circle of love eternal without beginning and without end, it was a tribute to the bride and to the matriarch of the House of Bismarck...and it surely was so. Since that glorious day, however, lingering in the recesses of Sigmund's mind was his steadfast conviction that a wedding band should be a precious and symbolic gift from husband to wife.

In his private thoughts however, he considered the gift to be somewhat disingenuous. Based on this strong belief, he would never accept the ring on Marissa's finger as his gift, and his alone to give.

He had been self-sufficient in his adolescence and into his early adult life, albeit mostly made possible by taking full advantage of the kindnesses and generosities of his family, his benefactors, and the opportunities he had been most grateful to receive. But on this matter, while he bore no resentment, Sigmund became profoundly moved to do something more.

He took it upon himself to explore the possibility of commissioning the crafting of a special gift to Marissa, from himself this time, to commemorate in her eyes his undying love and gratitude for her ultimate gift to him of their precious newborn daughter Annabelle.

Such was his state of mind when he confidentially made enquiries through Nicholai Fahrner, his best man. Nicholai's father, jeweler Theodor Fahrner, Jr., was a fine elderly gentleman, who happened to have been in attendance on the day Sigmund and Marissa were wed. Herr Fahrner was particularly taken by Marissa, as were most classic gentlemen of the times. Whether it was the lovely tone of her complexion, her style and grace, her entrancing demeanor, or her teasingly tasteful flirtatiousness, men were always drawn to Marissa. Herr Fahrner was honored to assist young Sigmund in the crafting of such a personal treasure.

The commissioning of this ring was a priority to Sigmund, and as such, he was intent on dedicating whatever time and effort was necessary to achieve his ultimate satisfaction.

After receiving a telegram from Herr Fahrner confirming his acceptance of such a delightful task, Sigmund and Nicholai departed Berlin for their full day of travel to the city of Pforzheim, located near the Black Forest of southwestern Germany. Nicholai had not seen his parents since the wedding, so was most anxious to accompany Sigmund on his sojourn. Besides, he was always eager to carouse a little with his companion, away from their wives for a bit of good times. He knew his return home was well overdue.

Herr Fahrner had taken over the Fahrner Company after his father's passing. Through his ingenuity and fine business acumen,

Fahrner, Jr. firmly established the company his father had founded in 1855, to become one of the most pre-eminent European jewelry designers of the late nineteenth century.

It was late in the day when the train pulled into the station. The young men were met by Herr Fahrner's driver at precisely 6:20 PM. Precision was very much a way of life for Nicholai's father, and it was apparent his fastidiousness for detail carried over to his personal life as well.

Upon the friends' arrival at the Fahrner estate, the attendant waved them through the gates to the fine old mansion nestled among the trees and gardens. The architecture was magnificent and very deserving of the lasting impressions that would linger in the minds of a visitor of any social status.

Herr Fahrner was as jovial and welcoming as Sigmund remembered. Despite the obvious distractions of that special day two years ago, this man could not be easily forgotten. He had the proud gait of a man of his bearing, but he was not standoffish in the least. "Bloody hell it's good to see you boys again! How was your travel? I trust all went well?"

"Yes Father, of course!" Nicholai responded as he wrapped his father in a genuine embrace of deep affection.

"Sigmund, my heartiest congratulations on the birth of your daughter. May I assume your darling Marissa has embraced the moment with her usual unbridled enthusiasm? She is a glorious catch, young man, and a fitting tribute to your fine taste in women!" He bellowed with unrestrained laughter. "If it were not for your telegram, this son of mine would still be in Berlin, feigning business commitments to keep him away from his mother and me—of that I have no doubt!"

"I doubt it, kind sir. He speaks of you often, and always in a loving and proud manner. You are deserving of the respect he holds for you and Mrs. Fahrner," Sigmund replied.

"Yes Father, I should write more often, and I do miss you both deeply. How is Mother?"

As Nicholai spoke, Madame Fahrner looking rather plump, waddled into the vestibule bearing the broad smile of the proud mother she was. "Hello, my dear boy! God bless us all for having you home with us again. We have missed you terribly…and pay no heed to your father. He tries not to show it, but he misses you too.

You already know that! Wonderful to see you again, Sigmund! You're in time for a late supper and we have prepared some of Nicholai's favorite dishes tonight, to celebrate his return home."

They were led to the parlor where cocktails were offered and enthusiastically accepted. It was a magnificent setting, tastefully encased in red mahogany panels that extended some thirty feet high to the twelve-inches-deep, plastered coffers crisscrossing the expansive ceiling above. The trim moldings were broad as well as deep, featuring no less than four-inch backbends, enhancing the perception of vivid depth of structure. Upon closer inspection, these finishing touches tastefully revealed decorative burled accents, befitting of such classical architectural design. Very classic indeed.

The regal fireplace was the main focal point however, and was of French provincial styling. It featured polished white marble, stretching from floor to ceiling, all of which was somehow both intimidating and inviting at the same time. This artfully sculptured structure had been patterned to subtly reveal streaks of natural greys, wisps of dark purples, and various hues of blue. Sigmund was mesmerized at the grandeur.

His awestruck gaze was politely interrupted as dinner was announced in the adjacent dining room. The warm and succulent aromas wafted gently to excite his palate and ignite his anticipation of what was to follow. As they passed through the double-arched passageway, Sigmund thought to himself, *is this indicative of the grand opulence to which young Nicholai is accustomed?* How different were the childhoods of these two best friends. Sigmund felt no envy, but rather he became more appreciative of Nicholai's friendship during which time Nicholai had never been pretentious about his privileged childhood.

The meal, as expected, was a culinary delight and superseded anything in Sigmund's recent memory. An assortment of fresh seafood, succulent and perfectly prepared, was accompanied by a fine chardonnay, crisp and sumptuous, evidently barrel aged but possessing only subtle hints of fine oak casks, while intentionally absent a predominantly oaky texture.

The entree was nothing less than superb, consisting of braised beef shanks with a rich, flavorful *osso bucco* sauce, featuring a perfect marriage of a delightful reduction of beef *au jus*. Parsnips and sauerkraut, expertly marinated with onions and red wine vinegar, tenderly accented the nuances of Austrian influences. An outstanding and full-bodied Syrah, from the host's private cellars, left no doubt the meal had been professionally and caringly orchestrated. The young men were unashamedly gluttonous, which delighted Madame, and did not escape the attention of her attending staff.

The evening was spent delightfully, as Nicholai and his parents caught up on family matters crossing both sides of Germany, fostering pleasant memories of times gone by and the promise of a bright future that undoubtedly lay ahead. Herr Fahrner was consumed by entertaining the young men with stories and reminiscences of the well-publicized history of Marissa's proud heritage.

Fahrner proclaimed his earnest admiration for Marissa's ancestor's shaping of the new empire, which he obligingly professed was due in no small part to the might and determination of her great grandfather. It was commonplace for these discussions to occur with some predictable frequency, but few had the loquaciousness and eloquence to express the content as capably as Nicholai's dear father.

As the conversation and conviviality wound down, tempered by the excessive consumption of slightly more than enough alcohol, the sudden realization tomorrow would be a long and hopefully productive day came upon them. The young gentlemen reluctantly decided to retire for the evening in the hope of achieving a sound sleep. Sigmund was most anxious to be at his best to address the matter of agreeing upon the perfect tribute to his dear Marissa and was confident that his trust in Herr Fahrner was well founded.

The following morning, Sigmund and Nicholai bade an appreciative and fond farewell to Madame, as they would be taken to the station directly from Herr Fahrner's offices. It was a thirty-minute-drive to The Fahrner Company and from there, only three city blocks to the train station.

Enroute, Herr Fahrner described some of the history of Pforzheim, which was well known throughout Germany for the prevalence of its jewelry and watch-making industries. It is located only an hour's drive northwest of Stuttgart, one of the largest industrialized cities in Germany, yet it was the reputation of this much smaller city that earned the nickname of *Goldstadt,* meaning the "Golden City."

Upon their arrival, it was not surprising to Sigmund that the offices of Herr Fahrner were of similar stature to his exquisite residence. It was a very identifiable and prestigious building for certain, and it appeared to be the very hub of the business district in the inner city.

Once they were seated in the finely textured settee in his opulent private office, coffee and pastries were presented as Herr Fahrner began to address today's primary areas of focus directly with Sigmund, who had already articulated the purposeful intent of this specific gift. Sigmund's genuine and heartfelt thoughts demonstrably pleased the elderly jeweler, who was excited at the prospect of the task before him. He was truly honored Sigmund had come to him personally.

"Young man, throughout the history of my company, we have taken great pride in our fashioning of numerous beautiful and highly unique items, most of which our clientele purchases out of impulse, or in a moment of fleeting fancy. It is always our pleasure to satisfy their requirements. But this task, as you have described it to me, my dear Sigmund, will be a rare one, unlike the typical demands for which we are often commissioned."

Sigmund felt comforted by Fahrner's comments.

"May I speak freely, young man?"

"But of course, Herr Fahrner." Sigmund replied.

"The very genesis of this thoughtfully conceived idea, as I understand it, is your fervent desire to personalize the occasion of Annabelle's birth, the topic of which I have been giving a great deal of quiet thought. Despite the specificity of the task, many may perceive there to be numerous options. However, as I have become better acquainted with you, I believe otherwise. Forgive me Sigmund…it is my humble opinion there is only one perfect solution."

"Please do tell, sir. I am eager to hear."

"To recognize Annabelle's birth is a noble gesture; however, may I also suggest the ring be crafted to forever be a strong reflection of both your love and your devotion to your sweet Marissa? Let me explain. I have recently obtained a lovely collection of desert diamonds by way of the De Beer Diamond Company. As you may or may not be aware, diamond mines in southwestern Africa have achieved global significance since the diamond discoveries only a decade or so ago in Namibia. Most of the operational mines are under the control and ownership of the De Beer family, with whom I am not only close personal friends, but also one of their premier distributors. Because of this fact, I can assure you I have access to the finest diamonds of our time. These hand-cut stones could be used to create a surround, all meticulously crafted here in Eastern Europe and fitted to perfection. I envision the shank itself should be nothing less than fourteen-karat white gold. What do you think so far? Am I taking you in the right direction?" He reached for the carafe of aromatic coffee and refilled Sigmund's cup. "Cream?" he offered thoughtfully.

"I am excited by the concept, sir! I am not particularly concerned about price, but I fear it may be too pretentious for Marissa's taste. Nothing too ostentatious either, as I worry the diamonds may achieve just that effect. She already has her great-grandmother's wedding ring, so I have no intention of even having the appearance of somehow competing with that iconic bauble."

"It is a magnificent piece to be certain," the jeweler solemnly assured him, "and my intent is to make this ring into something she will cherish forever, but which will also be more comfortable, or shall I say, more appropriate for her to wear on more frequent occasions with whatever subdued ostentatiousness this ring may attain. I believe we can achieve just that effect."

"I trust your opinion sir, and I very much appreciate your creative insights. As I really have minimal understanding of some of the terms you have described...could you...please go back to something you said about a surround? Can you please explain? Surrounding what?"

"To my next point. We must have something featured within the surround of diamonds, a gemstone that stays within your prescribed requirements, or shall I dare say, your self-imposed limitations. Here is my idea. May I ask, what is Marissa's birthdate?"

"September the 10th...why do you ask?"

"Since your desire is to truly honor her delivery to you of your precious daughter, should we not use the design of the ring to represent both the wonderful moment of Annabelle's birth, as well as a dedication to her mother as well? What better way than to place Marissa's birthstone on the mantle of the ring, nestled among the desert diamonds? In her case, it would be a magnificent, midnight-blue sapphire, somewhere between five to six karats, I would estimate."

Sigmund's eyes began to tear with anticipation as Herr Fahrner withdrew a roll of red velvet that encased about twenty such sapphires, each one more glorious than the next. "What could be more striking, I ask you?" Herr Fahrner said. "You understand it is said the sapphire is believed to protect your closest loved ones from harm. It is worn to represent trust, and most of all, loyalty."

He familiarly flipped the magnified monocle affixed to his spectacles and continued to examine the stones carefully. After several minutes of close examination and suspended silence, he decisively offered his selection. "This one without question...in my humble opinion!" He grasped the stone with his jeweler's tweezers and held it up to the sunlight. The refracted light dispersed vividly across the rosewood desk adjacent to both gentlemen. Simply breathtaking!

Nothing more needed to be stated, as evidenced by Sigmund's beaming smile and in the appreciative twinkling of his already moistened eyes. "I can only hope it will evoke in Marissa the same pride and thankfulness you have evoked in me, Herr Fahrner. I am confident it will."

Handshakes and firm embraces were exchanged when they had determined the delivery date and shipping details. Sigmund's confidence in his choice left no need to see the dazzling piece again until he could reveal it to himself in the privacy of his own home. His mission had been accomplished. It was indeed fitting to share another celebratory snifter of fine brandy with Herr Fahrner and Nicholai.

Satisfied his decision was as appropriate and consistent as his intention, Sigmund relaxed with Nicholai enroute to Berlin, sipping a few well-chosen snifters of glowing amber brandies. His head swirled in slight intoxication as he basked in the relaxation of the gently swaying parlor car, heading home to his sweetheart once again. He became lost in his thoughtful consideration of the next few weeks when the ring would be crafted and polished for presentation to his beautiful bride, Marissa.

CHAPTER SEVEN

♂

THREE WEEKS LATER, A NONDESCRIPT BUT SECURELY wrapped package was delivered to Sigmund's Cuvrystrass address. He felt it was more discreet to use the business address as it was imperative nothing be revealed to his unsuspecting Marissa until the actual moment of presentation. To this end, Sigmund had thoughtfully considered the location and specific moment to present his gift to her to create a romantic and memorable event.

He selected the delivery from Pforzheim from the assorted supply of shipments and other customary packaged items and politely but anxiously, excused himself from his office reception area to the private confines of his office, closing the door behind him. His fingers were visibly shaking with anticipation as he carefully removed the small jewelry case from its protective package. For a brief and fleeting moment, he hesitated to consider whether his high expectations had caused him to overestimate its much-anticipated content.

Before opening the case, he strode to the eastern window of his corner office and drew the sashes wider to flood the office with glorious September sunshine, hoping to recreate the moment the sapphire had been selected by Herr Fahrner. Slowly and deliberately, with his surgeon's delicate touch, he raised the hinged silver lid, which had been artistically engraved with Marissa's initials, and gazed for the very first time at the dazzling piece before him.

His heart pounded with complete and utter pride and satisfaction; the piece exceeded even his almost unattainable expectations. His eyes watered as he could only imagine Marissa's reaction to such an offering of his eternal love. It was sheer perfection! Sigmund's eyes welled up with tears as his lips trembled… "Very well done, Herr Fahrner! Thank you!" he exclaimed out loud.

It was September fourth, only six days before Marissa's birthday. It was Sigmund's carefully considered preference there would be no fanfare, no festivity, nothing nor anyone, to distract their attention from this personal tribute. There had been many such family moments in the past, as there might well be in their future together, but this was never intended to be one of them.

Weather permitting, he had decided to picnic under the magnificent old oak tree in the Tiergarten they had often frequented since their college days. He planned to present his unique offering to the love of his life, with only Annabelle to bear witness. It would surely be a fitting spot indeed.

It was all Sigmund could manage just to become fully absorbed in his medical practice. He had recently taken on a commitment to lecture twice a week at the Humboldt campus, and the preparation added immeasurably to his usual heavy workload. Despite the pressure of this task, he enjoyed the divergence from his daily routines. He was thankful to have these onerous responsibilities demanding so much from him at this time, as it preoccupied him so completely. In a way, it helped to alleviate his anticipation of this very special birthday and all he hoped it would be.

With the co-operation and support of Nicholai, he arranged for a former alumnus, one whom Marissa was not likely to remember, to occupy the specific bench Sigmund had selected until he and Marissa appeared. This arrangement was contrived to secure the spot, despite the park being so popular on such a perfect September afternoon. It was within proximity to the magnificent gazebo, which occasionally featured various musical concerts, often string quartets or soloist recitals. It was always predictably soothing and absorbing for grateful patrons of the park.

Marissa had scheduled a mid-afternoon hairdressing appointment to prepare for her birthday party at the Grand Hostel Hotel in the evening, as had become their custom each year. It was an intimate gathering of the usual close friends, and it had become a wonderful tradition for family and friends to be anticipated with great enthusiasm.

She protested strongly at the suggestion of the picnic, stating, "It is already such a full calendar today. Did you forget, we are to see

Jeanette and the baby today, even if ever so briefly? I was so embarrassed to realize we haven't seen them since Rebecca was born. Do you realize it was almost seven months ago, Siggy? Can you believe it?"

"Ahh, you are right, sweetheart. Forgive me, I had forgotten. Too much on my mind I suppose. Of course, we can defer the picnic to another time."

Within the hour Jeanette called, explaining apologetically she was unwell. Nothing serious, but she hadn't slept well the past few days and was a little under the weather. Graciously, as always, Marissa said she understood and thanked her for the call, wishing her a speedy recovery. Such a coincidence. Suddenly they could picnic after all.

Nothing was coincidental. Sigmund had, in his customary manner, carefully orchestrated everything, none of which occurred to Marissa until later in the evening when Janette and her husband would suspiciously appear at the Grand Hostel for cocktails. Sigmund was a lovable conniver and always had a flair for the dramatic. Yet another characteristic she loved about him.

The picnic was on, and within a short time the chef had carefully prepared a tasteful basket consisting of succulent grapes, a variety of tasty melons, an assortment of cheeses, and one of Marissa's favorites, foie gras and biscuits. He also discreetly enclosed a cold, crisp carafe of Riesling and of course, two crystal glasses for the occasion.

"You have thought of everything, my love! What have I done to deserve such elegant treatment? I'm suspicious you are up to something, but whatever it may be, I am delighted!" She squeezed his hand and kissed him tenderly, whereupon they bundled up Annabelle and tucked her lovingly in her pram. It was only a short walk to the park and within five minutes, they arrived quite unceremoniously.

"Oh look, Siggy, such a shame! Our bench is already occupied. We should have expected so, as the weather is truly wonderful...And look, there is a full complement of strings today; even a harpsichord!"

"How fortunate! Not to worry, sweetheart. Give me a moment and let me speak with them. They appear to be packing up in any event, so I don't dare miss our spot." Sigmund walked ahead and sure enough, was able to seize the bench. No need to feign the awkward request. Marissa was delighted and expressed her thanks to the couple for accommodating them so graciously.

Vivaldi's *Four Seasons* concerti had barely begun when the two lovers settled in next to each other, gently rocking the pram as

Annabelle was sleeping peacefully. Sigmund poured some wine and as he always did, toasted Marissa with the discernable ping of the crystal goblets as he kissed her succulent lips.

"You know Siggy, I'm certain Jeanette will be fine, but I must admit I feel a bit guilty for saying this…I am just so very content right now. I am pleased we were able to come here today after all."

"Sweetheart, I…"

"No, please, my love. Let me finish," she said as she held her finger against his lips. "You and I are so very fortunate to have our precious Annabelle and each other. I want you to know how truly thankful I am for all you do for us. You make me feel so loved, and you never fail to give me such a feeling of…how shall I say…yes…inner peace when I am with you. Nothing you could do or say could make me love you more, Siggy."

Tears welled in their eyes as they intertwined their fingers together with such deep affection. "There is something I must say to you too, Marissa, if I may speak now? Would that be alright my darling?" He teasingly smiled.

"Of course, my love. I just didn't want you to interrupt what I had to say. I fear I don't say those things to you often enough."

"Remember when Nicholai and I went to Pforzheim a few weeks ago, on business?"

"Yes, of course I remember."

"To be truthful… it was to meet with his father Herr Fahrner, who sends his congratulations and his deepest affections to you."

"That's very thoughtful of him, but whatever business did you have with Herr Fahrner my love?"

"I must confess, sweetheart, it was not about business at all. We went to see him to seek his expertise, to help me fulfill a strong desire I have had, burning inside of me since the best day of my life Marissa, the day you married me." His lips were starting to tremble.

"Oh Siggy. You mustn't…"

"No Marissa. Now it's my turn," he said as he mockingly placed his finger against her sweet lips.

They both giggled and sipped more wine. They were so absorbed in their intimate conversation they had no awareness of the activities of passersby, nor the progression of the orchestra into Vivaldi's third concerto. They were equally and totally entranced with each other.

"Since our wonderful day, I felt an urge, lest I say a passion, growing deep inside me, to find a special way in which to convey my obsession for you as my best friend, my companion for life, my darling lover…well…my everything! Since Annabelle came into our lives, this obsession has become most unbearable. You already know how much you mean to me, and you know I will love you for all eternity. But I have come to realize… well, in some way, shape or form, 'love' is just a word, Marissa, until someone gives it meaning. That is precisely what you have given me. You have given deeper meaning to my very existence."

Tears were openly streaming down Marissa's adorable cheeks, and she did her best so as not be too obvious to onlookers. As she gently dabbed her tears, she realized it was the first time she had even considered the presence of anyone or anything, since this conversation began. She took this tender moment to check Annabelle and thankfully, the baby had barely stirred.

Sigmund continued, and awkwardly reached into his cardigan pocket to reveal the engraved silver case.

Marissa's lustrous glistening eyes quizzically shifted to the shining case, and then in an instant returned to meet his loving gaze. Speechless, she pensively extended her hand to touch his as he slowly opened the case before her.

"Oh Sigmund. What have you done? This is exquisite!" Her weeping eyes overflowed with emotion and she sobbed uncontrollably with tears of thankfulness and overwhelming joy.

Lovingly he guided the precious golden masterpiece onto her sculpted delicate hand. It was perfectly fitted, and perfectly presented.

"You've made a fool of me you, you silly so and so. Evidently your kindness… and …your thoughtfulness…" she struggled, sobbing and laughing through her emotions, and fighting to regain her composure, "…they surely know no bounds. I never thought I would say this … but…you have just managed to make a fibber out of me, do you know that? I *do* love you even more!" Marissa eagerly lunged at Sigmund, wrapping her arms around her doting husband.

His powerful frame enveloped her delicate body as he held her tightly to his chest in his firm embrace, whispering intimate details of his next intentions, all of which were reserved for his lover's ears only.

Those noticing this emotional and deeply moving demonstration of affection, had quietly and inquisitively assembled and in so doing, attracted other intrigued patrons of the park to witness what they perceived must certainly have been a proposal and acceptance of marriage.

As if on cue, everyone spontaneously started to applaud and cheer the happy couple. Even the orchestra had ceased playing after the third movement, as directed by Sigmund when he had originally commissioned their performance. With a nod of his head they burst into the fourth concerto with the rousingly familiar "Allegro Con Molto" strategically timed to serve as an accompaniment for this loving couple. As the celebrity couple gathered themselves, they waved appreciatively to the smiling and respectful witnesses who remained, and the dozens of others who joined them. Sigmund placed the basket under Annabelle's pram and nestled Marissa's arm, which she had placed under his own.

The pair followed the walkway adjacent to the gazebo and Sigmund extended his hand to the maestro and a few other musicians. "Very well done indeed, Maestro! Your timing and incredible talents were nothing short of perfection. May I introduce my lovely wife Marissa?"

"Wonderful to meet you, Maestro. You have made this an incredible memory for us that we shall always remember."

"The pleasure was all ours, Madame. We were so fortunate to have such a glorious day for your special occasion. We are all pleased to have played a small part in this wonderful moment."

Sigmund and Marissa concluded their goodbyes to the respectful applause of the orchestra and numerous patrons of the park. Many walking on the pathway courteously stepped aside for the young couple, now slowly proceeding to the waiting horse and carriage. Most of them were unaware of the happening that had preceded them but were intrigued enough to continue admiring the handsome duo.

Sigmund graciously accepted his princess' extended hand, as she ascended the lowered step leading to the open door of the exquisitely crafted carriage. Once settled, he gingerly but expertly lifted Annabelle, who had now awakened, wrapping her tenderly and lovingly kissed her forehead before presentation to Marissa.

The day had been a suspended moment in time, a moment they would remember for the rest of their lives. As an added courtesy, one of the musicians graciously offered to walk the pram back to

Sigmund's office behind the slowly moving procession. It was such a perfect tribute to both Marissa and Annabelle, precisely as it was intended to be.

CHAPTER EIGHT

IT WAS A PERIOD OF THANKFULNESS FOR THE COMFORT-able lifestyle bestowed upon the Landesburg family and for their fulfilling love for their healthy and vibrant young daughter, all of which found them on the cusp of an excitingly gratifying career. For Marissa, her preoccupations were rightfully focused upon her maternal responsibilities, which she always embraced wholeheart-edly. Regrettably she was no longer an active musician with the phil-harmonic—such was the extent of her commitment to motherhood as well as to assisting Sigmund with administrative matters of his practice whenever it became necessary.

She and Sigmund were the perfect match for one another in almost every respect. Together they established well-defined objec-tives and had the ability and predisposition to carry them out to fruition. Then suddenly, as often happens, life took a different course when spontaneity threw them a curve. Marissa happily, but unex-pectedly, was pregnant.

It had only been ten months since Anna's birth, but when Marissa shared her suspicions with Sigmund, he was ecstatic.

"This is wonderful news my darling! I knew there was something else on your mind today. I could just sense it. Are you feeling well? When did you know? What is ..." Sigmund was as excited as the day they first met.

"Slow down, sweetheart. I am feeling well. I'm feeling...well... just amazingly happy!"

"When you said you had good news to share, I thought to myself, did Annabelle take her first step? Did she say her first word? But another child...I am speechless with pride!"

Over the course of the next six and a half months, Marissa was glowing and meticulous to a fault in closely attending to her nutrition, weight gain, and general well-being. In short, everything was by the book, so to speak. Sigmund closely monitored her daily routines, as would any doting husband, let alone one with his own medical practice. For the first six months, the pregnancy was normal and stable until, for no apparent reason to Marissa, Sigmund started showing signs of concern.

"Marissa, have you noticed anything abnormal about your health over the past week or so? Every day you tell me you feel well, but over the past ten days, you stated you are feeling more fatigued—not abnormal as your pregnancy progresses."

"Nothing noteworthy Siggy...maybe a little short of breath now and then. I thought perhaps a touch of a head cold what with the winter season and all. Why are you asking? I am very well aren't I?" Marissa was sitting on the edge of an examination table.

"Your legs appear a bit swollen. Please, sweetheart, extend your leg to me."

Sigmund tenderly but firmly squeezed her right and left calves to better determine his growing suspicion she was retaining fluids. It was confirmed. "We need more blood work my dear. Nothing to be alarmed about but I want to be certain."

"About what, Siggy? You must tell me, please my darling."

As he drew some vials of blood, Sigmund explained his concerns briefly so as not to alarm her. "Every day I take your blood pressure reading but over the past week it is slowly but definitively starting to rise. There is no imminent concern, but it is to the point it is no longer a temporary fluctuation. I suspect you may have early indications of preeclampsia. It used to be known as toxemia."

"I've heard of that but know nothing about it. Is it anything serious?"

"If we identify it early, we can keep it under control. Neither you nor your family are typical of those normally afflicted so the tests may show nothing at all, but there are always exceptions. Let's wait until the lab reports are completed before we get too carried away. However, in view of your blood pressure I want you admitted to the hospital, Marissa. If testing confirms toxemia, it needs our immediate attention. Try not to worry, sweetheart. You are in good hands."

His smile and a reassuring kiss on her forehead were not enough for Marissa to relax, but as always, she would agree with Sigmund's proposed course of action.

*****

By mid-morning the following day, Sigmund consulted with Dr. Schleschen and the resident obstetric gynecologist. The urine sample indicated the presence of protein, which was consistent with pre-eclampsia. It was Sigmund's worst fear.

The obstetrician summarized most of which Sigmund already knew. "Marissa's pregnancy is just entering her final trimester. As you are aware, there is no cure per se for this condition, other than to give birth. If we supplement her loss of protein and monitor her closely, she could carry for another four, maybe six weeks. We certainly don't want any chance of blood clots, so it is vital we keep the swelling of her extremities to a minimum. At the first sign of a seizure, we must proceed with a C-section without delay. Understood?"

The doctors were in complete agreement.

"You made a good call getting her in here right away, Sig," said David. "Do you want me there when you tell her what's happening?"

· "Yes, of course. I would feel better if you were there with me at the time. Let's do this, David. Thank you, Benjamin. Let's keep each other posted as we go forward."

Upon hearing Sigmund and David's evaluations, Marissa covered her mouth to hide her shock. *How is all this possible? What has gone so very wrong?* she thought to herself.

"Nature sometimes takes a twist we cannot anticipate. However, you are young and strong Marissa. You are in the safest place you could possibly be. The best thing you can do now is to maintain your customary positive outlook and have faith in the advice we have all agreed upon." Sigmund held her hand and remained calm to convey his own strength of conviction.

Marissa asked for confirmation. "So, if I understand what you are telling me, as long as we take the precautions you have outlined, the baby should have a safe delivery and lead a healthy life?"

"We have every confidence with each passing week that our baby will be just fine...as will her mother, sweetheart. Right now, the best thing you can do is to get as much rest as you can, alright? I'll check in on you later in the day. I love you, my darling!"

*****

Marissa did precisely what the doctors ordered. As expected, midway through her final trimester, it was unanimously agreed that while mother and baby were doing well, postponing delivery any further could place them both in serious jeopardy. Pushing their luck for more time would be foolish, especially having completed almost eight months of the pregnancy. The baby was close enough to full term.

And so, on July 20, 1900, Emilie Elisabeth Landesburg opened her beautiful brown eyes in the arms of her loving mother. She weighed five pounds eleven ounces and was perfect in every sense. When Marissa awoke after the surgery, she sighed with relief as she held her newborn daughter for the very first time. It had been a nervous ordeal for her, and Sigmund knew it.

After their few moments together, this very grateful young mother passed Emilie to Sigmund, who was beaming with pride. He personally took his tiny, newborn daughter to the neo-natal ward for further incubation. As he entered the room to hand Emilie to the nursing attendant, the staff applauded enthusiastically.

*****

By 1902, Dr. Landesburg had become a well-established general practitioner in Berlin-Kreuzberg. One of the youngest and brightest graduates from medical school, he occupied a small, main-floor corner unit in a rather large block of unpretentious apartments. Sigmund and Marissa were the proud parents of two equally lovely and joyful daughters: Annabelle who was now four and already quite precocious, and her younger sister Emilie, who was almost two years old.

As his practice flourished, Sigmund had wisely rented the adjacent two apartments the moment they became available. These he could now separate from his family residence. Within two months, and with consent of his elderly landlord, he had converted these units into his medical offices, which gave him the prominent exposure he had so deservingly earned, right on the main street of Cuvrystrass. Within two more years, he would purchase the entire building and rent it out to many of his medical associates of various disciplines, with his business thereby becoming one of the first private clinics of its kind.

This would signify the hardly modest beginning of a legacy that, within the next decade, would enable Sigmund and Marissa to raise Annabelle and Emilie as privileged children. The medical practice expanded quickly to become one of much acclaim and Sigmund was often the recipient of numerous awards at the renowned Friedrich Wilhelm University in Berlin. Along with these accolades came much-deserved honor and respect as the Landesburg family achieved the distinction of being an up-and-coming family of German aristocracy.

*****

Later that same year, Annabelle entered the *Vorschule Preparatory School*. Leaving her little sister each day meant Annabelle would reluctantly have to entrust Emilie's daily care to her mother. She was a very protective big sister and did everything she could to pay close attention to Emilie's every need. There was never a sign of disdain or impatience toward Emilie, as was often common between siblings, particularly when the eldest dealt with sharing what was once theirs alone—the total focus of the parents. No, this was genuine affection and deep-rooted care for her young sister's best interests.

Most of their younger days together were typically focused on private schooling requiring personalized tutoring from Marissa. The areas of study would consistently take the children's thirst for knowledge to whatever limit of understanding each of them possessed, and then exceed it. This pattern was eagerly embraced by Annabelle and was always beyond what her mother would ever have anticipated. Annabelle thrived on her mother's reading lessons and she would often continue reading passages long after Mother's absence to tend to Father's business needs.

School was not a place Annabelle had been reluctant to attend... until she did so. This precocious young child had such expectations upon her admission to the Vorschule that, other than her natural penchant for socializing, which was considerable, within months she became entirely bored with the curriculum. The tutoring of her mother had served her well but had also created discord for Annabelle at school.

She was a voracious reader of all things Marissa assigned to her, irrespective of subject matter. Such was the trust and faith she had in Marissa's direction. By the age of five, this fastidious child had been studying Immanuel Kant and Friedrich Nietzsche, and already possessed a level of understanding and comprehensive mental agility that would equip her for the challenges of the extraordinary life about to befall her.

As one would expect, Annabelle was not popular among her classmates, primarily as a result of her incredible intellect and even more so, the other students' apparent lack of it. The children were supposed to be of higher than average intelligence, or so Marissa had confided to Annabelle; hence Annabelle was understandably disappointed and frustrated by their innate limitations. It became exasperating to such an extent that after her first month she had become despondent at school and was clearly increasingly unhappy.

Thankfully, several weeks later there would be one fortuitous exception, in the person of Marta Elisabeth. A young colleague of significant repute, this astute young child proved to be the perfect antidote for Annabelle's dissatisfaction at school. Marta had arrived a few weeks after classes began and had in the past experienced her own difficulties being absorbed into the usual and customary classroom routines. It took less than a full first day together for these unique young girls to find each other in their common inability to fit in with the other classmates. Marta was similarly gifted in intellect and inquisitiveness as Annabelle was, but she was so much more mischievous and precocious than Annabelle could have ever become without her influence.

Figuratively the girls fed off each other and within a very short time became inseparable. In fact, each had the distinct self-awareness they were thriving in one another's company. It was as if their collaborative minds had only just started to blossom. With Marta's outspoken manner, she wasted no time in harassing not so much her classmates, but her teachers. This she did, not out of malice, but with a high degree of personal enjoyment and most certainly with clear intent of purpose.

Both girls had already been given an advanced curriculum intended to maintain some modicum of challenge for them. One morning, as a series of algebraic formulae were presented to the girls, the teacher was explaining the importance of breaking down each individual step to lead to the correct solution.

Herr Klaus Gottfried had already grown weary of Marta's pre-disposition to mocking his instructions in front of the class, often in open defiance of his guidance. It had become a source of constant frustration to him, and Marta's attempts at humor were frequently at his expense.

"Once you understand the fundamentals of algebra, you will be better served to solve much more complex solutions in the future. It is imperative you both follow my simple instructions, since it is not the correct answer I am seeking at this point, as much as you are demonstrating your grasp of the fundamentals," he instructed.

"Yes, Herr Gottfried, but if our intent is to solve the problem before us, I can only assume the correctness of my answers must be relevant? That would seem logical to me. Would you not agree?" Marta coyly offered.

He glanced at Annabelle, who was equally absorbed in this inter-action, but only passively, as she would never openly challenge any-one's authority, especially that of Herr Gottfried. "Yes, of course," he said. "Logic is a fundamental premise of algebra. But I insist I must see the logic of your reasoning in order to grant you perfect grade scores. Do you understand me, Marta?" Herr Gottfried could sense she was leading him somewhere he was determined not to go.

"Would you also agree with me that above all, accuracy and pre-cision are fundamental tenets of the algebraic process?" She looked at him quizzically with one brow raised. She was a child of almost seven years of age and was never reluctant to display her formida-ble intelligence.

Again, he shifted his gaze briefly to Annabelle and to the rest of the class to display his own confidence, confirming he was gaining Marta's favor and co-operation. "Yes, Marta, you are correct. It pleases me we are in agreement on these points." How sweet, how innocent, how very infuriating and manipulative Marta could become.

"Then, kind sir, if my final responses to your test questions are precisely accurate, my reasoning process must also be considered correct, as a direct consequence of their precision and accuracy. Would you agree?"

"Again, yes, I agree with such a statement." He smiled engagingly at the class.

"And, in the interest of my own understanding, algebra is specific to determining solutions to problems by way of accurately interpreting specific modes of reasoning in which each and every distinct step is fundamentally...logical."

Herr Gottfried shuffled impatiently and replied, "Marta, I am convinced you have a good comprehension of this subject matter, so may we proceed? We are taking too much class time. It is not fair to the other students."

Marta confidently looked him in the eyes and asked innocently, "Is time of the essence in algebra also?"

"Yes, Marta, it most certainly has now become so! Please just get on with your paper!"

At which point Marta passed him her quiz paper, absent the step-by-step breakdown he'd so steadfastly requested. Herr Gottfried surprisedly, and without looking at the examination, appeared confused. "What are you doing Marta? Do you refuse to take my test?"

"Of course not, sir! I have already completed it, accurately, precisely, correctly, logically, and timely, I might add."

The class erupted with laughter, not having even understood most of the discussion they had witnessed. All they knew was that Marta had gotten the better of him. He was incredulous as he scanned her written responses, becoming red faced with embarrassment. This little devil in disguise stared at him with a proudly irritating smile of satisfaction. Annabelle struggled not to laugh but feared his angry reprisal.

Herr Gottfried crushed the test paper in his fist and crossed to the doorway. In his haste, he tripped on the leg of a desk and stumbled briefly before regaining his balance. Embarrassed by the increased laughter of the class, he slammed the door behind him and was not seen again for the rest of the day.

*****

By the end of first term, the girls' mutual bond had become obvious and was quickly recognized by their families and faculty alike. In short order, following the determination and premeditation of viable options, it was decided in the best interests of the girls that private educational arrangements would be well warranted. Both families were of significant financial means and found it reassuring, as well as practical, to provide a common solution to better enable the potential for their young children to thrive under each other's limitless positive influences.

No fewer than three resident scholars were personally tasked with the creative responsibility of this private tutoring. These professional scholars would be overseen and coordinated by none other than Marissa, who had originally recognized and nurtured her daughter's talented and auspicious capabilities. A similar circumstance had occurred in Marta's upbringing as well, the only difference being a very demanding father from a military background.

The focus of the children's curriculum was to emphasize the base of philosophical knowledge already well established in their very early years: languages, specifically German, French, English, Polish and Russian; and finally, music, by way of mastery of both violin and piano. Music was intended to manifest an appreciation of the arts and perhaps to a greater degree for Marta, to establish a firm spiritual foundation to further inspire creativity and inner peace.

This final discipline of music and the arts was initially met with rebuke from Marta's father, chief of the German general staff, Erich Von Falkenhayn. He had little regard for the importance of such matters, perhaps influenced by his own pragmatic military education and training. Falkenhayn eventually acquiesced to the protestations of both his wife and his little princess, Marta. He was always viewed as stern and regimented, with the only perceivable exception being matters consistent with the happiness of his only daughter.

"Won't this be simply wonderful, Annabelle? I'm so happy Father said yes to Mother so we can always be together!"

"My parents are so fond of you, Marta, and I heard them say we were a good match for one another! I don't understand how their choice of words is appropriate, however. Do you think they are implying we should be competing with each other somehow? I never think of us that way, do you?" she asked.

"Nor do I! I suppose they must think we are happiest when we are together…which of course, we are!" Marta replied.

"Do you suppose we will still see our classmates at any time soon? I worry they will think us too snobby, although I must say I won't miss the frustration of their meaningless conversations."

"Who cares, Anna? Certainly, I do not! Father says we can always make new friends. He wants to be certain they are worthy of our friendship, whatever he means by that. Promise me we will always be the best of friends—will you promise?" she pleaded.

"Marta! Since when do you need such reassurance? Maybe you should get back to our old classmates right now, for heaven's sake!" Annabelle teased, as both started to giggle.

As the new daily routines became more entrenched, their intellectual development soared, and so too did their affinity for each other. They had become something much more than sisters, although Annabelle never once wavered in her ever-deepening love for her little sister Emilie. She tried desperately to spend personal time with her sister every day, but it became increasingly difficult as her scholastic workload increased.

Annabelle eventually made the adjustment and did her best to reluctantly accept what she must by entrusting her dear mother to devote even more of her time and attention to Emilie's needs. Marissa was a dedicated and loving mother to be sure, and Annabelle's concerns had already been well considered by her mother's maternal instincts. Out of respect for her thoughtful seven-year-old Mother Hen though, and her well-intentioned concerns for her young sister, she assured Annabelle she would see to all of Emilie's needs.

Less time with Emilie was without doubt, the only regret of Anna's new educational pursuits. As her academic agenda became increasingly onerous, both she and Marta were simply consumed by it, never once considering it too demanding. Anna's inability to find enough time for her beloved sister however was a sacrifice that often would haunt her. To understand the expansiveness of the daily subject matter was truly astonishing, and it often tested the extent of their parents' considerable knowledge—hence the need for their tutors' exceptional scholastic acumen.

*****

It was late spring 1911. Annabelle and Marta were now thirteen years of age. The proactive efforts of their parents' private tutoring had brought forth the harvest of their dedication and direction. Formal applications for admission for both Anna and Marta were duly completed and submitted to the *Köllnische Gymnasium*. Together they represented the youngest students to successfully complete their family and personal interviews, having earned qualification for such interviews by already passing the curriculum examinations, with distinction.

At this stage of their educational development and with their resulting mental maturity, there would be no more awkwardness in assimilating with these extraordinary intellectuals, each of whom doubtless had their own social difficulties, being identifiably gifted children with all that may have entailed.

The girls' prior personal trials and tribulations were no longer of relevance in their new reality. Those hurdles had already been left in the past. The children's parents no longer had to worry about such problems. There were now other matters of grave concern as the strong winds of change swept across the German Empire. These concerns would profoundly engulf the rest of Europe along with it.

Berlin was rapidly following the lead of London in becoming a major world city. One only had to observe Berlin's District of Siemensstadt to witness firsthand an example of Germany's industrial might. Siemensstadt was an electrical and manufacturing colossus, which became a city unto its own, employing tens of thousands of skilled and unskilled manual laborers, who worked and lived within this single district.

This giant of industry would become a model of success for other manufacturing businesses by attaining new standards of efficiency, quickly becoming the envy of Western Europe. By so doing it affirmed the status Germany had long sought by building piece by piece, a reputation which would shake the very foundations of the earth.

Offering the promise of stable employment, these monsters of industry primarily drew their labor from European immigrants. Entire families were absorbed within the endless rows of massive imposing walls, with buildings often spanning an entire city block to serve its insatiable needs. From the perspectives of these workers, there was no future here, just the monotony of backbreaking, assembly-line work for which they were abusively underpaid.

Many workers could be accurately described as fugitives running from extreme poverty, who were satisfied merely to survive as they toiled to be fed and housed for another day. The Industrial Revolution had radically and predictably altered the efficient economic realities of industry, but of equal significance were the drastic changes to family life, as it had once been. Massive personal fortunes were created for the rich, but very often at the cost of the broken backs of the impoverished.

The days of operating small family businesses not only in Berlin, but throughout industrialized Europe, gave way to automated piecework that proved to be unfulfilling for many. Very few at this time would ever be as privileged as Zeev and Dahlia Landesburg were at the turn of the century when they walked away from the life they once knew. Those opportunities were long since lost in the distant past.

*****

It was a beautiful October afternoon that same year when Sigmund's parents came back to the city from their country home to visit with the family. It was difficult for Sigmund to find the time to drive to their home in the village of Olper in Lower Saxony, which always required an overnight stay. He was always torn between taking time for his beloved parents and tending to the onerous demands of his thriving practice. The travel was difficult for his mother and their visits to Berlin were becoming less frequent over the past year.

"We are all so delighted to learn you were coming this weekend, especially Emilie. She has been talking incessantly about it since we heard."

Emilie, now eleven years of age, had already run downstairs from her room and raced toward her grandparents in leaps and bounds. "Nana, Papa! How we have missed you! I helped Mother in the kitchen this morning. Wait till you taste what we made for you!"

Emilie was still young enough to openly display her excitement whenever her grandparents visited. She was extremely close to them, especially since she had spent many of her summer months staying at their home in Olper. The last time she'd seen them was just before school resumed after the holidays.

As the family settled in to reminisce, Marissa prepared some tea and returned shortly thereafter with a wonderful display of fine cheese selections with biscuits and fresh fruits.

"We are so pleased Anna and Emilie could be home this weekend. Anna should be home shortly. She and Marta are most anxious to see you again."

"Here let me help you with that, my dear," Nana Dahlia offered. Even though she had become very overweight and short of breath, Dahlia was always eager to offer a helping hand.

"It's alright, Nana. I can help Mother now. You just relax. You have had a long day of travel."

"Thank you, Mother Dahlia. Emilie is right. We'll be right back with some wine too. A little something to celebrate the homecoming."

"Oh, how I've missed you, Nana! Do you remember this summer when we baked the banana bread with chocolate chunks, and Papa ate so much he couldn't sleep that night?" Emilie was giggling so much through her conversation Dahlia had difficulty controlling her own laughter.

"Yes dear. How could I forget? I had to sleep beside him, and he was up all night running to the bathroom and always moaning and groaning." Nana put her hand beside her mouth, whispering loudly enough so everyone could still hear her. "I never knew anyone could have so much gas! Whew!" She waved her hand back and forth to exaggerate the event.

"I didn't get any pity from either one of you the next morning. It was delicious, but to this day I still dare not eat another one." Papa Zeev pretended to grimace and grabbed his protruding belly as if to quell his pain.

As the family shared a few laughs at Papa's expense, the front door opened and both Anna and Marta burst in upon them. It was a happy scene, as it always was whenever they were reunited.

"My, my! Look how much you both have grown! Such beautiful young ladies you've become," Nana exclaimed.

"I'm so happy to see you both! Hi Papa!" Anna gathered her grandfather into her loving embrace and kissed his cheek enthusiastically. "How are you feeling Nana? Better, I hope. I pray for you every night," she confessed as she repeated the same affectionate hug.

"I'm just fine dear. You never have to worry about me. But thank you for your kind thoughts, Annabelle. It's so good to see you too, Marta. You both make such a fine pair. You two really are inseparable, aren't you? True friendship is such a wonderful thing."

"We have to stay close together, Nana Dahlia. I always do my best to keep Anna out of trouble," Marta stated so convincingly and sarcastically. Nana never knew any difference, which the family always thought so amusing.

"Anna could learn a thing or two from you, Marta. You are always such a good influence on her, and the family appreciates you looking out for her best interests. What's this you are holding so tightly Anna?"

"Oh, just a little something to celebrate your visit with us." Anna extended her arm to present a beautifully bound package from one of the high-end bakeries nearby."

"Oh, you shouldn't have. But thank you so much for your thoughtfulness, dear."

"It's from Marta too, Nana."

"Well then, thank you both! Whatever could it be?"

Dahlia sat back down while the family was intrigued with the presentation. As she removed the box from the ornately decorated bag, everyone was waiting in eager anticipation of a wonderful dessert for the evening dinner. Nana carefully pulled the tabs and opened the top in full view. To the dismay of Anna and Marta, however, everyone else broke into laughter.

"No! *Not banana bread!* It looks like another long night, Nana!" Papa exclaimed.

*****

The following morning after a hearty breakfast, before the young ones awoke, the four adults enjoyed their morning coffee while more serious discussions ensued. Sigmund had very little opportunity to reminisce with his parents, but when he did, the topics were often focused on the changing times, about which his father still had strong opinions. He was always eager to express them.

"Do you ever think back to those days, Father, and what life would have provided had you continued to work the farm?" Sigmund asked,

"...particularly now that you are retired. Life would have been so much more difficult."

"I cannot even imagine, son. All we knew was something had to change. Fate took over and were it not for your mother's support and confidence in me, I would probably not have tried. There was too much to risk, or so I thought at the time. As I look back, the benefits are so obvious, now that we have the advantage of hindsight. Don't you agree, Dahlia?"

"I do, of course. I think we were still so naïve. We had no idea what would happen. I think we were just at the right place at the right time. Fortune shined upon us."

Zeev continued, "The traditional family businesses are long gone, I'm afraid to say. I worry for these families now that the steady income once promised by big city industry is no longer enough. As I see the situation today, I am discouraged for the working class. I'm thankful my working days are behind me."

"What was your impression of the inner city on your drive today? It's been almost a year since you've come back. Do you miss it at all, Father?"

"As we drove closer to the city it was bustling with people. The restaurants and cafés lining the main streets and intersections of Unter den Linden were filled with customers. There were so many fancy hotels and expensive fashion shops. None of the names were familiar to us. I think the face of Berlin has long since left Mother and me behind. In answer to your question, it is an emphatic *No*. I do not miss the city at all. It is no longer recognizable to us."

Mother Dahlia sipped her wine and offered, "It is all so glamorous, and I imagine so very expensive to shop here. It's so different than what we have been reading about. Clearly someone is making a great deal of money from such beautiful shops. It surprises us that such fine shops are only a few city blocks away from the toil and stench of the blast furnaces of Siemensstadt. We could still smell the pungent odor as we drove closer to the city center."

After some time, Sigmund and Zeev excused themselves from the table to take a casual walk on this quiet Sunday morning. Sigmund had needed some time alone with his father since the moment they had arrived. The sun was beaming brightly as it reflected through the leafy canopy hovering over the side streets. It was a perfect autumn day for Sigmund to have a private and very overdue conversation with his father.

"I'm worried about Mother these past few months, Father. I speak with Dr. Warner quite frequently and he keeps me apprised of her medical status. Since her diagnosis of congestive heart failure, we are becoming increasingly concerned for her well-being. You and I spoke of these matters several times, but Dr. Warner and I agree her physical symptoms are becoming more apparent, especially now that I see her."

"She seems the same to me, son, but I don't really know what to look for. I see her every day, so maybe I don't notice the things you and Dr. Warner see."

"You must notice she is out of breath almost every time she moves about. She's wheezing more than I expected too. That's a sure sign things are not at all well. Her lower legs are swelling which started several years ago, but now it is getting much worse. It's another sign her heart is laboring to supply enough oxygen to her lungs."

"How bad is her condition Sig? She still thinks she is doing well. I don't know what to say. Please help me out here, son."

Sigmund had never seen his father so helpless. "I'll speak with Dr. Warner tomorrow morning. We must get her into the hospital for some additional tests and should keep a close watch over her for those few days. Now that I have seen Mother personally, I agree with his prognosis. I must be totally honest with you, Father. There is not much we can do at this late stage, so we must be prepared if she takes a turn for the worse. Her positive attitude never wanes, and that will buy her a little more time, but it is difficult to remain realistically optimistic. Do you understand what I am trying to say to you?"

Zeev's normal unflappable demeanor was starting to fray. His eyes moistened and he looked pleadingly at his son, who was also now on shaky emotional ground. "She is only sixty-three. Is she going to die, son?"

Sigmund didn't have to answer. One look at him and Zeev knew the answer he was dreading. In a shady spot on the quiet side street, they both silently embraced and for the first time in their lives father and son cried together. Less than four months later, Nana Dahlia succumbed to her failing heart. She passed away peacefully with Zeev still asleep at her side.

Chapter Nine

♂

Against a backdrop of growing political concern, Annabelle and Marta managed to remain relatively sheltered from the current conditions and steadfastly maintained their focus on their educational and social priorities. Both became highly proficient in their musical development, in piano and violin, to the extent they were often featured in the rigorous symphonic tours of the university, bringing increasing repute to the Köllnische Gymnasium.

Marta's father had become less involved in his daughter's development, something she often openly resented. He had become increasingly consumed by his ever-expanding military duties, necessarily sacrificing his home life, but not in any way excusably to Marta. She resented him for prioritizing the military above herself and to that end she became more openly rebellious toward him.

In the early days of July 1914, there was a noticeable element of increasing anxiety not previously existing among Berliners. More and more, people vocalized the growing concerns about the probability of war manifested through controlled demonstrations of the stress inexorably gripping their lives. It was as if the pot was being stirred as a conflicted mixture of conservative viewpoints tried to calm the growing swell of patriotism. This misplaced patriotism was often mistaken as pro war in sentiment.

Tension and uncertainty affected every Berliner to a varying but often vocal degree. As the threat from Russia and France escalated, so too did the shift to the preservation and defense of the empire, eventually creating a groundswell of common purpose.

Inevitably, as the threat of war became increasingly pronounced, panic overran the banking system when those who had, fended off those who had not. The liquid benefits of cash produced a feeding frenzy, forcing several banks to temporarily close their doors and escalating even more fear and panic.

During this period, Sigmund's father had been living a peaceful and quiet life away from the worries through which he had often struggled in his earlier years. His needs were modest and the strain on the economy and the banking crisis mercifully had no significant effect on him. The loss of his dear Dahlia had devastated him though, and he carried his loneliness with him every day since her passing. On the surface, he appeared content and remained self-sufficient despite continuing an almost solitary existence, except for a few maintenance staff who tended to his cooking and gardening needs.

His visits to Berlin became less frequent and despite Sigmund and Marissa's offers to have him stay in the city with the family, it no longer suited his modest lifestyle. It was as if he was slowly retreating from everyone, instead choosing to enjoy his remaining days one at a time until he would finally be reunited with Dahlia.

In the autumn of that year, one of Zeev's staff telephoned Sigmund to inform him of his father's death. His father had suffered what appeared to be a sudden stroke and had collapsed on his front porch. He was in his seventy-seventh year.

The family was heart-broken but even the children were old enough to understand it was what their grandfather desired. He was peacefully laid to rest beside Dahlia, as he had wanted. Emilie took his death the hardest, and in retrospect she realized how fortunate she had been to be such an integral part of her grandparents' lives. At their gravesite in loving respect, she rightly acknowledged this should not be a tragic moment for the family, but rather it should be a joyful celebration of the lives Dahlia and Zeev had led. How is it that maturity and character often tend to blossom amidst the most trying of situations?

*****

In response to these unsettling times, which were compounded by his father's death, Sigmund's concentration remained dutifully focused on those matters within his control: the care and safety of his patients and his family, not the helplessness and despair outside the sanctity of his home and office. Except for occasional moments of weakness and self-doubt, it was his fervent belief these turbulent times would surely stabilize, and any demonstration of his concern or panic would only serve to potentially make matters worse.

He and Marissa, however, kept close vigilance on the girls as the safety and security of the students and faculty at their school came under increasing scrutiny, particularly by the proactive initiatives of Marta's father, General Von Falkenhayn. On a campus populated by young, opinionated idealists, the boldness and bravado of youth had to be anticipated, but carefully controlled. As history had shown, youth does not understand the realities and human cost of war every generation before had to endure, until they truly endure and survive it themselves. It is always too late when the wisdom of their emboldened naïveté is called into question.

Numerous universities had heretofore witnessed among their student bodies, an aggressive enthusiasm for the announcement of war with Russia and France, primarily disguised by the colors of patriotism. Unsupportive articles and photographic evidence to the contrary were mostly suppressed and were generally regarded as anti-nationalist criticism. The silent masses, consisting of millions of peace-loving German mothers and fathers, were voices going largely unheard.

Despite the majority of Germans pleading against it, the vocal outcry for war by the overwhelming minority was falsely exaggerated to give the appearance of establishing a common purpose of national unity so sorely lacking in Germany at this time. The groundswell of supporting propaganda continued, as news of early victories on the battlefields was made public, and anticipation of a swift resolution to war seemed probable. For the German public at large, the vocal minority spoke for those who remained mute, creating the pervasive and mostly erroneous impression Germany in its entirety had become mentally acceptant of mobilizing for war.

Berlin had always been the epicenter of the German Reich, and it was never more evident than in 1914. A strengthening of military troop presence within the city redefined the urban atmosphere, serving to reassure the anxious populace orderly conduct would be maintained. In the interest of further easing their tension, by summer's end the public was kept very much unaware of the heavy losses this proud nation had sustained. Despite these efforts to control the press, the toll of war would become overwhelmingly evident in a manner Berliners had never experienced and were reluctant to accept.

Normally Germans were proudly welcoming and hospitable to outsiders from across Europe and America, to enhance the image and positive global perceptions of their homeland. The tide had now turned to one of suspicion and persecution of visitors. This paranoia was directed even more so against alien residents.

These people were treated as if they were treasonous spies and were punished accordingly. The paranoia was infectious and fueled by the German unpreparedness for their domestic circumstances. Despite their formidable military capabilities, domestic inventories and supply lines were considerably inadequate. Awareness of these facts was magnified by the imposition of powerfully effective military blockades by the British Navy.

Day by day, the shortage of everyday basics led to continuously growing lines of hungry customers, from the late-night hours to the following midday, when shops had already exhausted their supplies. Due to these overwhelming demands for the necessities of sustaining life, prices quickly inflated beyond the reach of all but the wealthy, further exacerbating the eroding fabric of society. In response, crimes of assault and petty thefts escalated and the once-orderly cultural Mecca that was Berlin, lost the reputation it could neither warrant nor sustain.

The natural result was the strictly enforced rationing of bread, milk, meat, and potatoes, which typically were set at amounts meeting only half of the quantities normally consumed before rationing was implemented near the end of 1915. A year later, when potato crops were decimated by poor crop production, turnips and other less agreeable crops were used to supplement the already sparse German diets. It was not long before Germany's faces of despair were re-sculpted to reveal visible signs of emaciation, in the form of withered physiques and protruding cheekbones, indicating certain evidence of physical malnutrition.

On a gradual basis, the malnourishment of their patients did not go unnoticed by Sigmund and Marissa. They too saw first-hand from a medical perspective, the toll that was taken on working people. At this chaotic time in history there were moments when Sigmund's shell of armor was tested. This was one such time.

It had been a particularly long and arduous day when the last patient had finally left the clinic. Sigmund slumped in his office chair, too exhausted to make sense to himself, let alone to Marissa. She was the only one to whom he could confide his innermost feelings at a time such as this. He was too tired to even go upstairs to bed.

He spoke slowly as he struggled to clear his mind. "You know, Marissa, I am coming to believe we are living through a time in our personal lives that must be a fantasy—a figment of our imagination, one could say." He paused haltingly and looked about the room as if seeking answers to questions he could not capably articulate.

"What are you trying to say, Siggy? Has something happened I don't know about?" Marissa stared at her husband closely to examine his facial expressions for a visual clue. Not comprehending his comment was a frightening feeling to which she was totally unaccustomed.

"Please my darling. I need a cold glass of water."

In only a minute Marissa returned to the room, visibly more anxious than when she had left.

Without saying a word Sigmund slowly downed the entire glass of water, trying to compose himself for what he was struggling to say. "It was always a dream of ours to serve our community in such a way as to make a positive difference in people's lives. We have spoken about this since before we were married."

"Yes, of course. I think we are still trying to accomplish that goal, are we not?"

"I thought we would get there someday, one family at a time. Now I am not so certain."

"It's the first time I've ever seen you so despondent. What has brought about this sudden change in you, Sigmund? Tell me please."

"Today was a day like most others this past year or so. It seems no matter how much we try to mend our patient's physical injuries and sicknesses, I am beginning to feel overwhelmed by even more than their broken and disfigured bodies—just as perceptibly, it is their broken spirits. Their sallow and exhausted eyes are windows to their souls, and I swear I can see the profound despair within them. It struck me that our own family lives stand in such stark contrast to so many of our working-class patients. It's hard for us to fully grasp the true depth of their anguish."

"I know we have so much to be thankful for. We are truly privileged Siggy; however, we certainly shouldn't feel guilty about our good fortune…" She thoughtfully paused and hesitatingly asked, "I know that's not what you are saying, is it sweetheart?"

"No of course not…well perhaps not directly at any rate." As he shared these confidences to Marissa, his eyes became misty as he continued. His lips were trembling now. "Sometimes I feel so entirely out of touch with our patients…and utterly helpless to comfort them."

Marissa had felt something similar too but had never confided it to Sigmund. He was always her rock, and she felt it to be much wiser to keep such feelings very much to herself. "No one is more dedicated and caring than you, my dearest. You are only human, Siggy. We must do all we can do—nothing more nor anything less. You yourself told me that years ago."

Marissa reached firmly under his arm and attempted to pull him to his feet. It was an impossible task, but he sensed her strong effort to shake him somehow from his growing despondency as he began to follow her lead and rose from his chair.

"Come! Help me get you upstairs. You will feel better after a hot bath. Please come, my darling. Tomorrow will be a better day."

*****

By 1917, the shortages of food were devastatingly apparent and felt by everyone except the wealthy among them. The rich could continue to purchase nutritious and fanciful foods, wines, cigars, and fine fashions, much to the chagrin of the lower classes. It was a constant source of domestic unrest and frequently caused life-threatening altercations owing to the growing desperation and frustrations of the constantly expanding and under privileged lower classes.

When the war ended, following the inevitable capitulation of Germany, many thousands of subsequent deaths were caused by the continued enforcement of the British naval blockades. These harsh actions caused famine and starvation to be the weapons of choice. Young children suffered a significant percentage of these deaths. Additionally, the numbers of unsuccessful childbirths escalated profoundly, often claiming the lives of the women delivering them.

Starvation and the resulting sickness and disease were not limited to Berliners, as these contagious conditions knew no physical borders, nor class exemptions. Influenza and tuberculosis ruthlessly attacked the poor and the homeless due in large part to the inability of their immune systems to fight off infectious diseases. In a futile attempt to stave off extreme malnutrition, field kitchens became prevalent throughout city streets, however even this well-intentioned effort failed to substantially offset the ravages of extreme hunger.

Desperation spawned vast numbers of homeless children and orphans to scrounge for food and coal to fight the oppressive coldness in makeshift shelters. There was no time or energy to attend schools. Education was only relevant if they had any concept of a future, of which there was no prior thought or consideration in such desperate times. Raging hunger always took precedence.

In the fall of 1918 Germany had lost the ability and the will to continue fighting. When her allies started to withdraw and the German people began to revolt, Germany sought armistice. It was granted in November of that year after having cost 17,000,000 lives.

It was a time of profound change in postwar Germany. Class distinctions became more engrained amidst the readjustment and humiliation of her abject defeat. The Treaty of Versailles, under the authority of the Allied Reparations Committee, imposed punitive reparations of $33 billion dollars against the German Republic, and an additional twenty-six percent levy was applied on all exports for a period of forty-two years. The debt load on this once-thriving economic colossus was crushing, as it was intended to be.

Discord on the streets of Berlin was continuous in the form of street fights, demonstrations, and general fisticuffs by gangs of the oppressed and the vanquished, often orchestrated by influential intellectuals with steadfast direction of purpose.

Confusion and new realignments of government representation were struggling to restore order to the floundering republic. The Social Democratic Party was challenged in this tumultuous time by the growing prevalence of the KPD, the Communist Party of Germany, which fed the tenets of Stalinism and Leninism to the disadvantaged lower classes. It was commonplace to witness the forces at play between the communists and the fascist conservative establishment.

The seeds of discontent had already been sown. The Social Democratic Party was dissolved and under the initiatives of party delegates, quickly evolved into the Independent Social Democratic Party of Germany. The returning German Army mutinied and under threat of a pending revolution, Kaiser Wilhelm II abdicated, triggering massive demonstrations that screamed in unison for new governance.

The first of many priorities of the new political leadership was to facilitate massive increases of food supplies, which were mercifully no longer restricted by naval blockades. While there would be disruptions of violence and turbulence as political and social norms were restructured, it was an auspicious beginning taking years to fully reconcile. The bitter revulsion of the Allies' decimation of the vanquished, however, would not be easily quashed.

CHAPTER TEN

♂

BY THE END OF THE WAR, SIGMUND AND HIS FAMILY had remained relatively unscathed physically, but emotionally and spiritually, they and millions of others were scarred by the traumatic impact of how the German Empire had zealously shaken the very fabric of Europe. The constant shroud of fear and disconsolation had eroded its citizens' faith in Germany's destiny to rule itself with dignity and empathy. In the light of public outrage now bubbling over like a tempest in a teapot, it was necessary to grudgingly reconsider their future aspirations, which they realized could only be achieved by new leadership.

Throughout this rebuilding process, Annabelle and Marta graduated among the best intellectual minds Köllnische Gymnasium had produced. Much like her mother, Anna, as her friends and fellow academicians now knew her, had fallen in love with a promising young alumnus in whom she had found her intellectual match. Jacob Friedman was a devout Jew from a well-to-do family of psychologists and theologians, the company of whom had reawakened in Anna the dormant Jewish ancestry of her dear father Sigmund, pleasing him more than she could have imagined.

Marissa, despite all her wonderful attributes, of which there were too many to count, had not been a practicing Jew and was less observant than her husband. Sigmund had always understood her religious devotion was based more as a matter of compliance of marriage than it was of deep Judaic faith. It was gratifying to him knowing the tradition of his parents' religious convictions would continue through Anna.

Marta, on the other hand, had enjoyed occasional romantic trysts from time to time that had been intended to be only flirtatious in nature. She took these developing intimate relationships lightly and her promiscuity, while often a concern for Anna, was a secret Marta knew would always remain safe with her closest of friends.

In recent months, however, Marta had been quite taken by Klaus, a strikingly handsome German officer, whom she had casually met at a social function with her parents. This was a man with a most promising future, who had also caught the attention of her father. He was born into a military family and had been educated at the Prussian Military Academy, the highest-ranking military college in Germany. Under the watchful scrutiny and guidance of his father, Field Marshal Walther von Brauchitsch, Klaus had been fast tracked and it was quite fitting when both families fully endorsed such a collaborative union.

Marta, not one to often acquiesce to her father's wishes, appeared to do precisely what he had hoped she would do, but her motivations were only of an opportunistic and sexual nature. Not to be outdone by Anna, or so it seemed, the announcement of Marta and Klaus' marriage came only three months after Anna and Jacob's engagement.

The two young ladies remained forever close and as was their habit, they were highly protective of each other. As they continued to pursue their professional music careers after their graduation and throughout their budding romantic involvements, they travelled in the same circles. This provided them the opportunity to maintain their bond of friendship as closely as they always had, although Anna did not remain as fully immersed in her musical career as Marta had continued to be.

By contrast, however, both Jacob and Klaus seemed to merely tolerate one another on those infrequent occasions they met. There was never a problem between them, but they were of much different character, education, and background, particularly when Klaus' military responsibilities often drew the ire of his very spoiled and self-absorbed, young wife. It surprised no one their relationship was frequently contentious, but over time both Anna and Jacob adjusted their expectations to frequently accommodate Marta.

Only a few months into their second year of marriage, both couples found a way to again keep pace with each other. This time it was Marta who described a romantic liaison with Klaus occurring in a quite unpremeditated manner when Klaus had been home on a rare furlough. She freely admitted to Anna her carelessness on this occasion when in an inebriated and careless moment of lust, she did not even consider birth control. She confided the details to Anna, and both friends giggled and laughed at her description of the intimate exploits of the evening in question. Marta was often impulsive and consistently found ways to deal with whatever life presented to her, usually to her ultimate advantage. Why should her becoming pregnant be treated any differently?

As was typical of their approach to life, Anna and Jacob, in a much more subdued fashion, planned their pregnancy. As with almost everything in their lives, their thought process toward life together was far less impulsive than Marta's. It was inexplicable at times, how these two young ladies continued to depend upon and to thrive in the company of each other, despite their contrasting approaches to life. This was, however, a friendship neither party would ever tarnish.

Both young ladies enjoyed routine pregnancies up until the final trimester when Anna experienced some minor, but potentially important difficulties her father cautiously advised she take seriously. Was this to be a repeat of her mother's pregnancy complications with Emilie?

Although there was ultimately no foundation for any alarm, at the time Sigmund strongly urged her to minimize her remaining travel commitments with the symphony orchestra and seek more time to rest, at least for the duration of her pregnancy. Anna was very much a woman of her own mind, but not when it came to medical matters. She and Jacob heeded her father's recommendation and reluctantly requested an absence from her travel commitments, which the Hungarian-born resident conductor Arthur Nikisch graciously granted.

By contrast, the most difficult issue for Marta during her pregnancy was to curb her drinking, smoking, and on infrequent instances, her cocaine indulgence. Since becoming a leading musical artist of significant stature, she continued to remain who she always would be...Marta; rebellious as ever, controversial among her followers, and a highly intelligent woman who had no reluctance in letting her strong opinions be known. Her legions of admirers fed on her bold audacity and responded positively to her growing charisma.

Anna did her best to encourage some element of moderation but was reluctant to do so for fear of jeopardizing her close friendship with Marta. It was a relationship she was determined to maintain as she had been throughout their childhood together.

"Marta you know I always have your best interests at heart, don't you?" Anna asked.

"Of course, my dear. Why would you ask such a silly question?"

Anna was hesitant to proceed but Marta quickly read her confusion and boldly pushed the issue. "What is it that you aren't telling me, Anna? What have I done now?"

"It's just that you are with child now, and you have more than just yourself to be concerned about. For the few months remaining in your pregnancy, why not consider shall we say, showing more moderation with your unhealthy tendencies?"

"Are you referring to my alcohol consumption?"

"Yes, and smoking now that you mention it. But the cocaine must be off limits."

"I agree Anna, and I assure you I would *never* use cocaine while I am pregnant. But surely if I drink only moderately, the cigarettes are harmless, aren't they?"

"Perhaps so, but my father thinks otherwise. Remember the impact Mother's pregnancy with Emilie had on her physical well-being. That had a profound effect on him. There is a definite lifestyle connection, I'm certain."

"I never considered smoking to be unhealthy for the baby until now. I suppose I just get so caught up in having a good time, I lose my usual objectivity. Sometimes one thing just leads to another."

"Forgive me Marta for addressing this but if I can't advise you, who else is going to do it?"

"You know as I think more about this, I recognize your positive influence has often tempered my more outrageous inclinations. At the very least you have urged me to rein in my temptations to at least a more manageable level. Were it not for your steady influence, there is no doubt I may have exceeded the boundaries of public acceptance, perhaps tarnishing my career by doing so. Anna you have earned my trust and confidence long, long ago. For all intents and purposes, your unconditional support for me has saved me many times over from my own self-destructive behavior. Thank you for this, Anna. I hope I'm not an embarrassment to you. Your opinion of me is really the only one I ever really care about."

"I'm so pleased you feel that way, Marta. And no, you never embarrass me. To be candid, I believe your approach to life perhaps protects me in some way to not experience many things I may occasionally be tempted to try, but even so I can at least imagine them. Do you understand what I'm trying to say?"

"Yes, of course. You were always a bit of a chicken shit waiting for me to go first!"

"Well, that puts it succinctly!"

*****

Marta's profound growth in popularity grew by leaps and bounds, particularly because she was constantly approached by the best fashion designers the world had to offer. Coco Chanel and Marta's names quickly became synonymous with each other while Madame Chanel's ever-expanding reputation reasserted her position as the undisputed leading fashion icon in all of Europe.

Going forward, most of Marta's gowns were those fashioned by the House of Chanel, which drew legions of wealthy admirers and elevated Marta's status to new standards of iconic popularity.

It appeared she could do no wrong and she did her utmost to make a conscious effort to remain in the spotlight of criticism without exceeding acceptable boundaries of motherhood, at least until the baby was born. She continued serving in many ways as a strong female presence to be embraced by women throughout Germany and Western Europe.

Being a dedicated and hard-working socialite throughout her pregnancy Marta continued to fastidiously prepare her recitals and fulfilled every symphonic obligation possible, including the hectic travel schedule to be expected for a rising young superstar.

It was about this time when regrettably, Maestro Nikisch passed away. He had served the symphony with distinction for over twenty years and his contribution helped to expand global awareness of the Berlin Philharmonic, which played a significant role in the advancement of this musical art form in Berlin. The city was now firmly establishing the reputation it had long sought, to be considered one of the pre-eminent cities of the world as it entered the era of the Golden Twenties.

The tasks of Maestro Nikisch's capable and dedicated responsibilities now fell to the leadership and guidance of Wilhelm Furtwängler, a resident Berliner who broke away from the conservative historical foundation upon which the Philharmonic had been previously patterned. He was particularly proud and very appreciative of the natural flamboyance and technical expertise of his rising young star; the beautiful, albeit controversial Marta. It was his firm belief her very presence furnished the potential of enhancing the popular appeal of the orchestra within the existing established base of concert patrons.

The young nouveau riche and the expanding middle class had their own exquisite sense of high-end fashion. Many were drawn to the symphony to eagerly witness Marta's newest fashion offerings. Large numbers of these devotees of haute couture would inevitably also become concert advocates, irresistibly drawn to the classical experience as much for the opportunity to showcase their tasteful and incredibly expensive gowns, as it was for the glorious music.

But it was the renowned Coco Chanel who stood the world of fashion on its ear when she revolutionized women's tasteful style away from the all-too confining and unbearably tight corsets...to women's ultimate delight.

Chanel's free fitting and less confining garments were eagerly sought by the wealthy women of Europe. Madame Chanel was known for radical but always tasteful design changes, to suit the new dynamics of women's comfort needs. As Chanel once said, "*Luxury must be comfortable, otherwise it is not luxury.*" When Marta's professional musical fame and naturally flamboyant persona were complemented by Chanel's design and marketing expertise, the dramatic benefits were mutually significant.

Chanel's astute attention to seizing opportunities had long recognized the potential value of capitalizing upon Marta's natural beauty and celebrity status. This awareness opened yet another significant market niche.

In 1921 Coco released a tasteful and seductive new perfume, *Chanel No. 5*. It was chemically formulated to "*smell like a woman*" to use Coco's own words. It was exclusively available in Chanel boutique shops, until the insatiable demand for the complex and seductive scent reached unanticipated proportions, requiring Chanel to extend its availability to surging global demand.

This added a significant touch of enhanced elegance to Marta and to the symphony she represented so admirably. She was described in the tabloids in and about Berlin, as a "woman in whom good taste and elegance are pronounced." By contrast, she was also known to be feisty and high spirited in her passionate and questionable defense of her various vices. These questionable tendencies did nothing to dissuade the colorful persona of Coco from her continued support and growing dependence upon Marta. These two formidable women were birds of the same feather.

Always having a discerning eye for the latest fashionable trends, Marta continually set the tone for others to follow, featuring gowns, shoes, jewelry, and now sensual fragrances on stage. It was not coincidental when sales skyrocketed in the wake of Marta's strong endorsement.

After so many successful styles of sophisticated dress wear had been introduced to the grand stages of the symphony, their collaboration was again reignited to an even higher level when they agreed to dare to defy the prevalent standards of the day. During this exciting time even Marta's pregnancy did not deter her from her electrifying and very demanding musical career. In fact, her pregnancy intensified it. Coco Chanel took her loose fitting and refreshing sense of style to design ultra-chic clothing ensembles for the pregnant woman. Who better to introduce them to the world stages than Marta?

Elsa Schiaparelli, Coco's Italian counterpart, followed Chanel's lead and introduced glorious knitwear to Marta designed to "*release women from the bondage*" of restricted movement and personal expression. Sighs of awe from the packed theatre audiences were always apparent from the moment Marta literally flowed across the stage. She seized the attention of her devoted fan-base, which was always anxious to absorb the visual delight and the seductive scent of this extraordinarily beautiful violinist.

Whether she was the featured artist on the program, or a supporting underscore to the evening selections, it was Marta who always received boisterous accolades and shouts of support amidst the raucous applause. The likes of such adoration had never been seen in the customarily subdued and reserved expressions of audience enthusiasm. These events had always been sophisticated with appreciative acknowledgements of good taste and quintessential elegance. Her unique influence was contagious and inspired spontaneous praise and a welcome breath of fresh air in each symphonic performance. Her performances delivered absolute delight to the orchestra, the maestro, and the fully absorbed audiences, who always retired from the auditoriums thirsting for more.

Marta's personal endorsement of high-end women's wear created a furor within the industry, causing other designers to fight for her attention. Paul Poiret, Jean Patou, and numerous others also sought to share in the limelight inhabited by Marta, all the while irretrievably catching their own fans and collaborators in the symphonic embrace as well.

The rapid pace of life somehow agreed with Marta, including her frequent fashion photo shoots continually endearing her to the public, even as her slender figure became more plump through the late stages of her pregnancy. It would seem that as her belly grew, so too did her popular acclaim.

It was May of 1922 when Marta, now twenty-four years of age, delivered a handsome little boy at seven pounds, eleven ounces, with glorious blonde hair and beautiful blue eyes—the image of both his parents. Despite his best intentions, Klaus was unable to be by her side when her water suddenly broke and labor commenced. As one would expect, Anna was at her bedside throughout the healthy delivery of her beautiful son. His name would be Manfred.

Although his and Marta's marriage was somewhat tempestuous, Klaus was a very proud and appreciative father who doted over his son and had newfound desire for his lovely bride. It was as if young Manfred had awoken something in his father, tempering the authoritarian military manner that had until now pervaded his habits and demeanor almost entirely. This was understandable, what with the way Klaus had been conditioned throughout most of his childhood. He was and always would be a dedicated military man, but over time a sensitive side also started to emerge.

Anna and her husband were as fulfilled and joyous as if this little boy was their own. Marta thought of no one better qualified to comfort her and attend to the baby than Anna, and Anna would have it no other way. It was frustrating to Klaus to have missed the event, however he found solace in the depth of support and comfort provided to Marta by her lifetime companion.

He had come to better understand this unique sisterhood and had, through this birth, even come to better appreciate the many kindnesses Jacob had extended to Marta and him. He had no such close friendships in his own life. Like his father, he seemed to lack any significant personal relationships other than those with military rank. Like father, like son...it was all they had known.

Less than two months later Anna gave birth to little Pietra, a lovable child with only slight wisps of reddish-brown hair and mystifying dark-brown eyes. Despite Sigmund's anxious concerns for Anna's health in the latter stages of her pregnancy, due in large part to Marissa's pregnancy with Emilie, she progressed through her final trimester with flying colors.

Pietra was a healthy and vibrant six pounds, six ounces, another of nature's small miracles that remind young parents of new beginnings, temporarily shifting focus from the reality and frequent tedium of everyday life. One could only imagine how these beautiful newborn lives would be intertwined but be surely destined for such contrasting pathways to the roads they would inevitably have to follow.

*****

Maestro Furtwängler was most accommodating in restructuring a less demanding personal appearance schedule for his rising superstar. During her maternity absence and the months following Manfred's birth, Marta's popularity did not wane. She continued to be a significant influence upon the maestro in reshaping the selections of various classics known to have featured some of the world's most talented solo performers.

When Marta was scheduled to perform on far less frequent occasions, her amazing charisma and colorful personality predictably drew even larger audiences, further enhancing and revitalizing not only her own popularity, but that of the classical music scene as well. Many younger generations of socialites discovered for the first time in Marta, an international common ground for her definitive taste for fashion, as well as a fond affection for her outspoken and often rebellious behavior.

Marta's magnetism and flamboyance were permanently ingrained into her image, but now her influence and insightful musical opinions, which were encouraged by her conductor, added immeasurably to her professional credentials. As a result, she was now requested to appear as a featured artist with not only the Berlin Philharmonic Orchestra, but also as a guest artist of the Brussels Philharmonic Orchestra, the Munich Philharmonic, and the Orchestre Philharmonique de Strasbourg. She was increasingly dismayed at her inability to accommodate these various engagements and reluctantly chose to strictly limit her appearances to continue caring for young Manny.

Although disappointed at her inability to continue her former rigorous professional agenda, her adoring fan base were moved by her more motherly identity; a side of her not seen before. It appeared she was human after all. Amazingly, this emergence of her softer side made her more relatable and garnered incredible respect from her devotees. It was a response no one had anticipated.

*****

One evening as the day wound down, Anna carefully placed Pietra into the warm bath water typically full of large bubbles the little one would always enjoy popping and smearing around her exposed chest. The yellow rubber ducks bounced about the dear child in complete disarray as she tried intently to stop them from slipping away from her tiny grasp. It was Pietra's favorite time of day and for Anna, it was approaching her private time with Jacob too. Life was truly joyful indeed.

Anna finished bathing Pietra and was rinsing shampoo from her tousled curls. "No need to be afraid, sweetheart, the water never hurts you. See!" as she poured fresh, warm tap water over her hair. "Whee! Look at my brave little girl! Mommy is so very proud of you!"

Pietra was still spitting and gasping for air. As with most young children, it was quite frightening in the moment, but always resulted in more giggles and laughter as soon as the flow of water stopped. Wrapping her in a freshly scented towel adorned with animal characters, Anna lifted her precious bundle to the dressing table and commenced to lightly powder her body from head to toe. These were indeed fulfilling moments Anna would cherish forever. "Come my little angel, let's say goodnight to Father. That's my good girl!"

She found Jacob in his usual spot, reading the newspaper beside the fireplace. "Hello Daddy. It's time for bed. Would you mind taking her and tucking her in for me? I'm already quite wet and I really must take a bath myself, my dear."

"Of course, sweetheart. I've read more than enough upsetting matters for today. I'm delighted to do so!" Jacob was a wonderful father and never refused to cradle Pietra in his arms whenever he was given the opportunity. Moments with their little one comforted him as much as they did Pietra.

Within the hour, Anna returned from the bath in her cozy nightgown and tiptoed quietly into the baby's room for one final check before preparing tea for her and Jacob, as was her custom. "So, tell me Jacob. You intrigued me a short while ago; something upsetting today, no doubt? What has happened now, pray tell?" She sat on the footstool near his feet, both hands grasping the steeping hot teacup.

"Yes. I once thought it may be nothing, but I am noticing more and more unsettling matters coming out of Munich…again. It is becoming most disconcerting, Anna. These extremists are getting more press with every passing day, and what was once just another glorified disturbance, is gaining serious political attention. You and I spoke about their disturbing attacks against the status quo months ago, but what was once perceived as just an exaggerated sense of bravado has been steadily gaining some roots of acceptance. What frightens me are the rantings against Judaism, particularly from this man, Adolf Hitler. It really has become quite perverse."

"Of course, it concerns me as well, but whatever it is, it is probably not going to amount to much. I have always believed common sense will inevitably prevail, and the collective good in the German people will suppress any serious threat of radicalism."

"I pray you are right, as you usually are. Well, I am ready for a good night's sleep. What say we call it a night? I have a very busy agenda tomorrow."

As they crawled into bed in the warmth of their sumptuous duvet, Anna laid her head on Jacob's chest as she reflected on the joy she felt for little Pietra. "You know Jacob, I don't think I could be happier than I am at this time in our lives. We both have such boundless love for our dear little one, that much is obvious. But do you ever wonder about what happens if we have another baby?"

"In what context? Tell me what's on your mind. We've had many discussions about this possibility. What makes this evening so different?" he asked inquisitively.

Searching for words, Anna thoughtfully articulated, "This sounds absurd but…do you ever worry we could not possibly feel the same love for another child as we do for Pietra?"

"Whatever are you saying, sweetheart? Of course, we would!"

"How, I ask, could we ever be capable of loving another child, without somehow taking some of our love away from Pietra? It sounds silly, but I cannot imagine having the physical and emotional depth to generate more love than I feel right now. How is it possible for us to reach even deeper into our souls to generate even more? Do you understand what I am saying, Jacob? Or am I just crazy?"

"I never quite thought of it that way, but I suppose nature will provide. It is a conundrum, but the day will surely come when we will face the reality, as the Lord provides. Perhaps it is unwise to think of love, and life for that matter, as being a zero-sum game my darling."

"Whatever do you mean? I don't follow, Jacob."

"Let me put it this way. The wonderful things in life will certainly enhance the memories of our lives, correct? Bear with me here. If so, does this mean the joys we may experience are only possible because someone else must have an equal and opposite element of sadness for example? Of course not! At least I do not see it being so."

"I think I understand what you are saying. Wherever do you find your logical solutions to my frequent illogical questions, Jacob?"

"I never thought about it much but…I'm sorry, my dear. I really must get some sleep. Good night and sweet dreams, my love." As he did every night, he gently kissed her forehead and stroked her hair reassuringly.

CHAPTER ELEVEN

♂

SINCE BEFORE THE GREAT WAR, BERLIN HAD CONTINued to become the source of Germany's very heartbeat, from which its politics, industry, ideology, and the arts felt its inexorable pulse. A significant exception would be the malignant cauldron of evil, the genesis of which was already festering in the distant streets and collaborative minds of Munchen, otherwise known as Munich.

This was a city in which former military troops had tended to settle after the war, having proven unable to be assimilated into civilian life. Many were enraged by the harshness of the terms of the Treaty of Versailles. In Munich they found tolerance and receptivity for their voices of growing discontent.

Significant among them was a former political leader named Anton Drexler, who founded the DAP, an antecedent of the NSDAP, which shortly thereafter became the Nazi Party. As early as 1919, Drexler was steadfastly recruiting like-minded individuals who were receptive to his party platforms. It was an environment rife with intolerance and the prevalence of numerous extremists seeking the strength of common purpose, mostly among the very much disgruntled military personnel. Common views of anti-Semitic, anti-Marxist, and anti-capitalist persuasions formed the tenets of their newly evolving manifesto.

It was typical for Drexler to organize relatively impromptu rallies of hardline members, those once drawn in themselves by outspoken, often inflammatory brochures and various underground publications posted about the streets of Munich. In fact, on numerous occasions, the flames of discontent were purposely fanned by Drexler's thugs, and were specifically intended as a demonstration of their constantly growing political force.

One such rally came under the verbal attacks of a visiting professor of political science, whose well-regarded intellect challenged the wisdom of Party criticism of capitalism. Among other related matters, he went on to suggest decreeing the separation of Bavaria from Prussia, to form an alliance with Austria. These issues were very much counter to the core beliefs of the proscribed doctrine of the NSDAP.

Before the professor could gain momentum and potentially sway the gathering, a young man, on his own initiative, took the stage to aggressively and profoundly destroy the professor's credibility by way of his own passionate, biased beliefs. In so doing, his skillfully articulate oratory resulted in the embarrassing admission of defeat by the opinionated educator, who was forced to leave the stage in shame.

The actions of this young man did not go unnoticed by Drexler, who immediately approached him, offering a copy of *My Political Awakening*, one of Drexler's more formidable publications. It was apparent the young man already possessed many of the same ideologies his publication espoused, and Drexler enthusiastically encouraged him to join their cause and become a Party member, an offer the young orator was only too eager to accept. He introduced himself as Adolf Hitler.

Drexler immediately recognized Hitler's unique capability to bring a stronger presence to the Party, to further the momentum of growth it so urgently required. He never doubted Hitler's ability to feed the growing hunger of his audiences with his powerful oratory. Shortly after this newfound alliance, it became a more common occurrence for frequent fiery demonstrations to occur, including physical altercations. The escalation of violence was not as spontaneous as it first appeared, nor was it coincidental with Hitler's newfound alliance with Drexler.

In the subsequent few years, the DAP continued to become more entrenched in its Party platform. A former captain named Ernst Rohm, who had served in the Great War, was instrumental in creating the accurate public perception of physicality and brutal force for which the Party became known.

His military influences were defined by the loyal support of the men who served under him, bringing with them strong-arm tactics that served to terrorize any resistance the Party encountered. Rohm was a strong advocate for Hitler, under whose leadership the Party became a force to be reckoned with. Hitler's powerful oratory resulted in aggressive recruitment of key military members such as Heinrich Himmler and Hermann Göring, the latter responsible for organizing what would eventually become Hitler's Storm Troopers.

Yet another controversial ally was in the person of Joseph Goebbels, whose publications and promotional flair for propaganda also caught the attention of Hitler. He recognized the power of the press, without which the Party could not possibly inspire the masses sufficiently to gain the national attention it strove so desperately to attain. Rallies were not enough. Hence, it fell to Goebbels to spread the established rhetoric of the Party far beyond the outskirts of Munich.

At this time the Weimar Republic was reeling. Solutions were not to be found by their decision to aggressively print voluminous amounts of currency, which was a feeble and temporary attempt to stimulate the rapidly dying economy. Instead, it triggered predictable and devastating hyperinflation, further feeding public discontent. The economic environment was a virtual tinderbox ready to ignite at the smallest provocation.

Into this tenuous fabric of trepidation and overwhelming uncertainty, the conditions were rife for drastic changes of political leadership. These conditions further enabled the rise of Hitler and Rudolf Hess who became Deputy Fuhrer and was named successor to Hitler and Goebbels. Their relationships quickly developed and together they espoused their vision of Party politics.

Through his newly found responsibilities, Goebbels fed the media with the goal and defining result of escalating political agitation. His skillful manipulation of the media included propaganda in newspapers, radio, theatre, and through the arts. No stone was left unturned. His personal reputation, which also represented the personality of the Party, was one to be feared, particularly by the Jews who were being increasingly targeted.

One such example of blatant antagonism, which became the hallmark of premeditated physicality typically seen at most rallies, occurred in November 1923, the Nazi's infamous Beer Hall Putsch. Hitler and his ardent military supporters marched into the public hall with Hitler climbing upon a table, whereupon he fired his pistol into the ceiling with the proclamation the putsch (coup) had begun.

His daring bravado seized the attention of hundreds of unsuspecting people.

The crowd appeared confused but inquisitive, until Hitler's captivating speech began to attract their interest. His fiery rhetoric relentlessly gathered momentum and when he screamed for their support with his impeccable sense of timing, the indecisiveness that once was, had been replaced with overwhelming support. The crowd roared with enthusiastic frenzy.

It would be reported he punctuated his speech by this closing declaration, *"You can see that what motivates us is neither self-conceit nor self-interest, but only a burning desire to join the battle in this grave eleventh hour for our German Fatherland...One last thing I can tell you. Either the German revolution begins tonight, or we will all be dead by dawn!"*

The Party's assumption of control and aggressive intimidation led directly to violence resulting in several killings, and among the victims were four police officers and several military soldiers. By the time local authorities managed to regain order, Hitler himself had sustained serious injury and escaped only briefly until his arrest a few days later. The attempted coup gained world attention but proved to be premature and failed miserably. It also resulted in Hitler's subsequent imprisonment under the charge of high treason, originally for a term of five years.

His imprisonment and those of other Party members, among them Rudolf Hess, had seemingly disbanded the nefarious and treasonous Party. Some of their fellow conspirators, most notably Herman Göring, evaded capture by managing to escape to Bavaria. Their headquarters were immediately raided, documents were seized, and the Party newspaper, *The People's Observer*, was banned from publication. One would suppose the uprising had been totally suppressed.

However, despite these actions, Hitler never hesitated to seize the opportunity before him. The courts provided the perfect, high-profile setting for the impassioned defense of his alleged crimes and misdemeanors, blaming the Jews, Marxism, and France for all the country's problems. The conservative-leaning judges refused to block Hitler's efforts to deflect the prime focus of the court and the prosecutors shrank from challenging the defendant.

The magnitude of his highly skilled rhetoric captivated many of the very critics on the world stage who chose to imprison him, none more effectively than the presiding trial judge, Herr Neithardt, whose own personal ideologies were already aligned with Hitler's strong viewpoints. Neithardt was admittedly impressed by this defendant's genuine motivations. His belief was, no one with such exemplary dedication, intent, and deep loyalty to the German Empire could be guilty of such treasonous crimes. As such, Hitler's sentence was summarily reduced to eight months.

During his brief incarceration, two significant achievements further strengthened the Nazi Party immeasurably. The first was Hitler's drafting of *Mein Kampf*, the first volume of his autobiography. Rudolf Hess, imprisoned with Hitler, assisted him with the drafting and printing of the book. Their wide range of deranged ideologies took form in this manifesto for Party policy. Of no less importance was the opportunity during his time of personal reflection afforded by his captivity, to more finely hone his radical beliefs.

Of note was his clear realization that if the movement ever achieved absolute power it would only be made possible by way of legal means. Hitler's relentless ability to adapt and press forward regardless of any obstacle before him enabled him to out-will his court conviction on the charge of treason. Because of this determination his conviction indirectly served to re-establish his political career on an even stronger footing.

History would show the learned opinions of many, who posited the obvious gravity of such an error in jurisprudence by the early release of this madman. Had Hitler served his full term, it is likely during those years of incarceration, Germany would have worked its way out of the economic and political uncertainty by more orthodox methodologies, sparing untold millions of agonizing and totally unwarranted deaths.

Upon his release from prison, Hitler and Goebbels quickly developed a very close relationship, and shortly thereafter in 1924, Goebbels became the district administrator of the Nazi Party. His impact was profound to the extent that within three years, he was personally appointed by Adolf Hitler to serve in the capacity of National Director of Propaganda for the Nazi Party. The cancer of hate was about to metastasize.

*****

In the late 1920's under the Weimar Republic, Germany had become more integrated, more interdependent somehow. Disciplines of human interaction such as science, education, philosophy, and medicine exposed the civilized world to all manner of knowledge and new ideologies.

Amid this swirling knowledge, expansion of new ideas and mind-boggling concepts of freedoms of expression, Berlin evolved into a city of many social contrasts. A large part of the population continued to struggle with high unemployment and widespread deprivation. Meanwhile, the upper class of society continued to thrive and spawned a growing middle class, gradually rediscovering prosperity and transforming Berlin into a cosmopolitan city.

During this period of relentless and growing political conflict, the rich continued to drive the economy throughout the Golden Twenties, with the resultant growth of expressionism particularly in the realm of art, music, philosophy, and general decadent behavior. Increasing popularity of the automobile routinely created vehicular traffic during the newly named rush hours that log-jammed the city streets.

Through it all there was always a time for love. Indeed, very often, life's best moments are the ones we do not plan for, and the birth of a son is surely one of them. In 1924, Jacob and Anna were thrilled to announce the arrival of their newborn son Dietrich. It was a joy that reminded Anna her prior concerns for a new abundance of love were unfounded. No objective rationale could defy the natural course of evolution. The miracles of nature had ways of its own that few should ever question.

Retiring from the symphony orchestra had been overdue for Anna, even in such a part-time capacity. There were no sacrifices to be made to accommodate her newborn child. The memories of her brief professional career would be kept very much alive within her through Marta's marvelous accomplishments and hopefully someday, Pietra's as well.

Meanwhile, Sigmund's success reached the point at which he opened a second medical clinic in the northern district of Berlin as his expertise and reputation quickly expanded across much of Western Europe and ultimately onto the shores of America as well. As a celebrated alumnus, he was frequently a featured speaker at medical conferences hosted by the Köllnische Gymnasium where he himself had attended. His clinics were acclaimed for their innovative research in both cardiovascular medicine and gastroenterology, both capably overseen by Sigmund's extensive expertise in these specific medical disciplines.

His pragmatic standards, insightful approach to research, and well-established reputation earned him international renown and public recognition from his colleagues locally and abroad, particularly those foreign guests from the United States who had attended several of his conference lectures in Berlin.

As a result of his outstanding profile, Sigmund was very pleased indeed to be personally invited to attend his first American Medical Association (AMA) conference on May 1927, which was hosted by the city of Washington D.C. He would become one of only a few such European physicians to be given such consideration and distinction.

Upon hearing of this outstanding opportunity, Marissa was overwhelmingly supportive in encouraging her husband to attend this conference, despite his initial trepidation. "I am so very proud of you Siggy. Look at all you have accomplished in your life, and throughout your medical career. You deserve this recognition, sweetheart! You have earned this! Think of it, by way of personal invitation, you are going to visit the capital city of the United States of America! This is truly amazing! Why would you even hesitate to go?" she asked incredulously.

"You know as much as I how very much I want to accept, but I grow increasingly concerned for your welfare and the children's safety and well-being while I would be absent. I grow more uncomfortable with each passing day about the frightful political circumstances in which we find ourselves. I am more disturbed about it than I let on Marissa."

"Not at all my darling. You are as always, far too protective of us. There's nothing to fear here. I insist you take full advantage of the opportunity you have been given. Who knows what all of this could lead to Siggy?"

What it led to was Sigmund boarding the SS *Leviathan* on May 7, 1927 bound for New York City. This marked Sigmund's first of many transatlantic crossings throughout his illustrious career, and always for the AMA annual events. A German ship-building company pioneering passenger travel across the Atlantic had built the *Leviathan* in 1914. One of three sister ships, the original TS *Bremen* had been seized by the American government during the Great War in 1917, at which time it was renamed the *Leviathan*.

Sigmund's itinerary anticipated five days sailing time to dock in New York harbor on the twelfth of May, and to subsequently board a train to arrive in Washington D.C. the following day. This plan allowed a few extra days to accommodate any potential travel delays, and hopefully provide ample time to see the sights and enjoy the architecture, historical monuments, and hospitality of America. It would not disappoint.

In fact, as the *Leviathan* was skillfully maneuvered through New York harbor, the grandeur of the Statue of Liberty, the solitary identifiable landmark known to welcome immigrants to the shores of America stood iconically, as if guarding the main gates to this new world. It was always considered to be a notable beacon of freedom to those millions of immigrants upon whom America would come to depend.

Following Sigmund's concerns about leaving the family in Berlin, Marissa's usual supportive encouragement was more than enough to convince him not to squander this unique and memorable moment in his life. It was the first and only time they had been apart, and although he silently ached because of her absence, the wonder of this profound moment reaffirmed their decision.

Pennsylvania Station, unlike any train station he had seen, except possibly those of London and Paris, required a roadmap of its own for him to find his way through the relentless, briskly paced, and hustling crowds. So many people and always, it seemed, in such haste to get somewhere other than here. With perseverance he calmly connected with the correct platform instructions and absent the pervasive stress of other travellers, he purchased his ticket for the early-afternoon departure to Washington for the following day. The customs and immigration process were efficient and without any undue delay, but it was getting late in the day and the exhaustion of the travel was starting to take its toll.

At his hotel, Sigmund enjoyed a pleasant meal and a glass of wine and kept mostly to himself. A good night of sound sleep would surely recharge him and provide enough time to write a thoughtful note to his beloved Marissa. The following morning, he did so.

This 16th day of May 1927.

My dearest Marissa.

Having safely arrived in New York last evening, I was quite exhausted and fell asleep thinking of you. I love you so very much.

I am excited about the prospects of arriving in Washington later tonight. There are so many talented people I am anxious to meet personally and there is so very much I intend to learn from them while I am here.

During my quiet times when I am alone, I think of you constantly. It occurs to me this is the first time we have ever been apart since the day we first met, and I now discover I never want us to be apart again. As I write to you, I feel the warmth of your breath. When you read my words, I imagine that you feel mine too. I need you always by my side. Any memories I may have of this adventure can never compare to those of you and me together.

You, and you alone are my best friend. You are my soul, my inspiration, my lover. I have kissed your beautiful body everywhere I could imagine. I have my visions of you indelibly burned so deeply into my memory, even blindness could never cause them to blur.

When I stop to focus myself upon you, I believe I can taste your very essence. My fingers tremble at the thought of touching you, my tongue longs for your sweetness. I am desperate to hear and feel your soft, sweet breath stimulating me into a glorious frenzy in a way only you can achieve…and yet, so naturally, so effortlessly. Marissa, I love you more today than yesterday, knowing our love will surely become even more enduring tomorrow.

You captivate me to the extent I bought my own bottle of Chanel No. 5 last evening, just to comfort me with your loving scent.

Please give all my love to the children. They are the most precious gifts you could ever aspire to give me. Know I will love you and our family always.

Your adoring husband,

Sigmund

Within the hour Sigmund posted his heartfelt letter of devotion, feeling content to have dedicated something of a tribute to his equally devoted partner in life, who made all things possible for him. He felt invigorated and inspired by his own gesture and his enthusiasm was difficult to subdue to manageable proportions.

The train was scheduled to arrive in Washington at 7:10 PM. He planned to dine enroute and would check in at his hotel with enough time to get his bearings before the event began in late afternoon of the following day.

His initial perception of the capital city was one of intimidation. It was a hive of human activity to which he was an irrelevant witness, playing no active role. Over the next few hours, he felt the experience to be surreal and dreamlike. His life had been so full, or so he had thought, until this experience triggered a dramatic shifting of his personal perspectives.

There was no nervousness or insecurity on his part, just a prolonged period of self-introspection. He was, after all, an already successful, intelligent family man from a distant but very real world so far away. This man was not naïve, nor innocently protected from the perils life had presented him, so his frame of reference was firmly based, all the better to interpret and shape his penchant for analytical critique, yet continuing to be guided by the well-established framework of his spiritual and softer side as well.

As Sigmund became more deeply immersed in his personal thoughts, he could not help but wonder why it was he so seldom had sufficient occasion, or even rare sporadic moments of fleeting time for quiet solitude and personal reflection. Was it a time to reload, to refocus his perceptions to better align with the direction in life he chose to follow, whether it required a resetting of course corrections or a reaffirmation of choices already made?

How can the joys and even the tedium of life, be consistently prioritized within our own mind's eye, particularly during moments of our most optimal capabilities? He became lost within the recesses of his mind, not once nodding off due to indifference and fatigue. Quite to the contrary, his mind and body were in complete harmony and all reference to time had long since peacefully dissolved within him.

After what seemed like moments, the conductor announced their arrival, at which point Sigmund calmly withdrew from his solace. In so doing he restated to himself what he had always believed, *I have not yet, nor do I believe I ever will meet, the person with whom I want to trade lives—all or nothing.*

This personal affirmation removed any of the tension and anxiety that is often prevalent for a traveler when alone in a strange new environment. It was only natural. Sigmund was determined to fully embrace this learning experience, to enhance his personal enjoyment of the actual moments at hand.

With a deep breath of satisfaction, he collected his baggage and proceeded into the slightly tepid night air. The line of available taxis barely had to slow to board passengers, so efficient were the porters assisting the orderly flow of travelers.

Once seated comfortably in the taxicab, he witnessed first-hand the beautiful city of Washington. It was something to behold. The White House was the epicenter of American power. His first view of it was at night and it appeared as a monument unto itself, shimmering against the darkened skies. Sigmund's focus was irretrievably locked in on the majesty of this architectural masterpiece as his taxi circled the gentle curves of Pennsylvania Avenue to his hotel.

He recognized the Capitol Building, which stood magnificently above the expansive tiers of illuminated steps serving to reassure the world that prosperity and order would forever be sacrosanct in this vast land of opportunity.

His arrival at the hotel necessarily disrupted the quiet, peaceful moments he found so intriguing.

The concierge posted outside the main doors was courteous and gracious in every respect as he promptly opened the rear door. "Good evening, sir. Welcome to The Willard Hotel. The porter will see to your luggage from here."

The personal and warm reception from the front desk was equally amiable and courteous. Within minutes of registration the bellboy was eager to escort Sigmund to his room. "We understand this is your first visit to America, Dr. Landesburg. Your room was selected for you because of the fine view. It faces the heart of the city for your viewing pleasure."

"That is very thoughtful of you. I trust I will come here again, but I shall not forget this first time. You are very kind, young man."

When the door closed softly behind the bellboy, Sigmund glanced about the tastefully appointed room and opened the balcony door to reveal the glorious architectural landscape. "Magnificent, my darling! I so wish you could be here with me, my beauty."

This was indeed a satisfying moment to savor. It had been a long day but once settled into his room, he quickly identified the bar fridge and scanned the plentiful varieties of whiskey and liqueurs.

"What the hell!" he said out loud to himself. "I'll be damned if I spend this night alone in my room! I'm heading downstairs to enjoy a drink or two! So many people I want to meet."

Sigmund took a satisfying shower and changed into fresh clothing. Within thirty minutes he was again awestruck by the splendidly designed Juliette balcony, wrapped embracingly around half the perimeter of the ground floor lobby. The elaborate black and gold iron railings were in distinguishing dark contrast to the shining and smoothly polished marble steps to the level below.

The staircase led welcomingly to the main lobby below, revealing a busily engaged group of distinguished looking gentlemen. The loud, boisterous laughing indicated the familiar re-acquaintance of many past friendships, of which Sigmund intended to become a part.

The jumble of conversations grew louder as he entered the bar area among the gathering patrons, most of whom seemed content to stand to be able to mingle and be better heard in ways the dining area could not possibly provide. It was only moments before he was extended a hearty welcome from a group of American physicians who had the same taste for fine cognacs. Life was good on this side of the ocean and it was quickly evident they would have a great deal in common.

*****

The following morning heralded sunny skies and the fresh fragrance of spring. Sigmund's day was briefly his own until a gentleman from the prior evening asked to share a table for some breakfast with him. Richard was somewhat older than Sigmund and disclosed some of the success he enjoyed in his established practice in Boston. He was a cardiologist as well and was appreciative of Sigmund's distant travels, which afforded a multitude of flowing conversation. An avid traveler himself, he and his wife had explored much of the United States, Canada, and even Hong Kong and China on a recent occasion.

"Never made it to Europe, though we plan to do so once things settle down over there. Neither of us intend to put ourselves at risk, but it is our hope this Hitler fella learns to keep his mouth shut. Let people just learn to get along with each other, I always say. Hell, we have enough of our own problems right here at home! Who am I to tell a German what to do?" They both laughed in unison at his brash comments, which were all taken in the right spirit.

"So, I suppose your lovely wife stayed at home taking care of the children while you enjoy a brief escape from Berlin? First time away from them?"

"That it is. However, my 'young wife' as you refer to her, is helping our daughter tend to our grandchildren," Sigmund replied as he sipped his hot coffee.

"Well, I'll be damned. That's wonderful! I didn't think for a moment you were old enough for grandkids. Congratulations! I remember my first time away, even after twenty years of marriage. You get used to it, Sigmund. Keep in mind that many of us here bring the wives along with us from time to time. It's a chance for them to see the cities and get to commiserate with the other ladies."

"I'm sure Marissa will accompany me one day soon. Thanks for the suggestion though."

"Here's my card. Call me anytime if I can assist you with anything, whether here in Washington or wherever the hell we'll be next time. Let's keep in touch."

"I appreciate that, Richard. Will do. Now, if you will excuse me, I'm heading out for a walk this morning. I'll see you tonight I'm sure."

These Americans seemed considerably more hospitable than Sigmund had imagined. He looked forward to sharing more of their hospitality later in the day. Guided only by a few tourist brochures, he decided most of what he intended to see was within walking distance of his hotel. The day was lovely, and he wanted a good long walk after being somewhat cramped on board ship for the better part of the past week.

His first stop was the Washington Monument. His impression was that it possessed a stunningly simple but highly definitive and timeless design. The obelisk was easily recognized by everyone throughout the civilized world since its construction had finally been completed in the late 1880's. The stark contrast of the white concrete structure against the deep blue and cloudless sky appeared bizarre, powerful, and somehow strangely intimidating. He took the time to sit down for a *Café Americano* in a street café providing a distant but prolonged view of the monument. He wanted a relaxed moment to allow the image to linger.

The remaining objective for Sigmund this fine day was to view the Lincoln Memorial, an edifice he had been anxious to approach and enter with a high degree of reverence. His studies of American history revealed the scarring America would forever bear from its oppression of African Americans tragically stolen from their families and homes, and their very way of life. It seemed so inconsistent with his limited understanding of its character of this present day.

His leisurely pace continued as he climbed the steps to this incredible monument, a symbolic tribute to race relations in America. Although dissention would likely continue to exist to varying degrees, the standard of tolerance it espoused would forever be built on shifting sands. Sigmund likened the solid and formidable foundation below its expansive pedestal to the inevitable resolve of the people, surviving the test of time to inexorably find their way to always endure.

He prayed silently to himself as he sat on the steps at the base of Lincoln's granite sculptured feet, for the same tolerance and humanitarian resolve to be discovered within the hearts and minds of the German people. There was no place for discrimination and persecution of others on either side of the vast ocean separating each of these prolific empires. Sigmund's eyes started to moisten as he reflected upon the dreadful conditions in which he'd left his family. He gathered himself and rose to his feet to slowly descend the steps to prepare for the evening's opening events.

*****

Late in the afternoon, after a brief nap and shower, Sigmund negotiated the opulent spiral staircase that extended to the lower mezzanine and was shocked to see the enormous assembly before him. Many hundreds of dignified American physicians had already started to gather into several registration lines in anticipation of the opening remarks of the evening. He presented the necessary identification and was directed to the appropriate line of registrants. Everything was professionally organized.

Upon entering the huge auditorium, he irrationally tried to search out a familiar face or two until common sense prevailed, and he stopped such foolishness. He was totally unknown here and so was unaccustomed to his newly found anonymity in the middle of a sea of humanity. Yet he remained mindful their common *Hippocratic Oath* bound him to this multitude of thousands of strangers. The swearing of that oath exemplified the very rite of passage to which every physician bore testimony. He was among friends he just hadn't met yet.

In the years ahead, he would remember of this moment, not the loneliness, not even the obscurity of his person, but the common pride of profession he had not acknowledged to himself since his graduation. Here of all places, amid the deafening din of thousands of conversations, each one trying to out-shout the other, Sigmund was poised in a moment of quiet reflection to again consider this unique moment of reaffirmation.

Within seconds in real time, he mentally re-engaged to personally become witness to the opening speaker, who was to be none other than the President of the United States, Calvin Coolidge.

The appearance of the president himself was both a fortuitous and significant advantage to the AMA decision in selecting Washington, the capital city of the United States, to host their annual event. The president's words of pride and encouragement for the steadfast accomplishments of the medical community extolled the numerous medical advancements of modern medicine.

He was quoted to have stated the "*conservation of human health and life [was] one of the greatest achievements in the advance of civilization.*" He went on to declare, "*The debt which we owe to the science of medicine is simply beyond computation or comprehension.*"

The greatest impact upon this gathering of the medical elite of America, and to no less a degree upon Sigmund, was Coolidge's plea to the medical community at large to always maintain inquisitiveness and the ability to develop a thirst for new knowledge. Without this essential direction of mental attitude, the exploration of new possibilities through research might diminish the pace of ultimate potential.

"By not closing ourselves off to new ideas and lines of inquiry, we can find truths and principles in all sorts of matters, including scientific ones. Americans have thrived because we have been exceptionally good at exploring new ideas and pursuing knowledge in whatever direction it may lead. The modern, broad-minded physician is willing to use or to recommend whatever methods seem best suited to the case at hand."

The captivated audience rose as one in appreciative and reassuring applause and support of America's head of state, upon whose platitudes of genuine sentiment the American Medical Association now attained a new level of unprecedented credibility throughout the world. For Sigmund, Coolidge's words opened his eyes to the potential future development made possible by these international collaborations, for himself and even more so for the benefit of all humanity.

Sigmund was profoundly taken by the Coolidge speech, to the extent he became a strong advocate of support for these educational conferences. In so doing, he became known to always be eagerly alert and very open minded to new technologies and diagnostic techniques developed in America. His continued close affiliation as a guest lecturer at the university in Berlin also enabled him to keep abreast of cutting-edge technologies developed within its walls. As such, he was eventually entrusted to extend his pre-eminent status to other accomplished European researchers and medical specialists who were, in his own opinion, worthy of similar honor and respect to present their innovative scientific research as well.

In the ensuing days, among those he met was Dr. Charles Souttar, who befriended him. Over drinks and several meals together they shared some of their most challenging medical experiences and discovered several areas of common interest. Charles was a cardio-thoracic surgeon involved with some exciting and creative surgical research. He proudly confided to Sigmund his close professional relationship with his older brother, Dr. Henry Souttar.

"Henry is a resident cardiovascular surgeon based in London, England, with an engineering degree as well." Charles proudly offered. "He has become well known for his inventive acumen and has designed numerous surgical tools already credited with demonstrable improvement to surgical techniques."

"This intrigues me, Charles. We tend to be so much more insulated in Berlin, and in Germany in general. Comparatively speaking, we are reluctant to share our own technical developments with the outside world, believing our achievements are vastly superior to those of the rest of the world. It's a short-sighted view in my opinion," Sigmund confided.

"My brother sees the world from a larger perspective than most. He's been that way throughout his entire life. Even more so since he became a medical practitioner. In fact, in 1925, he became the first physician to successfully perform open-heart surgery on a young woman with mitral valve disease. The post-operative results were encouraging and extended the life of the patient by almost two years before she eventually succumbed just four months ago. Unfortunately, shortly thereafter it was decided by my brother's colleagues the procedure was not justified, and he was no longer sanctioned to continue that course of action. He was understandably infuriated."

Sigmund was noticeably captivated by this illuminating discussion and respectfully requested Charles to arrange a referral to his brother, to allow him to keep abreast of Henry's progress. Even subscribing to Henry's published periodicals, and in fact, anything Henry would be willing to share by way of any non-published updates would be helpful. Sigmund's intention was to communicate more frequently with Henry on a direct basis, which Charles encouraged. When the convention was concluded, the two friends parted company and promised to keep in close contact in the months ahead.

Over the coming years, Sigmund's fervent support and enthusiasm for the AMA would become an annual commitment. He was proud to be an integral and proactive proponent of these ideals and knew he would make his own contributions to the AMA someday soon.

*****

Sigmund's return home was generally uneventful, and his reception upon arrival was most heart-warming, more than he could possibly comprehend. He worshipped his dear Marissa and was thankful for her constant dedication to their daughters and to their young grandchildren.

"This trip to America has caused me to take pause, much as you once suggested I should do now and then. It was several years ago under the oak tree. Do you remember?"

"I remember it well, Siggy. I am impressed that you do as well."

"On the rare occasions I manage to step away from the pace of my life, you are who I think about…every day; and who I dream about at night."

"Oh, Siggy. You say the kindest things to me."

Sigmund continued with his train of thought. "I want you to know how very privileged I feel for the wonderful life we have been given and I am determined to somehow give back the same encouragement and dedicated purpose I have been fortunate enough to have received. You made this all possible for me, Marissa. I don't acknowledge my appreciation to you enough for your support in all I do."

Sigmund would return to America again in 1928 and continued to rekindle his own friendships and associations of the previous year, but still very much as an eager spectator.

The following year, however, the commitment Sigmund made to personally contribute was a dream come true. In 1929, he was selected to not only attend the congress, but also to be a recipient of their esteemed offer to make his first appearance as a guest lecturer at the upcoming conference in New York City. Sigmund was deeply honored. When he'd passed very briefly through New York heading to Washington two short years ago, there had been no time to see the city itself. This occasion afforded very limited opportunity to do so as well.

New York was intimidating, as he had expected it to be. Sigmund was humbled to acknowledge the extent to which this city surpassed his wildest expectations. This was truly one of the greatest cities the world had ever seen. The towering skyscrapers seemed to touch the clouds, almost beyond his view. He realized after only moments of lost imaginings, he was the only person among thousands who was staring upward instead of forward.

He quickly changed his focus and tried desperately not to appear overwhelmed by the hustle and bustle of the overcrowded city sidewalks that appeared to weave their way through the omnipresent waves of very preoccupied American businesspeople. The streets were a cacophony of sounds: from horns and roaring vehicular exhausts; to the shouting and aggressive street vendors relentlessly pushing their wares, everything from fresh fruit to newspapers and record albums, and of all things, bed sheets!

His perception of the congress was far less intimidating than either the one in Washington, or the last event in Detroit, Michigan. Perhaps this impression was owing to the fact he now saw more familiar faces and those of welcoming friends and associates with whom he often corresponded and kept in touch with, mostly through shared articles and publications of common interest. One of the highlights of these conferences was Sigmund's ability to nurture his keen professional relationships from his past visits, not the least of which was his friendship with Dr. Charles Souttar.

CHAPTER TWELVE

In Berlin, the opulence of the rich flowed from within the revered architecture of the main hotels to outdoor high-end venues of popular cafés and bistros. Among these was the Terrace Romanisches Café, a personal favorite of Anna and Marta. It often provided them an overdue respite from the routines of motherhood. Anna had familiar longings for the frenetic city life from time to time, which had become so elusive to her over the past few years when her priorities were mostly focused upon the raising of the children.

Anna had just stepped off the carriage she often rode for short hops around the city. Normally these horse-drawn carriages were hired out to tourists, but ever since her father had solicited the service for special occasions, Anna often delighted in the experience when she was alone, or on occasion with the children.

Marta quickly rose from her chair with a beaming smile. "Anna, I'm over here!" cried out Marta, who was already seated at the table with the best view of the street on the opposite side of the park.

"Hello, sweetheart! You look beautiful, as always! Why you barely look old enough to bear a child, let alone two! You cannot possibly be the mother of a six-year-old, never mind your handsome little Dietrich. Are they both well?"

Their enthusiasm and warm embraces evidenced their very close friendship for one another. What with Marta's professional career and the necessary travel demands, the two friends had not seen each other in over two months, a rarity for them.

"The children are both well, thank you, and growing ever so quickly. As for you my dear, you are looking as vivacious as the last time we met. I think family life must suit you well!"

"Yes, I suppose so. I was hoping we could talk about that subject today concerning my recent state of confusion and overwhelming feelings of guilt. I'm in a bit of a mess, I am afraid to say. I have been struggling of late with this whole motherhood matter. If I can't be honest with you, I can't be honest with anyone."

"Of course, Marta. I can see the concern on your face. You know there is nothing you could say to me that could tarnish my love for you. You should always know that."

"I do know that Anna."

"Did we not already have this conversation? The only difference is that our roles are now reversed, so it would seem. I am shocked you would even think to hesitate."

Marta was reluctant to discuss her problems so prematurely on this fine day and did her best to briefly defer the matter, deciding it was not her original intention for this overdue luncheon. She resumed in another direction by temporarily changing to a more pleasant subject. Anna only presumed the deferral was to provide Marta with a moment or two of reflection in which to build up her courage before addressing this obviously sensitive topic.

"But first, let me say Klaus and Manny heard we were meeting today and they both send their love. We speak of you and Jacob often, and we hear Jacob has become head lecturer of theology. How proud you both must be! He certainly deserves the recognition. He has made such an outstanding contribution to the reputation of the university. And please tell me, Anna, how has your mother been feeling of late? I think of her frequently, but I never seem to remember to enquire about her whenever we are together. We always have so much going on in our own busy lives, I feel neglectful of her well-being."

"It has become somewhat of a struggle for her day after day, but her spirit remains strong. Father simply thrives on tending to her every need. He has always been so gallant in that regard. I'm so very proud of him. I think their greatest enjoyment is the time and attention they dedicate to Pietra with her violin. Mother's impact has had a very positive effect upon her."

"Her time with Pietra can be very therapeutic for them both, I'm certain. The last time we spoke Pietra was showing, shall we say, possibilities of greatness with her violin. I think of her often and I am so anxious to hear about her progress."

"Greatness may be a touch too exaggerated, but yes, she is playing mostly by ear. Jacob is 'over the moon' with pride, as are Mother and Father. To be truthful, Pietra was always so intrigued by the melodies I played over and over when she was barely able to walk. She just seemed to pick it up by memory until she mastered it. And she never appears to be frustrated. I believe she has such a natural affinity for music, but she also has the patience of Job."

"Just as her mother, I seem to recall," Marta declared. "Good for her! Listen, the orchestra is booked for most of this week on a three-city tour. I won't be touring with them and I am free this coming weekend. I was hoping to come see the children perhaps on the Saturday. Do you suppose Pietra would indulge me with a personal performance?"

"I will do my best to hold her back! She asks for her auntie more than you know, Marta. Saturday it is! So, tell me, is all well at home? And little Manny I assume, is also excited to be at school?"

"It was all he could speak of for the past few weeks. He said just this morning I should not worry about him today. 'I'm a big boy now, Mother!' he proudly exclaimed.

"Anna, this brings me back to my predicament. I swear there must be something dreadfully wrong with me. My life seems to be getting out of control, what with the demands of my career…and…and tending to Manny. You know how much Klaus and I adore our little man but…how should I say this…oh…I am so delighted Manfred is finally attending The Vorschule, mostly I regret to admit, for my own selfish reasons. Perhaps now I can finally have some time for myself!" she quickly blurted out, and embarrassedly started to laugh. "Does that sound awful of me?"

Anna grasped her hand comfortingly. "No one could love little Manny more than you and Klaus. I think you are too hard on yourself by feeling guilty about your strong natural desires for self-indulgence. You do have quite the reputation, as I seem to recall. Parenthood somehow robs us of things once so important to us. Mother tells me she often felt the same things we do."

"I suppose so, but I don't have much experience with feelings of guilt. I left that to you, my dear angel." Marta cynically responded. "I don't know how you manage two children, and I can barely handle one! You leave me in awe, Anna, you truly do!"

"Jacob and I have always wanted a full house of little ones since we first met, but I think it's safe to say that perhaps I am better suited for it than you. That's not to suggest you couldn't handle another baby, but I think we learn to adjust and remain thankful for the blessings we are given."

"Speaking of blessings..." Marta paused with perceptible awe as she couldn't help but notice the stunning ring on Anna's finger. "Is this the same ring your father gave to your mother so many years ago?"

"Yes, it surely is. Mother and Father gave it to me when Pietra was born, as he gave it to Mother when I was born. You don't remember me telling you this?"

"I do remember now! I must have been preoccupied with other things at that busy time, but I didn't realize at the time it was *this* ring! My word, Anna!"

"I suppose we started a tradition of sorts."

Marta took Anna's delicate hand and held it more closely to her view. "My goodness, it is glorious! To this day, the way your mother recounts that day has to be the most romantic pledge of love I could have ever imagined. I am so happy it touched her heart so deeply!" She squeezed Anna's hand affectionately.

"And now, for them to have passed it on to you is truly an honor Anna, and I know you regard it as such."

"Thank you for your kind thoughts, Marta. You are quite correct. It always reminds me how truly fortunate my family has been. You don't think it's too pretentious though, do you?"

"Not at all. Truth be told, anyone that may feel it is so would never be fortunate enough either in love, or in life for that matter, to possess anything quite like it. You must always wear it with pride and unreserved flair. I know I most certainly would!" She flipped her wrist nonchalantly.

"I often wish I had more self-confidence about things like that. So Marta, please tell me. You have brought up this predicament of yours twice this afternoon, and you keep averting our attention elsewhere. Be direct with me. What's going on in your life that's stressing you so much?"

"You are always so perceptive, but before I open that door, I need a crisp, cold glass of Riesling to fortify myself. How about you?" Without even waiting for an answer, Marta turned her head, raised her hand to flamboyantly gesture to the waiter, and quickly placed her order. "We talk about the children all the time, and as much as I wanted to pretend to be single again today and still live with at least a little reckless abandon, it is Manny I need to discuss with you."

"You said Manny was well. Is he or not?"

"Yes, yes of course. He's just fine but to be specific, it is more about me as a mother."

Anna stared quizzically into Marta's eyes and was mystified at whatever it could be she was about to share with her.

"School has barely begun, and a few days ago I found myself in front of the school a bit earlier than usual to quickly take Manny home. I was trying to make an extra rehearsal the maestro had booked on some rather short notice. As I was early and Manny was late exiting the schoolyard, I found myself unable to control my frustration. I took it out on the little one and he didn't understand what he had done to upset me so. There is so much more I want to do and standing outside the school for thirty minutes is not one of them! That incident was only one of several lately and now it has brought me to an important crossroad, leading me to conclude I must return to my career. Although I never left it, I want to return with the same level of determination and focus I once had. I must make my career my priority again, Anna. I've started looking for someone who is well experienced to take full time care of Manny, on a live-in basis.

I intend to broach the subject as soon as I can with Klaus. I'm praying he will understand my circumstances and the importance of achieving my ultimate happiness. We only see one another rarely, so it's not much of a marriage anymore. I don't know if I am willing to hold it together much longer by myself."

"Oh Marta, I'm so sad to hear you and Klaus are losing your closeness. I feel for you Marta, truly I do. We were all meant to do what we can to survive in search of happiness, but for many I fear, they never have the same opportunities as you and I have been so privileged to have. You are a good mother Marta, but you are also an *amazingly* talented musician possessing a true gift from God. If you are asking my opinion, you should chase your dream. To do otherwise would be irrational and wasteful. Manny will be taken care of, no doubt, and perhaps with more dedication than you are able to provide at this time in your life. It occurs to me your expectations of parenthood might have been unrealistic."

Tears started to roll down Marta's cheeks and she wiped away some sniffles. Through her genuine, heartfelt emotions she struggled to control her composure as she confided to Anna, "Oh Anna, you understand me! I think you are the only one on this earth who ever will. I have been wracked with confusion and frustration long enough, and I have no one else I could confide in. You have helped to ease my mind, sweetheart. How do you think Klaus will react to what I have to say? I have my own expectations, but you can be more objective. I am anxious to hear your thoughts."

The waiter had already poured the wine by this point and Marta was eager to enjoy it. "A small but sincere toast… to happiness, wherever we may find it."

"Truthfully, I think Klaus is a better man than you give him credit for. As long as Manny is properly cared for, I know he will support your decision. It is the right thing to do, and frankly, there is no reasonable alternative."

Marta reached across the table to place her hand on Anna's. "I pray you are right, Anna. I feel so much more relieved just talking to you about this. You always give me courage to do what is necessary, and you give me the confidence I am secretly lacking. Thank you, Anna. I love you so very much."

Anna had taken young Dietrich to her mother for the afternoon, and this luncheon was very much past due. With the air having been cleared from their heartfelt conversation, it was a sheer delight to indulge on some of the best foie gras Berlin had to offer, followed by a fresh garden salad with a basket of warm, baked scones. In no time Marta ordered another round of wine, despite the protestations of Anna. As was their habit, the extra glass of Riesling was never wasted when Marta and Anna were dining together.

The conversation shifted into light-hearted banter as the wine started to take effect, increasingly engaging them in robust laughter. The patio was full of smiling and partially intoxicated patrons enjoying themselves in the same manner until the chatter inexplicably began to subside. As if on cue, everyone's attention shifted to a loud commotion that could be heard near the intersection just adjacent to the hotel. The muffled sounds of street traffic and other patron's conversations had initially muted the altercation somewhat, but the general aggressiveness and visible body language had escalated.

Three young men were verbally assaulting an elderly Jewish couple, an occurrence becoming more frequent on the streets of Berlin. Whatever was said appeared to be menacing and after a few anxious minutes, the couple apprehensively retreated away from the bullies and faded from the patrons' view. Only then did two gentlemen diners begin to move to the exit nearest the street to feebly attempt to intervene. Seeing them approach, the bullies walked away briskly from the scene.

"You know, I heard some disturbing things said lately about situations such as what appears to have happened down the street. I must say it's the first time I have personally witnessed something like this. That was a defenseless couple not deserving to be treated in such a manner. They were completely vulnerable, and I fear I could do nothing to prevent it had the matter continued to escalate, which I am so very thankful it did not! Have you seen anything of that sort before, Marta?"

"Not personally, but Klaus has told me some terrible things I simply do not understand. There are some who say a movement is gaining support among some hooligans right here in the city. It appears to be randomly directed against Jews, Russians, Serbs, in fact anyone they seem to target."

"...But Jews? We are as German as anyone! Marta, if what you say is true, you are frightening me!"

"I cannot imagine it will continue, but there is no doubting there is a great deal of unrest. Even within the government, the communists are raising hell, and Klaus tells me they seem to be gaining more momentum with each passing day. He assured me something would be done about it, that's for certain."

The conversation shifted back to more reassuring matters and once again their delicious lunch became the subject of focus. As planned, there was still enough time for some shopping, and doing so with Marta was always an adventure. Anna knew her friend to always find ways to keep her sufficiently entertained. All the best shops were within walking distance of the city square and the two ladies found comfort in chatting about lighter concerns. And so, under the shade of their parasols, they eagerly strolled toward the shoe stores and dress shops farther around the block.

Nevertheless, Anna continued to feel a strange anxiousness within her stomach. It was very discomforting. Although Marta's dilemma at home seemed resolvable, it was the confrontation they'd witnessed and the gravity of it she still could not possibly comprehend. She was determined she would speak with her father about her misgivings before day's end. For the moment however, the diversion of shopping was what she needed most.

*****

Arriving home later the same day, Anna was bursting to recount to Jacob the incident to which she and Marta had been witness. He was shocked to hear what he had long been dreading. Was it possible this could happen in Berlin? He agreed the persecution was escalating and had potential impact on the family. The press was continually printing misleading information that was unreliable at best. Who better to consult about the truth than her father?

Without further hesitation, Anna telephoned Sigmund to express Jacob's and her growing concerns. Her father could feel her tremors of genuine trepidation and was eager to clear his calendar for a few hours the following day. The strength of the bond between father and daughter would forever be forged through the good times and, just as surely, the perilous ones. Of that there was no uncertainty.

Soon after arriving at her father's office, Anna and Jacob recounted the events of yesterday outside the café and spoke of Anna's immediate feelings of empathy for the old couple and her panic for the safety of her family. In the quiet hours of the evening her imagination had reviewed the terrible prospects of similar circumstances potentially befalling her own loved ones.

Sigmund reacted calmly to the details of the incident. The news was disturbing to him, but he remained outwardly reserved. Were Sigmund's suspicions of eventual endangerment to his family being realized? This potential threat was foremost among the reasons he had been initially hesitant to accept the AMA invitation two years ago and since then, it was evident matters had become much worse.

Anna's call had not come as a total surprise, but it did force Sigmund's hand to consider it was now time to acknowledge his own growing concerns. He recognized that preparing his family for potential harassment should be acknowledged but in such a way as to avoid unnecessary panic.

"You and Jacob were right to come to me, Sweetheart. You are both already aware of my close contact with many of our parliamentary friends. We have been watching intently the ranting of this radical Hitler fellow, believing as you do in common sense and dignity eventually winning over the general populace."

"Do they continue to maintain their deep convictions? Please tell me it is so." Anna pleaded.

"Many still do, but I would be misleading you if I suggested they are maintaining the same degree of absolute resolve they once did. There will likely be a necessary period of readjustment, but there will always be those who will initiate public confrontations designed to intimidate and disrupt the status quo. We must be prepared for possible disruptions to our present way of life. With so much growing discontent some change is inevitable."

"How so, Father?"

"I advise us all not as Germans, but also as Jews. Do not ignore the threats and abuse directed against us. Take them seriously by not underestimating the driving force behind it. Don't walk the streets alone, day or night. Keep a low profile and try to go about your business to avoid any direct confrontations. This may not be what you are expecting from me, but this temporary submissiveness will not last.

"My credible sources within the upper-class circles of our lives have always remained steadfast in their strong convictions the Nazis will never control parliament. In due course, the consensus is that their extremist views will eventually wither into abject failure. I continue to feel justifiably reassured by their knowledgeable parliamentary insights."

"This has always been our home, Father, and now I fear we are being potentially ostracized because of our ethnicity? Our family's lives have been woven into the fabric of this society; a society that one-day may turn its back on us? This is more than I can comprehend! Have you discussed these matters with Mother and Emilie yet? I must ask Father, as I worry about them constantly, especially as Mother has become more frail of late."

"No, I have not specifically discussed this with them. When you told me what you wanted to discuss, I thought it best to meet privately at the office rather than at home. Your mother and sister are intelligent people. We have similar conversations from time to time, but none of us have seen what you and Marta experienced. I will keep them both very close to me, but up to now I had thought it best not to unduly upset either one of them. I pray the need for such discussions will never become necessary."

"Of course, Father. I'm not sure whether I feel better or worse for having this discussion. I can only imagine they will feel the same confusion as we do upon hearing it. We appreciate you being candid with us, as you always are. I love you, Father."

"I promise to keep you both aware, Anna, but I urge you to let me determine how and when I speak to your mother about this. Is that fair enough?"

Anna agreed. She never had cause to question Sigmund's diplomacy and tactfulness. He always knew what was best, and her dependence upon his best judgment would never waver.

CHAPTER THIRTEEN

MARTA'S SATURDAY WITH ANNA'S FAMILY WAS GREATLY anticipated by everyone, but no one more than Pietra. Immediately upon hearing the knock, she raced to the door and jumped up and down with excitement upon seeing her Auntie Marta and young Manfred. Without giving them any time whatsoever to speak with Anna, in her enthusiasm the little one grabbed Marta and Manny's hands, refusing to let go until she virtually dragged them into the salon near the piano. "Wait until you hear what I can play Auntie! I hope you will like it too, Manny."

"I know I will, Pietra. Mother always tells me how well you are doing. I really want to watch and listen."

"We cannot wait, sweetheart, just let me put down my jacket and purse…there we go."

"Manny, how you have grown!" said Anna. "You look just like your father, and he's a very handsome man, you know! Do you think that after Pietra finishes her piece you could play the piano for us too?"

"Yes Manny. We don't come to see you as often as I would like. I hope we can change that because I miss you so very much," Pietra said sympathetically.

Meanwhile, Marta had turned toward Anna extending her arms and smiling broadly with the usual expressions of deep affection. Little Dietrich was perched on Mommy's lap struggling to escape her grasp to hug Auntie as well. "Good morning Anna!…And hello my little cutie. My, how he has grown, Anna! You're keeping him well fed, I see."

Marta kissed his chubby cheeks and he hugged her closely for fear of being placed on the carpet. Dietrich was a very loving child who, although given plenty of affection from his attentive and loving family, always appeared to be starving for more. Anna sat on the settee with Manfred snuggled closely beside her. He was all eyes and genuinely eager for Pietra to begin.

Marta sat down with Dietrich facing forward, sitting securely on her lap. "I think we have the best seat in the house. Let the performance begin!" Marta directed, as she raised her arm in the air. Dietrich looked up at his auntie and raised his little arms too, always mimicking those around him, as if very anxious to grow up and always be close to them.

Pietra proudly and most professionally placed her violin under her tiny chin, holding it firmly; withdrew her hand to tighten the hair of the bow one final time; and slowly drew a deep breath to help compose herself.

The first note was aggressively and properly attacked, as well it should be. She had selected "Hungarian Dance #5 in G Minor" by Johannes Brahms, one of Marta and Anna's favorite pieces. Pietra had been practicing this piece for weeks on end in preparation for her first national competition scheduled only two weeks away. She had dominated state competitions thus far and was now heavily favored to win the nationals.

She played the piece brilliantly, demonstrating the power and boldness of the melody. It was perfectly contrasted with moments of tender delicacy. The changes in tempo offered throughout the piece highlighted this child's brilliance. Her poignant pauses, once broken, were expertly rebuilt into incredible emotional crescendos. Her timing was pure perfection right up to the final note, which featured its distinctive and formidable punch.

Pietra's interpretation was almost flawless, subject only to slight corrections of technical improvement with the finger work. Her hands were so tiny but were still capable of delivering finer attention to her technique. These mechanics would be better refined with some guidance from Marta. Of greater relevance was her command of the melodic standard with such enthusiastic passion, having both eyes closed while she became totally immersed in the moment. It was a certain sign that even at the tender age of six years, this young child possessed a truly rare gift.

The family applause brought everyone to their feet, which Pietra acknowledged with a beautifully controlled curtsy. In seconds, she broke toward Marta, who quickly returned Dietrich to his mother and plucked Pietra from her feet and hugged her, all the while turning around and around. Pietra's little feet dangled about.

"Did you like it, Auntie? Did you really, really like it?"

"Yes, yes, and yes! I am always so very proud of you, but never more than now! I just have one question to ask of you, though…may I come to the competition too?"

"Mother, can Auntie Marta come too? Please Mother, can she?"

"Of course, my dear child, of course she can. I think that is a wonderful idea!"

Again, Dietrich struggled to return to Marta shouting, "Me too, Auntie! Me too!" Marta made certain she twirled the little boy around and around as she had done with his big sister.

Manny immediately rose from his seat and took both of Pietra's hands in his. "Pietra, you play like a professional! That was so very beautiful. I'm so proud of you, truly!"

"I'm so pleased I could play that for you. I've been working so hard to get it just so. Can we hear you play something now? Play a piece you especially enjoy. You must have a few favorite ones. Play anything you want."

"Alright. My very favorite composer is Beethoven and I especially like the "Piano Sonata No. 14." Would that be a good one, Mother?"

"Of course, Manny. I think that's a very good choice."

The little boy moved the bench to a comfortable position and the room fell silent as he tenderly caressed the keyboard with a fine performance of the adagio. He beamed with pride when the families erupted with enthusiastic acknowledgement of his beautiful interpretation of Beethoven's masterpiece.

It was an impressive performance by both children, demonstrating their individual gifts of talent at such a tender age. As soon as tea and coffee were served however, both Pietra and Manny raced to another room to play, followed in hot pursuit by little Dietrich—evidence that even musical dedication and talent should always leave time enough for children's other happy pursuits.

True talents come in all shapes and sizes but always share the same essential elements; to prevail they must be recognized, they must be nurtured, and they must be encouraged.

*****

The previous Saturday simply had not been the appropriate time and place for serious discussion, especially in front of the family. Marta had just concluded a rigorous week of practices in preparation for brief concert performances she was planning to attend in Paris and Brussels. The intense diversion had been satisfying, but now she was anxious to refocus on young Manny and the pressing issues plaguing Anna and her. It was evident how upset Anna was that day at lunch in Kreutzburg, and Marta hoped Sigmund had been able to calm her serious concerns.

As Marta anticipated, Anna's father saw no immediate need for panic and would be mindful to keep monitoring related developments coming out of Munich. In fairness there was not a great deal he could do at this point. His influential opinions and his confidence to express them were well thought out and rational but would not affect the destiny of Germany. In later conversation with Marissa and Emilie, he offered the same advice and cautious optimism.

Despite any remaining uncertainty, the girls still relied upon each other's personal reassurances as a coping mechanism, feeling that if all was well with their immediate families and each other for the time being, life would simply go on and the world would adjust.

Marta though, had difficulty taking heed of Sigmund's advice. As a non-Jew she had a very different perspective and was much more disturbed than Anna recognized since that day outside the café. To this point in their lives, these best friends thought they could openly share anything with one another but on this subject, Marta was strangely apprehensive and uncertain about expressing her serious concerns to Anna.

Anna being Jewish had never been an issue between them, nor would it ever be, but the peril Anna and her family could face some day was more than Marta could bear. She felt the desperate need to do something more proactive to draw attention to this baseless discrimination. In her opinion, her father-in-law, not Klaus, was the best place to start.

Marta took it upon herself to arrange a private luncheon with the field marshal near to but off the military base in Zossen. She was accustomed to being outspoken and opinionated with her father-in-law but never on matters of Nazi anti-Semitism. Her newfound passion about this subject had led her to believe she could be direct in her intended line of questioning. It would be a major miscalculation.

As their meal concluded, Marta's nervousness gave her the sense she was running out of time. *I must tell him what Anna and I witnessed. If I don't confront him about this today, I likely never will.* Foolishly, she summoned up the courage to just blurt out what had occurred as if he was personally responsible for orchestrating the entire event.

The field marshal was aghast. "Marta, where is this coming from? As a soldier in the service of my country, nothing shocks me any longer...however, the way you direct your questions toward me most certainly does!" The field marshal carefully looked from side to side, checking the positioning of his escorts, and he lowered his voice accordingly.

"There is a movement afoot in Munich that has gained public support. It wields more power and hatred toward Jews than had ever been anticipated. The winds of change are upon us that will assuredly affect my professional career. Say nothing but nod your head if you understand me clearly."

Knowing she had touched a raw nerve Marta did not utter a word. She only nodded in silent agreement.

"Permit me to be as clear and concise as I am able. This is none of your damned business, or mine quite frankly. You know me well enough to understand I hold no personal animosity toward the Jews, or anyone else for that matter...except the fucking communists. *Hypothetically speaking*, if I or others under my command ever behaved in a sympathetic manner about the persecution of Jews... let me rephrase that..." His eyes were bulging now and the veins on his neck looked as if they would explode. He continued to berate her through clenched teeth. "If these people *even suspected* we were, they could have us shot for treason, as they could our entire family; *and all without due process!* Do you grasp what the consequences of these treasonous attitudes would be, not only for me and Klaus, but also you and Manfred? I shudder at the very thought."

His jaws remained tightly clenched now. "On matters such as this, your opinions are of no consequence. Keep them to the world you know, classical music and fashion! You infuriate me sometimes Marta and have offended me deeply. *Do not speak to me of this again!*" he snarled.

The field marshal had worked himself into a fury and his face was visibly flushed from the rage within him when he attempted to stand up to exit the restaurant. As he did so he became disoriented and staggered to grasp the back of the chair beside him. Losing his balance, he appeared to black out and crashed unceremoniously to the floor, pulling the chair down upon him.

Marta screamed and jumped to her feet as the security detail pounced into action to assist their commanding officer. "Field Marshal, are you able to stand? Should we call a physician?"

"No! I don't need a goddamned doctor! I must have tripped over the chair you bloody idiot! Now help me to my feet! I am fine."

"Walther, are you sure you should leave right now? Perhaps a glass of water would help steady you."

Walther half turned his head toward Marta and glared intently into her eyes. She knew instantly to remain quiet in front of the security detail about what had really happened.

*****

Marta endured a very long and sleepless night stressing about her misplaced aggressiveness toward Walther. She had directed many accusations toward him in the past and whether deserved or otherwise, she knew she had crossed the line with him yesterday. Not only was it important to apologize for her behavior, of greater importance was her concern for his physical well-being.

Her heart was pounding, and her mouth was dry when reception attempted to put her call through to him. "Good morning Walther. Thank you for taking my call today. I was not certain you would."

"You are still my daughter-in-law Marta and you should know I will always love you like my own blood, but you tested me yesterday. I want no more of that discussion. Period!" In businesslike fashion he sarcastically asked, "Why are you calling me this morning? I have back-to-back meetings in the next ten minutes. What have I done that offends you today?"

As best she could, Marta calmed herself. She deserved the treatment she was getting. "I love you too and I want to offer you my sincere apology for my behavior yesterday. I had no right to take out my frustration on you so personally."

The telephone line was silent… "Walther, are you there?"

"Yes. Yes, I am here." He realized there was nothing to be accomplished by alienating his daughter-in-law. "I accept your apology Marta. I already stated what had to be said on this subject. Let's move on."

"Thank you! I acted impulsively without thinking about the matter from your perspective. I am truly sorry. Putting that topic aside, however, I am very concerned about your health after what occurred yesterday. You and I both know you did not stumble on the chair, did you?"

"That's what my men saw, and I expect you to keep the same story, Marta. It is critical that you do."

"*Critical?* Critical is why I am asking the question Walther. I want to make certain your health does not become so. Has anything like that happened to you before? Please be truthful with me."

"I appreciate your concern, but this is neither the time nor place for this discussion. I am short on time this morning anyway."

"I agree but promise me we can speak about this no later than tomorrow. I know there is more you can tell me."

"Fine. Tomorrow it is then. Marta, I appreciate your concern, but I really must go now."

True to his word Walther telephoned Marta the next day and quietly confessed his concerns for his health. He was not at all himself, feeling unduly fatigued, light-headed and often unwell. The outburst yesterday had almost killed him, and he was becoming fearful for his longevity.

"Please let me speak to Klaus and Anna about what happened. You are operating under significant stress and it is likely to cause these unpleasant episodes to recur more frequently. Why not have a conversation with Anna's father? You met him at our wedding. You know he is a top-ranked cardiologist. I'm confident he would be thorough as well as discreet."

"I know it is something I should do, but there is no one here I can trust. Discretion is the key, and I don't know where to turn."

"I'll call Anna right now and see how this should be best handled with her father. Please don't worry, Walther. He will have the answers to your questions. You are doing the right thing."

Anna was most receptive to Marta's suggestion for a meeting with her father, who had first met the field marshal at Marta and Klaus' wedding. They had appeared to develop a comfortable bond with one another, and she knew Sigmund's expertise made him best equipped to advise Marta's father-in-law should he choose to accept it. The girls agreed it would certainly be worth investigating.

It was late autumn 1929. Although reluctant to meet openly with Sigmund, for reasons not quite understood at the time by either Anna or Marta, the field marshal agreed to a clandestine appointment with Sigmund at a discreet location not far from Kreuzberg, near to, but not at Sigmund's clinic. Sigmund's willingness for discretion and confidentiality impressed Field Marshal von Brauchitsch, as Sigmund expressed no apparent interest in what may have been the basis of such a secretive meeting.

On the day of their somewhat mysterious meeting, Sigmund was quite surprised by the three-car entourage of military security, which safely delivered the field marshal to the rear door of the hotel and provided armed escort to the inside tavern in which Sigmund had been waiting. *So much for low-profile discretion,* thought Sigmund.

It was mid-morning, and other than a few staffers readying the tavern for another day, the room was absent any other patrons. The tavern was somewhat darkened by the subdued daylight passing through the ornately colored glass windows. It was an innocuous setting indeed.

"Good morning, Herr Landesburg. It is indeed good to see you again!"

Sigmund rose as soon as the small escort entered the room and noticed the field marshal not addressing him as *Doctor*. He took no offense and extended his welcoming hand. "And to you as well, Field Marshal," he offered respectfully.

"Let us dispense with such formalities shall we, Sigmund? Please call me Walther. May I call you Sigmund?"

"Yes, yes of course. Thank you, Walther. I trust the family is well. My congratulations on the birth of your little grandson! I hear Manfred is now in school and keeping Marta fully absorbed with the joys of motherhood." Sigmund chuckled harmlessly, not aware of Marta's recent disclosures to Anna or how sarcastic his comment may have sounded.

The usual pleasantries were brief, and out of respect for time Sigmund directed the conversation to the matter of Walther's call.

"How may I be of service, Walther? I understand you have had some health concerns recently."

"Yes, I am concerned that may be true and, as I touched on so very briefly on the telephone, I am anxious to get to the heart of the matter, so to speak. However, before we commence, I must confirm and trust that whatever we discuss today be kept in the strictest of confidence. It is essential we be direct and speak candidly with each other. Is that agreed, Sigmund?"

"Of course, Walther. I can assure you whatever we discuss will be kept strictly between us, and specifically not for our daughters' ears, just to be clear."

"Excellent! Precisely what I wanted to hear." The field marshal stretched his tight tunic and sipped his black coffee as he was evidently composing himself. He continued. "As you can appreciate, the military has preoccupied me continually throughout my career, much to the dismay of my family as you are already aware, and now more than at any other time in my past twenty-seven years of service. Recently my command responsibilities have been increasing daily, details of which I must not disclose."

"I completely understand. Please continue, Walther."

"You are no doubt as aware as anyone of the recent events in Munich. Disturbing to say the least." He paused briefly, continuing again. "Whether I personally agree or disagree with these potentially grave issues is not for me to decide. I must do as I am instructed, irrespective of any personal conflicts I may feel. I am, first and foremost, a loyal and dedicated soldier."

Sigmund nodded in agreement but did not interrupt. He saw the field marshal struggling.

"I pray your family and loved ones will always be safe, and if there is ever a problem, I assure you I will do everything in my power to assist you to whatever extent I am able. I am not without significant influence."

"Thank you, kind sir. Let us pray it will never become necessary."

Walther continued. "My health seems to be slipping. I am continually fatigued, I have been gaining weight, as you can see quite visibly." He adjusted his broad black leather belt uncomfortably. "I am frequently short of breath and generally, if I may be so blunt, I feel like shit!"

He sipped his coffee and began again. "Probably nothing serious but, due to my rank, I must always appear fit for my duties. How can I expect those under my command to by physically and mentally prepared if I cannot maintain those same standards for myself? It troubles me Sigmund." Walther held up his finger momentarily. "Hear me out though, before you comment."

Sigmund was an attentive listener, as was his practice, and he was intrigued as to where the discussion appeared to be heading.

"This young upstart in Munich has stimulated more than a ripple of change, particularly within the military. I have worked too long and hard not to be an integral part of Germany's rise to reclaim its position as a world power. I am determined to be an important part of it. If I have a fear, it is the possibility my failing health could preclude my proactive involvement. It is for this reason I come to you."

He leaned forward and lowered his voice to further ensure not to be overheard by his escort. "I cannot trust our own medical personnel to investigate my fitness for duty at the first notice of a problem I can no longer hide. Can you do whatever tests you deem appropriate to determine what the hell is happening to me? That much I know you can...but can you do so confidentially, without the customary disclosures?"

"What you are asking is possible Walther, but highly irregular to be sure. You already trust me as a capable physician, but will you trust my personal judgment as well?"

Walther nodded in agreement.

"I suggest we investigate the problem and do our best to reconcile what I already suspect may be the cause for concern. I can submit your clinical information under a fictitious name, and most of the workup can be completed at my own clinic. There is no reason at this point to suggest involvement with hospital treatment, at least not yet, so your name will not appear on any public records to possibly arouse suspicions."

Walther reached out to squeeze Sigmund's shoulder with confident assurance.

"Thank you, Sigmund. I knew you of all people, would be discreet. This means a great deal to me, my friend, and I am in your debt."

"Let's just make your health our priority and see where your tests may take us. Based upon clinical results, it will enable us to determine the best course of action. You are still stationed at the base in Zossen, I presume?"

"Yes, another reason for contacting you. I can commute easily on short notice. It's only an hour drive and won't draw any attention away from my usual travel habits."

As they rose, handshakes were exchanged, and nods of acknowledgement were shared silently with the guards. Not one word had been spoken by any of them. Walther respectfully requested Sigmund remain behind for ten minutes or so until the field marshal had left the area, a request Sigmund was pleased to follow as instructed.

CHAPTER FOURTEEN

♂

MARTA HAD BEEN ENDURING HER PERSONAL CRISIS FOR some time now, most of which she had previously confided to Anna that day at the Café Romanisches. Throughout most of her life since her adolescence, it had been her well-established habit to confront her personal challenges directly and without hesitation. In fairness, this matter had to be handled in a sensitive and tactful manner, face to face with Klaus whenever he eventually returned home. When that would happen was under the control of neither of them, as he often deferred to his military obligations that frequently took precedence.

The stress of continually dividing her attention between her fulfilling career and her numerous responsibilities to Manny's needs had become draining and simply had to stop. There had been no opportunity for her to engage in any discussions with Klaus on this topic, or any other for that matter. The very idea of prearranging a discussion of this nature was an absurd consideration.

Finally, and on typically short notice, she received the news she had been anxiously awaiting. Klaus was scheduled to be home for the next few days. His continual absence from Marta had become frustrating for each of them to be certain, but for Marta it had become intolerably so. She genuinely missed his companionship, and she was excited and stimulated at the very thought of him coming home to her.

The spark between them was still very much alive, but life was simply getting in the way, inexorably sucking the oxygen that fed the flame. As much as she wanted the man in her life to love and nurture her, it was imperative to be candid with him on this visit to address and put to rest her internal confusion. Her spirit had been noticeably buoyed since her confession to Anna, and Anna's understanding of her dilemma; would that Klaus was of the same mind, she thought.

Marta thought intently about how she would take this opportunity to re-stoke the fading fires of passion between them while at the same time, gain his support for a new arrangement for Manny. Marta presumed their upcoming and probable contentious discussion would ruin any chance she had to reconcile their passion for one another. She decided she would have to leave those complicated matters to the following day. Tonight, she was intent upon enticingly offering herself to him to reaffirm their love for one another.

In preparation for the ultimate evening of romantic decadence, Marta took the initiative to have Manny stay overnight with Anna, Jacob, and the family. He and Dietrich didn't see one another as often as they hoped but despite the age difference, they were always quick to resume their friendly relationship. Manny would return home the following morning to share some valuable time with his father, but Marta needed some time alone with Klaus first. The staff was also informed the parlor was to be kept private and there was no need to greet Klaus upon his arrival, as they normally would do.

The stage was set that evening when Klaus arrived home, marking almost a month since his last leave from duty. Much like his beautiful wife, his dedication to his career was never more ardent than it had now become. It totally preoccupied his mind to the point of becoming an obsession. This evening Marta would prove to become the single exception that would entirely disrupt his focus.

As he entered and closed the door behind him, Marta walked unhesitatingly to the vestibule in such a sultry manner he knew instantly this would be an extraordinary welcome home.

"Hello my gorgeous man! I've been counting the weeks to hold you in my arms again. I am so happy you are home, my love." Marta wrapped herself around Klaus and kissed him passionately, not for a moment giving him the chance to say a word. He simply dropped his valise where he stood in surprised delight to return his own impassioned embrace, no doubt having only been expecting the customary peck on the cheek.

"My, my! This is a marvelous welcome Marta! You look ravishing! I don't understand what I could have done to deserve this, but I don't really give a damn. I trust you don't object to me being unusually receptive this evening?"

Marta said nothing, but her response was more than adequately expressed by her sumptuous kisses with slightly parted lips, encouraging his tongue to touch hers.

She was seductively attired in a full-length, ivory-white peignoir set, elegantly caressing her curvaceous and delicately toned body. She wore precariously high heeled shoes which added an additional two inches of elegant stature to her already majestic figure. Her shoes were finished with fine white silk, accented by an appropriate plumage of white ostrich feathers. The familiar scent of Chanel No. 5 effused her very essence.

In stark but effective contrast to the purity of her innocent, virginal image, her ruby-red lipstick, tastefully applied eye shadow, and a slight touch of blush, off-set by her cascading, glowing blonde hair, totally intoxicated her formidable lover. Klaus knew neither how nor why he was being so thoroughly smitten in this wonderful manner. It was irrelevant. Some things in life a man need not question.

Within minutes they staggered into the parlor locked together, the room still basking in the early evening sunshine, which was barely diffused by the luxurious sheer curtains, offering little to no privacy to mask their passionate interlude.

They both stumbled and laughingly maneuvered their way to the finely crafted, gold-embroidered lounge that beckoned them. Marta was already kicking off her shoes, hopping on one foot while struggling with the other, as Klaus was tearing at his jacket. All the while Marta was directing Klaus closer and closer to the lounge, at which point she forcibly pushed him onto his back. As she calmly straddled him, her soft spreading thighs revealed her silk stockings and garter belt, also in matching pearl white. She had saved the best for last, as she slowly but self-assuredly raised her impeccably chic lingerie to reveal her shimmering love spot in the absence of her panties.

Marta did not give Klaus any opportunity to undress. She leaned forward toward him to resume inflaming him with another series of deep-throated kisses. Gradually and by design, she slowly shifted herself from her position on his still clothed abdomen in his full military regalia. Without uttering a word between them, and carefully guiding the train of her lingerie behind her, Marta moved toward his upper torso to nestle herself ever so gently upon his astonished and now welcoming face. His tongue penetrated her gently as she slowly rose ever so slightly... and settled back down in rhythmic ecstasy.

Marta silently amused herself by thinking, "Now that I have your undivided attention, my dear..." She was torn between the humor of the thought, and her lustful craving for his touch, and could only groan with delight at the prospects of what was to come from this seductive experience.

She raised her arms above her shoulders to firmly grasp her head as if being self-possessed. She became transfixed by the absorbing pleasure of this intimate moment between her and her lover. Her convulsive orgasms were suitably announced when Marta lost all control, shouting to him not to stop pleasuring her in this way. Her groans became screams, as if finally being unleashed from within her during his period of absence. This was something she had been longing for, for far too long.

Entirely satiated, Marta collapsed onto the sofa couch, struggling to regain her breath. It was a glorious moment she would never forget. Klaus knew his own unbridled pleasure would soon follow, but this was a moment in which both lovers wanted only to bask.

*****

The following morning found Klaus and Marta exceptionally tender and attentive to one another from the minute they awoke. It was gentle; it was genuine. It was extraordinarily romantic. However, Marta was on a mission this day and there wasn't a better time to address it than this morning. As they were finishing a sumptuous late breakfast, the moment for serious discussion had arrived.

"You know, Sweetheart, I have been thinking a great deal about my future of late."

"It isn't the first time. What's different about this one? Is everything all right?"

"Yes of course, in fact it's more than alright. I spoke to Maestro Furtwängler this past week about my reawakened desire to once again become totally immersed in my professional pursuits, as you have with the military. I want your opinion Klaus, and even more so your support for my ultimate decision."

"Your decision? Whatever have you done now, Marta? I thought everything was good for you now, and you do know how very much

I count on you to attend to Manny. Is he becoming too much of a handful? We can always hire some help."

"Just listen to me Klaus, please. You are very kind, sweetheart, but I need more than occasional help regarding Manny. I'm thinking of transferring the full-time responsibilities of our beautiful son to a more capable custodian than his own mother."

"Whatever are you suggesting?"

"Just hear me out. With you being away so much the past few years, I'm not prepared on my own to keep myself available and seeing to his every need. We both love him dearly, but I will never feel truly fulfilled unless and until I can resume my career as it was before he was born." *There, I've finally said it out loud,* she thought. It felt so very good to do so.

Klaus was speechless and despite his momentary silence, his tension and anger were visibly apparent, as his eyes remained totally focused on Marta's.

Marta continued. "Since Manfred started attending the Vorschule, I think the time has come for his day-to-day care to be allocated to someone better suited to his attentive care than myself. I have interviewed several qualified candidates recently and checked their references, of course. Among them, I met a very loving and well-qualified, middle-aged woman named Lena. She is a very capable and dedicated woman, Klaus. I am certain you will be impressed when you meet her."

Klaus paused contemplatively and reached for his second cup of coffee. "It sounds to me the decision has already been made, Marta. Why were you not compelled to speak to me about this before?"

"And when exactly did you give me the chance to do so, Klaus? It's been a month since I've seen or heard from you...this time! Before this, I simply lost track of the time. When we are together on rare occasions, the last thing you want to do is address other matters such as these. You customarily leave them to me, as you are far too pre-occupied with more important issues. How many other wives are as understanding as me, I wonder?"

"Stop Marta! How can you be such a self-absorbed, bloody bitch? Is this what last night was really all about? This is our little boy we are talking about, not a simple frivolous distraction! I never would have believed we would need such a conversation between us. How fucking dare you!"

"You are entitled to be upset with me, Klaus, but this is not a matter of frivolous whimsy. I have been agonizing with myself for the past two years, and I cannot endure it any longer. I want to return to the symphony in the same capacity as before, and I want your support to do it. I deserve to have my career, Klaus, as much as you deserve yours! I won't have it any other way. Please Klaus."

"I had no intention of coming home to this. All I wanted was to see you and Manny again and relax by taking my mind off the bullshit in my life." Klaus sat despondently and took a few deep breaths as he sought to calm himself.

Marta was wise enough to give him some space and understood she must not keep attacking him if she ever expected a positive resolution from him.

Klaus excused himself and stepped out to the balcony overlooking the street below. He lit a cigarette while he quietly contemplated his situation. About a half hour later, he returned and called to Marta, who by now had started preparing for her shower. She had evidently kept occupied by removing the few dishes and clearing the table. It was probably the first time in years she had done so.

"Please come back to the dining room and sit down, Marta. I just needed some time to carefully consider what you said. I don't want this to linger between us until the next time we are together."

"Thank you, Klaus. I don't either," she replied.

"I must get this off my chest, so please don't interrupt what I have to say." Klaus poured himself another cup of coffee and thoughtfully topped up Marta's as well. "As often happens, you are right. I'm not about to argue with you. I hardly know my own son, let's admit that. And I trust your decision, Marta, as well as your judgment about this woman you found. All I ask is that you properly introduce her to me. I will be home even less frequently now, so how often would I see either of them anyway? It no longer matters in the scheme of things, I suppose. My life is no longer my own."

Klaus sat rather dejectedly as he made these admissions to his wife. He had already sensed they had been drifting apart as well. He'd imagined something like this would happen sooner or later and upon reflection, was thankful she'd finally opened up to him.

Marta went on to calmly explain that despite her temporary loss of focus from her professional music career, her global popularity continued to grow, though its momentum was slowing appreciably.

She was as aware of this as anyone and was gradually becoming mentally erratic and unsettled by this apparent trend. She was figuratively starving to death without her music and she craved the adoration and popularity to which she had become accustomed. Klaus hadn't been home enough to have noticed.

As Anna had suspected, Klaus' gentle side emerged and he graciously supported Marta's request, without further reservation. He knew that continuing to argue with her would only drive them further apart. Her happiness was important to him and he co-operated fully. This was the wonderful man Marta had fallen in love with.

After meeting with Lena, Klaus and Marta mutually agreed Manny would do well in her very capable and loving hands. For Lena, staying home idly was not fulfilling enough to suit her purposes. Having raised a family of her own, she confessed genuinely that caring for Manny would give her life purpose again. It was all she wanted to do.

After numerous references were carefully considered, it was only weeks before arrangements were made for Lena to move into the von Brauchitsch mansion. She would be compensated admirably and had no difficulty adjusting to her new life of splendor and opulence.

Lena's enthusiasm for taking on such a responsibility was encouraging. She was grateful to help shape Manny, while still young, and set a safe and productive course for his life to make his parents proud of him. She was also thankful to Marta for deeming her capable of such a noble task. "Madame von Brauchitsch, I am honored you have selected me. I will not disappoint you or give you any cause for concern for Manny's welfare."

"Your references spoke very highly of you, and I believe I am a good judge of character. We are happy to have you become an important member of our family. And please, Lena. Just refer to me as 'Miss Marta.' There is no need for formalities behind these doors."

*****

It was not long before Marta collaborated further with Maestro Furtwängler to restore herself to prominence as the preeminent emissary for the Berlin Philharmonic. Box office sales soared when her return was announced, which was a significant development reflecting their co-operative effort.

Furtwängler requested enough time with Marta for his meeting with her. He very much wanted her learned opinions and feedback on programming design right from the very outset of her much-awaited return to the public eye.

By his tone, Marta understood this luncheon was much more than a private celebratory one. There was something more she sensed. Her modest apprehensions quickly dissipated when his exuberance was evident upon learning of her firm resolve to re-establish herself in the symphonic spotlight.

"I cannot adequately express my excitement at having you become such a vital cornerstone of the Philharmonic once again. It was all I could do to not pressure you to return after Manfred's birth. I owed you the respect you rightfully deserved to place your family before your career. If I may be candid with you Marta, it was a decision I accepted reluctantly."

"That was so kind of you, Wilhelm—even I did not realize how torn I would become. I have since decided to stop my unproductive feelings of guilt and accept who I am, a musician as much as a mother, if not more so. With Klaus' support, I intend to dedicate myself fully to pursuing my dreams again. Thank you for keeping the door open for me."

From the elevated VIP table they shared, the opulent dining room spread out before Marta and Maestro. Numerous diners who frequented the restaurant were accustomed to seeing celebrities, but this time the hype surrounding Marta's return piqued their curiosity more than usual.

Since the announcement Marta's impeccable image had again been prominently featured in newspapers and magazines throughout Berlin and across most of Western Europe. On this day her familiar profile was highlighted so naturally by the afternoon sunshine, it exuded a mystical golden glow befitting the occasion. Her loveliness did not go unnoticed.

Among the gathering patrons, a few excited and enthusiastic admirers broke with tradition to approach Marta's table, despite the usual police security normally reserved for political and media dignitaries. The general fuss about Marta's return was never one of a threatening nature, but rather an over-exuberant prelude to what her entourage would have to deal with in the years ahead.

A young family politely approached within the generally secured perimeter when a burly security guard impeded their advance. A handful of other patrons had followed suit in hope of meeting Marta, and no one was being disorderly.

"Please Officer. Would you mind letting these few people through? I would very much enjoy meeting them. Please."

The maestro acceded to Marta's request and two or three small groups were directed to approach their table.

"Thank you so much, Madame von Brauchitsch for being so kind. Our son is a young aspiring violinist. I hope you will forgive us for interrupting your meal, but it has been our son's dream to meet you one day. It was a chance I had to take."

"Of course! Please come here, young man." The young boy, not more than ten years old, approached Marta with wide beaming eyes and his mouth was agape with excitement.

"What is your name, young man? I must say you look very handsome this fine afternoon. Please come closer," she said as she beckoned him to stand beside her.

"I am Alexander Kazmierez. It is an honor to meet you Madame. I listen to you on the radio as often as I can, and I saw you once in concert when my grandpa took me to see the Philharmonic for the very first time. I shall never forget it as long as I live. I pray that one day I will be on the same stage as you. You inspire me more than you could know."

"Well, it is certainly my honor to meet you personally, Alexander. You remind me of my niece. Perhaps you have heard her play too. Her name is Pietra. She is about your age I would guess."

"Pietra Friedman? Yes! I have seen her play at various competitions! She plays beautifully! I remember her well. Seeing her gave me confidence that I too could be much better than I was at that time. Because of her I am working even harder to achieve my dreams!"

Marta looked over her shoulders from side to side to create just the correct amount of expectation from the young boy, and softly whispered into his ear, "Let me tell you a little secret, Alexander. I am still chasing my dreams too!"

It was the beginning of an entirely new side of Marta. Although she had never been the least bit standoffish in the past, her magnetic personality was beginning to blossom again—an absolute marvel to watch. Her absence had sharpened her appeal. Maestro Furtwängler was of the same mind and smiled with genuine admiration for the kindness and consideration she had just shown.

"Your gesture to that young boy was very thoughtful Marta. As always I am very proud of what you have just done." He raised his snifter of cognac before her. "Bravo my dear."

The discussion returned to the business at hand while enjoying pastries and coffee. Programming matters had to be addressed before resumption of the upcoming season, which was now fast approaching.

"I have been considering doing something unique to celebrate your return to the spotlight. What are your thoughts on devoting opening night to acknowledge ethnic diversity and the profound contribution it has brought to classical music? I'm thinking of perhaps opening with Dvorak's New World Symphony followed by your interpretation of the Tchaikovsky Violin Concerto in D Opus 3 immediately following the intermission."

"Wilhelm, that sounds exciting! I am pleased to do so, however why in the second half? It is so uncustomary isn't it?" Marta enquired.

"The piece would provide an incredible beginning to appropriately announce the new resurgence of the orchestra as well as highlighting the resumption of your own career. I want to break with precedent, thinking that your adoring followers waited so patiently by adjusting as best they could to your appearances that became less frequent. What say we make them wait just a little longer...until after intermission? By so doing, you can make your long-overdue grand entrance in more dramatic fashion to perform such an emotional signature piece."

"Wilhelm, you flatter me with your thoughtfulness. I am deeply moved..." Marta paused only momentarily to consider the opportunity. "Yes of course! It will be delightful to break with tradition and tease the audience a bit, I agree."

Maestro reached for Marta's hand to tenderly kiss it in true gentlemanly form. "That evening is sure to be another highlight of my career, thanks to your graciousness, Marta. I am truly honored to be an integral part of it."

Marta had a quizzical look of concern as she explained to the maestro, "I have but one concern, however." Maestro took pause. "And that is concerning...?"

"I want to acknowledge to you personally how very well Gilbert Back has stepped up so capably as first violin in my absence. He has proven his talent time and again. What will happen when I am not a soloist with respect to those responsibilities, Wilhelm? I do not want to cause any friction between him and I. Have you considered this in light of my return?"

"I have, Marta. In fact, Gilbert thoughtfully broached the subject following your initial discussions with me. As the true gentleman he is, he has accepted a subordinate role and will continue to serve in the capacity of first violinist when you are touring or soloing. He has always considered his role to be of a temporary nature until such time as you eventually returned. I must add that from the moment you left us he was hopeful you would come back…stronger than ever."

"Wonderful! I am so relieved, Wilhelm."

*****

This was the day Pietra had been preparing for since she'd first held her violin at the tender age of three. More accurately, it was the aspiration of her mother and Aunt Marta, who had both dreamt of this eventful day coming to pass, both having the hope Anna's talent would carry over to her young daughter.

Critics were attracted to little Pietra, as they followed the career and numerous publicity appearances of her highly visible aunt. Essentially, Pietra was regarded as a supremely gifted young prodigy of note. Today was a significant opportunity to bring public acclaim and deserved recognition to this very charming little girl. She would not disappoint.

The weather was quite dreary on the evening of the performance, with grey overcast and heavy, intermittent storm showers forecast. Nevertheless, the private cars and taxi cabs lined up to deliver their passengers, mostly parents, friends, and family members of the competitors, to the steps of the magnificent Konzerthaus Berlin in the central district of Mitte.

Despite the dismal weather conditions, the lower level of the auditorium was packed to the last row. It was an auspicious beginning for these youngsters ranging from five to eighteen years of age, all of whom would be accompanied as required by various members of the Berlin Philharmonic orchestra. Patrons and sponsors of the music and arts community had funded the concert and their generous contributions to these competitions assured the longevity of such outstanding annual events.

Typically, specific age groups competed with other children of similar age categories. The final grouping, however, was always reserved for the infrequent few who graced the stage specifically recognized as possessing prodigious talent. This year there were two such candidates for the National Championship.

Josef Menuhin was an accomplished young pianist of seventeen years of age. A round of polite applause welcomed him as he strode so elegantly across the stage. He was a majestic young man who carried himself so very well.

He flawlessly delivered the first movement of Tchaikovsky's First Piano Concerto in B flat major. His flowing, shoulder-length black hair was tossed, and he snapped his head with flourish, throwing his hair away from his handsome young face, making the triumphant melody come more to life than the concert goers had imagined. His slender body displayed his intensity of emotion, which was vividly apparent right to the final row of concert attendees.

Upon completing the rousing and hauntingly familiar final notes of the movement, he sagged momentarily against the keyboard in utter exhaustion. The audience stood in loud appreciation for this incredible young man who had delivered every ounce of passion the piece demanded of him. It was a compelling performance.

As he acknowledged the crowd, he bowed repeatedly to the cheering, appreciative spectators until the applause diminished and he disappeared from view. The stage was hastily reset for the final performer, as the audience murmured their admiration for what had just been witnessed.

It was now time for little Pietra.

When she took the stage in her white and elegantly embroidered, knee-length dress, the audience became hushed and politely applauded her arrival at stage center. A pianist assumed his position near the grand piano to accompany the young child, and he respectfully gestured to her by bowing his head in acknowledgement of his appreciation for Pietra and that of the audience as well. The accompanist began to applaud lightly, awaiting the nod of the head from the lovely child to indicate she was ready to begin. The final murmurs of the audience quickly ceased, and the hall fell totally silent.

As she had done weeks prior for her private recital for Aunt Marta, who was now sitting front row with Klaus, Anna, Sigmund and Marissa who was holding little Emilie on her lap, Pietra's eyes closed. The family seemed to have held their collective breath. From the opening note, she exploded with the fervent attack Brahms had intended. Her passionate interpretation was barely contained as this beautiful child touched the heart and soul of everyone in attendance, many of whom were already clutching their tissues at the ready. The mellow tones resonated throughout the theatre and captivated the same mothers, fathers, friends, and family in breathless anticipation of what they were witnessing, and only imagining what was yet to follow.

Skillfully she demonstrated the impeccable technique Marta had capably refined, as she confirmed Pietra would be capable of achieving. The gathering was stimulated to new heights of emotion evoking complete awe for this most capable virtuoso, for whom "prodigy" seemed inadequate to fully describe. Pietra performed so comfortably, so effortlessly, and so naturally, as if the instrument had become an extension of herself. To the final note, her admirers were captivated beyond the limits of their artistic experience, leaving no possibility for those present to fully comprehend the magnitude of Pietra's absolute mastery.

She paused trancelike, just momentarily, but genuinely, and not solely for dramatic effect. She was lost and fully absorbed in her music. The audience shook the auditorium as everyone rose to their feet, applauding, shouting, crying, and a few even fainting, only to fall back upon their seats, having become emotionally drained. To personally bear witness to such a marvelous expression of this unparalleled art form, delivered so memorably by such a young child, was hard to grasp. But it was the only way Pietra knew how to perform. It was…as if the very hand of God guided her.

Auntie Marta was so overcome with pride she rose from her seat and exited to the backstage entrance, not to steal or share Pietra's moment in any possible way, but to stand in her presence to publicly applaud her, and to personally endorse the outstanding mastery of her craft. She did so with silent, tearful, and prideful admiration and affection.

When Pietra became aware her Auntie Marta was standing slightly behind her, she transformed from a professional virtuoso to become a little girl again as she ran to embrace Marta. As at home, she was swept up in her famous auntie's arms, igniting another surge of delightful acceptance from not only the audience, but most notably Josef Menuhin, who had entered the stage to enthusiastically acknowledge both Pietra, and one of his professional inspirations, Marta.

The applause continued for several minutes more until the various dignitaries began to assemble on stage bearing the second prize for Josef, and reserving their final presentation to the National Champion, Miss Pietra Elisabeth Friedman!

In the years following, Pietra was in constant demand. The press broadly covered each of her successive concert performances. Newspapers and music critics raved about her musical genius to the extent that Anna was forced to consult Jacob, Marta, and of course, her parents as to finding ways to shelter her from the constant distractions of celebrity. Anna's only desire was to allow her precious daughter to enjoy her childhood. It had not occurred to her yet that the only thing capable of sustaining Pietra's passion in life was to continue to caress the one true love of her life...her violin.

CHAPTER FIFTEEN

♂

THE MEDIA WAS BUZZING IN ANTICIPATION OF MARTA'S homecoming performance, and equally as much when the programs were published. It was September 30, 1929. It would be a propitious season opener featuring Marta, the violin virtuoso, delivering her touching interpretation of the Tchaikovsky Violin Concerto, a stirringly emotional and melodious classic by Russia's finest composer. As previously agreed, her personal entrance would be deferred to the second half of the performance.

Most of the excited patrons had been comfortably seated and were alive with boisterous discussions among fellow patrons reunited once again with so many other appreciative musical devotees. The spontaneous clamor of incomprehensible and indiscernible chaos gradually became louder, and even louder still as the grand old theatre continued to fill.

When the curtains opened and the orchestra took their places for a final tuning, the audience continued to converse but in a more subdued fashion. It ceased entirely when Maestro Furtwängler entered stage left. The applause was respectful as expected and quickly subsided when lights were dimmed, and Maestro turned to face his musicians from his rostrum.

The Dvorak selection was notably the Austrian composer's most famous work. Its melodious structure remains unique throughout the pages of history and is most identifiable to classical music enthusiasts.

It was played to perfection, as always by the BPO, but the atmosphere in the theater was markedly apprehensive in the wake of their delayed gratification that hungered for Marta's presence. Few members of the audience left the auditorium at the break, almost to indicate they were guarding their reserved seats from other intrusive patrons. When the moment they were waiting for arrived, as signified by the dimming of the house lights, the anticipation was palpable. The instant the side curtain moved, before Marta could be seen, the crowd exploded with pent up delight. An instant later, finally... it was Marta! She was back!

She was adorned in a ruby red strapless gown highlighted as usual by her ruby and diamond necklace and stunning earrings. Even after the remaining lights were fully dimmed, Marta's iconic image glowed in the featured performer's spotlight shining from far above her. She was a mesmerizing sight for everyone to behold and definitively delivered the intricacies of Tchaikovsky's creation with her customary ease and sensitivity.

Her performance was entrancing in how she negotiated her way through the hauntingly lovely melodic masterpiece. Her styling and grace suitably embraced the perfect congruency of the performance, and the performer, in such a way few could explain or understand.

*****

In the weeks following their initial meeting, Field Marshal von Brauchitsch became a high-priority patient for Sigmund, as numerous blood tests and complete medical examinations enabled Sigmund to confirm what he had already suspected. The field marshal had developed clear signs of congestive heart failure, caused by possible arterial blockage of the heart. In most other aspects, he was muscular and remained in reasonably sound medical condition. But the heart, if left to degenerate without some remedial treatment, would continue to take its toll on his overall well-being.

Walther took the news from Sigmund as would be expected by a domineering and disciplined man of his military stature. He possessed an almost inhuman disregard for the news of this imminent threat to his realistic prospects of longevity. Without hesitation, he insisted Sigmund do all he could, to at the very least, give Walther some hope and expectation for a reasonable period of time to fulfill his destiny and become revered for his service to the Fatherland.

At Walther's urging, Sigmund disclosed some research he had discovered that offered more than a glimmer of hope for a possible and temporary remedy to the field marshal's inevitable premature demise. It was agreed Sigmund take the time he required to further determine the possible implications for Walther.

During his investigation, Sigmund learned from numerous discussions with Dr. Henry Souttar that Souttar had continued to privately design and develop a short, flexible tube, which had not previously been available. By carefully implementing some clinically tested modifications, both Dr. Souttar and Sigmund were cautiously optimistic that a similar procedure utilizing the insertion of the tube could dramatically improve blood flow and potentially extend the heart function necessary.

Based upon Dr. Souttar's extensive mathematical and technical evaluations, the appropriate dimensions of the tube were configured to be appropriate for Walther's specific requirements. Henry Souttar was a man of significant medical repute, evidenced by his valiant military service and his subsequent appointment as assistant surgeon to the London Hospital, not to mention that he was a recipient of the Order of the Crown of Belgium. Sigmund was enthused about the possibility of this collaboration with him.

Walther confided to Sigmund his fervent belief that he "had nothing to lose that wasn't already lost." At Walther's forceful urging and determined insistence, and despite his own cautious reservations, Sigmund agreed he would undertake the necessary arrangements to complete the procedure employing the subterfuge of some amended paperwork to protect the identity of his patient. Walther agreed to sign waiver documentation of liability, something not typically done at the time, and the procedure was categorized as emergency, life-saving cardiac surgery.

This so-called emergency procedure was purposely scheduled for a typically quiet time in the operating theatre, and Sigmund arranged for his personal staff of assistants and anesthesiologists. The same three military officers who had delivered their field marshal to the tavern meeting also escorted Walther to the hospital entrance. They were his most trusted and loyal security detail and were aware of the risks to their commander, and to Sigmund as well. The operation lasted five hours, after which the formidable patient was taken to private recovery for close and constant monitoring. Other than during the surgical procedure, the guards never left his side.

Despite their challenging relationship, Marta and Klaus took alternate shifts as best they could to remain by Walther's bedside. The subject of Marta's premature mid-life crisis was blithely ignored and seemingly dismissed by both parties in deference to Walther's circumstances. Klaus was severely restricted as to his availability to be present with his father, since any undue absence from his duties would have logically signaled something was amiss. The field marshal was in and out of consciousness, but each time he awoke, he found Marta within arms-length to dutifully reassure him for the better part of the first week of post-surgical recovery. Sigmund had submitted paperwork describing a severe case of pneumonia to explain the extended absence of his patient, hence no one at Zossen was any the wiser.

The invasiveness of this unsanctioned surgery presented significant risk to Sigmund personally and to his career. The overall physical vitality of Walther, combined with his determined will power, most certainly provided an unquantifiable advantage to achieving a positive surgical outcome.

Within the next ten days, Walther's recovery fully stabilized and slowly but steadily his health began to strengthen. Despite a predictable weight loss of some twenty pounds, he was fully alert and enjoying full respiratory function far in excess of his pre-surgical condition.

Walther's recovery was time for thankfulness and cautious optimism. Over time, his stamina and appetite were restored, and he agreed to heed Sigmund's advice to rest. Under medical supervision he was gradually reintroduced to moderate physical activity. For such a strong and domineering character, he fully submitted himself to the care and watchful eye of Sigmund's most trusted medical team. Walther knew he was very fortunate to be alive.

Although this was an incalculable risk Sigmund had uncharacteristically undertaken, he was enthused by the adrenaline rush of success, but equally exhausted by the stress and anxiety he needed to endure to ultimately accomplish his goal. All the while Sigmund knew he could never speak of the procedural violations he had masterfully manipulated to make it happen. The AMA would never hear of this, of that he would remain determined.

It was a grand moment of suppressed and secretive jubilation for both Henry Souttar and Sigmund. Henry's brother Charles was the only person aware of the confidential complicity of Henry and

Sigmund, and he had pledged his silence. Sometimes, the course we follow is counter to our instinctively ingrained habits, to be altered only by our fervent desire to achieve greater significance in our lives. This was such a life-changing experience for Sigmund.

In the years following, Sigmund remained actively supportive of the AMA's contributions to strong standards of excellence, the development of strict ethical guidelines, and the credibility of their publications in the *Journal of the AMA*.

Despite Marissa's ever concerning and slowly progressing physical frailty since the birth of Emilie, she attended many of Sigmund's honorary presentations at the university. She would even manage to visit America with him on one of his medical conferences hosted in Philadelphia in 1931. This opportunity provided Sigmund and Marissa the opportunity to expand their global perceptions after having been previously confined to Central and Western Europe. Comparatively speaking, the American experience reaffirmed to them both the precarious gravity of their family circumstance within Germany.

*****

It was 1932. Hitler had become a frighteningly capable politician. His persuasive oratory frequently featured his charisma and fierce determination to seduce his adversaries, forcing them to unwittingly drop their guard. By so doing he consistently took from them far more than his fair share of advantages.

As an example, his strong advocacy to protect German business interests against Marxism and social democracy was closely aligned with the best interests of business and industry leaders. These protectionist ideals provided significant economic advantage to immensely wealthy business icons and were eagerly embraced by them. Despite remaining repulsed by Nazi ideologies regarding unjust persecutions, their financial support of Hitler curried favor from him they could ill afford to challenge.

This assured the Nazi Party of having access to vast political funding, thereby subsidizing their common interests to further solidify an extremist and very much secure political presence, particularly on the world stage. During this time Sigmund's worst premonitions were becoming closer at hand.

The poor economy, combined with fear of Marxism, created a conducive environment for Hitler's ideologies to thrive. The Nazi Party gained momentum, emboldening its leadership and wreaking a reign of terror that was no longer a hypothetical fabrication, but the new reality. In democratic elections that year, the Party achieved close to one-fifth of the general vote, consolidating their hold on governance in ways that had not been experienced in Germany since the Great War.

There were reports of the bullying of Jewish shopkeepers and tradesmen, and even professional services such as legal and medical had become unwary targets of serious oppression and violence, sometimes even leading to death, often without retribution. Munich was not the only city to be affected. Numerous cosmopolitan cities were forced to endure similar terror and uncertainty among the populace. The randomness of these assaults struck genuine fear and panic among many more than those personally enduring the callousness of these attacks.

This powerful instigator of Jewish hatred, of people whom he often referred to as parasites and a menace to society, continued to be a central point of relentless focus. Hitler openly held Jews totally accountable for every social and economic failure to befall Germany. Thousands of the German electorate, heretofore having never drawn a breath of anti-Semitic animosity began to espouse their newly developed hatred with no apparent motivation other than out of abject fear of serious reprisals for believing otherwise.

Despite Hitler's personal agenda, specifically these seemingly illogical and irrational tirades to persecute the Jews, business leaders continued to facilitate his ability to embrace a broader range of social classes and religious followings, all of which diversified his public appeal. It was as if the impact of anti-Semitism was simply regarded as the cost of doing business, or worse still, immaterial, and the scale of it was never intended or comprehended by anyone except Hitler's closest and most powerful henchmen.

*****

Sitting at home after sharing a late Friday evening dinner with the family had become a weekly ritual for Sigmund and Marissa. Against the backdrop of the familiar clatter of dishes and relaxed conversation, the telephone suddenly rang in the parlor. Sigmund excused himself to take the call. It was one he had been anticipating.

"That's odd. Whoever could that be at this hour?" Marissa casually wondered aloud. The gathering of dishware continued as she and Anna prepared some fresh coffee and pastries with no further thought given to the intrusion of the call.

Sigmund's muted conversation was barely apparent and could not be clearly overheard.

Within ten minutes he returned to the kitchen bearing a somber demeanor that was definitive. "Please everyone, I need to speak with you. Perhaps the children can play upstairs for a short while? It is important that we talk."

"Oh, my dear. That sounds ominous," Marissa offered.

"Perhaps it is something about the election?" Jacob whispered.

Everyone obliged Sigmund's request and joined him in the parlor. Sigmund began to speak but he did so pensively and with a measure of obvious reluctance. "As I promised to do some time ago, I have always tried to keep you apprised of relevant information on matters of potential consequence. A few minutes ago, I received a call that I must share with you. There is no other way than to be direct, but I am saddened to say, the Nazi Party has now officially become the second-largest party in parliament."

"Oh, my dear!" Anna exclaimed. Marissa and Jacob just sat in temporary shock while they processed the devastating news.

"The election results will be announced publicly within the hour. We are no longer questioning whether our own political efforts can continue to quell the groundswell of general discontent. It has now become apparent the Nazi Party has become a credible threat to our democratic republic. If they continue to be unopposed it will only be a matter of time before parliament concedes control of the House to these Nazi renegades."

He paused and reconsidered his wording. "I correct myself...*renegades* is actually no longer an accurate term to describe these persons. Their growing popularity has been fairly supported by the people! That, is our most serious problem."

*****

Over the course of the last few years, the Nazi Party had become legitimately entrenched in the German electoral process. This was not a coup d'état. Since the failure of the Beer Hall Putsch and his incarceration in 1923, Hitler understood the only course of action was to take power through the legal democratic process. He had played his cards brilliantly to this point, orchestrating events that caused his personal popularity to escalate before the horrors of his actions surfaced like some infectious disease screaming for attention.

As predicted by Sigmund's parliamentary advisors, Hitler received more than a third of populace support through the second ballot in his opposition to the incumbent, President Hindenburg. At the urging of many key members of parliament, Hindenburg acquiesced to Hitler's demands and offered Hitler the only role he would accept. Adolf Hitler lawfully became Chancellor of Germany on January 30, 1933.

The democratic process secured Hitler's position as chancellor but did not provide the majority control he sought so insistently. He still sought the support of other opposition parties, which would continue to require co-operation and compromise to effectively govern. This was unacceptable if Hitler was to achieve complete autocratic authority.

With this intent in mind, Hitler assigned ultimate control of the Prussian police, the largest police force of its kind throughout the German Empire, to his long-time ally, Hermann Göring. In doing so, the new chancellor had provided himself with his own private army.

On February 27, 1933, the parliament building known as the Reichstag caught fire. It was not by fortuitous co-incidence. Nazi leadership was immediately summoned and upon Göring's arrival moments later, a Dutch communist was arrested fleeing the scene of the fire. Göring shouted to the onlooking press, "*It is a communist revolution!*" This singular event gave the Nazis the opportunity to stoke the fears of communism by further stimulating the growing belief of the middle class in the imminent Communist uprising. It established the general perception of a successful national revolution.

Under the guise of securing emergency powers to quell the revolution, Hitler needed and was granted broad, sweeping, autocratic power by President Hindenburg, the implications of which were not fully understood by most German voters until it was too late.

Once these powers were granted, Hitler himself took immediate and firm control of the Reichstag crisis and by so doing, the following morning he convinced President Hindenburg to institute emergency measures by issuing the Reichstag Fire Decree. This declaration gave Hitler absolute control and a long-sought-after dictatorship, with the instant implementation of drastic, unprecedented restrictions on human and civil rights, including outlawing anyone or any group foolish enough to oppose the Nazi Party.

Within weeks of the Fire Decree, arrests were frequent and unrelenting to the extent that over ten thousand communist supporters were beaten, killed, or sentenced to concentration camps known to use excessive punishment and torture with little or no chance of survival for the victims. Dachau would become the first of many such camps. Soon after, parliament was moved to Berlin and the Enabling Act was issued. This enactment effectively assured Hitler of unlimited and unfettered power no longer requiring prior approval from either the president, or the Reichstag.

Effective immediately, all potential opposition to the Nazi Party was essentially eradicated. Trade unions were banned as were all political parties, and equally devastatingly, cultural and scientific cleansing was being seriously considered. Often overlooked among the authoritarian decrees was the systematic process of barring Jews from artistic life.

This decree understandably struck a nerve deep inside Maestro Furtwängler, who strenuously objected to any dismantling of his orchestra on religious or any other ethnic grounds. As it was, there were four Jewish musicians employed by the Philharmonic: including the first violinist, two cellists, and concertmaster Goldberg.

Marta was furious about the decree and was not at all timid in her support of the maestro's protestations. Despite the field marshal's strenuous outburst several years before, the wounds of which had finally healed over, she remained very outspoken in her defiance of the intrusive and unwarranted persecution of her Jewish colleagues. After all, her father-in-law had stated that her opinions, while not valid on military or political matters, should be restricted only to matters pertaining to *classical music and fashion.* Perhaps therefore, she felt some justification for ignoring his warning.

"I knew you would find this repulsive, Marta," said the maestro. "The entire orchestra is outraged, but they feel helpless about what can be done to stop it. They depend upon me to do all I can to keep this from happening."

"Just to be clear Wilhelm, I've stood back from the persecution I have personally witnessed time and again. It seems to me too many of us have been standing in the shadows afraid to speak up for fear of reprisals. I'm not accustomed to holding my tongue—you know that about me more than most, but I am at a loss to know what I can do. I have some influence with the media. Perhaps it is time my voice should be heard on this important matter."

"Listen to me carefully, Marta. I believe this will be a losing battle for us both if we do not tread carefully. You cannot underestimate the will and determination of the Fuhrer. He is not a man of tolerance. You must take this into consideration. He can destroy us both based upon nothing more than a whimsical impulse."

"It is frightening to hear of this, Wilhelm, but I have heard it all before. Will no one stand up to this egomaniacal monster?"

"Let me give you some perspective on the situation we are facing. I have been a close personal friend and colleague of Bruno Walter since we were children. He telephoned me yesterday from Leipzig and told me the chief of police has already closed down the dress rehearsal, and under threats of violence has forbade the concerts if Bruno attempts to conduct. In Bruno's mind he has no other choice than to reluctantly step away from the Gewandhaus Orchestra to depart for Berlin. He is scheduled to conduct the Philharmonic here next month."

"This is preposterous!" Marta exclaimed.

"There is more, my dear. When Minister Goebbels learned Bruno would be appearing on our March program, the minister made it clear there would be unpleasant demonstrations and more violence at his concerts. None of us can handle such threats.

Bruno can be a hothead sometimes and does not willingly back down. He has faced his share of persecution for most of his life. My point is, that if Goebbels can stop Bruno from performing, do you really believe he won't do the same or worse for you and me?"

Marta was stupefied and again, for the first time since the episode with the field marshal, she was frustrated beyond words at her inability to be heard. Dejectedly, she proceeded to gather her things to return home. The maestro did the same.

"For what it is worth, Wilhelm, I will support you in any way you ask. You do not have to stand alone to fight this oppression. If I can be useful to your defense of the orchestra, you only have to ask."

It had been a long and arduous day, but it was not over. As they exited the theatre together, they heard a commotion just up the street with hundreds of people shouting and running not away from, but toward a large but controlled fire. Masses of people were screaming and cheering as they threw hundreds of items into the growing blaze of orange and red. Out of inquisitiveness Marta and Maestro cautiously approached the scene.

Suddenly, in shock, Marta shouted above the growing pandemonium of noise, "Oh my God! They're throwing books into the fire Wilhelm! Has everyone gone mad?"

The cheering throng had become caught up in the paranoia, though many of its participants neither knew nor understood the rationale of such unprecedented behavior. Was this the true nature of mob mentality?

"I want no part in this, Marta. It is time to leave."

They had seen enough. Their fear had become all too real and so painful to bear. At that moment, seeing the crazed look on the people's faces, Marta knew Maestro's assessment was correct. Without saying the words, it had become clear this was not a fight they could likely win.

The Bible says God created the world in six days. It took Adolf Hitler only twice as long to fundamentally destroy it.

*****

Most Germans did not celebrate the news of Hitler's rise to the pinnacle of ultimate authority, but anyone in opposition to him knew the wisdom of maintaining apparent acquiescence. Too many were in abject fear of terrible potential consequences to anyone foolish enough to speak up against the Nazi regime. This was no time for bravery. This pervasive perceived acceptance, considering no apparent alternative, enabled Hitler to implement his reign of terror, assuring it of becoming a horrific reality.

What once had seemed preposterous to those who erroneously assumed common sense and humanitarian reason would ultimately prevail, under these new circumstances was now reluctantly accepted. It was time for many to seriously consider initiating proactive strategies to realistically enable their families to survive the upcoming ordeal.

Sigmund and Marissa epitomized those in the upper class who were highly exposed to persecution on religious grounds, with one significant advantage. If not for the discreet but powerful protection afforded the family due to the field marshal's indebtedness to Sigmund, they too would have been exposed to the common perils of the oppressed.

Despite all odds, Hitler's power was now absolute. This acknowledgement caused both Sigmund and Marissa to ask each other, *"How long can our family continue to cower under the field marshal's protective shadow?"*

Having pondered this once improbable circumstance over the past several months of Hitler's meteoric rise, the answer to their question became increasingly obvious. Although Sigmund and Marissa had conspired together to put certain opportunities into place, it was time to reveal the details of their plan for Pietra to Anna and Jacob. Ultimately, if anything were to be agreed upon, it would be Pietra's parents' decision, and theirs alone. Regrettably, the options before them were not at all currently clear for young Dietrich, who was now just ten years old. He was still very much dependent on the nurturing of his parents and grandparents.

Many doors of possibility had been opened by way of Sigmund's participation in the annual AMA conferences and the incredible talent of his granddaughter Pietra. It was time for some dramatic but well-conceived measures to be implemented.

Over the next weeks and months, after numerous gut-wrenching discussions, Anna and Jacob both agreed. "Father, our family always understood the day would come when Pietra's rare talent would take her far away from us and most importantly, she knew it too. Since we all met with Richard Ellis after her first win at the Nationals, it is what she always wanted. She is ready for this. You have seen it for yourselves. None of this is at issue with her," said Anna. "We agree with you that we should downplay the dangerous circumstances she is leaving behind. Each of us understands that the cost of delaying this incredible opportunity any further could unthinkably be paid for with her very life. She must never be aware of the danger that still confronts us while we continue to live in Berlin."

Jacob was totally supportive by adding, "Frankly, she is so pre-occupied with her music, and she remains naïve to the persecution that will now separate her from us. There is no point to be served in delaying this any longer."

"For all of us, our greatest remaining concern is little Dietrich", interjected Marissa. In support of her, Sigmund handled the more delicate realities. "Our fear is that after news of Pietra's defection becomes public, any chance we will have to do anything similar is now nigh impossible for him. There is no question the authorities will be watching us like a hawk. Hence, it is clear we cannot easily remove him from Germany, but there are some less obtrusive alternatives Mother and I have already explored."

Sigmund was understandably disturbed about this topic and rec-ognized both Anna and Jacob were at odds with what to do about their young son, but neither one was willing to expect more from Sigmund and Marissa. They did not have to ask.

"For the moment we must focus on Pietra. In the ensuing two weeks, before our departure, Father can finalize some arrangements you should be comfortable with. For now, let's agree the upcoming conference may be our last window of opportunity, correct?" Marissa confirmed. "I don't think we dare wait another year. Too many things are happening here to restrict our rights and freedoms. Your father and I could be restricted from international travel anytime soon. We simply cannot take the chance."

Sigmund added, "The upcoming AMA conference is June 14th in Cleveland, Ohio. That gives us almost three months to prepare. Mother and I have already spoken to my cousin Grace and her husband, Richard. I haven't even met Richard, but I understand they would both be delighted to share their home with Pietra. They feel as though they already know her from various press reports and so on, and are only too happy to serve as her guardians."

In attendance at Pietra's first national competition and at several of her subsequent appearances, were a select few emissaries from highly ranked schools around the globe. Their purpose was to seek out the best musical talent the world had to offer. One such emissary represented the famed Julliard School of Music in New York City.

On behalf of Julliard, Richard Ellis had approached Pietra's family shortly following her glorious debut performance in 1927 at her then-tender age of six years. The events of that day, specifically her most memorable performance, established this gifted young musician as having the potential to become a major force within the world of music, and potentially to achieve new standards of creative excellence.

Mr. Ellis confirmed Julliard would be scrutinizing her development by his commitment to attend many of her public performances in the following years. He did so with dedicated and frequent consistency. Each successive year Julliard developed greater resolve to one day enroll the promising young lady at their esteemed school of music.

"Jacob, you and Anna should approach Mr. Ellis to notify him of your intentions to enroll her in the upcoming semester. I don't imagine there is any change of plans from Julliard?"

"Not at all, Father. We have developed quite a unique relationship with Mr. Ellis over the past few years. Julliard remains as determined as ever to have her enrolled. He will be thrilled to hear the news; of that we have no doubt."

"Excellent. Our travel documents should be in perfect order. Please prepare Pietra's documentation as well. I already checked with the passport office and you will both need to sign permission papers for Mother and me to take her out of the country. It is crucial we pay attention to every detail. The last thing we need is an administrative error that could delay matters."

So, in 1934, based upon Pietra's increasingly devout and steadfast dedication to her artistic gift, and motivated by the increasingly growing concerns for her safety and well-being, Jacob, Anna and her parents proceeded to accept the generous scholarship offered by Julliard. Pietra would be enrolled forthwith.

*****

With plans for Pietra's defection well underway, it was now time to address a creative medical circumstance that would attract no suspicion from military or security interests concerning finding a safe haven for Dietrich. Sigmund's trusted friend since graduate school was Dr. David Schleschen who had kindly assisted Sigmund on his mother's failing heart condition. He was always Sigmund's first and most reliable authority for any family or client care. The matter of Dietrich was no exception.

Based upon their collaborative effort, there was seemingly nothing they could not accomplish. Their impressive reputations and established medical authority were never open to scrutiny or debate. Within days of finalizing Pietra's arrangements Sigmund, Marissa and David sat with Anna and Jacob to discuss the unique opportunity they were proposing for Dietrich.

Sigmund prefaced the meeting with a general overview. "With David's help, our partnership has already utilized the medical services of Dr. Hans Asperger, a visionary who has devoted several years to a psychological condition closely related to autism in young and adolescent children. He has a well-established clinic in Vienna that has received numerous accolades for their amazing accomplishments. Our personal experience with him and his incredible staff has earned our genuine respect."

"Forgive me Father, but are you suggesting Dietrich be somehow institutionalized?" Anna asked in astonishment.

"Not at all Anna, but that is the usual reaction of most parents with children so afflicted... and also those who are so very gifted." he replied.

"And what about Austria? Would that not attract diplomatic attention?" Jacob inquired.

"Excellent question Jacob. The answer is a definitive *No!* This is a medical condition, not an emigration issue. The relationship between Austria and Germany has always been a close and amicable one, but even that fact is most certainly of no negative relevance here. David, perhaps you would prefer to explain the clinic further?"

"Most certainly Sigmund. What distinguishes Dr. Asperger's clinic from every other is the recognition that for every child suffering from the aberrant social stigmas usually associated with extreme autism, there is one who is at the extreme opposite side of the autism spectrum; in other words, they are clinically brilliant. To use Dr. Asperger's words, they are very high functioning individuals. His staff has the training and appropriate psychological expertise to work responsibly with those who are truly afflicted.

However, his clinic also identifies with the full range of autism by separating and nurturing those whose intelligence is identified as being quite extraordinary. The clinic is fully equipped and staffed to customize special tutoring for these children found to be so gifted.

While Dietrich is not their intellectual equal to the clinical extent these children are considered to be, he is nonetheless a very intelligent young boy. We are assured by Dr. Asperger he will fit in nicely among others of a similar age."

"Thank you, David. Your explanation leaves us intrigued. I think I speak for both of us, do you agree Jacob?" Anna asked.

"Very much so. I am anxious to know more. Please be so kind as to continue."

Sigmund felt compelled to continue to feed their apparent open mindedness and needed to specifically address an important advantage that had to be articulated. "Your initial reaction was a natural one as you mentioned the term *institutionalized*. It is precisely what everyone thinks, including the Nazi physicians. It is a stigma of the diagnosis. I must say, the gifted children thrive on their personal tutoring. In fact, this group has every expectation to be capable of becoming fully functioning when they return to society, at a much higher level than would otherwise have been attainable had they not been admitted."

"That's incredible Father! It sounds more like a private school for the privileged!"

"In point of fact, it is just that for those specifically selected. Clearly young Dietrich is a fully functioning and intelligent boy, and his customized education assures his time there will be highly productive and serve him well as he continues to mature. I want to clearly emphasize that his 'institutionalizing', which is more accurately his 'enrolment', would only require medical authorization from David, myself, and of course Dr. Asperger, to which he has already agreed. Most importantly, this enrolment will ensure Dietrich's safety as well; hiding him in plain sight, so to speak."

It seemed Sigmund's creativity and reputation could solve almost any problem. Anna and Jacob were overjoyed at the solution but understandably the painfulness of the timely separation would be agonizing to be sure.

*****

Sigmund was aware there were new restrictions on international travel that had been implemented over the past few months. Rigorous documentation was strictly enforced despite the fact Sigmund and Marissa were already established as regular visitors to America whilst frequently attending annual AMA conferences. Taking their granddaughter to see America surely would not be perceived to be out of the ordinary for a young lady of her age. Such was their thinking. They were about to receive a rude awakening.

Sigmund personally approached the passport office to follow the usual process to which he had become accustomed. It was a necessary requisite prior to arranging international travel and he knew his usual documentation was in perfectly satisfactory order. He procured a numbered ticket and took a seat among thirty or so others ahead of him. One by one the numbers were called to the teller booths as per usual procedure.

Today, however, there appeared to be a few contentious discussions between several customers and the tellers, more accurately between the applicants and numerous police officers becoming atypically involved in the process. Frustration was apparent and tempers flared as several conversations became extremely animated. This was not what anyone had expected. When Sigmund's ticket was called, he discovered he too would be one of those to be singled out for closer scrutiny.

As he approached the booth, he continued to believe his calm demeanor would best serve him to avoid being singled out from the inquisition many others were now facing. As he and the teller were about to engage, a policeman stepped unexpectedly toward Sigmund and authoritatively smacked the back of his hand on Sigmund's chest. Understandably it startled him. "Is there a problem, Officer? I travel regularly and I always keep my papers in good order."

The officer rudely snatched Sigmund's passport from his hand and perused the document before uttering so much as a word. "There are security matters we must consider, Doctor…Landesburg?" the stout policeman read from the passport.

"Security for what possible purpose, may I ask?"

"That is not any of your business!" he barked. "However, it is very much ours."

He turned to another junior officer standing close by and ordered, "Take these papers to the lieutenant. He has already been summoned to speak with this man."

Sigmund looked incredulous and started to calmly protest. He had no intention of surrendering his passports without just cause. Within minutes a stately and rigid lieutenant exited a rear office followed by a soldier of lower rank, his helmet still secured about his chin. They approached Sigmund face to face, in public view of the gathering of people still waiting to be called.

"Do we have a problem, Doctor?" The lieutenant stared directly eye to eye, uncomfortably and intimidatingly close to Sigmund.

"No sir, I trust we do not. I simply do not understand what the problem may be with my request for travel, and in particular I must know for what purpose you are demanding our passports. I travel to America almost every year to attend a conference and I am expected to be there within the times I have specified on my documentation."

"This year you will not be attending your conference. Do you understand that? Take this man to my office!" With that, the other soldier moved Sigmund in the direction of the office by shoving him unnecessarily with the brunt of his rifle. Being a solidly built former athlete, Sigmund was still a formidable man and took the gesture with obvious disgust, while remaining mindful that any demonstration of resistance here was not a wise choice.

Sigmund was instructed to close the door as the lieutenant assumed his seat, not once even gesturing for Sigmund to take a chair as well. The officer picked up his telephone for a brief instant, only uttering a single word, "Come." Two brief taps on the door preceded the entry of a second soldier, who took position beside Sigmund in a very threatening manner as the conversation continued.

"You are a Jew, are you not?"

"I am, sir. I was born here, and I am proud to be a German, like yourself, I assume."

The officer in command gestured to the guard with a brief look and a nod of his head. Sigmund did not see what was coming as he was struck from behind and collapsed from his chair to the floor, whereupon he was kicked repeatedly in his belly. Grimacing, he fell back from the shock of the unexpected forcefulness of the blows.

"Do not *ever* equate yourself to me, you fucking filthy Jew! We will do as I wish. I will keep your passports…indefinitely, until I alone determine if you are a security risk. Now wipe your pig blood from my floor and get the fuck out of my sight…without a word, or I will put you in a dirty hole where you belong! Get this pig out of my sight!" he barked to the guard.

Sigmund wiped his blood from the floor, struggling to focus his blurred vision on the simple but degrading task. Then he was unceremoniously and repeatedly shoved away from the office to the front door of the passport office. Remaining disheveled and groggy, he descended the steps to return home like some beaten dog.

When he arrived to face Marissa, she was alarmed at what she was witnessing. In shock, she pushed him for immediate answers. "Whatever has happened Sigmund? Were you accosted on the street? We must get you examined my darling. Your face and especially that cut over your eye needs immediate attention!"

Never had she seen her husband in such a condition. She wept openly and immediately summoned the staff to tend to his injuries. Sigmund sat in silence without wincing as he focused on what he had to say, being mindful of the presence of the attentive staff.

As soon as he was cleaned and bandaged and was alone with Marissa, Sigmund confirmed his determination to get his family out of this hellhole they had once called home. He spoke haltingly as he described the incident to her, after which he made his intentions clear. "We must get Pietra and Dietrich out now!"

After they'd shared the terrible situation with Anna and Jacob, Anna, never one to quietly acquiesce to any wrongdoing, approached Marta, who was equally distressed and shocked at Sigmund's mistreatment. Marta immediately insisted Sigmund approach her father-in-law, who after all was deeply indebted to Sigmund. It was something Sigmund had considered in the recesses of his mind, but he was uncomfortable at having to do so. But for Pietra's safety, he knew it was his only remaining choice, and time was running short. The conference was less than two weeks away.

Sigmund was not aware Walther had been promoted to a command position of the East Prussian Military District shortly after the Nazis had seized power the previous year. Walther evidently had the ear of the Fuhrer himself, extended to him as a privilege of his military posting in Prussia. Sigmund was pleased about Walther's accomplishment as he recalled his determination to play a role of significance in the new movement. It appeared he had accomplished his goal. His involvement could be more influential than Sigmund had initially imagined.

To no surprise, the field marshal was most eager to assist in any way possible. He profusely apologized for the attack Sigmund had endured but would not reprimand the lieutenant for doing what was required of him. It was after all, within his jurisdiction to carry out his responsibilities in whatever manner he so decided. It was most unfortunate Sigmund had been the victim, but Walther encouraged Sigmund to move forward from this unpleasant episode. With that said, Walther was confident a well-placed and respectful request of his Fuhrer would achieve the desired results. He was correct.

No one objected or questioned the immediate granting of permission to attend the Cleveland conference. Perhaps more importantly was the inclusion of a letter of personal reference, signed by both Walther and the Fuhrer himself. The confiscated passports were immediately returned to their door and the necessary documentation was expedited, not only for Sigmund, but also for Pietra and Marissa. It was logically presumed Marissa was required to tend to the needs of her granddaughter while Sigmund attended to his business obligations in America.

Among preparations for this journey, Sigmund prearranged that his cousin, who resided in New York City, accept Anna and Jacob's request to formally appoint her and her husband as custodians of young Pietra. It was a responsibility they accepted without reluctance or reservation. It was critical they did so as a condition of the Julliard School's granting of the scholarship, and to provide the confidence and peace of mind to those at home knowing Pietra would be with family.

Grace and her husband Richard had never met this rising young star of world acclaim and were both delighted to play such an important role in the continued development of her unique talents. Most importantly, everyone was relieved to know Pietra would always be safe in Grace's capable care and custody.

The family of three arrived safely in New York on schedule. Marissa and Pietra enjoyed the kind hospitality of Sigmund's cousin and her loving family, whom Sigmund had only met once as a young child. Grace had been named appropriately, as she exuded a natural grace befitting of her name and demonstrated a genuine and deep affection for young Pietra, as did Pietra for her Aunt Grace. It was

impossible not to be delighted by this young, albeit sometimes precocious, young child.

Meanwhile, Sigmund carried on by train to Cleveland, staying at
the Hotel Carter in which the medical conference was being hosted.
His network of American contacts had continued to grow over the
years, and he never again would experience the loneliness he vaguely
recalled on his first visit. He did his best to shift his focus from the
stresses of his recent ordeal and welcomed the chance to get reacquainted with his circle of familiar colleagues.

Among them of course was Dr. Charles Souttar, who introduced
Sigmund to another of his colleagues, Dr. Frederick Thompson, a
renowned Doctor of Pharmacology. Dr. Souttar had been instrumental in originally referring Dr. Thompson to his brother Henry
several years ago and had endeared himself to both by arranging such
a fruitful collaboration.

Over the next few days, Sigmund became thoroughly enamored
by Frederick, and particularly of his subsequent introduction to two
pharmacologists. These highly regarded medical scientists had been
assigned the onerous responsibility of ensuring the standards of
research for submissions of articles for publication were consistent
with the criteria established by the AMA. It was an honorable task
they capably embraced.

It was through these gentlemen that Sigmund was introduced to
the works of Dr. Gordon Alles, who had earned both his masters
and PhD at the California Institute of Technology. A frequent lecturer in pharmacology, Dr. Alles had recently been recognized for his
research on the psychological effects of amphetamines and published
numerous articles about them.

His ground-breaking study had apparently led to his partnership
with the pharmaceutical giant Smith, Kline and French (SKF). He
became a consultant with SKF Laboratories and eventually would
construct his own Gordon A. Alles Laboratory for Molecular Biology.
With financial backing from SKF, amphetamines were transformed
from an experimental compound to the status of wonder drugs.

These activities were perfectly legal at this time. With virtually no
government oversight, SKF could introduce its new product absent
additional testing. But gaining the support of doctors necessitated
advertising in the American Medical Association journals, which
ultimately required their support. To gain the AMA's approval, a drug

had to be proven both safe and effective, which meant commissioning studies that could convince an impressive body of highly qualified doctors and scientists, specifically the AMA Council on Pharmacy. That said, safety standards were a relative formality.

Extensive animal studies were completed to determine appropriate dosages for human consumption, and the potential side effects. This phase was essential before the conducting of human testing to determine the drug's best application of usage within prescribed limitations.

After extensive testing, the research confirmed no apparent ill effects and later appeared in the highly regarded *American Journal of Medical Science*. That was proof enough for the AMA; amphetamines' safety stood confirmed.

Sigmund remained particularly fascinated by this new era in pharmacology. There were potential benefits for a few of his patients in this category of drugs. He was determined to keep abreast of the continuing research as it became available through the publications in the *Journal of the AMA*.

As the conference wound down, farewells were extended with promises to keep one another abreast of any new developments. Well wishes were particularly and thoughtfully extended from Sigmund's numerous friends and associates, who remained concerned for his and his family's continued health and well-being considering the current political climate within Germany. They assured him they would be closely following the formative years of his young granddaughter as well.

CHAPTER SIXTEEN

LESS THAN THREE WEEKS AFTER THEIR DEPARTURE FOR America, Sigmund and Marissa returned to Berlin without their beloved Pietra. It was a very frightening time in Germany. They were thankful they had acted so swiftly and decisively in removing her from this place when they had.

Upon their return, Sigmund promptly contacted the field marshal to confirm his return to Germany and again, to convey his gratitude for his kind support without which the journey and Pietra's emigration to the U.S. would not have happened. Although Walther was otherwise preoccupied, his personal assistant assured Sigmund his message would be relayed directly to the field marshal. He deliberately omitted any reference to the fact his granddaughter remained in New York.

*****

In the relentless and unimpeded tyranny of Adolf Hitler, the first of his many priorities was to eradicate opposition to the Nazi Party using whatever method he believed to be necessary. By his estimate, the greatest threat was no longer from opposition parties in government, nor from the general public electorate. It was from within the Party itself, in the form of the faction of prior support known as the Storm Troopers (SA) and their commander Ernst Rohm, a formerly loyal supporter of Hitler.

Ruthless brutality was about to befall even staunch supporters of his own party, those Hitler perceived to become a potential threat to his authority. His growing insecurity and paranoia were beginning to redefine him in more frightening ways, which even exposed his own allies to groundless reprisals.

Certain policy issues had been challenged by Rohm, and his more moderate tendencies were potentially creating opposition to Hitler's extreme radical decrees. This became the most pervasive focus of the newly assumed dictator. On the evening of June 30th, 1934, a purging of the SA was ordered by Hitler, leading to the arrest and immediate executions of the entire SA leadership, including most notably, Eric Rohm. As a direct result of these executions, the Secret Service (SS) under Himmler and the Secret Police (Gestapo), under the direct command of Göring, both carried out the purge, and in so doing they fell next in line within Hitler's chain of command.

The death toll was estimated to be a thousand, and at least a thousand more were arrested based upon suspicion alone. Hitler had seized complete, unopposed control of the entire German military forces and with it, the absolute ability to enforce it.

*****

Despite Sigmund's spontaneous decision not to inform Walther's assistant about Pietra's emigration, he knew the news of her defection would receive broad publication, sooner than later. When the inevitable happened, it was only a matter of days before he was summoned to Walther's office, under a security escort. It was not a request from the field marshal; it was a direct order.

Sigmund was taken by car to the command headquarters in Zossen, about an hour's drive north of Berlin. He did his best to calm his nerves to ease the knot in his stomach. Had he underestimated the eventual consequences of his decision to take Pietra away from here? He reasoned that even if such were the case, he was now more certain than ever the removing of Pietra from Germany altogether was the correct decision. This was no place to raise a family under these oppressive conditions. He stood by their decision. Pietra's and Dietrich's safety was all that mattered.

It was the first time Sigmund had witnessed such tight security, which he suspected was customary for a facility such as this and the powerful leadership personnel it housed. To their credit, the guards were courteous and respectful but barely spoke a word. They sensed Sigmund's apprehensions and made it clear he was not under arrest.

The main gates led up an incline to the fortified barracks, appearing stark and stoic against the natural backdrop of the majesty of the forest. A series of gates were mechanically withdrawn to reveal the modest but functional main entrance. Armored military vehicles and a multitude of cargo trucks and camouflaged jeeps were too many to count.

Automatic machine guns and what Sigmund assumed were other assault weapons were within his view, as were numerous elevated watch towers manned with sharp shooters strategically located near and about the perimeter, ranging as far as Sigmund could see. It was impressive and even more so, intimidating.

As the car pulled up to the main building, guards instructed Sigmund to follow. Two sentries stood at each side of the steel-reinforced main doors, which they opened to allow entry inside the unwelcoming bustle of activity.

The rattling of typewriters and the ringing of telephones were incessant and served to suppress the constant chatter of conversations. Two more guards took position behind Sigmund's escort to cover their flank, and all of this within the walls of this fortress! Sigmund wondered what they could possibly expect an unarmed man to be capable of doing in this circumstance.

The field marshal did not immediately exit his office when Sigmund's arrival was announced to him, and Sigmund was indifferently left to wait in reception. It was clear this once amicable relationship had been strained.

Waiting twenty minutes or more added to Sigmund's already mounting anxiety, precisely as was intended. Finally, an officer in full regalia with his cap secured impeccably under his arm, strode from the commander's office to direct Sigmund to the austere and uninviting office from which he had emerged. The field marshal did not rise but remained in front of the window with his back turned to Sigmund. He said nothing in response to Sigmund's "Good afternoon, Field Marshal."

Von Brauchitsch continued to drag another deep breath from his well-rolled cigar, exhaling meditatively before slowly turning his chair to face his personal physician. "You have greatly disappointed me, Sigmund. Why am I reading newspapers to discover your granddaughter did not return to Berlin?" He appeared calm and prepared for this inquisition. "What do you have to say for yourself?"

"Field Marshal, I attempted to tell you upon our return but felt it inappropriate to inform you using formal channels through your assistant. It was most certainly not my intention to disrespect you, sir. I sincerely apologize if I have done so." Sigmund remained calm and did not demonstrate fearfulness, but simply awaited Walther's response.

The field marshal rose from his seat, placed both fists firmly on his desk pad and glared at Sigmund in a red-faced rage. "Do you have any fucking idea what the Fuhrer may think of this clear abuse of the courtesy I have shown you and your family? I stuck my neck out for you, at the behest of my daughter-in-law, and despite my better judgment! The Fuhrer even signed your diplomatic papers for Christ's sake!" He paused to snatch his cigar out of frustration and dragged on it to control his flaring temper.

He continued, as he replaced the smoldering cigar in the ashtray. "I have heard nothing from his office yet, so by almighty God I demand a damned explanation from you! Do you hear me, Sigmund? Was this medical conference just bullshit? Was it? Yes or no?" He was now berating Sigmund, screaming with furious all-consuming disgust.

"No sir, not at all! I attend these conferences every year, and the contacts I have established in America are critical to my base of knowledge. In fact, Walther, that was how I discovered the physician who guided me throughout your procedure! I remind you, Walther, were it not for those conferences, I would not have been able to achieve what we did in collaboration with Dr. Souttar's expertise!"

The field marshal took pause to walk toward Sigmund and perched himself on the corner of his desk. He sat adjacent to his visibly shaken physician and said nothing as he gathered himself. "Was it your plan to leave your granddaughter in America before you left Berlin?" he enquired calmly.

"I will not mislead you, sir...Yes it was, but would you have approved such an intention if I had asked you?" Sigmund looked directly into Walther's eyes. He knew the answer he was about to receive.

"...No, I would not have done so."

Sigmund continued hesitantly. "Walther, we were in fear for our family, and we continue to be, particularly so after the events pertaining to my visa approval. The offer from Julliard was a genuine one, and it also gave us a brief window of opportunity to save Pietra from potential harm. This decision has ripped our family apart, but we are firmly resolved it was the only option before us. Consider what you would have done if our roles were reversed? I appeal to you…as one grandfather to another."

Sigmund's eyes began to tear up despite his best efforts to control himself, and his lips trembled slightly as he fought to regain control of his emotions. He turned his focus from Walther and dropped his head in abject sadness to avert Walther's gaze. Neither man spoke a word for what seemed an eternity.

Having reflected on Sigmund's comments, the commandant moved to the chair beside him and nudged it a little closer to him. He spoke softly despite being behind closed doors in the privacy of his office. "Perhaps you can give me something…something I can offer the Fuhrer when he inevitably calls me, so I can justify my faith in you…You say you have these connections in America. If they are as good as you say, is there anything, any new research…or developments we can use for ourselves for the war effort? Think Sigmund! I need to give him something to demonstrate your loyalty to the Reich, not as a Jew, but as a German."

It rankled Sigmund that Walther considered it necessary to distinguish him as a Jew, as if he was something separate and distinct from that of a German, something perhaps less than a German. But his mind raced for what seemed like an eternity and within minutes he considered a possible solution. He carefully weighed his options, of which there were few. Despite his initial thought, which was now becoming more obvious to him, he took another moment or two to silently consider his response before speaking.

Walther waited patiently.

Although it was still early in its development, Sigmund believed the potential benefits of amphetamines could have application for the German military. It was possible he could use this knowledge and the initial test results, supported by the recent approval of amphetamines for limited distribution by the AMA. This could give him some significant leverage…if he seized the moment before him.

"What do you have for me, Sigmund? Speak to me. I can see something is on your mind."

"I will caution you up front, Walther, that research is continuing on what I am about to disclose; however, it could hold great promise for the military. If, and I emphasize *if*, the military confirms by way of its own independent research the appropriate application of this potential wonder drug, as Americans have already hailed this discovery, the positive implications could be extraordinary."

The commandant smiled and patted Sigmund's shoulder with assurance. "I am intrigued, my friend. Tell me more." Walther's demeanor had become noticeably more subdued, a sign that indicated Sigmund had piqued his attention.

"What you are asking me to do could be interpreted as being espionage against the Americans. If I do co-operate with you, can you assure me my family will always remain safe from harm? I am sorry to have to ask this of you, but I fear I must."

"If you do not do as I am asking, can you imagine the unwanted attention the Fuhrer could impose on your family, despite my most strenuous protestations?"

They sat in contemplative silence as each one played another chess piece in their game of high-stake negotiations.

"Tell me what you have, Sigmund. I will do my absolute best to accommodate your most reasonable request. If what you tell me has the realistic likelihood of positive impact for us, I will grant what you are asking. But you must tell me now."

It was an agreement contrived to assure the protection Sigmund so desperately needed, despite his own perceived breach of his Hippocratic oath. He had come to the realization the impact of this new technology, if implemented properly, could potentially shift the battle lines of war to some immeasurable degree. In sharing this discovery, Sigmund could not possibly understand what ultimate effect it might have on the course of the war. Alas it was his only bargaining chip to play. In the interest of his family's potential safety and security, he knew he had no choice other than to share it.

*****

Amphetamines continued to be studied by American research scientists to determine what effects, if any, they would have on the enhancement of performance, either physically or mentally, particularly as it related to human fatigue. Although rigorous research did not initially correlate with noticeable improvement, in the experience of many test subjects, the drugs' mood-altering effects increased confidence and aggression with subsequent feelings of elevated morale and a feeling of well-being.

This qualified endorsement was more than enough for Hitler to order extensive testing of amphetamines on humans as quickly and as aggressively as his scientists deemed to be appropriate. Unlike those in America, his inventory of human specimens was considered dispensable and would provide more than enough test subjects for this unregulated and potentially dangerous pursuit.

*****

Dachau opened its gates in March 1933 and was the first of 42,000 concentration camps created for the imprisonment of those declared to be political enemies of the state: communists, social democrats, trade unionists, and in very short order a wider range of persecuted undesirables. Dachau was located to the northwest of Munich, and in a few short years it had become a model for constructing future camps. In the press release it was announced to the guards and staff *"that we have no room for sentimentalism. If anyone here cannot bear to see the blood of comrades, he does not belong and had better leave. The more of these pig dogs we strike down, the fewer we need to feed".*

Sachsenhausen-Oranienburg was also opened the same year. Constructed on a much larger scale, it was located just a few miles north of Berlin, and was initially designated a central administrative training facility for administrators, guards, and forced-labor management and enforcement, to establish operational guidelines for thousands of future camps.

Although its primary focus was not on matters pertaining to executions, primitive methods in use at the time, which consisted of simply forcing the victims into deep ditches to be summarily shot or hanged, were further refined. This secondary responsibility did not conflict with Sachsenhausen's most urgent priority, specifically the use of forced labor conscripted for the purpose of brick manufacturing. When the number of executions became more pressing due to the overflow of detainees, thousands of prisoners were sent to other nearby camps dedicated solely to mass extermination.

In Hitler's mind, his next priority was to address the drastic economic impact of the Great Depression, which had created millions of unemployed people from every walk of life. In response, Nazis leadership made a determined effort to rebuild the crumbling infrastructure by employing this massive pool of labor to initiate major public works, such as roadways, bridges and specifically, the Autobahn.

Adolf Hitler was not the first to conceive the concept of a high-speed, unimpeded motorway. It was the mayor of Cologne, Konrad Adenauer, whose own ingenuity initiated and financed the first twenty kilometers running from Cologne to Bonn. Initially Hitler was not a strong proponent of this massive motorway, as he felt certain the structure would only serve the interests of the relatively few aristocrats able to afford automobiles. He eventually understood there were many more reasons to reconsider his position, as the aspect of increased mobility for all citizens would keep pace with similar motivations already being touted throughout the industrialized world.

The Nazis were delighted to take full credit for the decision to restart this costly but high-profile project to affirm German construction capabilities and in so doing create massive and gainful employment. The goal was established to complete about 1,000 kilometers of roadway each year to specifically reduce the crushing numbers of unemployed workers in Germany after the Great Depression.

At the peak of construction only 120,000 jobs were created for the Autobahn, far short of the 600,000 Hitler had promised. The public at large had no awareness of the severity of the punitive working conditions, which often caused the deaths of thousands of broken workers. Strikers who strove to improve the inhuman conditions were sent to the newly built concentration camps to effectively suppress any further rebelliousness.

At about the same time, millions of potential young workers resorted to a life of crime, theft, and violence, simply to feed themselves and their families. It was apparent to Hitler that enlistment in the military was a far more viable alternative. Shortly thereafter, thousands more were forcibly conscripted into the armed forces. This growth caused massive manufacturing demands for military hardware, tanks, artillery, munitions, and various support services. The booming arms business was the single most important factor that reduced the number of unemployed.

Nazi popularity grew steadily when the vast labor force transformed into income earners and income spenders, feeding the economy as much as their stomachs. As they fed their own economy, they redefined the people's self-esteem, their sense of direction, and the confidence for which Germans had always been known.

About this time, German leadership continued to be enticed by the potential psychological benefits of amphetamines being researched in Sachsenhausen, and subsequently became extremely interested in exploiting these effects further. In June 1935, it was no coincidence that Walther von Brauchitsch became the first commanding general of the 1st Army Corps by way of special appointment by Adolf Hitler. This promotion was perhaps in part to acknowledge the contribution and insight provided by Dr. Landesburg.

German leadership knew human testing was already the primary focus of a few of their existing concentration camps located mostly in Germany, and shortly thereafter in Czechoslovakia, Poland, and Austria. Human test subjects were intentionally pushed beyond their limits of tolerance and often with wanton disregard for the negative consequences of exceeding responsible dosages.

In certain designated death camps, incarcerated prisoners were given performance-enhancing drugs to field test army boots on behalf of shoe manufacturers. They were forcibly used to run incredible distances over rough terrain day after day. When they were physically and spiritually broken, the test subjects would be executed and quickly replaced by other unwilling prisoners who would face the same abusive torture—being overdosed on amphetamines and literally run to death.

By contrast, the acceptable American standards and humanitarian approach to prudent and responsible testing of subjects adhered to strict limitations and meticulous data collection. This more responsible process was more time consuming, and consequently the Americans lagged behind Germany before appropriate dosages were determined for cautious usage throughout their own military.

*****

It was at the Brandenburg Euthanasia Centre and the Chelmno Extermination Camp that Hitler chose to further expand the Nazis' continued search for the effective applications of amphetamines. Despite his dubious medical certification, which appeared never to have been earned, Dr. Wolfgang Christian Wirth personally oversaw the development of gas chambers disguised as shower rooms, which would eventually consume millions of innocent helpless lives.

Wirth was described as a crude and gross man, who demonstrated no respect or humane predispositions. He would openly laugh and was quoted as *"doing away with useless mouths,"* stating that *"sentimental slobber about such people makes me puke."*

Often referred to as Christian the Terrible, Wirth would later direct the forcible use of numerous experimental drugs, one of which was referred to as D-IX. This complex drug was specifically designed to increase stamina and endurance. Methamphetamines were used to enhance mission performance in which longevity and exhaustion became pertinent issues.

Whether these events were a direct result of the attention given to amphetamines by Sigmund, or the positive impact upon General von Brauchitsch' career, Sigmund himself personally struggled with the disclosures he had originally made, despite never knowing the way amphetamines were to be tested.

Nevertheless, Sigmund's family received the protection he had sought from General von Brauchitsch, and more indirectly, the supreme commander, Adolf Hitler. Without specific awareness of his influence, Sigmund had left his mark for history to judge.

CHAPTER SEVENTEEN

THE BOOK BURNING INCIDENT WAS LIKENED TO A STAB in the heart for freedom of speech and creative expression, in all cultural pursuits including not only literature but music as well. The maestro urgently needed to address sensitive political matters with Marta that had come to light. He considered it unwise to speak with her near the theater or his office. To ensure an extra measure of confidentiality, he extended an invitation to Marta to attend his home for this discussion.

"Thank you so much my dear friend for coming here this evening Marta. I assure you I am not intending to appear theatrical by doing so. There is so much more to discuss that I am compelled to tell you. Here, let me take your coat and fetch you a glass of fine cognac."

"You sound ominous Wilhelm. It appears I will need more than one to hear what is on your mind."

Maestro directed Marta to follow him to the kitchen and carried on his discussion, briefly turning to speak to her over his shoulder. "I know I need a few to brace me for what I have to tell you. Come, have a seat here by the fire."

They sat facing one another and after a brief clinking of glasses, he began the task before him. "It is not pleasant for me personally to convey all of what I am about to say; however, you and I have always been direct with one another. Nothing will change between us in that regard."

"I am concerned by your wording. I pray I am not the cause of any unpleasantness."

"Quite the opposite, Marta. You are the solution!"

"You have piqued my interest, I must say. What's happening, Wilhelm?"

"As you recall a few months ago, in fact this past February, the orchestra started to flounder…financially. The threat of war has taken its toll on everyone. The orchestra has not been exempted from this disruptive chaos. It is time to bring you current on recent events as they pertain to us both."

"This sounds so worrisome, Wilhelm. You have my undivided attention."

"Lorenz Höber was appointed on behalf of the BPO to approach the new government for emergency funding. Marta, we were on the brink of ruin, even more so were it not for your featured performances. Your flair for the dramatic has always captivated your adoring fan base. Although there are other contributing issues, your extended absence from the stage was a major factor in our declining attendance. You are a force, and your influence is palpable Marta. Now that you have returned to us in a more prominent role, the excitement you personally bring to the stage is something the Fuhrer and Minister Goebbels wish to build upon."

"You are too kind, Wilhelm. I am overwhelmed."

"Those facts are self-evident and not based upon idle flattery. Nevertheless, permit me get to the more contentious issues. You know how much I am personally opposed to the mandates of the Nazi government and Hitler's insane predilections for the persecution of the Jews. I despise the man and I will not bend to his decrees, particularly when it places restrictive policies that suppress the artistic form. I want no part in his politics. Many of our musicians share these same sentiments. If you recall, Hitler's initial intent was to ban five players from the orchestra, which would have included Anna had she remained with us, simply because they are Jewish; Gilbert Back being most notable among them!"

Marta listened intently in absolute disbelief to Maestro's upsetting disclosures. He saw the tension building in her face and feared she would most likely take this discussion in a very different direction if he gave her the opportunity. It was essential he maintained control of the conversation. Just as she was about to unleash a tirade of angry responses, Maestro quickly intervened.

"Please Marta, let me finish what I have to say, as I believe we have reached some middle ground that will result in a viable compromise.

Just hear me out, I beg of you." Marta nodded affirmatively to allow him to continue without interruption. "There is a great deal at stake here, and you and I must stand together to have any chance to find a workable solution with the minister."

Amazingly, Marta controlled her impulsive temper. It was never directed at Maestro. He was just the messenger. She respectfully gave him the time to further explain. She realized anything she was about to say at that moment would only exacerbate the situation, so she hesitantly submitted to Maestro's request.

"I have met personally with Joseph Goebbels, Hitler's propaganda minister. As of November of this year, the State now owns and totally controls the Philharmonic." Maestro took another sip of his cognac and lit himself a cigarette, during which time Marta explained "My financial advisor contacted me about the shares I hold but I postponed any such conversations until I could speak to you first."

"All the shares are being purchased outright from the previous shareholders or they are being forced to sign proxies. We are now a public corporation and the BPO has been officially appointed Nazi Germany's flagship cultural ambassador. Our mantle of responsibility as the pre-eminent ambassador of Germanic culture is one we should embrace. Our countrymen need this as much as the orchestra, possibly even more so."

"I couldn't agree more," said Marta supportively.

"We struck a tentative arrangement. With the direct financial support of the state, we have been commanded to escalate our global profile by participating in considerably more international tours in the interest of enhancing diplomatic relations on the international stage. We have also been directed to perform, if called upon, at domestic political rallies and in the opening ceremonies for the upcoming summer Olympics in '36 and…to occasionally perform at various celebrations and Party anniversaries."

"Surely you must be joking!" Marta responded. "What does all this mean for our freedom of expression and our diversity of heritage among our musicians? These are the most relevant issues."

"Excellent questions, Marta. Permit me to be blunt. Our popularity, yours and mine specifically, have provided some leverage in my negotiations with Minister Goebbels. In return for our co-operation, he and the Fuhrer have agreed not to unduly restrict our creative expression on matters of musical selection and general programming content. The notable exception, however, is the strict forbiddance of Jewish guest appearances on our stage, as we already witnessed with Bruno Walter. They are willing to permit our current Jewish musicians to quietly remain."

Marta remained pensive for a moment and thoughtfully considered her response, knowing how much Maestro desperately needed to reaffirm her alliance with him considering recent political events. It was clear to her these compromises had to be expected. This appeared too simple; there was a catch somewhere she thought.

"Before I respond, Maestro, please clarify for me their meaning of 'not to unduly restrict' our programming content."

"It was their wording Marta, not mine. But as we had anticipated, since the orchestra and the musicians are now state-owned property, they are reserving their right to review and if necessary, to edit our scheduled programming prior to every performance. It is their mandate to ensure we adhere to certain guidelines to be consistent with Nazi ideologies. In my view, I see our relationship with them as being a slowly evolving work in progress, considering which their current compromises are not totally unreasonable.

Their final concession to us is their clear reassurance that our performers will be exempt from conscription for military service to the Fatherland. These absolutions are intended to maintain the integrity of our past traditions and protect our musicians from persecution and physical retribution."

Marta responded in a conciliatory tone, which was understandable for a woman whose passionate dispositions knew few compromises. "Well, at least that takes some of the sting off their list of conditions. At first blush I believed we would not survive without preserving our personal rights and our artistic license. I had expected far worse but as I see it, we must be pragmatic about this relationship. These conditions appear to be reasonably unreasonable to my eye, if there is such a thing. So, am I reading you correctly by saying you are comfortable with these compromises to ensure our longevity, at least for the moment?"

"Yes. I am satisfied for the present, and only time will determine if additional conditions will be forthcoming that may further undermine our integrity. Either way, I am not prepared to propose anything more at this time until and unless it becomes necessary to do so. I agree with your assessment, Marta. We are of the same mind."

Maestro Furtwängler went on briefly to conclude, "For you personally, it also means the demands of your vital role with the orchestra going forward will be much more onerous than they were before Manfred's birth. You are being asked specifically by the Fuhrer to make more frequent guest appearances with other prestigious world-class orchestras. This will further increase your travel commitments, providing even less time with your family than you may have anticipated. If the BPO is to continue as the National Ambassador, you and you alone are our orchestra's ambassador. Are you up for the challenge?"

Marta did not hesitate to answer Maestro's question and made her point unequivocally. "You and I have the same ethical and political reservations as we contemplate our new circumstances. Our compliance will catapult the BPO to global prominence, which is our ultimate objective. If we are to be successful as artists, we must apply unwavering focus and creative expression despite our trepidations. These requirements cannot be accomplished dispassionately. I think you know my answer, Wilhelm. I intend to do everything in my power to fully embrace what you ask of me."

*****

It was most gratifying to learn the theatre was completely sold out; however, it was not solely because of Marta's preeminent performance. It was announced the Fuhrer himself would be the guest of honor along with numerous of his chiefs of staff, including Martin Bormann, Heinrich Himmler, and Minister of Propaganda Joseph Goebbels.

Hitler and Goebbels in particular, were insistent in requesting they be suitably recognized at the prestigious event. Since they had recently assumed state ownership of the BPO, it was their foremost intention to see a unified demonstration of support from both the audience and the musicians, led by Maestro Furtwängler. It would be the first public test of resolve between the Fuhrer and the maestro, with Hitler demanding the Nazi salute by everyone in attendance, including the members of the orchestra, as part of the playing of the National Anthem.

The maestro had earlier decided he would not succumb to the personal shame he would experience by being forced to make such a visible gesture of support for the Nazi Party. This crucial moment was a major reason he had offered, for the second time in her career, to defer Marta's grand entrance until after the intermission.

It was in fact Furtwängler's hidden agenda to ensure Marta was not publicly compromised by the awkward symbolic gesture. It was more appropriate in his mind for Marta to avoid the situation altogether to save face, rather than make such a concession by acquiescing to the Fuhrer's demands. The press was closely covering this event and Maestro knew a photograph of Marta saluting the Fuhrer would not be an image she could accept. But not to do so would be tantamount to making a bold statement of disrespect. Either way, postponing her introduction to the second half absolved her from being ensnared in the trap.

Outside, at the foot of the immense base of the majestic concrete and flagstone front entrance of the Philharmonie Theatre in Kreuzberg, a military fleet of armored vehicles descended upon the scene. Armed troopers leading the caravan quickly sprang into action to assume unmistakable control of the immediate perimeter. Only a few latecomers continued to ascend the staircase, observed by innumerable interested onlookers from a vantage point on the far side of Bernburger Strasse. These onlookers could only imagine being part of the pomp and circumstance of the gala event unfolding deep within the palatial building.

Within minutes the Fuhrer himself arrived in his armored car, fully ablaze with Nazi swastika banners that had been fully unfurled during his procession and now lay flaccidly at rest when his car came to a complete stop. A phalanx of about a dozen motorcycles surrounded the three cars, each with machine guns at the ready. The second and third vehicles were parked immediately behind the Fuhrer's car and prior to the four doors of each car being thrown open, the honor guards assumed their position before it was deemed to be safe for the officers of German High Command to exit their respective vehicles.

From the crowded sidewalks a loud roar was spontaneously released when the Fuhrer first appeared, smiling and waving to the throngs of people. As they were instructed, thousands of the well-choreographed gathering raised their arms in tribute to their Nazi savior. It was a chilling and emotional experience to witness.

Inside the amphitheater, the loud chatter became immediately subdued and broke into a very controlled, almost apprehensive applause to recognize the entry of their dictator, who with his closest officers was directed to the VIP seats reserved in the front and center bank of seats.

Only Hitler acknowledged the applause by raising his hand and gesturing to his appreciative subjects. The implicit understanding of his staff was to confirm the impression the applause of respect was intended to honor him, and him alone.

As if to suggest the audience's fear of disrupting the staged demonstration of affection, no one uttered a word until the orchestra finished their ever so brief but final tuning, to signify it was time for Maestro Furtwängler to enter the stage. As the maestro approached the podium, the gathering erupted with frenzied applause. It was discernably louder than that for the Fuhrer. This did not escape either man's notice.

Maestro subtly acknowledged his gratitude and made no attempt to suggest the applause should cease until it reached its natural conclusion. He did not move a muscle to stop them as his inaction was intended to reinforce Hitler's probable dismay. Once the adulation naturally subsided, he composed himself as he cast his glance from his expansive audience, to nod his head politely in the direction of the Fuhrer. It was likely interpreted as a courtesy, but his purpose was as if to say, he and only he was in control of this event. The message was effectively delivered.

As he turned to his set position facing the orchestra, total silence engulfed the entire setting while the house lights were dimmed. Holding the baton in his right hand with his left hand touching the tip, Maestro nodded, released his hand from the tip, and pulsed his baton silently four times to the appropriate beat, before stabbing the baton into the air when the orchestra erupted into the National Anthem. The full house stood to raise their right arms in salute to the Nazi regime for the entire duration of the anthem. It was no doubt a very significant moment for the Fuhrer, as he proudly stood erect with his salute remaining solidly affixed and locked into position for everyone in attendance to emulate.

Hitler continued to hold his position until the anthem ended, and the Maestro and the orchestra stood to return the salute. The precise moment of resolve had arrived. The musicians rose as one and saluted with but one exception. It was Furtwängler. He chose not to place his baton on the easel but rather continued to hold it in his right hand, as he had always done in these moments. He did however raise both his arms together, more to respect his adoring audience than Hitler himself.

He also chose not to return the penetrating glare in Hitler's eyes for fear of unnecessarily antagonizing him. It was a wise choice.

As the contentious moment passed, Maestro readdressed his musicians and guided them methodically through the magnificent Egmont Overture, keeping his attention away from his subtle triumph to focus solely upon his artistic leadership. For the duration of the evening performance, he dutifully remained fully absorbed in his musical and creative pursuit of artful perfection.

As the Overture came to a powerful conclusion, the applause again rose enthusiastically. After three or four minutes it began to subside while the musicians reset themselves for Beethoven's Symphony #3, the Pastoral. The lights remained dimmed.

It was written by Beethoven himself about the Pastoral that one *"should sit back and appreciate nature without wanting to hug it. What we hear is human interaction with the universe"* when Beethoven begins his sentimental romp through the Viennese countryside.

From beginning to explosive ending, the audience was mesmerized by the range of emotions drawing the appreciative listeners into the fantasy, and away from complex political considerations. It was a glorious respite for the audience and musicians alike and was a common bond to be savored.

The applause finally diminished when the house lights were gradually raised as many of the patrons exited to the refreshment area to resume their conversations over a fine selection of fine wines and various cocktails. The clamor of noise was more subdued than it had been an hour or so earlier.

Behind the closed curtains, the musicians relaxed and refreshed themselves in preparation for the main event of the evening. Maestro, Marta, and Gilbert Back were reviewing the final details that required attention when a distinguished officer approached, apparently sent by Hitler. Without introducing himself, he respectfully interrupted the small but private discussion and directed his words specifically to Furtwängler, though making certain all three participants in the conversation clearly understood his comments.

"The Fuhrer wishes to inform you of his disappointment in your actions earlier this evening. What he perceived could be taken by many to have been your indignation directed toward him. Perhaps it was simply the Fuhrer's misinterpretation, Maestro. He suggests, however, you tread carefully with him from this day forward."

As the officer turned away to leave, he stopped himself to add, almost as an afterthought, "Oh, the Fuhrer wishes to add his sincerest congratulations to you and the orchestra on an exemplary performance. He and his staff enjoyed it thoroughly. We remain eager for Madame von Brauchitsch to appear shortly." He nodded respectfully to Marta and quietly withdrew, saying, "Have a wonderful evening, my dear lady and esteemed gentlemen."

There had been no response from Maestro whatsoever and he simply returned to his prior conversation.

While the orchestra started reassembling and retuning their instruments behind the closed curtains, Marta remained offstage with Maestro as per normal protocol.

Not that any was needed, but after a final few words of personal encouragement from Maestro to Marta, the tuning ceased and Mr. Back signaled they were ready to resume. The entire building fell silent. No announcement was required that could break the anticipation of this moment. …until Marta graced the stage.

As soon as the audience perceived the slightest movement of the side curtain they ignited into a frenzied explosion of adoration for their beloved Marta. Maestro was formally escorting her, hand in hand, both beaming with pride. The very sight of her lovely, golden presence inspired many to break into tears of gratitude, and respectful outbursts of cheering soon out distanced the rousing and unrelenting applause. This ultimate show of respect and admiration only served to make Marta more determined than ever to deliver a truly unforgettable experience.

She elegantly curtsied not once but twice, and when control was restored and the din began to wane, she prepared herself by drawing a deep breath. She stood quietly and calmly, subtly signaling Maestro Furtwängler by a single nod of her head that she was ready to begin.

The theatre lights dimmed, leaving only the stage lights remaining as thousands of music lovers simultaneously held their breath.

From the opening four beats of the timpani, the grandeur of the concerto became evident, and its distinctive melody was clearly articulated by Marta's impeccable command and masterful artistry. The hauntingly delicate tones gave justifiable cause for every focused attendee to experience the poignant and powerful theme, which was repeated several times throughout the extended first movement.

Beethoven created one of the most sublime concerti in the history of music. This evening it was Marta's interpretive gift that brought it to life. The violin concerto was forty-five minutes of glorious diversion from all other concerns of life; the political and strife-filled world continued to wait unabated for those who sought peaceful refuge within the revered walls of this magnificent edifice.

As the formidable music drew to a close, the bassoon took up the final theme with a repeated and familiar cadence, ending on a magnificent crescendo. Sheer perfection had been striven for and duly achieved. The house shook with repeated rounds of thunderous ovations offered up to the entire cast of wonderful musicians, each of whom had set new personal milestones of musical perfection.

Despite Marta's attempts to deflect some of the adulation to these world-class musicians, there was no doubt it was her career moment, to be savored and cherished for all time. Both Gilbert Back and Maestro Furtwängler offered their public congratulations to their star performer with kisses on her cheeks and on the back of her delicate hand. The crowd erupted to even greater heights of enthusiasm when a stylishly dressed young girl presented a bouquet of beautiful white roses to "Her Majesty" causing a barely discernable blush in Marta's lovely, sumptuous cheeks.

Maestro took Marta by the hand, holding it tenderly with both of his hands about waist height, and securely escorted her to the foot of the opulent rising staircase. It was a new feature of the stage, created especially for this performance to symbolize Marta returning to the heavens from whence she came. It was also a fitting opportunity to better display her gown's fifteen-foot train of golden silk embroidery as it played out to full splendor during her ascension.

As gracefully as she appeared, Marta withdrew from sight as softly and majestically as she had arrived. She was riding on the wings of angels.

The crowd continued to applaud for another extended curtain call but for the first time in her career, Marta had to deny the moment. She wept uncontrollably with deep gratitude behind the stage, forever thankful her family and friends understood the struggle within her that had finally been put to rest.

She knew at that moment her decision to return was the correct one.

*****

Marta re-gathered herself within a few minutes in the comfortable confines of her private dressing room and she was graciously extended some additional time to touch up her make-up and so forth before Maestro Furtwängler's and her scheduled press conference. Before entering the pressroom, however, she was informed there was a special guest waiting to meet with her. This was quite unexpected, but as it was an evening of firsts, she ceded to this strange happenchance, more out of intrigue than courtesy.

There outside her private dressing room were several bodyguards, Propaganda Minister Goebbels, and none other than the Fuhrer himself. Marta was taken aback but walked unabashedly toward them and curtsied as she offered her extended hand.

The Fuhrer was eager to accept her gesture and gently kissed her hand respectfully. "Thank you for seeing us in such an unannounced manner. I trust you will forgive me for such an intrusion."

"But of course, Mein Fuhrer. To what do I owe this esteemed honor?"

"I merely wish to meet you personally to commend you on your outstanding performance this evening. You have made every German citizen proud… none more than myself."

Marta was careful not to patronize the Fuhrer himself and was determined to save her flattery for the role she was undertaking on behalf of the orchestra. "You flatter me sir. I will remember this moment always. I am privileged to represent Germany's historic cultural richness and will always strive to enhance it as much as I am able."

"I trust we will meet again, Madame von Brauchitsch. Now I understand why your father-in-law speaks so highly of you. Your beauty does take my breath away and that does not happen often in my lifetime, I assure you. Please don't let us delay you any longer than we already have. Your adoring fans await you. Again, my heartiest congratulations to you and your supporting cast of fine musicians."

With that said, the small military escort led the Fuhrer to the private exit doors behind the theater where the highest security was already fully deployed.

*****

The following morning while enjoying a cup of fresh-brewed coffee from Lena, who had by this time settled nicely into her role as Manfred's caregiver. Marta's first call of the day was to Anna. "Good morning, my dear! I trust you are all doing well." She paused while Anna greeted her. "No, I'm not terribly tired this morning. I suppose it is the adrenalin rush carrying over since last evening. It was a marvelous event. You and Jacob were sorely missed. Did you listen to it on the radio?" Marta listened while sipping her coffee. "Oh, I'm so glad. I do wish so very much that you had been there…Perhaps next time. Has Jacob recovered from his bout of influenza?"

She listened attentively while Anna informed her of her husband's gradual recovery. Then she said, "Excuse my early call this morning but I must tell you who came to see me last evening after the concert. As much as I cannot stand the man, it was none other than the Fuhrer himself! Yes, can you believe it?"

Marta sipped her coffee and twisted a curl absent-mindedly while listening to Anna's mixed reaction.

"He was extremely chivalrous I must say," she continued. "The man has a special charisma that is quite difficult to describe. For someone of such diminutive stature he absolutely exudes power and supreme confidence. He surprised me by bringing his entourage backstage. He's quite a flirtatious person, Anna." She went on to describe Hitler's mannerisms down to the last detail.

Anna was stunned to hear of this encounter and reflected on how far Marta had come in her world of fame and influence. "You know Marta, this only reconfirms the wisdom of your decision to return to the theater. You are flying on the wings of eagles. I am happy for you.

I pray you always enjoy these moments, but you must remain mindful none of them sink their talons into you one day, sweetheart.

Forgive me Marta, I must rush off as I am taking Dietrich to see my father this morning. As always, he makes time to see the boy, but he only has a small window of time today to do so. I mustn't be late. He's giving him a quick examination to be sure he's not coming down with the same thing Jacob has. Let's resume this discussion later. I love you, Marta. Let's talk again soon."

*****

True to her promise, Marta was thrilled to be thoroughly absorbed in reassuming her role as the "First Lady of the Philharmonic," as the press affectionately dubbed her. It was a logistical nightmare preplanning her itinerary, which now included several guest appearances for numerous deserving orchestras of world renown. Among these were the Vienna Philharmonic, which she had previously graced with her presence, the Royal Concertgebouw in Amsterdam, and the London Symphony Orchestra (LSO), a stage debut to which she had long aspired.

As the tour was in the process of being finalized, both Goebbels and Hitler insisted they be consulted to give final approval to the travel itinerary for the orchestra and Marta's overlapping agendas. The BPO assumed it was a reminder to Furtwängler that he would always be required to be at the Fuhrer's beck and call. Little did they understand Hitler's intentions, nor did they expect that on this occasion, it was something much more involved.

A meeting was arranged for Furtwängler to meet privately with Minister Goebbels; however, it was very much sanctioned by the Fuhrer himself. Furtwängler reluctantly agreed to meet the minister at the Reichstag building the following afternoon.

"Good afternoon, Herr Furtwängler! I bid you welcome. The Fuhrer offers his apologies for being otherwise pre-occupied. Please, sit down. May we offer you a coffee, or something stronger such as a brandy if you wish?"

"No, no Herr Minister, a coffee would be most appreciated, though."

Goebbels only had to nod to the attendant and he prepared the maestro's coffee in a matter of moments.

"We have been very impressed by your cultural contributions of late, Maestro. I assume you have been pleased with our decisions to continue facilitating your demands for unfettered musical expression, which I recall was a very critical aspect of our newfound relationship."

"Yes, very much so. Your latitude has been greatly appreciated. What may I ask has required me to visit you this fine afternoon?" Maestro paused and sipped his aromatic, freshly perked coffee and readjusted his seat ever so slightly, patiently waiting for Goebbels' response.

"The Fuhrer and I have been reviewing the itineraries you were kind enough to provide. They both meet with our approval, of course; however, we want to request a brief extension of two days for Madame von Brauchitsch to accommodate an important extra performance during her stay in London."

"Regrettably I believe we would be hard pressed to make any adjustments to what has already been decided upon. I am sure you understand."

"Will you just hear me out? I am confident you will find a resolution that will be acceptable to all parties."

"As you wish, Herr Goebbels, as you wish."

"Very well then. Sir Thomas Beecham has been consistently co-operative in previous years by way of his open-mindedness with our carefully measured requests from time to time. He and the Fuhrer have developed a relationship that transcends business matters between them; one could say they have developed a friendship of a personal nature. It is imperative we nurture our strong associations, particularly with people of such high profile within Great Britain."

"I understand your request. I know Sir Thomas well. In fact, I am a great admirer of the man. What is it you are asking of me, Minister?"

Goebbels continued to explain. "As you are aware, his reputation and amazing ability to use his well-established contacts throughout the music industry have consistently re-enforced his importance to the Fuhrer. We informed him Marta would be performing with the London Symphony Orchestra on this tour and he was disappointed the London Philharmonic was not extended the same courtesy. The competition between the two predominant London-based orchestras has been well noted. Sir Thomas Beecham has taken the standards of excellence to new heights since the inception of the Philharmonic only a few years ago—clear evidence that healthy competition is critical to exceeding previous pitiful British standards. I'm sure you would agree."

Maestro paused reflectively, thinking to himself that Sir Thomas' ambition since 1932 had been to establish an orchestra reflective of the best Europe had to offer. To his credit, Beecham was widely acknowledged to have achieved his goal. Maestro remained attentive but did not so much as twitch, nor blink an eye.

Goebbels continued. "We have decided to once again level the playing field. As such we wish to reward Sir Thomas for his support of the Reich and agree to honor and respect his supportive friendship with us by engaging the co-operation of the BPO in the same respectful manner you are demonstrating toward Sir Hamilton Harty and the LSO. Our program director of cultural affairs has already commenced discussions, and Sir Thomas was most receptive. Can we count on you to make this happen, Maestro?"

"Sir, with respect, this should have been handled directly by me. Are you subrogating my authority, Herr Goebbels?"

"Not at all, Maestro. We know your workload has been onerous and merely wished to investigate our options to determine the possibilities for Marta's upcoming tour before involving you unnecessarily. I am sure you understand."

Maestro could barely contain himself. This was a deliberate attempt to undermine him. He was visibly troubled despite his efforts to disguise it. He felt as if he was being controlled by the Fuhrer through his extremely tactful and manipulative minister.

"I see you are, shall I say, reluctant to comply with this opportunity. Is this going to be a problem?"

"Let me be direct with you, Minister. Perhaps I have misinterpreted your actions, much as the Fuhrer misinterpreted my own at our premiere performance. If I can convince Madame von Brauchitsch to comply with your request, which I do not believe would be an obstacle, can you assure me that any such future modifications to our itinerary are run through my office first? I am willing to work hand in hand with your program director, but I am strongly opposed to being brought into these discussions after the fact. My proven credentials have never been in question, nor should they be now."

"Agreed Maestro!" Goebbels extended his hand and grasped Furtwängler's firmly and confidently. Maestro responded in kind, choosing not to release his firm grasp until Goebbels released his own; a small gesture, but an effective one.

"Perhaps you would courier the amended details to my office," said Goebbels. "I will inform our cultural director to co-ordinate with your lead from this day forward. You have my word. Please extend our sincerest best wishes to the orchestra and Madame von Brauchitsch as well."

Soon after, as Maestro sat in solitude in the rear seat behind his driver, he contemplated the wisdom of his support of Goebbels' initial request. He had vowed he would always remain independent of any political issues. Although this could certainly be construed as political in nature it was only a modest compromise the maestro was in the position to grant, more out of respect for Sir Thomas than for the Fuhrer he so despised.

He knew Marta would be more than eager to comply with what was asked of her. However, the second matter of undermining his authority was extremely upsetting. Nevertheless, he convinced himself his response was as insistent as he dared.

CHAPTER EIGHTEEN

THE 1936 SUMMER OLYMPIC GAMES SIGNALED THE first time since Germany's defeat after the Great War, that it would once again be welcomed onto the world stage. Despite the genuine efforts by the United States, Great Britain, France, Sweden, and Czechoslovakia to boycott the games due to Germany's alleged human rights abuses, almost fifty countries attended the games.

The beautiful and picturesque district of Charlottenburg was the site of the main arena, a fitting district of Berlin to display the splendor of this upper class and impressive locale. The Opera House, and numerous museums and art galleries throughout the city established the image Hitler sought to create. These Olympics would become the first such event being broadcast live on black and white television. While the world audience had been very limited, many could now bear witness to an inside look at the sophisticated culture and the superficial triumphs of the Nazi regime.

Once Berlin had secured the heavily contested decision to host the event, only those German athletes of pure Aryan blood were permitted the opportunity to participate in the games. Numerous world-class talents of Jewish ancestry were immediately deemed unfit to represent Germany, irrespective of their athletic excellence, except for one such athlete. Helene Mayer would ultimately win the silver medal in women's individual fencing and despite her ancestry would stand on the podium in front of the world and present the Nazi salute.

The prevalent displays of anti-Semitism and militarism were carefully subdued throughout the games to avoid any hint of human-rights violations from the already suspecting international press corps. On opening day of the XI Olympic Games, Hitler's motorcade passed along streets lined by thousands of cheering people, all of whom were presenting the Nazi salute, including children of all ages up to and including the uniformed members of the Hitler Youth Brigades.

In the front row among these adolescents was Marta and Klaus' son, Manfred, who had just turned fourteen years of age.

It was his first year in the Hitler Youth and he had been selected among other teenaged adolescents to occupy a position in the front row lining the street closest to the procession. Only those boys with the most striking Aryan features would be so honored. Manfred, a very handsome young man, was certainly qualified in this regard. He was only a few feet away from the Fuhrer as he passed by in the motorcade and Manfred proudly presented his proper Nazi salute.

Hitler beamed with superiority and embraced the crowd support as confirmation of his profound accomplishments. It was a proud moment for Hitler and the leadership of the Party, as Nazi banners had been strategically placed throughout the arena and across much of Berlin for this highly publicized affair. Throughout this procession of self-absorption, there were no visible signs of protest along the route of the motorcade, nor inside the arena.

The pageantry continued when Hitler's entourage entered the massive stadium constructed for this specific moment, to proudly signify the industrial might of the German Empire. The adoring adulation of the crowd inside the arena was profoundly tangible.

Having been long since agreed upon, the Berlin Philharmonic was prominently featured at center stage, which was adorned with more than fifty enormous floral displays around the expansive perimeter on all four sides, as one would expect for this unique spectacle.

The stage had been constructed in such a manner that a seventy-five-degree angle softened the customary right-angle corners to accommodate yet four more elevated garden boxes. They were a sight to behold, having been transplanted from the Berlin Horticultural Society displays. The exterior facing of each garden projected its softly curved majesty extending well beyond the daunting boundaries of center stage. This created the effect of having floral balustrades further fortifying the overall appearance of formidability. It was an awe-inspiring display of nature's prolific splendor.

As to be expected, between each floral bouquet were Nazi banners affixed to the stage walls featuring the revered Nazi swastika for the entire world to see.

The Berlin Philharmonic Orchestra suitably accompanied the Fuhrer's entry into the stadium. Herr Furtwängler and Marta were conspicuously absent but had been excused from this event to accommodate Germany's own Richard Strauss, who had composed and would now conduct the BPO playing a fanfare of a variety of his own renowned classical masterpieces. Hitler and Minister Goebbels conditionally granted Marta and the maestro's absence from this grand event to accommodate their guest appearance with the Vienna Philharmonic. For years the BPO had been the main rival to the Vienna Philharmonic as the world's greatest orchestra.

Since Hitler had become chancellor, the Vienna Philharmonic had established a particularly supportive relationship with the Nazi Party and Hitler saw the opportunity to recognize its support by graciously loaning the amazing tandem of Furtwängler and Marta. The co-operation of these two high-profile musicians was seen to be a personal courtesy to the Fuhrer.

That year a new Olympic tradition was born when, for the first time, a lone runner would enter the stadium to light the torch to signify the official opening of the Olympic Games. It had been carried by hand by a series of runners from the very birthplace of the games in Athens, Greece.

A series of prominent politicians including, of course, Minister of Propaganda Joseph Goebbels, Heinrich Himmler, and the mayor all gave impassioned accolades to their Fuhrer for the restoration of might and world acclaim for the German nation.

As the minister closed out his inspiring message he stated, "*This day will not be forgotten for what it is, a reaffirmation of Germany as the indomitable economic and political leader of our time. We have achieved global recognition politically, militarily, and culturally through principles of fairness and respect for the peoples within our borders, and from those outside our borders who can only aspire to be one of us.*" He paused only briefly as his eyes scanned the throngs of people, raised his right arm and shouted, "*Heil Hitler!*"

Simultaneously forty-five thousand Germans rose to their feet shouting, "*Heil! Heil! Heil!*" with arms fully extended to honor their seemingly adored national leader. Hitler himself bore a calm and self-righteous smile, exuding his satiated narcissistic cravings.

Press reports were overwhelmingly positive about the image of Germany as a most gracious host, representing an orderly restoration of lawful order to what had been perceived to be a very troubled Germany. The *New York Times* reported the consensus of world opinion about welcoming "*Germany back to the fold of nations,*" stating the success of the event made the Germans appear "*more human again.*" There were only a few that understood the Berlin glitter was merely a façade hiding a racist and oppressively violent regime.

Within weeks of the closing ceremonies, amidst mostly positive world acclaim, Nazi Germany dismantled its false pretense and resumed its prior intended course—one of persecution and intolerance.

Over time even the general public became more receptive to the Nazi conviction the Aryan race was the master race. Only the purest of Germanic bloodlines were desired, to the notable exclusion of all others. As a result, the seeds of racism, those sown specifically to encourage anti-Semitic persecution, soon became the official ideology of the German regime. This fostered renewed confidence and a more unified direction to hundreds of thousands of Germans. Business leaders benefitted greatly from dropping unemployment and improved economic stimulus. These factors in turn caused the Nazi party to become increasingly popular.

By 1937 the looting and desecration of Jewish-owned businesses had become increasingly commonplace. The Star of David was spray painted on shop windows and on the front doors of Jewish homes to easily identify places to be forbidden to customers and former patrons. The star conveniently marked who was to be evicted by the SS troops, who were given absolute authority as to what was to be confiscated. This was carried out against the Jews by force, to whatever extent was deemed necessary. Resistance was futile and frequently led to arrests, physical assaults, and even executions, all without charges or trial by law.

More and more, the intensity of persecution continued to exceed even the worst of possible imaginings. It was as if a switch had been flipped to ignite the horror of more pain and degradation. The continued destruction and looting escalated. Soon after, it was extended to include more unprovoked attacks against homosexuals and the physically or mentally disabled, the latter regarded as a genetic and economic blight on the Aryan genetic pool.

Confiscation of all assets and personal properties left thousands without homes, and without businesses to support themselves. Almost half of the Jews living in Germany were essentially forced to emigrate to other countries willing to accept them. For many choosing to remain, mass arrests led to overcrowded police cells and a total breakdown of due process. Prisoners were forced to build their own death camps, as the pace of executions could not keep up with the rate of arrests and extended detainments.

To further exacerbate these escalating injustices, about this time a teenaged Jew named Herschel Grynszpan entered the German Embassy in Paris and shot a young German diplomat named Ernst Vom Rath without warning or provocation. Upon his immediate surrender, the young assassin openly confessed his motive for the shooting was out of love for his parents and for his people, who were subjected unjustly to outrageous treatment at the hands of the Nazis.

Eighteen thousand Polish Jews had suffered deportation from Poland to Germany only weeks before Grynszpan's act of violence. His parents were among them. Neither Poland nor Germany wanted these refugees within their borders and many, such as his parents, had to endure living like animals, dependent upon what nature could offer them. This harsh and totally unprovoked maltreatment of Jews became an accurate reflection of the very real extent of the pariah status these people had to endure throughout Europe.

As young Herschel passionately stated to police and news media, *"It is not, after all, a crime to be Jewish. I am not a dog. I have a right to live. My people have a right to exist on this earth."*

What defined this single moment in history was the fact the Vom Rath shooting was the act of one young man. The Nazi Party, however, eagerly seized the moment to represent this relatively ineffectual event as being a strategic offensive in the war between Germany and international Jewry.

Subsequent propaganda from Goebbels' ministry to the media did not insinuate, but rather insisted the motive was another step by the Jews toward the extermination of National Socialist Germany. The influence of Nazi propaganda on the persecution of the Jews was never more profound than its new claim this event was proof of the international conspiracy that justified the victimization of Jews in the first place.

When Vom Rath died of his wounds just days later, he became known as the newest martyr for the Nazi cause. The highest Nazi leadership immediately called for a nationwide pogrom, and in effect declared open season on the Jews. An emboldened Hitler increasingly vilified his actions, as he no longer saw any further need for 'discretion' in matters of Jewish policy.

*****

It was astounding that in the midst of the horrors of 1937 Berlin, flowers continued to bloom; soft, welcoming rainfall cleansed the streets and gardens; sunshine continued to unveil its majestic glory; marriages sanctified newfound love; babies were born amid abounding joy and thankfulness; and music continued to echo throughout happy homes and concert theaters across Europe.

Still being led of course by the inimitable Marta, the predominance of the BPO was never more apparent than during these times. Its increased visibility and almost unfettered access to world-class cities because of the unlimited budget provided by the state, magnified the press coverage. Marta's work ethic was unwavering.

The demands placed upon the orchestra itself were all consuming for its member musicians, particularly after the development of vinyl disk recordings and concert broadcasts on radio. Through these radio broadcasts the British Broadcasting Company (BBC) became a leader launching the BBC Symphony Orchestra. Most of these recordings were pressed into vinyl in the broadcast studios in the absence of viewing audiences.

This technological innovation now exposed the popularity of classical music to private homes and millions of middle-class families who could now enjoy the musical standards once previously reserved for the privileged minority through live concert hall performances.

Repeat performances in London and Vienna served first-hand notice that the BPO standards of excellence, achieved almost effortlessly, were now forcing other world-class orchestras to re-evaluate their competitive position on the shifting global stage. Many of

the elite world orchestras were driven to perfection by the obsession and unflagging dedication of their conductors to meet these
new standards.

Most notably among them was Sir Thomas Beecham of the
London Philharmonic Orchestra and Willem Mengelberg of the
Royal Concertgebouw in Amsterdam. Arguably, only the Berlin
Philharmonic could rival these magnificent orchestras as the best in
the world.

Marta's overlapping personal performances as a touring super star
were not diminished by her already onerous commitments to the
orchestra. Her home life, however, was faltering and becoming badly
neglected by circumstance, more than she had originally envisioned.

Manny had become an excellent student who was very self-
motivated. He thrived in the environment of the Hitler Youth
Brigade and took his training seriously. He saw an opportunity to use
his keen acumen to fulfill his destiny as a top-flight fighter pilot in
the Luftwaffe. He was driven and extremely determined to proudly
follow in the footsteps of his father and grandfather in the military.

On the home front, Manny was well attended by Miss Lena and
he adjusted admirably to his daily regimen. For the most part, the
young are adaptive when their bellies are filled and genuine endearing love and encouragement are plentiful, regardless of the provider.
Lena fulfilled that role admirably, as was her duty on behalf of his
high-achieving professional parents.

Manfred became so preoccupied with his friends at school and
his perceptions of his new reality, he appeared indifferent to the long
absences of his parents. Within a few months and thereafter during
the passage of time, his questions about Mother and Father became
far less frequent. It was not a consequence Marta easily accepted.

Predictably, Marta and Klaus barely had time for one another.
They eventually reached the point of giving up trying to book
what had become intrusive appointments each with the other, only
to have last minute delays and re-bookings cause continual and
abject disappointment.

*****

The final months of 1937 wound down following an unprecedented series of outstanding performances that had spawned exceptional accolades from the press, the general populous, and Minister Goebbels in particular, all of them clamoring for more.

In accordance with protocol now being routinely observed with the cultural director, the minister summoned Herr Furtwängler to another meeting.

"Welcome Herr Furtwängler! It has been far too long since we last met."

"To you as well, Minister. Marta wanted me to offer her best wishes to you and the Fuhrer, and to acknowledge her appreciation for your thoughtful support of her."

"That's very kind of her. We know how much you and she are so very dedicated to your craft and we cannot imagine the extent of success she has achieved, much of which we are certain, is attributed to your wonderful leadership and direction."

Once the formalities were appropriately addressed, it was time the minister once again asked for maestro's co-operation, and his input. "The Fuhrer has been so impressed with Marta's and your support for him. We can think of no people more deserving than you both to have represented the Fatherland so capably. With this in mind, we must make another request for your consideration."

Maestro had no inkling as to where this conversation was heading and wisely decided to offer nothing in response at this time.

"Global tensions continue to escalate due to a series of remarkable achievements by the Reich. These tensions require the Reich to be more proactive by initiating suitable but subtle gestures of diplomacy; like those of a few years ago, with Sir Thomas Beecham's kind co-operation. That collaboration between BPO and London Philharmonic effectively bridged a looming discord with Britain."

"Yes, that effort was beneficial to all parties at that time. I dare say I too was pleased with the success of the events and the alliances that were so capably forged. What do you have in mind for me at this time, Minister?"

"This matter specifically concerns Madame von Brauchitsch. The Fuhrer has been quite taken by her, to say the least. Her violin virtuosity is only surpassed by her stunning beauty and genuinely formidable personality. In his opinion, she emulates what every aspiring German woman can only dream to become. It is evident her extensive fan base is totally inspired by the woman. We want to further capitalize on it. There is no one else who could be a more influential emissary in international relations for the interests of Germany, say…for example, with America."

"Those are flattering but also appropriate descriptions of Marta. Her talents know no boundaries… but America, Minister?"

"The Fuhrer wants to set in motion arrangements for Marta to take her larger-than-life personality to the shores of the United States, ideally by this coming year's end. We want the opportunity to showcase her extraordinary talent and incredible beauty internationally. He is insisting upon guest appearances with the Boston Symphony and the New York Philharmonic, although the latter's availability is presently in question."

"Have we not crossed this awkward bridge before, Minister? It appears you have again already put the wheels in motion without my prior input. I understood we had an agreement about this matter, did we not?"

"It may appear so, Maestro; however, we are merely following the lead of a few fellow accomplices who must remain nameless for security reasons, which I am certain you will understand. Safe to say though, we have influential friends overseas. We take their intelligence seriously and as such could not disclose any of this to you sooner until the information was verified."

"I will take what you say at face value, since you have always treated me with the honesty and respect to which I feel I am entitled. I do ask, however, that you bring me current on the present status of your confirmed intelligence. I need to know exactly where this matter stands. Once I am fully apprised, permit me to address the matter with Marta, and we can move forward from there. My people will make this a priority, as I am sure your people will also. Time is running short, I must warn you, but we will do our utmost to make this happen. If there is nothing more at this time, I must bid you good day Minister."

Goebbels beamed with satisfaction and graciously extended his hand in appreciation as he escorted Furtwängler to the door of his stately office.

*****

In a matter of weeks and after some creative readjusting of prior itineraries, Marta was delighted to comply, as she had never been to America. Not only was her excitement based upon her upcoming American adventure, this was a now or never opportunity for her to finally visit young Pietra. It had been three years since the travel ban had been strictly enforced on Jews. It was a visit she had promised to Anna since that time and it was her intention to fulfill it.

First-class accommodation was promptly requested by Minister Goebbels' office on Cunard's newest luxury liner, RMS *Queen Mary*. It was scheduled to depart Cherbourg, France enroute through Southampton, UK to arrive in New York City on December 15th. Since it was the midst of the holiday season, passage was nigh impossible to obtain on short notice, let alone in one of the private suites.

To make matters worse, since the loss of the *Hindenburg* only a few months earlier in May, public confidence in trans-Atlantic dirigible travel had significantly declined, placing considerably more strain on the demands for overseas travel to America. It was the only cruise available and the ship was fully booked.

Cunard was delighted with the successful introduction of its state-of-the-art vessel and provided a highly professional level of reliable service for its passengers, until an urgent call was received from Minister Goebbels on behalf of the Fuhrer to request an exception. Cunard respectfully refused to comply.

Upon learning of these scheduling difficulties, Goebbels consulted with the Fuhrer, who despite all odds, strenuously refused to cede to failure.

"I refuse to be denied the opportunity before us, Herr Minister. See to it that this scheduling bullshit does not stand in our way. Whatever it takes, Madame von Brauchitsch *will perform* in America this holiday season. Do I make myself clear?"

"Of course, Mein Fuhrer! I could not agree with you more. I may need one or two days to properly incentivize those whose co-operation is required to make this request happen. Will that be a problem, Mein Fuhrer?"

"Two days, Minister. Two days!" Hitler's steely gaze spoke to his unflagging resolve.

*****

Huge conglomerate takeovers and mergers since the turn of the century had shaped the world and evolved in such a way as to create opportunities for those powerful enough to take advantage of them. Minister Goebbels, having gained full insight of this corporate wheeling and dealing, seized upon the opportunity before him.

American financier J.P. Morgan, a major player in global trade at the time, had founded the International Mercantile Marine Company (IMM), initially incorporated in New Jersey in late 1902 as a trust. Its purpose was to operate as a holding company to monopolize the shipping trade by eventually acquiring and incorporating existing shipping lines into the trust, some of which were British.

British law at the time prohibited foreign citizens from direct ownership of British ships. As a corporate entity, IMM was able to circumvent the law and acquire ownership on behalf of an American citizen. This structured arrangement enabled IMM to own and control British shipping companies, most notably the Leyland Line and White Star Line, and other foreign companies as well.

In 1912 when the *Titanic* became the flagship of White Star, it was owned and controlled by IMM. Her sinking on her maiden voyage drastically affected the organization of the trust and drew unwanted attention of the government to disband the growing monopoly. After the death of J.P Morgan in 1913, IMM remained under the control of JP Morgan & Co.

The tragic sinking of the *Titanic* and the founder's death, though significant, did not directly bring about the failure of IMM. These events were followed by a series of financial setbacks, including the Wall Street stock market crash in 1929. Acquisitions and mergers followed throughout the Great Depression, but many were seriously over leveraged and did not create the desired financial stability.

In 1931, Kermit Roosevelt, son of the soon to be elected American President, and founder of the Roosevelt Steamship Company, spearheaded a merger with IMM to form the Roosevelt International Mercantile Marine Company (RIMM). Despite the merger, RIMM remained undercapitalized and continued to struggle financially.

By 1935, RIMM began closing and selling off many other failing operations under their umbrella. The remaining profitable divisions were merged into United States Lines, still owned by the parent company RIMM.

As history would show, later that same year the largest two German shipping companies Hamburg-Amerika, and its once formidable competitor Norddeutscher Lloyd were both under ownership and fifty-one percent control by the state. Together they were given lucrative construction contracts for state-of-the-art German battleships, which were financed by the Nazi Party. Deservedly so, they became ranked among the world's greatest shipping conglomerates.

Among the ships constructed under this unique partnership were the *Scharnhorst* and the *Gneisenau*. As the course of the war would unfold, these two battleships would wreak havoc on British and American transatlantic supply lines due to the financial backing of the Third Reich, which was seemingly unlimited.

Within just two hair-raising days, Minister Goebbels and his brilliant advisors understood the relevance of these fortuitous developments. The ruthless cunning and power of Goebbels' office knew no limits and seized the moment to deliver what Hitler had sought. The Fuhrer was only too anxious to reconnect with Minister Goebbels about this critical issue.

"I believe I have found a way to solve the apparent impasse Mein Fuhrer. If I may?"

"But of course. I am listening, Minister."

"As you instructed, I have taken it upon myself to learn that RIMM, the holding company owned by the wealthy American company, J.P. Morgan, has once again become over-leveraged. The loss of the *Titanic* twenty some years ago, and numerous other unfortunate financial catastrophes have caused their business interests to bleed cash. Our friends at Hamburg-Amerika and North Germany Lloyd Lines (HAPAG) are in a strong cash position, with our help, to potentially ease RIMM's financial pain, subject to certain conditions being met."

"I am aware they are thriving following the successful launches of our new transatlantic fleet. What are they proposing, Herr Goebbels?" Hitler queried.

"A few years ago, out of necessity, RIMM merged with the Roosevelt Steamship Company, owned by the same Roosevelt family presently sitting in the bloody White House. If we can convince Hamburg-Amerika and Lloyd Lines to strike a deal, in exchange for say…profit shares in RIMM, the ensuing financial leverage we could achieve would be very much to our advantage. Who gives a shit if they lose some money along the way? We still retain interest in the Morgan/Roosevelt alliance and can always offset any possible losses suffered by our shipping consortium. That should be enough influence to purchase a fucking first class round-trip for Madame von Brauchitsch, should it not?"

Hitler displayed a wide grin and began to laugh loudly. His uncontrollable laughter was contagious as Goebbels delighted in the moment with his Fuhrer, having seemingly found a way to accomplish the impossible.

Within days, ticketing was promptly furnished for Madame von Brauchitsch when Cunard Lines was regrettably forced to revoke the tickets for a VIP family in her stead. It was proof that with enough leverage even Cunard could move mountains to comply with the Third Reich's request.

Although details of the final agreement would take several subsequent months to complete, the merger of both multi-national companies was now well within Hitler's inevitable grasp.

CHAPTER NINETEEN

IT WAS A MASTERFUL STROKE OF GENIUS BY GOEBBELS to instinctively interpret the series of fortuitous events history had so kindly provided. While he had no power to control the past, his cunning manipulation of circumstances was perfectly aligned with his dutiful intentions. It was as if fate itself had intervened to tempt his insatiable appetite for personal advantage.

Only one minor setback remained. It was the impossibility of appearing with the New York Philharmonic on this American tour. Regrettably they were contractually indisposed for Marta's limited availability, although their concertmaster was a close associate of Arturo Toscanini, the resident conductor of the NBC Symphony Orchestra at this time.

It was a perfect fit! The NBC Orchestra was already booked for its inaugural broadcast concert on December 25th of that year at Rockefeller Center's Radio City Music Hall in midtown Manhattan. Vivaldi's *Four Seasons* had been selected for the program and the resident first violinist, who was originally scheduled as the soloist to interpret the masterpiece, graciously stepped aside to accommodate Marta's New York debut. Already a devotee of Madame von Brauchitsch and despite having never met her, he was honored to appear on the same stage with her eminence.

The venue for Boston had already been confirmed for December 18th and in place of their chief conductor, Serge Koussevitsky, who was booked for a medical procedure at that time, the resident assistant-conductor Manuel Rosenthal was his more than capable stand-in.

Rosenthal had served very successfully as chief conductor for the Orchestre National but had been immediately dismissed when

Lucien Rebatet, a prominent French journalist, discovered Rosenthal was a Jewish sympathizer. Rebatet was a very influential pro-Nazi, and a fervent anti-Semite, who forced Rosenthal's fall from grace, inadvertently making him available when Koussevitzky called.

It was this series of unexpected coincidences that enabled the collaboration of Rosenthal and Marta, without which she would never have met this amazing young man. He was six years her junior, but the attraction between them was immediate.

From the moment of their initial meeting prior to their first rehearsal, when their eyes met and their hands touched, there was an unmistakable and genuine connection.

"Madame von Brauchitsch, Manuel Rosenthal at your service." He lowered his head slightly and gently took her hand in his. "It is an honor to meet you. As with most of the classical music scene, I have followed your career closely and was delighted to learn of your return to the stage. To perform with you here in Boston is a dream come true for me. Welcome! Welcome, my dear lady!" He raised her hand to his lips and kissed it ever so tenderly.

Marta beamed and replied as demurely as her nature would allow. "Maestro Rosenthal. Flattery will get you everywhere!"

"Please call me Manuel, I insist. I understand this is your first visit to America. You must allow me to show you the city when your time permits. It would be my honor to accompany you. I look forward to getting to know you better during your brief stay."

"I would be broken hearted if you didn't, Manuel. Truly."

Marta was known to constantly exude natural sex appeal, but when she feigned bashfulness, she became even more alluring. During those moments, she could have any man she wanted. This was one of those moments, and Rosenthal could sense it. Never had Marta confused her professional career with the intimacies of her personal life. It appeared that was about to change.

Boston's Symphony Hall was widely considered to be one of the top concert halls in the world. Steeped in history, it had hosted the best musicians the world had to offer. It would now revel in the musical styling of one more such brilliant performer.

The walls of the concert hall sloped perceptively inward by design, intended to focus the sound more clearly. Even the numerous side balconies were abnormally shallow in structure absorbing very little of the orchestra's collective genius to maintain the purity of the audience experience. Replicas of iconic Greek and Roman statues appeared strategically placed in numerous skillfully crafted niches, giving cause for many to refer to the glorious structure as Boston's "Athens of America," a reverent honor bestowed upon it since the nineteenth century.

Upon making her grand entrance to this hallowed hall for her first time, Marta bathed in the endless waves of adoration being bestowed upon her. Evidently her stellar reputation had long since preceded her to an entirely new world she had only half imagined, as it was so very distant from the world she knew.

Music had evidently crossed the expansive divide separating these two formidable nations. The task before her was to reinforce the strength of a unifying bridge of communication and musical appreciation that evidently knew no cultural boundaries. She did not fail to deliver.

When Maestro Rosenthal received Marta's subtle gesture indicating she was prepared to begin, the masses of enthusiastic patrons quieted on cue. The Allegro Moderato of Tchaikovsky's Violin Concerto resonated softly within the amphitheater, gently caressing the attentive gathering with wave after wave of magical emotion. Within seconds the pace and intensity of the orchestra slowly gained momentum. As the piece reached its initial crescendo, the shifting of the spotlight was seemingly handed off to Marta's capable control and her melodic tones of perfection.

Any attraction she may have felt earlier to the gentleman with the baton remained safely and assuredly in her recently faded memory. Once she settled in to her customary and dutiful focus, she seized her moment of glorious proficiency and dismissed any trace of her prior distractive thoughts of desire. Those would be held in check. All her passion was now appropriately absorbed and redirected into her musical expression. Nothing could interfere with her exquisite emotional interpretation of this iconic musical masterpiece.

The orchestra once again took the spotlight only briefly from their gifted soloist and built a magnificent crescendo that had patrons helplessly swaying in their seats, slightly but oh so perceptively. Eyes began to moisten and the exhilaration of personal involvement of spirit became unmistakeable. It was a touching seduction for every Bostonian to heed. As Marta again regained the spotlight for her solo, the supporting musicians sat in absolute silence for what seemed a moment frozen in time. No one so much as twitched. It was a breathtaking and unforgettable mystical experience.

The seductive affect her creative interpretation had on Rosenthal himself seemingly energized his own authoritative task. Seeing her so immersed in her passionate veil of sensuality, Maestro was becoming overwhelmed with desire, for both his music and his lead performer. When the piece traced its inevitable path to the height of sheer perfection, skillfully directed by Marta's lead, the final notes became indelibly etched in the minds of everyone present for the spectacle.

The audience exploded with waves of thundering applause, made even more profound in this perfect acoustical setting. Numerous patrons stood on their seats, loudly shouting to proclaim their enthusiastic expressions of respect and adoration for what they had just witnessed.

Maestro Rosenthal gestured to the audience to continue their acknowledgments of Marta's gift, and the volume increased to new proportions. As Maestro descended the rostrum and walked to stand beside her, Marta extended her hand, which he eagerly accepted.

Typically, when a conductor kissed the hand of a gifted female musician, he would lower his head in a fully bowed position. On this occasion however, Maestro raised her hand slightly and from his prolonged and partial bow he raised his head slightly to gaze into her captivating blue eyes at the moment of his prolonged kiss. The gesture did not go unnoticed.

*****

The customary reception that followed featured an opportunity for the orchestra to celebrate and mingle with very special guest performers. This evening, the press unanimously agreed Marta and Rosenthal were a formidable combination that had brought out the best in each performer. High profile guest soloists among the best in the world often have that effect on the supporting cast.

Several VIPs who attended the much-anticipated event were also invited to bask in the presence of the very talented musicians for cocktails. It was a strategic exercise in public relations to foster on-going support for the symphony from several of the attending benefactors as well as various VIPs. Marta was the guest of honor, and everyone gathered around her to further enhance the mystique of her already well-established global celebrity.

Maestro Rosenthal stood by her side continuously, being the gracious host he was. It was a responsibility to which he had been well accustomed throughout his career. This was also his debut performance here in Boston, a fact almost overlooked. He made no effort to detract from Marta's spotlight and was both flawless and attentive to the guests and his musicians, whom he barely knew. The process demonstrated his natural adaptability, charisma, and effusive charm.

"Madame von Brauchitsch, it is indeed a pleasure to be in your company. I am Brian McGrory, chief editor for the *Boston Globe*. I am delighted to welcome you to Boston. May I say, Symphony Hall has hosted thousands of featured world-class performers throughout its long history, none of whom have outshone your performance here this evening. I am in awe, Madame."

"Those are lovely words, Mr. McGrory. I thank you sincerely. Is it safe to say you will be publishing a favorable review tomorrow?"

McGrory, Maestro, and those nearby all broke into spontaneous laughter. Marta was within her element as she seized the moment knowing his review would be seen by the Fuhrer and Goebbels, something she had never considered until this moment.

"I believe I can assure you of that, madame." The light humor and sipping of champagne continued in earnest.

"Madame von Brauchitsch is our guest tomorrow and must regrettably leave for New York on Monday to visit her very talented young niece. She is scheduled to perform with the NBC Orchestra on Christmas day." Maestro Rosenthal proudly proclaimed.

"Ahh yes, in Rockefeller Center! I just heard yesterday. It should be a wonderful venue for the orchestra's inaugural performance. We will all be watching on television; I can assure you! Pardon my thoughtlessness, Madame. I am Maurice Tobin, mayor of our fine city; such a pleasure to meet you. Your beauty has graced our stage without doubt."

"The pleasure is all mine, Mr. Mayor. As this is my first visit to America, I am very much looking forward to seeing more of your beautiful city tomorrow. I am certain to be very impressed."

The attentive waiter thoughtfully noticed Marta's glass was close to empty and promptly replaced it with another.

Maestro interjected by adding, "Before becoming mayor, Mr. Tobin was our representative in the House of Representatives in service to our great state of Massachusetts. We are all very proud of him."

"My, my, that is quite an accomplishment, especially for such a gallant but obviously very capable young man," Marta replied.

Marta had a way about her and was never at a loss for words. Her natural charms were never more evident.

Within about an hour, the gathering was tactfully ushered to the coat check and the exits. "This has been an exhausting day for everyone, but none more so than Madame. Ladies and gentlemen, we bid you a wonderful evening and as always we thank you for your kind and generous support."

Handshakes and respectful rounds of kisses on her lovely, manicured hand were affectionately extended. Everyone knew they were in the presence of greatness and were eager to display deep respect and affection for her; none however more than Maestro Rosenthal.

When only a few guests remained, Marta and Maestro gathered their coats and proceeded to the main exit together. They should have known better, but Marta insisted she could not simply escape through the rear doors. It was her only visit to this historic city and she was determined to make every effort to satisfy the fascination the Americans seemed to have for her.

The remaining crowd had finally begun to dissipate but still numbered in the many hundreds, and as such the police presence remained in full force. The last thing the city of Boston wanted was to risk possible harm upon their visiting virtuoso.

When Marta and Maestro came into view and commenced descending the awe-inspiring staircase, cheering and chanting of "*Marta! Marta! Marta!*" echoed throughout the assembly. She smiled engagingly and waved graciously in response to their adulation.

Unnoticed at this time was a heavily bearded and burly man who had positioned himself near the front of the friendly crowd. At this point it was evident the police had been lulled into complacency by the non-threatening and peaceful gathering. Suddenly and totally unprovoked, the large man pushed his way to break through the apparently unsuspecting line of armed policemen. The intruder, in an attempt to get closer to Marta took them by surprise and began to scream, "Go back to Germany where you belong, you stinking Kraut! We don't want you here, you Jew-hating bitch!"

In only a matter of seconds the protester was seized upon by the armed guards and abruptly forced face down to the concrete ground. He was a remarkably strong man, and it required several police to sufficiently subdue him. As he fell, his outstretched arm fell within inches of Marta's feet.

The officers closest to the breach scrambled to prevent his further progress. The security perimeter started to collapse from the protectively gathering crowd, but Maestro remained in firm control of Marta holding her closely to shield her from impending harm.

"I've got you Marta. Are you alright?"

"Yes Manuel. I think I am fine. A little unnerved I think, but I'm alright."

"Thank God!" he responded.

Even as the security detail cuffed his hands behind his back, the captive man stared up menacingly to see Marta's face just before he was efficiently pushed and pulled against his will to a waiting police van.

Despite being totally subdued, the man was continuing his right of self-expression, shouting with frustration and overwhelming emotion for his cause. It was not something Marta was accustomed to seeing or hearing. It was apparent to her that not only had her music touched the world, so too had Germany's reputation for racial intolerance and indiscriminate oppression.

The crowd loudly responded by a mixed chorus of booing, mostly against the man's attempted assault, but also at the injustice meted out against Jews in Germany. It was a strange yet nervous acknowledgement from many who were sympathetic to the intruder's cause and plea for justice for Jews everywhere.

The shock of being so close to the attack shook Marta's usual air of confidence. It was a spontaneous reaction that exposed something with which she was totally unfamiliar, a sudden awareness of her genuine vulnerability.

The waiting limousines shone brilliantly, reflecting the light from the full moon and the powerful light fixtures in front of Symphony Hall. Maestro and Marta moved as one, surrounded now by much tighter security as they were escorted directly to the safe confines of their car. After their final waves, the frazzled celebrities tried to relax together in the rear of the vehicle, both sighing with relief knowing this memorable day could have ended so tragically.

"Marta I am so very sorry about what happened here tonight. It is more than you should have to bear. I trust you know that despite the outburst, it was not intended for you personally. There are many people here who demonstrate openly against the German oppression. We read about it every day here in America, and they are not all Jews who feel that way. I'm so dreadfully sorry you had to see that."

"It did take me aback, Manuel, but I had been warned these demonstrations could happen. It is the first time it has ever happened to me, though. I am thankful because I know it could have been much worse. I was comforted knowing you would stay close to me." She took his hand in hers and squeezed it tenderly as her eyes remained fixated on his own. "Thankfully it's all behind us now and I am anxious to get to the hotel to relax…Can you stay with me a while Manuel, please? I need a few strong drinks to calm my nerves."

"Driver, can you please pick up the pace? The lady is getting rather fatigued."

*****

The Boston Park Plaza was yet another landmark of the city. It was a befitting, luxury hotel that could be assured of meeting the exacting standards the Boston Symphony had demanded for Marta's stay in Boston. The location for her stay had not been disclosed to the general public, to provide her with the peace and quiet she so deservedly sought on this extraordinary evening.

While her luggage was being organized by the bellboy and delivered to her suite, Marta invited the maestro for a nightcap in the main floor bar area. "Forgive me, Manuel, but I have been working tirelessly for the past three and a half months. I am overdue for some time off. I hope you don't object to keeping me company for a short while. I'm somewhat emotionally drained."

"You know I will, Marta. I enjoy being with you—very, very much I might add."

"Delightful!" Marta exclaimed, at which point she happily placed her arm under his and Maestro proceeded to escort his stunning companion to the grandeur of the magnificent bar lounge adjacent to the main lobby.

Within minutes she lifted the first of many vodka martinis to toast her newest companion. "To new beginnings, Manuel. I'm parched!" she enthused.

The bar was alive with idle conversation and laughter abounded as its numerous well-attired patrons consumed their various libations. It was evident many had been drinking for some time and Marta was determined she would not be left too far behind them.

The chatter continued and as often happened, some of the patrons who had attended her concert recognized her and the Maestro and eventually approached their table. Some of them appeared sufficiently well lubricated. They found Marta most receptive to their profusely flattering comments, initially to the general dismay of Rosenthal.

It was enjoyable and harmless flirtatiousness, but Marta gave back as well as she received. The alcohol did not numb her quick wit, or her outlandish sense of humor. She teased a few of the most boisterous men relentlessly, and purposely reserved the most ruthless quips for the slovenly drunken, and those less attractive among them, to discourage overstaying their welcome at her table. Sure enough, in less than an hour no fewer than three handsome and distinguished gentlemen, who evidently had no self-confidence issues, were personally catering to her every need.

Manuel remained undeterred by the men's respectful advances, but he quickly assessed there was one need only he could provide for Marta on this eventful evening.

As the hours passed, the chimes in the lobby signaled it was now three o'clock in the morning. Management, to allow Marta some additional time to enjoy herself, had graciously extended closing time. This hotel had indeed thought of everything!

"Maestro would you mind escorting me to the lift? I cannot imagine there is any remaining booze we haven't already managed to consume. I must bid you gentlemen good evening. Now all of you…" She pointed her finger scoldingly at each of them, "…get your asses home to your waiting wives before they notice you're missing! You're a sorry lot, which is probably why I enjoyed myself with you so much tonight. I thank you for making me feel so much at home here. God bless you all!"

It was a final slap in the face for these inebriated friends and was taken as it was intended, without malice or disrespect. Marta could have said anything and not offended these male admirers. It was her inimitable style and they wallowed in it.

When Maestro navigated Marta to the elevator, it was apparent she had become unsteady on her feet. Without a word and supported by Maestro, she steadied herself on his shoulder and flippantly bent over to remove her high heeled shoes, looping their delicate straps on two fingers while tucking her purse securely under the same arm. Every move this dynamic woman made displayed her natural sex appeal. It did not go unnoticed by her still leering male companions. Maestro held her opposite arm securely and protectively as they ascended to the top floor.

While still in the presence of the elevator attendant, Marta began to caress Maestro's handsome face and kiss his neck affectionately, cooing and groaning as she lowered her hand to grab his already aroused crotch. This would be a night to remember, thought Rosenthal, but he rightfully determined this was not the way to seduce this now defenseless woman. That was out of the question, at least in his mind.

As he fumbled with her key and unlocked the door he reassuringly stated, "Come now Marta. We have both had too much to drink. Let me get you comfortable. Trust me. I will keep you safe, sweetheart."

Closing the door securely behind him, Rosenthal guided Marta to her bedside and removed her silken shawl, which had cascaded to her tiny waistline. As she sat in a slight stupor on the side of her bed, he thoughtfully began to undo the satin buttons on the lower back of her dress, exposing her silk-like delicate white skin right down to the seductive curves just above her no doubt glorious buttocks. He briefly imagined one day having her permission to further explore her loveliness in more intimate detail, but again he shook his head to quickly whisk away such lascivious thoughts for now.

He struggled to carefully remove her dress completely and did so as best he could to not disturb her growing fatigue. As he pulled the dress above her head, he powerlessly paused for only a few seconds to fully absorb her perfect profile. This was an angel from heaven he wanted desperately to savor.

He placed her dress across the closest chair and looked with absolute wonder as her brassiere still supported her supple breasts, leaving her slender, toned tummy exposed as well as her stockings, garter belt, and panties for his inadvertent viewing pleasure.

In loving fashion, Rosenthal delicately placed her head onto her fragranced pillow and gently lifted her limp but exceedingly gorgeous legs onto the bed. Marta was sound asleep. Maestro experienced such profound longing for this rare beauty and thoughtfully pulled the duvet over her limp body tucking her warmly in its embrace. The moment was one of potentially deferred but deserved gratification, only when and if she was in complete control of her senses. Rosenthal would not have it any other way.

Marta was completely and helplessly passed out from the combination of alcohol and exhaustion. Maestro quickly discovered a blanket from the hallway closet and laid himself out full length on the living room couch, uncertain whether his decision to stay would be interpreted as overstaying his welcome. Within minutes, he faded into restful and nourishing deep sleep, satisfied he had acted honorably and maintained both his own and Marta's dignity and self-respect in the eyes of this amazing woman.

*****

Marta did not even stir until almost midday. It was the welcoming smell of eggs, freshly baked croissants, and aromatic coffee that finally aroused her from sleep. She had no memory of finding her way to her room nor climbing into bed…and undressing. She looked about and fumbled with a delicately perfumed housecoat, which had been neatly laid out on the opposite side of her bed. Wrapping it snugly around her waist she opened her bedroom door, not knowing what to expect on the other side.

"Manuel…what in the world?"

"Good morning my dear. I trust you slept well. May I pour you some fresh coffee, or orange juice perhaps?"

The very sight of Marta fluffing her hair was incredibly sexy and Manuel became discreetly and uncontrollably aroused. Her golden, tousled hair remained in some disarray until Marta turned her head smartly to unfold her loosened curls around her beautiful neck and shoulders as she responded, "Yes, thank you. Coffee would be lovely."

Manuel rose from the table at which he was already seated to present her cup and saucer, rightly assuming she wanted her morning coffee black. He took hold of a chair and presented it to her as he helped her adjust it comfortably.

"This is quite a surprise Manuel; a lovely one I must say." Marta looked toward the open bedroom door and asked uncertainly, "Did you...Did we...?"

"Nothing of the sort, Marta. You can relax. I did assist you in getting into bed and took the liberty of removing your gown. I didn't so much as peek, I assure you... Well, perhaps just a little, if truth be told."

"You are a rare gentleman Manuel; much more so than I probably deserved. Did I do anything inappropriate last night? I know I wanted you badly last night. Who restrained you? Someone must have. I did my very best to get us both laid."

Rosenthal spewed his coffee all over his white shirt from the night before as he laughed uncontrollably at her wicked and always outrageous humor.

Marta just sat back and watched him clean himself most embarrassedly as she nonchalantly sipped her coffee.

"You are a handful, aren't you?" he teased in a matter-of-fact manner.

"Too bad you didn't find out for yourself last night, Maestro!" Finally, she started to giggle. "I'm so sorry for being such an ass, Manuel. It's just who I really am. I cannot express how much I appreciate your tender care and thoughtfulness. You have distinguished yourself in my eyes like no man before. As I think more about your gallantry last night...yes...I have decided that this afternoon I shall fuck your brains out. Would that be alright, my dear?"

And so, it was the beginning of an afternoon of sheer delight and unbridled debauchery, as Marta so eloquently worded it. The interlude was inevitable and at least a day or two overdue. Surviving deliciously upon room service, neither lover left their room for the next two days until it was time to depart for New York. So much for seeing the sights of Boston, although the sights Manuel experienced outshone anything historic Boston had to offer.

All was well until they exited the hotel together with the intent that Manuel would whisk Marta away to the train station in a discreet fashion. The timing was perfect for her trip to New York.

Much to their shock and dismay, a large throng of reporters descended upon them, having patiently waited two days for *someone, or anyone* to eventually exit the hotel. As the crowd approached with cameras and microphones in hand, but before they were within earshot, both lovers looked at one another and simultaneously exclaimed, "*Oh shit!*"

CHAPTER TWENTY

♂

DURING HER COMMUTE TO NEW YORK'S PENNSYLVANIA Station, Marta obsessed about dropping her guard that evening. It had been an ill-advised personal decision, but it had happened before, just never with a professional colleague. Marta had always survived the inevitable suspicions, both at home and with her legions of admirers. This intimate act though, was more than a simple indiscretion. She had desperately needed a night of intimacy and had reveled in each moment of the experience. But it was a flagrant breach of her professional ethics and the fallout for her marriage could be devastating.

Although her indiscretion was of great potential consequence, she was never one to dwell on her weaknesses and was determined to deal with the matter as soon as she returned to Berlin. There was nothing she could do or say to change what had occurred, so for the moment she focused on enjoying some well-deserved personal time with Pietra and her Aunt Grace and Uncle Richard.

The taxi driver knew the area just on the outskirts of New York well. Despite it being a lovely, well to do neighborhood, Marta was surprised at the relative simplicity of the architecture and the excess space around each home. It was a style to which she was unaccustomed, having spent almost all her life in historic European theatres and residences occupied by the privileged upper class. This was an eye-opener for her sheltered perceptions.

The driver waited thoughtfully at the curbside after he escorted Marta to the front door with her abundant luggage. He did not recognize his mysterious but obviously well to do passenger and was intrigued by her elegant appearance and natural aloofness. She did seem very much out of place, at least to his naïve and inquisitive state of mind.

Marta rang the doorbell and only had to wait to the count of ten before young Pietra wrestled the door open and lunged at her with open arms. "Auntie Marta! Oh, how I have missed you! I have been counting the minutes till your arrival!"

"As have I, my darling! I only wish I could have come to see you sooner, as does your loving mother, Pietra." They pulled one another into an embrace amidst the expected release of tears of joy. As they did so, Richard and Grace were rushing from the upstairs to enter the central hallway.

"Hello Marta! Welcome to our home, and *welcome to America!* I am Grace and this is my dear husband, Richard." Again, more hugs and affections were shared. It was a wonderful moment for Marta to enjoy the closeness of this affectionate family.

Marta quickly surmised they were a very closely-knit family and they hospitably directed her further inside to close the still partly opened door. It was a typical winter day in New York, and it was evident the rapidly approaching holiday would feature a white Christmas, judging by the heavy accumulation of shoveled snow running the full length of the driveway.

"Please let me take your coat, Marta," Richard kindly offered. "My, my, it is indeed a lovely one. May I ask, is this mink?" he enquired inquisitively.

"Actually, it is not. Truth be told I think its chinchilla, although I don't even know what kind of animal that is. I don't suppose I could even tell the difference."

Pietra interjected enthusiastically, "Nothing but the very best for Auntie. We are in the presence of German royalty, Uncle Richard."

"Not at all!" Marta chided embarrassingly. "Please don't make a fuss over me. I am simply delighted to be here. Sigmund and his dear wife Marissa send their kindest personal regards. They are so very thankful for all you are doing for Pietra, as of course is Anna."

The small reunion was heart-warming, and Pietra was glowing with both pride and satisfaction at the prospect of having her aunt and uncle getting to know her Aunt Marta, up close and personal.

Over cocktails and a succession of numerous topics that were eagerly discussed, it had become late afternoon as the darkness of night was fast approaching. The aromas of a home-cooked feast emanating from the kitchen were becoming most evident.

The meal was a satisfying treat for Marta, who only enjoyed home cooking on extremely rare occasions. She found it to be delicious but was dismayed at the amount of time and effort that must have been expended by her hosts to prepare such a wonderful meal. She sang their praises and awkwardly offered to help with the dishes. Thankfully Grace declined her kindness because Marta had no idea what that process entailed. It would have been most embarrassing for her.

Marta was easily convinced she should remain seated, not protesting for a moment. She sat at the table with Grace and sipped a fine cup of coffee while Pietra and Richard handled the cleanup.

"I must say you have a beautiful home. Do you take care of it yourselves? Everything is so neat and tidy."

"The hired help attends to those matters, Marta. I will give him your compliments." Turning her head to face her husband, Grace stated very enthusiastically, "Thank you so very much for all your hard work, Richard."

Everyone enjoyed a good laugh, but Marta was initially uncertain as to what had just occurred until Pietra explained her aunt and uncle were just teasing. This was normal upper middle-class America. Marta was not intended to be the brunt of the joke and took it all good-naturedly.

"Let's all retire to the living room, shall we? We enjoy sitting by the fireplace after dinner." It was the same room that was displaying a meticulously decorated Christmas tree. It was evident Richard and Grace were not practicing Jews. Richard, as it turned out, was Roman Catholic.

"The tree looks wonderful. I cannot imagine a lovelier one, not in my humble experience I must say," opined Marta.

"My cousin Peter and I helped. It was a total family effort," Pietra proudly proclaimed.

"Speaking of Christmas trees," Richard interjected, "we were thrilled to hear about your engagement in Rockefeller Center on Christmas Day. Wait until you see the famous tree in the center of the square. Now *that's* magnificent! I understand its fifty feet tall and features more than 5,000 lights! It's simply amazing to see."

"I am very much looking forward to it. I have seen pictures of course, but to be there personally will be a wonderful experience for me."

"What time is Peter expected, Aunt Grace? Is he still working?"

"Yes, sweetheart. He should be home shortly."

Grace diverted her attention back to Marta. "Our son has become one of Pietra's biggest fans, Marta. He is eager to meet you based upon all the stories Pietra has told him about you."

"Oh no! I sincerely hope she didn't tell any of my bad ones!" After a few laughs and when Marta had a chance to relax, the conversations resumed.

"So Auntie, please tell me about Emilie and Mother. And Papa and Nana. And let's not forget about Klaus and Manny...and Dietrich! I only receive a few letters from Mother. I know she is terribly busy, but I do wish she could write me more often. I miss her so very much. Oh, there's so much I want to know, and so very little time for you to tell me. Please try, Auntie."

Marta did her best to help Pietra catch up on her family's various trials and tribulations. It was difficult for Marta because she was not fully aware as to what Anna had shared with her daughter, and more so with what she had not. She did her best to be open and candid but was careful not to convey undue concern to Pietra for her family's safety. The hours passed quickly; each person fully engaged by what they were learning about the other.

It was evident Pietra had become very attached to this lovely family and the affection between her and her older cousin Peter was unmistakable. She was in a happy place here and her career was blossoming under their guidance and the close tutelage of the Julliard School of Music. She was particularly fortunate to be one of only a few students offered a full scholarship with one of the benefits being housing on campus. She had grown accustomed to returning home to her extended family on most weekends, and of course during the holidays. It was fortunate Marta's itinerary enabled them to reunite during the holiday season.

It was getting late when Pietra finally bid goodnight to the family and headed upstairs to prepare for bed. Despite Marta's exhaustion, she was determined to outlast her dear niece.

It was Marta's first opportunity to speak confidentially with Richard and Grace on matters she could not speak of in Pietra's presence. "Please forgive me for not speaking up earlier but there is a matter I could not address in front of Pietra. I hope you understand."

"Of course, Marta. Whatever it is, we will treat it with whatever privacy you deem necessary," Grace assured her. "Is the family back home alright? We speak with Sigmund on occasion and he has already cautioned us to be mindful of what we disclose to Pietra, if that is what you are concerned about."

"The family is well, yes, but I must express from myself and the family that without you both stepping up on Pietra's behalf to permit her to live in America, her life would be drastically imperiled, as are the lives of those who still remain. You both have made all things possible for Pietra, which would not have been so had she remained in Berlin. I am certain Sigmund has already told you these things, but I want you to understand that also of significance is the incredible amount of stress and worry you have taken from Marissa's and his shoulders, and especially from Anna's, knowing Pietra is safe from harm. Dietrich is being well attended in his private school in Vienna and appears to be very happy there, but it is unbearable for them to not be able to take Emilie's family away too. It haunts them every day of their lives. They endure it as best they can, but your support has eased their suffering immensely."

"Thank you for your thoughtfulness, Marta. Richard and I hear radio and news reports, which we understand are strictly controlled. We cannot imagine the truths you must have to deal with daily. We shudder to think of it."

Richard also added, "We have come to love Pietra as our own. We are thankful for the opportunity to have her live with us and have her become part of our family." As he said those comforting words, he and Grace held hands in appreciative acknowledgement.

The following day would be another hectic one since Marta was invited to join them on a personal guided tour of the "Big Apple". Although Marta was delighted at the prospect, her energy was visibly fading as the midnight hour approached. She appreciated their kindnesses and realized perhaps this would not be as restful a visit as she first anticipated.

*****

It was almost mid-morning when the family boarded their four-door sedan to take Marta to the city for the bus tour scheduled for eleven o'clock sharp. Richard was always meticulous about being punctual and the drive was a relaxing experience, albeit somewhat more crowded than Marta was accustomed to. She was totally immersed in their company and took this new experience in full stride.

Marta did her best to dress down for the occasion but even at her worst, she stood out very conspicuously among the thousands of ordinary Americans. She was beautifully and tastefully attired in custom-fitted tan slacks, high heels, and a gorgeous suede jacket. Her hair and makeup were impeccably styled to the extent that not only the men noticed, so did the women—some of them no doubt with some element of resentment.

Grace commented to Richard when she knew she would not be overheard, "Marta is a vivacious woman to be sure, and I really enjoy her company, but she sticks out like a sore thumb! Don't you think, honey?"

"Did you really think I wouldn't notice? I feel sympathy for her. Despite trying her best, you simply can't put a square peg in a round hole. I don't know whether to laugh or cry for her, really I don't."

Throughout the tour, Pietra and Marta were inseparable. When the tour was complete and the passengers disembarked, they found themselves in the middle of downtown Manhattan. The streets were jammed with holiday shoppers, tourists, and the general buzz of excitement watching the NBC stage being constructed for the outdoor Christmas Day concert, scheduled for that same evening. Who among them knew it would include this colorful and distinctively overdressed woman of such significant cultural stature?

One person did. Out of the bustling crowd a man with a microphone and a film crew, who had evidently been filming a promotional piece for NBC, spotted Marta. She was impossible to miss. He was no more than ten feet away and started hollering her name as he aggressively pushed through the dense gathering of shoppers.

"Marta! Marta! Please, over here!"

Marta couldn't help but turn around. This man holding a microphone was waving frantically to her.

Who could possibly know me here? she thought to herself. The reporter continued to fight his way toward Marta and the now-obliging onlookers were allowing him to pass through. Their attention was focused on the man with the microphone, and his small entourage with numerous cameras set at the ready. *Is there nowhere in the world to hide?* Marta thought. God forbid if she ever did anything evil enough to have to.

Without thinking, Marta stood confidently to face the approaching man, still holding Pietra firmly and protectively beside her. Her concern was more for Pietra than for herself. She knew this was nothing compared to the incident in Boston.

"Thank you for stopping Madame. I am a reporter for NBC and could not help but notice you in the crowd. I never expected to see you here until your concert on Christmas Day. May I ask you a few questions, Madame?"

"Yes, I don't see why not. Only a few minutes though as I am with friends and family here."

"Of course, you are most gracious. I understand this is your first visit to New York. What is your initial impression?"

"I am only here in the city for a few hours, but I'm enjoying every minute of it. The size of the crowds is somewhat intimidating, but I am delighted to be here."

The reporter continued, "More than a million New Yorkers will be here on Thursday evening watching you and the orchestra live, and millions more on televisions at home. Does your popularity here surprise you?"

"Yes, I have come to expect this in Europe. I can only assume my reputation preceded me to America's shores. This is overwhelming and quite surprising to my mind. I am most appreciative for the attention."

"One final question Madame, if you don't mind. Do you think your reputation has been tarnished since your romantic liaison with Maestro Rosenthal was discovered in Boston?"

Marta was stunned by his disturbing and provocative question though her calm demeanor displayed no evidence of being upset. Without batting an eye, she responded accordingly. "I suspect people will interpret whatever they want from my meeting with the maestro that morning. He was kind enough to escort me to the train to ensure my safe departure to New York. He is a very fine gentleman I respect immensely. Thank you for your time, young man. I look forward to seeing everyone again Christmas night and I wish you all a happy holiday season!"

The reporter was taken aback with disappointment and he briefly reflected on the original news report that could have misinterpreted their version of the inflammatory story. Either way, he gained much respect for this amazing woman who kept such poise in the face of potential adversity.

"What was he talking about, Auntie? What happened in Boston?" Pietra enquired.

"This happens all the time, sweetheart. I meet with many, many famous people. Everyone is entitled to his or her own opinions about things that happen I suppose. It is what is called the cost of fame. You will come to understand it better when your time comes, my darling, and I assure you it will."

As Marta redirected her attention to rejoining Richard, Peter, and Grace, they were swept away in the crowds much as before. This time dozens of tourists immediately formed their own procession, closely following the now identified superstar among them, clicking cameras and shouting words of encouragement to Marta. Word was being communicated from person to person about how openly and courteously she had responded to the intrusive reporter. Many were oblivious to the basis for his inappropriate suggestion of whatever had occurred in Boston.

"My goodness, Marta, how do you deal with the constant pressure from the press and from people in general? Do you ever grow tired of it?" Grace enquired.

"All of my adult life has been like this. You get used to it over time. No harm done today. It would be worse if I tried to avoid them. The press will write what they must to sell newspapers whether I comment or not. Sometimes though, I will freely admit, they can be such a pain in the ass."

Later in the privacy of their home, Grace commented to Richard that "Marta never seems to talk down to people. It is as if she knows within herself, she is superior. She exudes natural superiority and supreme confidence in her demeanor that many could react to as being arrogant, but I see no evidence she intends it."

Neither Grace nor Richard broached the matter of what had occurred in Boston. They would read about it eventually and make of it what they would. Klaus and Manuel were the only ones Marta truly worried about. She would have to address those repercussions soon enough.

The gathering of fascinated onlookers continued to keep pace in whatever direction Marta chose to take. It was not likely they knew much about her, since they were not part of the classical culture scene, but whoever she was held their growing interest. The clicking of cameras was frequent and seemed to attract others into her magnetic pull. Her flair for fashion and the self-confident way she held herself, were increasingly apparent.

As they continued their family tour, Marta was awestruck by the massive bronze statue of Atlas. "My goodness this is an imposing piece of art! What is he supposed to be holding, Richard? Is it the weight of the world I wonder?"

"Close Marta. It represents Atlas holding the heavens on his shoulders. Isn't it a wonderful piece, especially in this setting? It is said that it rises a total of forty-five feet including the pedestal on which it stands. I find it quite imposing."

"Yes, I agree. Most impressive," Marta responded.

As they returned to their car, Richard and Grace were disappointed they were unable to show Marta more of what New York had to offer. The crowds were quite oppressive and for Marta's own safety the family agreed it was best to cut the private tour short.

In two days, it would be Christmas Eve and it would be another eventful day before Marta's scheduled return to the city. Maestro Toscanini had scheduled rehearsals, and full attendance was necessarily implied. Marta was eager to participate, but for now she was perfectly content to enjoy a few hours of peace and quiet with the family, hopefully in front of the fireplace one final time.

*****

The following morning found Marta longing for Klaus and Manfred. At this time of year, the world typically stops turning to provide for close family times, forging special warm memories of those gatherings that remain in our hearts forever. As was her custom, Marta quickly shook off her brief melancholy and was content to enjoy her last few hours with her newly discovered American friends.

Upon her descent to the main floor from the bedrooms above, the wonderful aromas of a traditional American breakfast of bacon and eggs, coffee and toast stirred within her now growling stomach. Even celebrities are not exempt from their gastronomic urges.

After a satisfying meal Grace asked Pietra to announce their intentions while there was still enough time before Marta's limousine arrived at eleven.

"Aunt Marta, in honor of your visit with us we want to do something very special this morning so you will always remember how very much we have all come to love you."

"My goodness, what is this all about?" Marta replied in surprised fashion.

"Please, let's all go into the living room, if you please, madame." Pietra curtsied and raised her arm very pretentiously directing Marta to lead on.

"Because you won't be able to be with your family over Christmas, we decided we would bring Christmas to you a few days early. We hope you don't mind."

Marta was unprepared for this overwhelming gesture. It took her totally by surprise and she looked about frantically for some tissues as her eyes were starting to openly stream down her lovely cheeks. "I don't know what to say, and that never happens to me." She started to giggle as the others followed her lead, doing the same. "You all honor me too by taking me into your family. I shall never forget this moment. I thank you from the bottom of my heart, truly I do."

Some perfectly wrapped gifts were thoughtfully presented to Marta from the base of the tree and set on her lap for her to open. "And presents too! How very lovely they are. Beautifully done! Thank you so very much!"

Being so far from her home at this time of year had not been forgotten and Marta was visibly touched by their extraordinary sentiment. "I have something for all of you too!" Marta exclaimed. "Pietra, my dear. Would you please go to my room? I have set aside some gifts of my own after packing my luggage this morning. Please bring them downstairs for everyone. Thank you, sweetheart."

Marta had been thorough in her preparation for this moment. She gave Peter an American football, a sport of which she knew nothing at all, but he was evidently a big sports fan and gushed with gratitude for her kind gesture. There was a very beautifully designed collector edition bottle of fine cognac for Richard and Grace to remember her by, and there was but one gift remaining for Pietra. It was a rather long and imposing package that had been elegantly wrapped, although certainly not by Marta as she freely admitted.

"Auntie Marta, what have you done? I cannot even begin to guess what is inside. I think perhaps it's too beautiful to open, don't you think, Aunt Grace?" she teasingly suggested.

As the exquisite paper was peeled away, it revealed a magnificent leather violin case. On the center of the lid was a brass engraving that read, "*Pietra Elisabeth Friedman*".

"Oh, my word! This is beautiful Auntie Marta! I love you so very much for all you have done for me…and now this! I shall always cherish it."

She rushed to her beloved aunt, who rose from her seat to properly receive her, and hugs and kisses abounded. It was a lovely moment for everyone.

Within a half hour, the arrival of the limousine was announced a bit sorrowfully, and soon after Richard and Peter assisted in loading the luggage into the massive trunk to ensure everything was safely secured. So too were the deep bonds of friendship that would hopefully last a lifetime.

As the car slowly backed away to the road, and began its departure, Marta could be seen waving enthusiastically and wiping a few remaining tears away. Her admiration for the family she had only met days before would be effectively conveyed to Anna upon Marta's return. Anna could rest easy that Pietra was in very capable and loving hands.

CHAPTER TWENTY-ONE

REHEARSALS FOR THE CHRISTMAS MUSICAL EVENT OF the year were an intense yet fulfilling experience for every participating musician. The NBC Orchestra had been created specifically for Arturo Toscanini's artful leadership. The National Broadcasting Company described the orchestra's inaugural performance to be "*the greatest radio event since the abdication of Edward VIII.*" For the first time in America, the greatest composers' music would now be available to millions of remote farmhouses throughout the land.

NBC offered the highest known salaries of any orchestra at this time enabling the hiring of the most prominent musicians, who had been lured from major orchestras across America. Marta was among the elite performers in the world and was paid an incredible wage, which reflected her high stature in the industry.

She was a true professional when she set foot upon the stage, even for a rehearsal. There were no diversions, personal or otherwise. Her dedication and work ethic were noted by Maestro Toscanini and conveyed to each of his already outstanding supporting musicians. Marta was someone to be emulated in Toscanini's more than humble opinion.

The venue for this performance, which was being recorded and broadcast live, was the NBC Studio inside Radio-City Music Hall. The concert hall programs distributed to every attendee, who numbered in the thousands, had a specific request at the bottom of the printed copy. "*Since the modern microphone is extremely sensitive, your co-operation in maintaining strict silence during the music is urgently requested.*"

Recordings of a live performance are quite unlike studio recordings which occur in a soundproof, controlled environment. Any sound whatsoever from the audience, a cough, sneeze or an uttered word of enthusiasm no matter how brief, is picked up by the microphone in a live recording and could not be edited from the master recording.

From the opening note of Vivaldi's *Four Seasons* Overture, Toscanini enthralled his audience and similarly his orchestra, by demonstrating unparalleled power and ferocity, as he had become known to do. No one ever forgot his sunken brow and the dark eyes shining beneath. He put his very blood into each note, as he used to say about himself. He expected no less from his musicians.

As the acclaimed guest performer, Marta was very much at ease that evening. She had supreme confidence in her craft, and a clear, dedicated mind to command it. She had long since removed from her mind the potential embarrassment of her personal misjudgments. No doubt the negative fallout from her ill-advised behavior would have debilitated even the best of musicians, were they foolish enough to have committed a similar error in judgment. But Marta held fast to direct her emotions to the task at hand.

She performed brilliantly under Toscanini's astute attention to detail as expected, capably demonstrating in both Boston, and now New York, that her celebrity status was well deserved. She set a new standard of excellence previously unseen in American theaters and auditoriums. This was indeed a woman to be revered throughout the civilized world. It was the most publicized musical event in the history of classical music, due in large part to the innovative new technology then available.

As anticipated, the audience co-operated fully with the request for absolute silence during the performance. They did well in suspending their pent-up emotions until Maestro extended the completion of the final note, and appreciatively turned to face the audience to open the gates to the vociferous and prolonged acknowledgements of appreciation. Although Marta had grown well-accustomed to similar accolades in the past, she had learned long ago never to take them for granted. She always knew fame was a fleeting thing and she was determined she would earn it every time she performed.

Just before midnight, when the musicians gathered on the outside stage in the Rockefeller Center, to be recognized one final time by the waiting throng, Marta was again struck by the amazing opulence of the festive décor. It was her first time to see the spectacle in the dark of night. The majesty of the much-celebrated fifty-foot Christmas tree shone brilliantly, even more so because its many lights were reflected by the surrounding glass and concrete towers surrounding it. This famous tree had become what Rockefeller Center labelled "*a holiday beacon for New Yorkers and visitors alike.*"

A massive skating rink had been built just below the elevated base of the tree facing the recently completed thirty-six-story Time & Life Building, which had been fully completed just one year before. The entire center, which included the skating rink, was now packed to standing room only, by close to a million onlookers.

Following a private celebratory reception with the musicians and NBC management, Marta uncharacteristically retired to her suite for some much-needed sleep. Tomorrow she would begin to address the potential ramifications from the Boston affair and prepare to return home absent any additional fanfare.

Marta savored a few well-prepared martinis from the very obliging room service and sat alone in her suite in the stillness and peacefulness overlooking the people far below. The entertainment and excitement had long since shut down and the remnants of the bedraggled and weary crowd continued to empty the once congested square. Marta was mired in her self-enforced solitude, content to serve a small penance for her past and most recent indiscretions.

For Marta, moments such as these were wild vacillations in time from those of fame and public adoration, to periods of extreme and frequent loneliness. It seemed to her that oftentimes her family had become strangers, and strangers had become her family. Is that how life was intended for her, or was that just her own distorted perception?

She vowed to take a proactive approach to address her growing anguish for the sins she had committed and privately asked God for guidance. On her leisurely voyage home, she would finally dedicate her attention to unravel her complicated predicament to find an appropriate resolution.

Upon reflection, it was neither Boston nor New York that troubled her; it was Berlin. If he didn't know already, it would only be a matter of time until Klaus would become aware of Marta's suspected infidelity. No doubt he would be devastated. He deserved better from her, much better.

Marta reconciled to herself that what was done was done, and nothing in her power could change past transgressions. The severity of her disclosure however was not something to address with him over a long-distance phone call, likely requiring her to leave a damned message. No, she would address the matter face to face with him in hope of their relationship moving forward. She knew it was not a likely proposition he would want to consider.

Manuel, on the other hand, was a very different matter, and one of comparative simplicity. Owing to his sensitive nature, he had no doubt been anxiously awaiting some communication from her. She would make every effort to contact him by mid-morning before his day fully occupied his attention.

*****

"Yes, thank you, and a good day to you as well. May I speak with Maestro Rosenthal if he is available please? Yes, I will wait." She was reluctant to give her name unless specifically asked. She wanted to avoid stating any information that could be leaked to any potential loose tongues, especially until she established some understanding of Manuel's circumstances over the past week.

The administrator returned within minutes. "I apologize madame. Thank you for waiting. The maestro is otherwise presently engaged. If you leave a message, I am certain he will return your call promptly."

Reluctantly, Marta responded abruptly, "Please inform him it is Madame von Brauchitsch calling. I will continue waiting if I may."

Within half a minute, the woman returned to say, "Please hold, madame, for a brief time. Maestro will take your call in his office."

Unknown to her was that Manuel had terminated his meeting abruptly and was racing to the adjacent building where his private office was located. The two minutes of waiting were anxious ones for Marta.

Suddenly she heard the fumbling noises of the phone that had evidently fallen from his grip in his over exuberance to speak with her. "Hello Marta! Thank heaven you called, my dear! Are you well I trust?"

"Yes Manuel, I am fine. I'm so very sorry I took so long to contact you. My schedule did not afford me the time or the privacy I needed to speak with you personally. I hope you understand that my delay was not for lack of consideration."

Marta could hear the clearly discernable gasps for air as Maestro was still struggling to catch his breath.

"My goodness Manuel, the last time I saw you in Boston we were both noticeably out of breath, as I seem to recall."

Both she and Manuel shared a good laugh. Clearly, he understood her reference to their sexual exploits of that now problematic day.

"You don't have to worry about me Marta. If I could be with you in the same circumstances, I would do it all again, without hesitation."

"I'm very happy you feel that way, my sweet man. I feel a connection between us Manuel that I have not experienced with anyone in a very long time. The press caught me off guard in New York but I neither confirmed nor denied our tryst and simply deflected to other matters. As I explained to my niece, the press will write whatever they want, truth or fiction is within their mandate to decide."

"I watched the broadcast on Christmas night. You were fantastic as usual. I am very proud of your amazing performance. Have you spoken to your husband yet? That was and continues to be my greatest concern for you, Marta."

"I decided that whether Klaus already knows or otherwise, I will not discuss this with him until I am safely home. It cannot be any other way I'm afraid. The biggest problem will be his lack of availability, but one way or another once we have our discussion, which will no doubt be heated, I will land securely on my own two feet. I pray he does too." Marta paused only briefly and continued. "If I may ask Manuel, what has been the reaction in your home, and in and about Boston?"

"First and foremost, my wife Claudine and I have been separated for the past year and a half and are no longer accountable to each other. Sadly, though understandable, I must admit my close friendship with Maestro Koussevitzky was soured somewhat by our indiscretion."

Marta waited patiently allowing Manuel to direct the conversation from this point.

"His concern was not about the personal choices I have made since my separation, but much more so with my outlandish behavior in becoming intimately involved with you as a guest of our orchestra. I overstepped a well-defined line between me as maestro, and you as our star performer. He considers my actions to be reprehensible. I am not certain as to how this will affect my career in Boston, and of greater importance, my valued friendship with Serge in particular. It is a friendship I cherish Marta. I do not want to lose it."

"I feel for you, Manuel. Does this mean we should just consider our tryst to have been a temporary misjudgment and move on?"

"Let me be clear, Marta. I would crawl a mile through broken glass to be with you again. You make me feel like a young, testoster-one-charged adolescent again. You are magical, Marta! I cannot stop thinking of you and I relive our time together repeatedly. Does that answer your question?"

"Yes, sweetheart. I am comforted to hear you say that Manuel. But I am boarding the Queen Mary early this afternoon to return home. As much as I am anxious to do so, I am disappointed I cannot see you again before leaving. There simply wasn't enough time."

"There is still so much I want to ask you. I thought often about your reunion with Pietra and her American guardians. I pray all went well for you. Please tell me we can catch up sometime soon. Promise me, Marta."

"Of course, sweetheart. I have thought at great length about what I am about to say to you. I have concluded I will not likely return to America any time soon. Perhaps our best opportunity to be together again will be if, and when you return to Europe. I am not pressuring you Manuel; I am simply stating a fact we should both consider. I will write you soon, I promise you."

"Thank you, my love. I will find a way to be with you again soon. I am at your beck and call, as always. I love you my darling."

*****

The five-day journey was a welcome respite, particularly since precious few of those on board had any awareness Marta was somewhere among them. Marta was travelling incognito, using the quiet time to recharge her energies that had been sapped by her American adventure. The extensive passenger list included mostly first-class travelers of significant means, who were also returning home to reunite with family and friends.

The vast majority was extremely well dressed throughout the daylight hours, not formally but always fashionably. It served to allow

Marta to go largely unnoticed, with the exception being the part of the evening when more formal wear had become the norm. Those were always her moments to shine.

The first evening when Marta approached her pre-assigned table, it was shared with five fellow passengers. She was stunning to be sure and caught the eye of everyone in view of her. Once everyone was seated and cocktails had arrived, the guests took turns to briefly introduce themselves.

"A pleasant good evening everyone. I am Kurt Wagner. This is my dear wife Amelia and our son Konrad. We are heading to our home in Munich and are looking forward to getting to know more about you as we enjoy our dinners together."

The gentleman on Kurt's left spoke up as well and graciously introduced himself as Martin Hylton and his mother Estelle. "Mother and I have been sharing the festive season with my sister and her family in the suburbs of southern Connecticut. We enjoyed a wonderful family reunion; I am pleased to say."

"Well that just leaves me. My name is Marta and I reside in Berlin, in Kreuzberg to be precise. I was visiting my niece who is living just outside of New York City. I have been very close to her since she was born and missed her terribly since she moved to America four years ago and was very pleased to be reacquainted with her again."

Marta purposely did not offer her surname, and no one asked. It was better this way, she thought.

The buffet offered a very fine array of cuisine, delighting every discerning palate. True to the reputation of Cunard's *Queen Mary*, the buffet tables featured an outstanding variety of popular dishes for their most distinguished European clientele.

As the dishes were cleared and a round of brandy and cognacs was offered, numerous one on one casual conversations began at many of the tables, creating a general and subdued muffle of indistinctive chatter. Martin Hylton, who was seated beside Marta, was the first to engage her in some social and inquisitive banter. "I travel overseas quite often on business, Miss…? I'm so sorry I didn't catch your last name."

"Oh, please just call me Marta. There is no need for such formalities, Martin."

"Very well then, Marta. If I may be so bold as to say, it is not often I see such a beautiful woman as you travelling alone, especially on such a long transatlantic journey. Is there a Mister…"

Marta quickly interjected a second time. "Oh yes. My husband and our son are awaiting my return as we speak."

Martin's mother, likely approaching her seventies, was less inclined to oblige Marta's apparent evasiveness. "Martin's wife passed away almost two years ago, and he has two wonderful children to care for without her." She tried to speak softly but as with many elderly people her whisper still carried across the dining table.

"Between you and me dear, he's always looking for a suitable mother for the children. Especially one as lovely as you."

"Please excuse my mother, Marta. She often says what is on her mind, no matter what people may think." He looked scornfully at his mother for her frequent intrusive comments.

"Well Mrs. Hylton, I'm sorry to disappoint you, but I certainly would not be the appropriate candidate. Regrettably, as much as I try, motherhood is not my forte."

"So, what is it that you do, my dear lady? Everyone has a passion for something. Don't you agree?"

"Yes, I do agree. I suppose you could say I am a devotee of music and the arts."

"I knew it! I'll wager you are a singer, with a voice like an angel. Am I close?"

"I am a musician. And you were correct, it is my passion."

It was only the first night on board, and already Marta had become evasive, as if ashamed of having soiled her pristine reputation. This was not who she was, nor ever strove to be. Shortly after the meal was concluded it was time to put an end to this line of questioning. Without unnecessary delay, she rose from her chair.

"It was such a pleasure to meet all of you, but I really must excuse myself. I think I shall enjoy some fresh cool air before we get to the open sea. My very best to all of you."

"Good evening to you, my dear. Sleep well." Although perhaps too inquisitive for Marta, nevertheless Mrs. Hylton seemed such a lovely and amiable person.

*****

With the dawning of a new day, the passengers gathered in various groups gambling, drinking, and eating. While at sea, the winter winds were bitterly cold keeping everyone inside the protective and beautifully decorated confines of the marvelous vessel. Marta spent most of her day reading in the comfortably appointed lounge, keeping to herself mostly as she savored her time near the welcoming fireplace. Since sharing the hearth with Pietra and family it was a habit she could certainly learn to embrace more often.

Following a luxurious afternoon nap, she awoke refreshed and set out her eveningwear for the upcoming formal dinner. Her table was scheduled for the later seating and on this night would feature the company of the captain, who typically shared the dining experience with a different table of VIP guests each night at sea.

An hour or so later, when Marta had finished impeccably applying the finishing touches to her hair and makeup, she entered the dining area. She strode effortlessly and majestically across the expanse of the luxurious room. Her very presence further enhanced the elegantly styled décor. Much like the night before, conversations became profoundly muted, as her loveliness and distinctive presence no doubt captured everyone's undivided attention. Even the captain was comfortably seated at the head of the table, further highlighting the conspicuous patrons already present. As Marta drew closer, Captain Irving rose to personally welcome her, followed immediately by Mr. Wagner and Martin Hylton.

"Welcome to the Queen Mary, Madame von Brauchitsch. It is my honor to finally meet you. I am Captain Irving. This is an evening I have eagerly anticipated since I learned you were coming aboard."

"You are too kind, Captain. It is I who am so honored. Please, just call me Marta."

"That's very kind of you Marta. I imagine you are all acquainted by now?" as he scanned the table.

Martin and Kurt remained standing and Martin was the first to interject. "May I compliment you on how truly lovely you are this evening, Marta."

"A sight to behold to be sure, Marta! It's wonderful to share your table with you once again." responded Kurt. None of the gentlemen sat until Marta was comfortably guided to her seat by the attending headwaiter.

"*My table*? Good heavens, Kurt. As I recall this is *our* table, is it not? However, your flattery and thoughtful gesture are most appreciated."

Captain Irving was a stately man of more than six feet in height with slim proportions. Clean-shaven, he was most dashing in his dark-blue uniform and he had a very charismatic manner that suited his station. He was not the least bit pretentious, but he frequently allowed his focus to return to Marta, whether consciously or subconsciously. Throughout the meal, conversation flowed freely between them while the others in the party for the most part, simply listened and enjoyed being entertained by the two obvious celebrities.

After another sumptuous meal and a round of compliments to the chef and staff, Captain Irving rose to leave the table, but before doing so he commented, "Along with most of the civilized world, I enjoyed your stellar performance in New York on Christmas Day. It was nothing short of electrifying, Marta. I shall remember it always and cherish the memory of your company this evening even more because of it." He took her hand in his and respectfully kissed it softly.

Then he turned to the others. "It was a rare pleasure to meet all of you. I trust you will enjoy the rest of your journey with us. If there is anything my staff can do for you, please do not hesitate to ask. I bid you all a wonderful evening."

The captain had barely left the table when Martin and Estelle resumed their brief interrogation of the evening prior, much as Marta had expected now that Captain Irving had inadvertently let the cat out of the bag.

"We knew there was something much more to you than you let on! We didn't realize the extent of your celebrity until now. Why did you not tell us, Marta? You must be proud of your accomplishments. Are they not something to be shared?"

"Certainly, I am very proud of my accomplishments Estelle, but truthfully sometimes I wish I could be anonymous, particularly during my travels. I did not mean to offend, I assure you."

"None taken, Marta," Martin offered. "We apologize if we made you feel uncomfortable."

"Not at all. I thank you for your understanding."

*****

It took only till mid-afternoon the following day for Marta to note something had changed. While once again enjoying her quiet seclusion by the glowing hearth as had become her habit on board, she became perturbed by what appeared to be secretive or sensitive conversations taking place in her general whereabouts. Her ridiculous suspicions that she was the topic of many of these discussions, she thought to be a sign of her increasing paranoia she knew she had to curtail.

Nevertheless, she couldn't but pay closer attention to the body language of many of the passengers in the lounge, and noted they averted their eyes from her general direction, as if to confirm she was indeed a topic of discussion. Marta found this to be quite disturbing. Was it simply her celebrity status that had fascinated them, or was it something far more sinister?

Despite shifting her focus back to her book, she found herself becoming even more troubled by these strange goings on. It was pointless to continue staring any longer at the damned book. Time to change the setting and find something decadent to eat. Hopefully that would settle her mind as well as her growing appetite.

Gathering up her bag, she smoothly glided past the gawking awkwardness of those around her, as they tried to back away ever so slightly from her path of exit. She purposely made direct eye contact with a few of them, reflecting her genuine confident self-assuredness. It was her way of intimidating the meek and mindless. Some were so sheepish it was laughable.

The feelings were similar at the buffet table. Everyone in line seemed completely normal but within seconds of only a few recognizing her, their idle conversations gave way to more silence and awkwardness. It appeared to wash over them, not because she was so well known by them, but simply because silence begets silence. It was infectious. It was obvious to Marta that her once understanding and compassionate dinner companions had drawn their own conclusions about her Boston tryst and had thoughtlessly spread the pandemic of negative opinion.

She passed the balance of her day pondering an appropriate course of action for the dinner table that evening. This was no time to be a shrinking violet. It was not her style.

That night as everyone reassembled, Marta entered the room much as before, looking as beautiful as ever, but on this occasion even more so; with a stunning strapless gown of midnight-blue satin highlighting her beautiful blue eyes. Her elegant bare shoulders and plummeting neckline exposed her flawless cleavage, for more than one table to admire. As her hips swayed gently from side to side, the side slash was open to her silken thigh, no doubt being burned indelibly into the lascivious minds of both the women and the men, who both envied and delighted in her mesmerizing beauty.

Without anything more than a sultry batting of her deep-blue eyes to her table companions, she bent over purposely to showcase her more than ample breasts when the attendant offered her a chair, into which she gracefully placed her shapely bottom. But for the few dropped utensils that dinged off the hardwood floors, and one well-timed, shattered goblet, the silence was demonstrable.

It was Marta's inimitable way of indicating to anyone who may have harbored any disparaging thoughts about her, that she was unflappable. In her opinion if such was the case, anyone feeling those disapproving sentiments could simply kiss her gorgeous ass.

Compared to her personal moment of vindication at dinner that night, the rest of Marta's journey home was uneventful…thankfully. She had effectively reaffirmed, to herself more than anyone else, that she was not a woman to trifle with, now or ever!

CHAPTER TWENTY-TWO

Upon Marta's safe return home, Manny and Frau Lena immediately embraced her. The relevance of the bothersome opinions of irrelevant strangers had already melted into oblivion, precisely where they belonged. Manny now sixteen years old, did not attempt to conceal his delight over seeing his mother again. It had been several months since they last saw one another, an inordinate length of time.

"Mother, I am so relieved you are finally home." He reached out to his mother and was immediately wrapped in her outstretched arms. "You must be tired after such a long journey, but I am so happy you have returned safely. Here, let me take your things."

"It's wonderful to see you again, sweetheart. I missed you more than I could bear. I love you so very much my son."

They both walked arm in arm to the parlor while Frau Lena pre-pared a light meal and pastries she'd purchased just for the occasion. It was approaching 10:30 at night. It was gratifying to be home at last and to enjoy the next few days together with her son. Within moments together Marta reassumed her role as his love-struck mother.

Her intent was to dedicate as much time as possible to Manny for the few days she would be home. Most of her newfound obsession with him was to overcome her profound feelings of guilt at having stepped back so far from his everyday life. It was rare for him to openly complain about it, but she could still feel his underlying pain.

"Seeing you every month or so for only a few hours at a time, has been an adjustment I struggled with initially. Frau Lena and I have become much closer over time though. She does her best and I've come to care about her deeply…but she will never be my mother."

"I'm so thankful you are both getting along well together. It was a decision I had to make for reasons I hope you will come to understand. Given time, at some point you might find it in your heart to forgive me. I could not have had a finer son, but I just wasn't built for motherhood. None of my shortcomings ever subdued my love for you. You must always know that Manny. How are you managing to cope with my absence now?"

"The simple truth is that I missed you more than I could bear. After speaking with Father as often as we could, together we decided the best course of action was to keep myself busy in constructive ways. So, I focused myself on school and my effort was reflected in my grades. Who would have ever thought it possible?" he added sarcastically.

"Your father and I always knew it, Manny. You just needed a little more incentive. It appears you found it. We are so proud of how well you responded."

Manny continued. "I also became more dedicated to my time in the Hitler Youth program. I've made several new friends there and we have come to really enjoy it. It keeps me physically fit and focused on my purpose."

"Good for you, son! Your grandfather informs me your accomplishments there will give you a decisive edge on where you want to eventually serve in the military." The grandfather clock began to chime signaling it was now midnight. "My, my! It's already past midnight for heaven's sake! Forgive me son, may we continue this in the morning? I am becoming extremely weary and really need my beauty sleep, my darling."

*****

Enjoying a late breakfast, the two chatted about Manny's preoccupations, avoiding Marta's almost exclusively. Throughout Manny's childhood Marta habitually shifted the focus of their conversation back to those topics most relevant to her. She could not change the wrongdoings of the past, but she wanted desperately to make the necessary adjustments to stop them from happening again.

She tried leading the flow of discussion back to Manny whenever possible. He had opinions she wanted to hear about, which would have been most difficult if she continued to dominate the flow of their conversation. It was a much more difficult task than she imagined. "I must say you are looking very well. You are gifted to become a natural leader with a sharp mind and a strong, dominant personality Manny. Keep doing what you enjoy, and you will see doors of opportunity open for you."

Very premeditatedly, Marta took a sip of her coffee and poured another fresh cup, hoping desperately the brief interlude would dismantle his apparent defenses. Although it was becoming awkward at this point, she was intent upon feeding him a variety of leading questions hoping sooner or later he would take her bait and open up to her. It was much more difficult than she had imagined. "You look strong as an ox and appear to be almost as tall as your father. I imagine you have met a young lady by now who has caught your eye? You must be the envy of many beauties at school."

Finally, he started to respond "Oh, I do alright. I have no reluctance about meeting girls. I rather enjoy their company. There are several I am fond of, but right now Father tells me those relationships will come to pass naturally. A career in the military will take effort and focus. I tend to agree with him. Thanks to Grandfather I'm already taking introductory flight instruction with a very select few of the Hitler Youth. With Grandfather's influence he saw to it that I was noticed as being among the elite of the class. It's my goal to join the Luftwaffe one day. You know it's all I ever really wanted."

"I do remember. I just worry that we are living in such dangerous times. I have already lost your grandfather and your father to the military. I pray I won't lose you in the same way. The cries for war are growing stronger and louder with every passing month. I fear we will all pay dearly for whatever it is the Fuhrer is seeking."

Manny interjected trying to calm her concerns. "There's nothing to fear Mother. The German Wehrmacht has become the greatest military the world has ever assembled. I am confident that my dedication and training will earn me a command position. If anything should happen to me, at least I will know I did everything I could to build a stronger Germany. I am willing to do my part, Mother. I hope you can respect that about me."

"I do very much Manny, but there is more to life than world domination. Whose purpose does it really serve? Certainly not the youth of the Fatherland. Oh! Speaking of the Fuhrer, I forgot to tell you I personally met him and Minister Goebbels after one of my concerts a few months ago. They met me backstage to acknowledge my cultural contribution to the German people."

"That's incredible, Mother! What did you think of him after meeting him personally? I am anxious to know."

Old habits die hard, and true to form Marta slipped back into directing the dialogue. At least it was no longer a one-sided conversation. "He was charming, charismatic, and exuded his power of determination and control. He is a very persuasive man, no doubt about it. In retrospect I can only wonder now if Europe, or even global domination is his intended objective, how many lives will it take to achieve it?

Aunt Anna and I have witnessed first-hand, displays of discrimination and persecution on the streets of Berlin and most recently its impact within the cultural world. I have spoken up against it time and again, but I appear powerless to make a difference. The stress and frustration I carry inside of me is difficult to abide."

As if in defense of Hitler's actions Manny stated, "In order to achieve great things, people must make great sacrifices."

"… But not at the expense of someone else's sacrifice. You appear to have all the answers, Manny. You sound more like your father than my son. You do remember that Aunt Anna and her family are Jews. Have you given that serious consideration? I cannot help but wonder."

Manny paused to reflect and could only express uncertain dismay. No answers were forthcoming to that question.

Marta wisely surmised it was better to change the subject for fear of starting an argument with her idealistic young son. This was not an enjoyable way to pass time with him as she had initially envisioned. She was finding it extremely difficult building bridges with her son that had not previously existed. Nevertheless, she pressed on. "So, have you seen your father recently? I know he has been fully preoccupied with his work. I understand his passion for what he does, but he continually justifies it by accusing me of having made the same commitment to my career. It's difficult to argue his point. I think we have both accepted the fact that nothing we do is likely to change our common circumstances."

"He used to call me once or twice a week but not as frequently lately. When we are together for dinner all we speak of are military things. I find it interesting, though. The same thing happens when Grandfather joins us. The military is all they know," Manny confessed.

"I sent a wire from America to advise him of my scheduled return. He has not seen fit to even respond. We are clearly having our problems. I don't want you in the middle of it, but if you could please leave a message for him on my behalf, I am certain he would take your call before any of mine. Can you please do that for me, Manny, and tell him it is rather important we speak?"

"Of course, Mother, but even for me, he may take days to respond, and it's not as if I call him very often. We've become nothing more than strangers who happen to share the same blood."

"That's not good to hear but perhaps that's just a sign of the times in which we live. Please at least try for me and let me know."

"Of course, Mother. Try not to worry. Somehow things always work out, even if not always for the best in the short term."

Marta was struck by her son's newly developed maturity. He had enormous potential to realize amazing achievements. She was immensely proud of him but not necessarily of who he was becoming. Her greatest fear was the cumulative effect of Nazi propaganda that had become evident in his deeply ingrained mental conditioning. It was to be expected but not necessarily welcomed.

By the late 1930's more than ninety percent of German boys had been conscripted into the Hitler Youth Brigade, numbering in the tens of millions. It was tantamount to the indoctrination of teenaged children during the most impressionable time of their lives. Marta knew it was futile to try to interfere with the influence of the movement upon Manny. Parents of adolescent male children no longer had the right to choose how to raise their own young sons. That was now mandated by the state.

In the weeks and months that followed, when Klaus finally returned Marta's persistent calls, she was unavailable, either at rehearsal for local concerts or touring throughout Europe. It was frustrating to be sure, but his general non-responsiveness only confirmed he had seen or heard something about her infidelity. They never properly addressed it again and as a result they continued to inevitably grow further apart.

Strangely, the next time they would communicate it would be a matter of more dire consequence than their marriage issues.

*****

On the streets of Berlin rioting escalated substantially, and the targets of abuse were not only Jews personally, but for the first time, their places of worship. These holy landmarks of history now became subjected to defacing, vandalism, and general destruction. Police and fire departments were directed by Goebbels himself to restrain from any interference, unless Aryan property was endangered. The ensuing attacks were not random ones of civilian disorder; rather they were primarily incited by Storm Troopers, who zealously smashed and burned down Jewish homes, businesses, and for the first time, synagogues.

On the evening of November 9th, 1938, the Neue Synagogue became a primary target for desecration and intended destruction. It would seem to have been an obvious symbol, the sacrilege of which would penetrate deep into the remaining spirit and faith of the Jewish people. Riotous crowds of frenzied hooligans started to gather on the sidewalks and steps outside the magnificent edifice, as if being drawn by an impulsive call to chaos, yet still hesitating to overcome their last shred of decency to commit this insulting travesty.

As Goebbels had instructed, the police and fire departments reluctantly obeyed the order to stand down, although many could be seen farther down Oranienburger Strasse, no doubt conflicted between their apparent moral anxiousness to assist, but to also obey their commanding officer's orders to hold position.

Sigmund was among those inside the main prayer hall that evening, along with several elders of the congregation about to conclude a vestry meeting on the matter of Jewish tolerance, of all things. They had no awareness of the impending chaos that was about to befall them until the distinctive sound of shattering plate glass upset the peace and calm of the synagogue's reverent silence.

In that horrifying instant, an instinctive visceral fear closed in upon them. It signified the reality that this sanctified place of holy worship was no longer outside the boundaries of violent persecution.

Sigmund sensed and shared their understandable fear and shouted authoritatively to assume immediate control. "Listen to me everyone, please! Do not panic! Alfred and Martin, please investigate the broken glass but for your own safety, you must stay together. Report back to us on the situation as quickly as you can. I remind you, keep the doors locked and *do not leave the building*. We should be safe if we stay inside. Do you understand?"

To further investigate the circumstances, a few of the sixteen or so congregation members still inside the hall rushed to the windows overlooking the street below only to witness the commotion outside, replete with loud chanting and burning torches being waved threateningly. It appeared the synagogue itself was the object of the rioters' vitriol.

Sigmund encouraged his friends, some of them senior advisors and benefactors of the synagogue, to remain calm inside the protection it afforded them.

As they huddled together in abject fear, more breaking glass could be heard from the annex and in the following minutes, the familiar smell of smoke now became perceptible. The two who had been sent to investigate came back, choking on the smoke from the scene of destruction to report there were two vandals inside and some chairs and wooden furnishings had been set ablaze by the violators.

At this point there was no need for a report to the elders as the smoke announced itself when it began to billow into the main hall, engulfing them from the rear annex. It was now beginning to overcome the elders, most of whom were now coughing and gasping for air. Despite Sigmund's previous urging not to do so, instincts prevailed, and the frail group heeded his instructions to the contrary and apprehensively began to exit the once-protective confines of the synagogue.

"We have no alternative. We must leave. Stay very close to the wall of the building as best you can and maintain your balance. Do not try to run if you are unable to do so. You must stay on your feet and keep moving forward. Just walk carefully at a safe pace until you reach the far side of the building away from the trouble outside. I will stay beside you the entire way, I promise you. I will not leave you alone. We will get through this together. Here we go!"

When they pushed the heavy door open, the cool, fresh air temporarily rejuvenated them as they wiped their tearful eyes, which had been seared from the smoke they left behind. Half blindly they attempted to get their bearings and tried desperately to hear Sigmund's instructions to move farther away from the general commotion. They were understandably frightened and confused as they looked pleadingly to Sigmund for his protection and direction. They were frozen by fear and totally unable to think for themselves.

In response to their appearance outside, there was a sudden hail of rocks and glass bottles hurled at the cowering elders. Sigmund covered the old men as protectively as he was able, absorbing the painful impact of thrown projectiles as he caringly ushered them across the front of the synagogue to find safe haven.

For several elders, their pace was agonizingly slow and hampered by their advanced arthritis and lack of mobility. Two of them were struck by rocks and staggered by the attack but managed with Sigmund's help to reach the supporting embrace of some compassionate onlookers.

Sigmund quickly returned to the fray to assist a man who had fallen. The assault continued as more rocks were indiscriminately thrown in their direction. Within a few interminably long seconds one of the rocks struck a direct blow to the side of Sigmund's head, dropping him immediately to the ground. A stream of blood quickly formed a pool of dark red reflecting the light of the moon, a startling omen his injury was more than superficial.

At that instant, and perhaps fueled by the sight of these desperate and overwhelmed elders, a singular police officer became witness to the quickly amassing crowd. Without hesitation, and with no apparent thought for his own personal safety, he disobeyed his orders to stand down and immediately rushed to the top of the stairs of the synagogue to brandish his handgun. He menacingly fired a round into the cold night air, threatening to die before he would allow the infliction of any destruction of this sacred place of worship.

Officer Otto Bellgardt's historic gesture of bravery and honor in protecting this historic landmark and the very lives of those whom it served, briefly delayed the imminent assault upon this Jewish institution and the subsequent assault of human dignity about to unfold. As a direct result of Officer Bellgardt's noble intervention, the fire brigade and supporting police seized the moment by following the police officer's defiant lead and were able to break through the crowd to minimize irreparable damage to the synagogue.

It would serve as evidence that a single voice of dissent, from one who is unafraid to be heard, can change the negative tide of history. There was no doubt the synagogue would have been destroyed without his courageous intervention.

His bold intercession in opposition to his direct orders to the contrary, while unpunished by his superior officers, would never receive the compassionate distinction for bravery to which Officer Bellgardt was so valiantly entitled.

In the ensuing maelstrom, when the barrage of glass bottles and rocks was finally controlled, Sigmund continued to lie face down and motionless on the concrete ground. The yelling and shouting of obscenities gradually diminished into wailing, and tearful cries of pain and anguish. Officers circled the offenders, preventing them further access, and safely enabled more men of the fire brigade to gain access to smother the growing flames. Emergency medical help immediately tended to the injured, who except for one, were administered treatment for relatively minor injuries.

Sigmund was barely responsive and was expeditiously placed on a stretcher once the bleeding was contained. Without regaining consciousness, he was carried down the steps to be secured inside the waiting ambulance. The wailing sirens served notice to the crowd to clear a pathway, as he was rushed to the very hospital in which he served his community for over forty years.

Emergency staff recognized Sigmund immediately, yet true to their duties they tended to him with undeterred composure and professionalism, showing no visible indications of emotion or panic. There was no time for human distractions at a time such as this. The man on the gurney was Sigmund, after all, the man who had trained and mentored most of the hospital staff; the man who had lectured them at the university and had inspired so many of them to become who they were today.

It would be determined that blunt-force trauma had shattered the back of Sigmund's skull, impacting the brain with bone fragments caused by either the impact of the thrown projectile, the impact of him falling on the concrete, or most likely a combination of both. It was unlikely he even felt the severity of either trauma.

In the ensuing five and a half hours of surgery, the bleeding was eventually controlled, and bone fragments were removed, but only after significant blood loss. He was stabilized and remained alive. Although it was too soon to know for certain, the chances of recovery appeared to be highly unlikely.

Dr. David Schleschen as the chief of surgery, personally attended to Sigmund's care. They had remained close personal friends and colleagues since shortly after Sigmund and Marissa became sweethearts. For the first time since attending to his professional obligations that evening, David retreated to his office in solitude and wept uncontrollably.

He had performed thousands of surgical procedures over his long and prolific medical career but knew this was a wound from which neither he nor Sigmund would ever fully recover. He composed himself as best he could under the circumstances. His thoughts were now of Marissa and the family, who were waiting anxiously outside his office door.

"My dear Marissa…Jacob…. ladies. I regret to say…that, that our dear Sigmund has sus…has sustained irreversible injuries…The damage and blood loss are extensive. I am so terribly sorry, for all of you." David paused briefly trying to choke back his emotions.

He drew a deep breath and continued, "He remains alive but, non-responsive. We are doing all we can so he may rest comfortably." David wiped his profusely sweating forehead with a paper tissue to look directly into Marissa's disbelieving eyes. She remained speech-less. "True to his character, there is no doubt he saved many lives by his actions last night. I am so very sorry for your loss, Marissa."

Marissa, Anna and Emilie were prepared for the worst but upon hearing David's words and witnessing his emotional reaction, Marissa was completely overwhelmed with grief and collapsed in David's arms. In anticipation of her understandable broken-heartedness, David held her tightly and eased her into a chair. An orderly was summoned to elevate her feet and provide her with water.

The room was vacant except for the family, which at this point included Marta and Gertrude. Not a word was spoken among them. It was a suspended time of deep anguish as they gave in to the confir-mation of Sigmund's imminent passing. The sobbing and remorseful overflow of emotions evoked deeper compassion from David than he could possibly bear. They embraced each other with heaving chests as the pent-up fears of the worst of possibilities had finally come to pass.

Sigmund had been the steady helmsman, the proverbial patriarch of the family long before his late father's passing. Who would take up the cause and steady the reins now? The family bond had always been unbreakable because of Sigmund's irrepressible devotion and reliable counsel. For this loving family that night, coherent thoughts were only fleeting images with dizzying flashes, alternating between con-fused and powerless solutions. The family's minds and consciousness were irretrievably locked in helplessness and abject shock.

*****

Before leaving the hospital that morning, the family was permitted to see their father. Marissa was placed in a wheelchair for her own safety and escorted through the various medical attendants and administrative staff who were aware of the circumstances, as many were well acquainted with members of Dr. Landesburg's family.

They were downcast, and had no awareness of the profound sadness and intense sympathy felt by the dozens of staff and friends so deeply affected by this tragic event. Out of respect, there were no words offered by staff that could not be expressed later at a more appropriate time.

An attendant held the door open as the grieving entourage entered the room. Their pace became more hesitant, and slowly eased to a stop at Sigmund's bedside. Supportively, the girls stood behind Marissa as she reached out to her dying hero, the love of her life.

Marissa took his right hand into her own, caressing and softly kissing him with what little control she had left and finally succumbed to cry out loudly and quite uncontrollably. "What have they done to you, my dear sweet Siggy? This cannot be! I am the one who is supposed to go, not you! Please don't leave us!"

Anna placed her hand on Marissa's while Emilie rested hers lovingly on her mother's trembling shoulder in compassionate support of her painful ordeal. Sobbing and sniffling permeated the room, affecting even the pretense of emotional stability of the orderlies. The only sound breaking the tearful expressions of pain and sorrow was the intermittent paging for doctors to respond elsewhere throughout the hospital. It was a melancholy place in time.

The deepest grief cannot be softened by words, and no story or remembrance can extinguish such profoundly anguishing pain.

They returned home together shortly thereafter. The family had been praying for a miracle since the first news of Sigmund being taken by ambulance services directly to emergency. Although exhausted, no one was able to sleep apart from Marissa, for whom David had prescribed sedatives. Her despondence was to be expected but remained of concern to David, as her overall health had become fragile at best. It had long been suspected she would one day be the first to pass. Sigmund's physical well-being and healthy vitality never gave the family cause to prepare for this sudden loss.

In the days following, the family drew strength from the close ties that bound them through good times and bad. David and his advisory team explored every available avenue of hope, but each path taken served only to reaffirm the initial prognosis.

Sigmund had been a compassionate, loving, and much-respected pillar of strength within the community and within the medical profession. The family was also intelligent and pragmatic in their eventual acceptance of facts. Delaying their reconciliation to this dreadful and senseless loss only perpetuated the agony of false hope.

They continued to keep careful vigil on Sigmund's monitoring by the hospital attendants, who had already done everything that could be done to sustain the life of their fallen hero. On the morning of November 15th, just six days from that fateful night, Sigmund passed peacefully with his loving family at his bedside. As his spirit faded from this world, so too did Marissa's.

Since Sigmund's fatal injury she had constantly clutched the love letter he'd sent her from New York almost eleven years prior, re-reading each word over and over, remembering the depth of their constant mutual adoration. This once-vibrant beauty delighted in the happiness and joy of being Sigmund's adoring focus of attention. There was always a constant and palpable interdependence between them, predestined from the moment of their first encounter.

Her quick wit and intelligent repartee gave unequivocal depth to the enduring extent of their love and eternal mutual support. In a quiet moment together, Marissa had once confided to Anna and Jacob that she and Sigmund seemed to draw their very breath from one another. They were the essence of each other's existence. One pulse...one purpose.

As surely as this almost mystical bond sustained them, in ways few would ever understand or imagine, Sigmund's passing took with him her very spirit and purpose for living. A month to the day after his death, Marissa slipped from the bonds of this earth to be with him. Records would show there was not a specific physiological cause of death. Perhaps it was her inability to persevere and get past her despondent sadness and despair. It was as if she had succumbed to the ravages of a broken heart.

Her loss was devastating to the family but had not been totally unexpected. Medications, though well intended, served only to prolong her agony over Sigmund's passing. Since his death, her life force had been visibly dissolving with every remaining breath she took. It was better this way. It was what she wanted.

Sigmund's diplomatic papers were later discovered among his personal effects and were returned to the family; so much for the protection he and his family had been afforded by his diplomatic status. What protection did his privileged status provide against a stray rock thrown from an angry crowd? This was the collateral damage of war...senseless and wasteful.

CHAPTER TWENTY-THREE

♂

THE PAINFUL DEPTH OF LOSS EXPERIENCED BY THOSE who have survived the insanity of ruthless persecution, or that of war, cannot be imagined by those who have not. If anything, once the initial grief eventually becomes reconciled, it surely must serve as a stark reminder of the fragility of the human condition. For the sake of order, and for the remaining family so cruelly afflicted, unwavering courage steadies the way for those left behind. For many it requires a hero to suddenly appear to assume the mantle of responsibility for those of a more dependent posture. For the Landesburg family, Anna would prove to be such a person.

Other than a few initial letters shortly after Pietra's escape to America, the prelude to war had severely restricted civilian communications with the outside world. The Fascist Nazi regime closely monitored and controlled foreign access to the knowledge of the atrocities and inhumanity within its borders, perhaps with the misguided belief the world was too naïve to fully grasp the wisdom of Hitler's dedication to serving the Master Race.

From the moment of Sigmund's unanticipated passing, and even more so from Marissa's fragile and not unexpected demise, Anna fully understood her first and most arduous undertaking; to sensitively communicate the sorrowful news of Pietra's grandparents' passing to her very unsuspecting and innocent child. This devastating news was not a matter to address through her Aunt Grace.

Passage to America for a Jew was an absolute impossibility at this time. Successfully posting a letter overseas was almost as difficult a task, resulting in confiscation, or worse, attracting attention and having the address of the sender traced, followed thereafter by arrest.

Surely General von Brauchitsch through Marta's request, could post a letter from Anna in a diplomatic pouch from which his staff could confirm the content was of a personal nature and bore no defamatory accusations against the Reich. Her confidence was bolstered by the general's promise to assist. Once Anna was assured of such co-operation, she commenced to draft the most difficult letter she would ever write.

Of all the times in Pietra's young life, this should be one event requiring close personal contact, face to face with her loved ones, lamenting the loss through common tears and the tender comforting of those who shared the same genuine and profound emotions. On the surface, writing a letter seemed so inadequate, so heartless, so agonizing. Nevertheless, Anna had no other option.

This 21st day of December 1938

My dearest Pietra,

I trust this letter finds you well, my sweetheart. As usual, too much time has passed since our last correspondence. It has been very difficult to post letters from Germany during these terrible times. Even more reason you were safely removed from this terrible circumstance.

This is the most difficult letter I will write in my lifetime. However, I cannot be less than direct in sharing the grievous news of your dear grandparents' passing. During an altercation at the synagogue, Papa was critically injured through no fault of his own. He was protecting the Elders from harm when he was struck on the head and lost consciousness. He was rushed to the Charité but never regained consciousness. Without doubt, your Papa's unselfish actions saved the lives of the Elders in his care, and his close friend Dr. David Schleschen confirms he thankfully never suffered any pain.

As you know, in the last few years Nana had become increasingly more frail. Papa's passing was more than she could possibly bear. She passed away peacefully in her sleep shortly after Papa, with the family by her side.

I am so very sorry to tell you these terrible things, but we should be grateful for the time we had with them. We will forever cherish their memory. Know we are all very proud of you and your accomplishments. The decision to send you to America was a sacrifice for all of us, but especially for you, my dear sweetheart. It was one we would decide upon again to keep you safe. The insanity in which we find ourselves here with each passing day, only serves to reaffirm the strength of our conviction.

I say this to make certain you understand that you must not return to Berlin to be with us to share our grief, under any circumstances. Your safety serves as a beacon of perpetual hope for our very uncertain future. The past is gone, and nothing we do can change it. It is imperative you remain with Aunt Grace until we are together again. I promise you that day will come.

Your loving father and I, with Dietrich, Aunt Emilie, Gertrude, and of course, Aunt Marta, send our deepest, eternal love. Stay strong my princess. We love you always.

Your loving mother.

It took Anna several hours to meticulously write and rewrite her letter, each draft considering Pietra's delicate reactions to reading such a melancholy message from her mother. Pietra had maturity far beyond her years but this dreadful news would surely test the limits of her emotional resolve.

The thoughtful and premeditated decision to place pen to paper at a time such as this is an exercise involving an intense degree of reflection and introspective review. Absorbing and modifying the thought process is not so naturally spontaneous as straightforward conversation. It is a process that can be likened to an internal conversation

with oneself. Anna's contemplations would not have taken this direction were it not for her decision to script her communication with
her dear daughter.

Only then did Anna take pause to feel the full impact of her own
loss. The crafting of her letter to Pietra was a cathartic experience.
The meticulous searching for words was painful as well as therapeutic, and caused her to search deeper within herself to feel the true
depth and magnitude of the loss of her parents. The grieving process
seeks whatever time and manner are required to find resolution,
acceptance, and reconciliation.

Finally, as satisfied as was possible, Anna delivered the letter personally to Marta. It was reviewed by the general's staff and expedited
to the German Embassy in Washington, D.C.

*****

The night raid on the Neue Synagogue, which history would
come to refer to as Kristallnacht, the "Night of Broken Glass", was a
portent of the beginning of the Nazis' "Final Solution to the Jewish
Question". There were many passive onlookers that fateful night, and
through their apparent indifference they had further enabled the
violent rioting to persist unabated. Most Germans disapproved of the
atrocities but remained too fearful to speak out against it. The Otto
Bellgardts of the world are few and far between.

In less than two years, there would be more than 14,000 synagogues across Germany and Poland that would be desecrated in
similar, violent fashion. Most of them were completely destroyed—
wiped from the earth upon which they stood. One can be assured
there were thousands upon thousands of passive spectators who did
not share the hatred. Many, no doubt, did not consider themselves
to be complicit, but chose instead to simply watch these disgusting
displays of anarchy and sacrilege. By so doing, the masses enabled the
offenders by not intervening in any way whatsoever.

To say the very least, it was painfully ironic that while many
synagogue elders quietly and persistently prayed they be granted the
ability to be more tolerant of those people whose actions continued
to oppress them, they did not pray for tolerance of themselves by

their oppressors. Humility, compassion, and forgiveness are the cornerstones of the faith that shaped their approach to life itself.

Equal rights no longer applied to Jews. Among government, police, and fire departments, up to and including non-Jewish neighbors and former friends, Jews became the common enemy, with no claim of protection under the law. Suppression of ideologies deemed to be incongruent with Nazi decree resulted in attacks on numerous places of worship, irrespective of specific faith.

As these targeted assaults became widespread, Muslim, Protestant, and even Catholic churches, braced for potential repercussions for unauthorized sermon content. Julius von Jan, a small-town pastor, spoke up against the violent oppression of the Jews to his congregation. He offered statements of fact, never intended to incite civil unrest, and yet, suffered immediate attack by a Nazi mob and was summarily taken into custody by the Gestapo. In the months and years ahead, educators and universities suffered similar maltreatment.

Amidst this religious and academic persecution becoming endemic, Jacob Friedman was lecturing at the Köllnische as he had done masterfully for almost twenty years. His offering one day was an introspective insight to his undergraduate students on the importance of maintaining and restoring the fervent belief that balance and appropriate judgment would once again be restored. He assured them their steadfast faith would become even stronger, by virtue of having eventually prevailed against those forces opposing them.

As with Pastor von Jan and numerous other priests, ministers and rabbis, there was nothing Jacob said that day that incited opposition or enflamed passions of antagonism toward Nazi ideology. Nonetheless, fifteen Nazi Gestapo officers entered the lecture hall of the university with the intent to terminate any discussion deemed to be less than consistent with proscribed standards of intellectual content. Jacob was one target among many designated for arrest.

Upon entering the lecture hall, the officer in charge commanded his armed guards to secure positions around the hall to obstruct anyone from exiting. Two of the officers escorted their commanding officer to approach Jacob at the lectern.

"What is the problem, Officer?" said Jacob. "We are in the middle of class here."

"Am I correct in assuming you are Jacob Friedman?" the officer enquired indignantly.

In disbelief that they were asking specifically for him, Jacob responded, "Yes sir, I am he."

The officer, without hesitation or explanation, bellowed, "Take this man into custody!" to the guards stationed on the stage. Whereupon two of the guards accosted Jacob and pulled him forcefully from the lectern, disgraced in full view of the entire student body.

"Under what charge am I being arrested? I am a member of faculty and I have not committed any crime!"

The presiding officer, now glaring indignantly, approached the lectern. The room fell silent. "I am Commander Manfred Groteluschen. Under supreme authority of the Fuhrer, I command those whose names I am about to call, to step forward beside your self-described faculty member," he said, as he mockingly gestured to Jacob.

The list began: "Abraham, H., Abrahm, B., Abrasha, M. Brugenheim, V., Cepora, M., Chanouk, H...." The list continued as those named rose from their seats, some in apparent shock, some still clutching their books and paperwork, still others tearfully escorted to the front of the room, "...Danil, D., David, P., Ekatarina, V., Estera, N., Evdokiia, B., Franziska, F., Gitla, V., Iosif, B."

No one resisted; no one attempted to run. No one dared to try. Additional troops were summoned to oversee the assembly of the damned, the vanquished...the innocent.

"... Ivan, H., Konstantin, K., Lodz, A., Makar, O., Marina, G., Mikhail, F., ..." and on and on it would go. Those named had slipknots fastened to their clasped hands. It was only then, there was a collective loss of emotional control among those being detained, as well as those who remained seated awaiting their names to be called. There was still no visible protest from anyone, only submissiveness and shock.

"...Nukhim, S., Ol-ga, H., Petr, U., Seigfried, R., Trofim, T., Vogen, P..." It became agonizing, but the ordeal continued, until sixty-five names had been read aloud.

The commander smiled maliciously while announcing to the remaining students seated about the room, "Those you see before you are being detained for treasonous crimes and misdemeanors against the state. Be thankful you are not among them. I wish you all a pleasant day, hmm?" His sarcasm was laced with malice.

Unknown to those in the lecture hall was that numerous other assemblies throughout the university were also raided that ill-fated day, with numerous arrests and similar contagious passivity.

*****

Anna returned home that afternoon with no awareness of the events at the Köllnische. Jacob was always fastidious to a fault, arriving predictably within the same hour of each day. As dinner was served, however her worry about Jacob started to peak as he had yet to arrive.

Within the hour, the ringing telephone broke the mounting tension and Anna eagerly took hold of the receiver, not waiting for a word as she exclaimed with relief, "Jacob! Where have you been? ... Hello, Jacob?"

The administrator, acting on behalf of the head of faculty who had also been taken into custody, was unnerved and groped for his words. "Hello Mrs. Friedman, this is Conrad Belken at the university."

"Hello Mr. Belken, is everything alright?" She corrected herself realizing something was clearly amiss. "Is Mr. Friedman alright?"

"That is the reason for my call, madame. I trust he remains well, however, the university was raided this afternoon, without prior notice or justification. Many of the students and faculty were forcibly removed from the premises by Nazi troops."

Anna was speechless and tried to assure Mr. Belken, and more so herself, there must be some mistake.

"I think perhaps not, madame. More than three hundred people were bound and escorted by armed security to vans brought onto the campus. Unfortunately, Mr. Friedman was one of them. It was a very well-orchestrated effort by the Gestapo, I am afraid to say."

"Do you know where they were taken, or even why they were taken?"

"No madame, we do not, though I can assure you the university is making immediate enquiries. I promise to communicate with you the moment we obtain new information. I very much regret that is all I can tell you at this moment, and I personally apologize to you, but I have more such unpleasant calls to make this evening. I pray all will be sorted out soon. I wish you well, Mrs. Friedman."

Still reeling from the loss of her parents, Anna was beside herself with concern. Naturally, her first call was to Marta.

*****

Choking back tears, Anna did her best to remain coherent to explain the circumstances in which she found herself.

Unhesitatingly Marta offered to accompany Anna. This was now her priority as well.

Upon Marta's arrival, the very sight of her elicited another flood of tears from Anna. As Anna held Marta closely, in hushed tones only Marta could hear, she whispered in her ear, "I cannot endure much more of this, Marta! Whatever is happening to my family?"

The maid prepared tea as the two friends reconnected as closely as ever. They had remained close throughout their adulthood, but the gravity of the tragedy Anna's family had suffered established new depths of their genuine compassion for one another.

This was just the first night without Jacob, and neither Anna nor Marta were optimistic the university would have any realistic information in the next few days. The friends agreed they had to be proactive to have any hope of reducing the risk of harm to Jacob. Their imaginations could only conceive the worst of possibilities.

"Promise me, Marta, not one word of this must be said to Pietra. My only salvation is that she is safely away from here, and we must keep it that way, for now. There is no point at all in her returning to Germany. I am no longer certain she would listen to me but returning to Berlin would only endanger her and serve no positive purpose in our efforts to have Jacob released."

"I absolutely understand, Anna. I have already spoken to Klaus and his father. If anyone can locate Jacob, they will be able to do so. But Klaus was quick to emphasize we must move swiftly if we are to right this dreadful wrong."

"I am so frightened for him, Marta. He's a very gentle man as you know, but he has very strong opinions too. Opinions I might add, his students are all too familiar with. I pray he has the common sense to keep quiet and not attract too much attention to himself. He will defend his students to his last breath. That is what frightens me the most."

"He is an intelligent man, Anna. He will do what he must. We will find him within a few days, I am certain."

*****

The general had not been aware of Jacob's arrest when the Köllnische was raided. He knew it wasn't on account of his own oversight, as his responsibilities were already burdensome. Rather it had fallen to his administrative staff, who should have immediately identified Jacob's connection to the Landesburg family. For this egregious error, the general was furious.

"Do you mean to tell me the purge of our most prestigious universities throughout Berlin did not trigger the slightest possibility that some of our most important diplomats might have family members in attendance? What do we pay you people for, you sons of bitches?"

"General, I personally investigated the oversight. If I may explain?" The general stood before his personal assistant for diplomatic affairs, arms crossed, and scowling as he looked not at him, but through him, over the rims of his eyeglasses.

"Sir, it appears Dr. Landesburg's diplomatic status was terminated shortly after his regrettable death, as is customary in such matters. The family continues to be under protective privilege, but I fear Herr Friedman was omitted in error. Although Herr Friedman's wife Anna and their children remain automatically protected by way of their bloodlines, this was not the case for him. Under a specific but different section of diplomatic status, his documentation had not yet been processed for reinstatement. It was, I very much regret to say, a matter of terrible timing."

"Timing? Timing you say! God damn it, Richard! Do you realize this man is the husband of my daughter-in-law's lifelong friend? I have a great debt of gratitude to Dr. Landesburg and to his family that simply cannot be overlooked. To add insult to injury, I am in for a shit storm of trouble with my daughter-in-law! Where was Friedman taken? Where is he now?"

"He was arrested for treason, as a proponent of antinationalist propaganda on the university campus. As such, he and several of his students were taken directly to Buchenwald."

The field marshal turned to gather himself. "Buchenwald...Is it Otto Koch that is in command there?"

"Yes, that is affirmative, General."

"...I know this man. He is a sadistic pig! His bitch wife is worse, so I am told...We have to get Friedman out of there, now!"

"I will start the necessary paperwork, sir, but may I respectfully suggest a phone call directly to Commandant Koch may be in order, to potentially expedite the matter?"

"This man is no friend of mine, Richard. I have nothing but contempt for him, as he is already aware. Nevertheless, I dare not trouble the Fuhrer with any of these affairs, at least not at this time. Get me Koch's contact information! I will make the call personally."

It was three days before SS Commandant Karl Otto Koch returned even one of several of the general's calls, each successive one becoming increasingly more frustrating and seemingly antagonistic toward the general. The delays had been intentional.

General von Brauchitsch was livid upon hearing that the very day of Jacob's arrival in Buchenwald, he and three other faculty members had been singled out as leading perpetrators, totally responsible for misguiding their young and impressionable students. As an example of their ultimate responsibility for leading and inciting ideological insurrection against the Nazi Party, all three had been hung naked, in plain view of their students and tortured by the agonizing *Strappado* method; hung by their wrists with their hands tied behind their backs, as the ultimate penalty for their alleged crimes. This was a degrading and inescapable punishment designed to inflict maximum pain and torturous agony, typically reserved for rebellious instigators among interned prisoners. It was intended to discourage any witnesses from displaying similar offenses.

The deed was done the day of the general's first call, or so it was recorded and later documented. Had Karl Koch set his personal dispute with the general aside, and heeded his first request, this tragic error may have been averted. Notwithstanding this, every individual who was incarcerated with Jacob that day, even those who never knew him, had their own tragic story to be told. Such was the nature of this Final Solution.

The general was incensed but was determined to maintain his dignity and never acknowledged his specific disdain for Koch to the Fuhrer, considering such a response to be beneath his dignity.

Other commanders could perceive him as being no better than Koch himself. There would come a time and place to even the scales of retribution. If only Marta and Anna would eventually be as forgiving in these circumstances. He felt so responsible and became uncharacteristically despondent.

Walther barely slept that night and could not reconcile his dilemma. He was accustomed to being decisive, and in total control of his military responsibilities. But this! This was the first time in his illustrious career he had crossed the invisible line that separated the military from his personal life.

As he considered his options, he remained steadfast in his conviction that, while he'd taken personal interest outside of the military when he had solicited the expertise of Sigmund, it was to better enable himself to serve his country and to fulfill his mandate as a commanding officer. Nothing he had done was in any way a conflict of interest, or a compromise of his objectivity. Of this he was self-assured.

Having absolutely no one with whom he could discuss his circumstance, Walther reflected alone, in the dark of the night, becoming more exhausted by the hour. He arose from his sleepless state as he continued to stress, and though he seldom sought refuge from such a source, retrieved a bottle of whiskey. In a matter of hours, a possible remedy came to mind.

Nothing could change the events of the past week, no matter how devastating they would always be. He knew he had to be forthright in delivering the painful news to Marta and Anna's family, irrespective of the consequences. Jacob's death was horrific enough, but there was no need to disclose in any manner his torturous and humiliating demise. It would serve no purpose other than to inflict more pain and suffering upon Jacob's loving family. Better if Jacob and his three faculty members could be remembered as martyrs, who died to save the lives of their students. Records could be sealed and left intact to reflect this fact.

Walther's concerns had to be properly prioritized to definitively protect the surviving members of the Landesburg family. This much was firmly within his control and his personal relationship with Hitler continued to be close. He was certain the Fuhrer would support whatever ultimate decisions Walther was about to offer on behalf of Sigmund's family. Thankfully the specifics pertaining to the Landesburg family were no longer asked of him in his direct conversations with the Fuhrer. On this specific matter, they were better off remaining that way.

It was time for some creative collaboration between the Landesburg and the von Brauchitsch families.

*****

Walther confirmed Marta's availability to meet with him privately the next morning to deliver the devastating news to her personally, and to outline his plans for redemption with Anna's family. As he further reflected upon his meeting with her, he was not certain as to what to expect from his outspoken and often volatile daughter-in-law. She was, and always would be a formidable woman and would no doubt be up to the task of facing Anna and eventually, her children. The more difficult test would surely be her ultimate ability to bury any animosity between herself and the general, for the sake of what was potentially at stake for Anna.

"Marta I can be no other way than direct with you. I have been agonizing over what has happened at the university, a raid about which my office was previously not made aware."

"What is it, Father? Please tell me Jacob is alright!" Her eyes were already welling up with heartfelt dread.

Walther looked briefly away from her piercing eyes to brace himself for what was to follow. Marta read his visual signal that things would not be as they had desperately hoped, and immediately sobbed uncontrollably. He refocused and clasped her hands in his. Sitting before her, he demonstrated remarkable control befitting his steadfast self-discipline and broke the news of Jacob's death.

Marta remained seated and raised her head pitifully as if to say, *How could you allow this to happen?* though she did not ask. Her pleading look of disconsolation said all that was necessary. Her body language spoke volumes. She repeatedly stomped her feet in frustration while she remained seated, as if not permitting herself to accept his deepest sympathy and heartfelt condolences. It was the awkward moment Walther had been expecting and was forced to endure.

As they both rose to stand in front of each other, he embraced her and held her tightly to his chest. She protested briefly and pounded her fist repeatedly on his shoulder in complete and utter exasperation.

In a moment more she relented, and just became a little girl again, crying in Walther's arms as if seeking to be genuinely and affectionately consoled by her own father, whom she barely remembered.

In the next hour Walther stayed with her, waiting for Klaus to arrive, and Marta began to finally regain her composure. Since the strained relationship between Marta and Klaus evolved after the Boston affair, it remained an unresolved matter. Neither one had spoken to the other or even considered addressing that problem in this tragic setting.

The request for Klaus to be in attendance meant there were no other options available to him, so accordingly Klaus had taken personal leave at his father's request. The timing was essential for what Walther needed to say.

Klaus was visibly shaken by Jacob's demise and although not close to Jacob, he knew he was a fine man of distinction and a loving father and husband who did not deserve the fate that befell him. Klaus was very determined to maintain his composure as best he could manage in the presence of his proud father, who would never accept anything less of him.

As for his personal feelings toward Marta, they were currently of no apparent consequence. As a true measure of his character, his focus was dutifully reserved for Anna's family circumstances. There was no other priority, nor division of purpose.

Walther's wife had been estranged from the family ever since she had walked out on Walther and her son when Klaus had entered military college. She had very much resented the military taking precedence over their marriage and was equally discouraged to learn Klaus had dedicated himself to the same profession. When Klaus proposed to Marta, Walther had been delighted at the prospect of his son's marriage to Marta, and of her becoming the daughter he never had. What Walther was about to propose today, however, could prove to be a problematic decision to orchestrate. He anticipated Marta would initially object to his plan, but he remained optimistic she would ultimately support it.

Whether this was an appropriate time or otherwise, difficult decisions had to be made quickly for the sake of Anna, to find a viable solution to prepare for what the future may hold for her.

"At the risk of being blunt, Marta, Anna will have to reconcile this devastating matter in whatever manner she is able. My timing is unseemly, but we must dispense with emotional considerations. Our support will be the cornerstone of a strong foundation to enable her to move forward."

Still harboring feelings that Walther should bear much of the responsibility for Jacob's untimely death, Marta interjected, "Walther, you speak as if we are building her a new house. Either be more tactful or just get to the goddamned point!"

"Very well then, we can all agree Anna's safety is paramount and I understand her children are already safe from harm, for the time being. Their home, however, is not...The Reich has already designated it for compulsory confiscation. I am not willing to interfere with those matters—my sole focus today is to assure Anna's ultimate safety and longevity, and any dignity that may remain."

"I agree her safety comes first," said Marta, "and knowing Anna's pragmatic approach to life, I am cautiously optimistic she will understand her predicament, as well as our apparent insensitivity. She has far greater priorities needing to be addressed. But where will she go? What are her options, if any? And what do you mean by saying *for the time being*?"

"Just bear with me. I will address that point once I explain my thoughts pertaining to Anna. Please may I have a drink? This may be difficult for you both to hear."

"Of course, Father, what do you..." The general interrupted Klaus mid-sentence. "Anything with ice!" was his response.

"I can arrange for Anna to be offered a posting at your office, Klaus. We are always seeking mathematicians, analysts, and reliable and trustworthy translators, particularly German, French, Polish and English, and of course, Yiddish. Didn't Anna major in languages at Köllnische?"

Marta confirmed that in fact, in those languages Anna was totally fluent.

Walther naïvely asked. "Which ones, Marta?"

"All of them! She is an incredibly intelligent woman."

Walther shook his head in amazement and continued, "Klaus, she will handle certain security matters based upon both your and my specific recommendations. She cannot fuck this up. You and I are backing her, one hundred percent! Serious responsibilities necessitate serious security protection. To be clear, Anna would be employed by the Reich, but not as a Jew. She would live modestly under an

assumed Roman Catholic identity under extreme security protocols
to the extent she will reside entirely inside the base. She must be as
impressive as you say, Marta, or suspicions will be aroused as to her
special security status. I pray she can distinguish herself and prove
her worth in due course."

"If anyone can do it, Anna will, I assure you. The Reich has no
idea what she is capable of doing for them, if given the opportunity,"
Marta confidently replied.

"That will absolutely ensure her safety, and make no mistake, we
will demand and enforce her loyalty."

"Whatever can we do to *enforce* her loyalty Father, and why would
we have to do so?" Klaus enquired.

The general continued to speak. "I would never question her
honesty and trustworthiness for such an assignment, but will she
work for the Reich after what has befallen her mother and father, and
now Jacob? That is my greatest concern. I have made enquiries giving
me the necessary assurances I sought to ensure she will be receptive
to what we are about to propose."

"Whatever are you proposing?" Marta enquired.

"Just hear me out. I insisted we meet privately today because I
need your full co-operation. By that, I mean the two of you, together,
despite your differences. Are you both willing to formally adopt
young Dietrich and to raise him as your own? Anna will no longer be
part of his daily life."

"Father how..." Marta protested.

Walther did not allow her to interject and continued. "In fact,
her communications with anyone outside of the limited confines of
her duties would necessitate this. She would have the peace of mind
knowing Dietrich will remain safely within your care and custody,
on the explicit condition she does not compromise her obligations to
the Reich."

"But Dietrich is already safe from harm is he not?" Marta correctly advised.

"Let me explain something to you." the general offered. "You
must already be aware of the recent talk about the extent to which
the purging of Jews, homosexuals, and the physically and mentally
disabled has been escalated as part of the Jewish Solution." Klaus did
not move a muscle, as he was already privy to what his father was
about to disclose. Marta nodded she had heard of such possibilities.

"Well, it has recently become fact." The general held up his empty glass to Klaus and paused for Marta's reaction to his comment.

"But again Walther, Dietrich would remain safe from harm, wouldn't he?" Marta repeated in an even more urgent tone.

"It is my belief that he would, based upon two probable exemptions. The first is that his status is one of high functionality, meaning he would possibly serve in some protective capacity for the Reich, and would not be included in the extermination of the less fortunate. The second factor is the location of the clinic being in Vienna, which could be looked upon more favorably."

"But can this be guaranteed Walther?" Marta asked hopefully.

"No, it cannot. It is me and my adjutant Richard's impression that would be a likely scenario. We do not think we can afford the risk. It would be safer to remove him... and place him in... well, to place him under your adoptive care."

"The very thought of separating Dietrich from Anna disturbs me more than I can say! I have absolutely no concerns about taking him into our home. He is a wonderful young man to be sure...but to separate him from Anna by taking her rights as his mother would cause them both further devastation. Klaus, what are your thoughts?"

"I agree with you, Marta, but I don't believe Anna has any other realistic options. It won't be me raising the boy, as it will be on your shoulders more than mine. I am happy to support the lad, of course, in any way asked of me." He paused pensively to digest the full import of this awkward circumstance. "You must know this strategy would never imperil him, and would in fact guarantee his long-term safety, which the clinic could never fully ensure, given the Fuhrer's cleansing campaign. To my mind, it is by far the best of the two scenarios. Do you agree?"

"Yes, in light of that perspective I would agree."

"Permit me to ask you another question. Will you break the news to Anna? I think my father may not be the one best suited for that task."

"Yes, of...of course Klaus. But I ask that we speak with her together, as husband and wife...as her lifelong friends. Please do this for me, Klaus. She would need to know by your presence that you are in support of this arrangement."

"I agree with Marta, son. However, this is not simply *an arrangement*. This will be a documented adoption. As such, Dietrich would be untouchable. But you must speak to this matter with Anna and Dietrich immediately. I have had the paperwork for the repossession of their home misfiled, however it will only buy us a few extra days before it happens."

Marta broached yet another related topic, with some noticeable apprehension. "There is one more important consideration that I must ask of you, Walther, which you have not mentioned. I hesitate to ask but I must…Can you also do something for Anna's sister Emilie and her daughter Gertrude? They must also be protected by new identities or whatever other resources you can provide, should they not?"

The general rolled his eyes slightly and drew a deep breath of exasperation knowing he could not expose Emilie's family to a similar fate as Jacob. He turned away and scratched his head searching his mind for yet another complication he had not fully considered.

"Please Walther. I beg you."

He turned with resolve etched on his already furrowed brow. "Yes. You are right to have asked, Marta. It will be done. I need a day to clear my mind, but I will find a solution. Forgive my oversight."

Marta eagerly rose and hugged him kissing his cheek. "Thank you, Walther. Thank you." As she sat down again, she gently dabbed the corner of her eyes and resumed more minor clarifications. "Should we bring Anna here with us before the house is taken over? What do you think?"

Walther paused to consider the circumstances, and quickly determined the urgency of Dietrich could be temporarily subrogated to Anna's. He took out a cigarette and stood facing the front window of the luxurious flat facing the main streets below. The vehicles and pedestrian traffic reminded him life carried on normally…for some. After a few minutes he took a final drag of smoke and with his burly index finger butted the cigarette in the finely cut crystal ashtray. "I must confess, I had not considered this moment thoroughly until now." He paused again reflecting on the appropriate strategy for a matter of such delicate deliberation.

"As soon as you and Klaus break the tragic news about Jacob to Anna, regardless of her grief we must act quickly. I am very sorry, but I must insist on this. We can deal with the legal matters concerning Dietrich over the upcoming days *after* Anna has been appropriately documented and placed under security protocols. Anna must be alone at her home when the Gestapo arrives. I will give you notice as to when the time is at hand."

The general continued. "She will not be harmed in any way; I swear before God Almighty. She will be taken into secure custody and delivered to a safe house for her interrogation, which I will personally oversee. Marta, you and Klaus must be certain she accepts and fully understands our conditions each step of the way. I pray she cooperates with our terms and trusts our judgment. She is an intelligent and practical woman. If anyone is capable of doing all that we ask, it would appear it is indeed Anna."

CHAPTER TWENTY-FOUR

♂

THERE WOULD BE NO STAR OF DAVID PAINTED ON THE front door of Anna's home. Marta and Klaus had nothing but dread and apprehension about their ensuing discussion and the obvious heartbreak about to befall Anna and Dietrich. Both were thankful for the absence of the desecration of the home that had already suffered so much pain and suffering.

As Anna opened the door, Marta and Klaus could see the apparent devastation and heartbreak in her eyes. She had anticipated the worst, particularly after learning Klaus would be joining them that morning. While she appreciated his thoughtfulness, she sensed a foreboding of what was to come, and immediately embraced them both. Even Klaus, the steady and unemotional "man of iron" as Marta referred to him, sobbed sympathetically in their embrace. It was the first such time he'd ever shed a tear in Marta's presence.

As they entered the house in the comfort of the main room in front of the fireplace, long gone were the lovely warm memories of the times that hosted many happy family gatherings. In fact, it was the same room in which Pietra had performed her private concert for her Aunt Marta so many years before. Who would have suspected their happy life could turn so terribly awry?

None of the painful details of Jacob's death were ever disclosed to Marta, and Klaus remained obviously tight lipped about the subject. It no longer mattered. It was simply the untimely death that preoccupied their discussion, not the circumstances under which it happened.

Anna was numb with despair, never for a moment imagining Jacob being taken so suddenly from their lives. So soon after the death of her parents, Anna's world had changed more quickly than her ability to adjust. She held herself accountable for never seeing the obvious, and for waiting too long to accept the inevitable. She should have seen something like this coming.

"Anna, I cannot imagine the pain you are feeling. We are committed to you and your well-being and will do anything in our power to ensure you and Dietrich are safe. I'm your sister in life. You know that." Marta took Anna's hands and held them in her own.

"You're mine too," mumbled Anna softly, not looking up and too overcome to speak clearly.

"I was supposed to be the strong one and yet, I can barely function." Marta spoke slowly and distinctly so as not to be misunderstood. "You and Dietrich have enormous strength too and should draw upon it for each other in honor of Jacob's memory. Jacob would expect no less from you. Forgive us if we appear insensitive Anna, but we must discuss something of urgency with you, for Dietrich's immediate safety."

Anna lifted her head slightly and through her puffy eyes and broken spirit, she simply nodded affirmatively and continued to rest her hands, and perhaps her fate, in Marta's.

In the ensuing hours, Marta and Klaus painstakingly walked Anna through their discussion with the general and described as tactfully as possible the stages of his plan, to which she passively acceded. What was said may not have been fully comprehended in her current state of mind but there was no point in reiterating the complexities that had entangled her life, undeservedly or otherwise.

Anna knew she was overwhelmed and had no strength remaining to resist. It was simply a moment of numb acceptance—the deadening reality to which she was helpless to consider any alternatives. She mumbled something unintelligible, but obviously of great importance.

"I'm sorry Anna," said Marta. "I don't understand. What are you asking?"

She lifted her head and cleared her throat. "What about Emilie?" she whispered in a hoarse voice.

"Emilie and Gertrude are being well taken care of; I promise you. Walther is handling the details personally. It will be explained to you soon, but for now just rest easy. I will stay with you here until tomorrow. Is that alright?"

Klaus headed to the residence on the base and very reluctantly left Marta behind with Anna for the night, despite the general's explicit instructions to the contrary. Arguing against Marta's insistence about the matter would have been pointless, particularly when everyone was so emotionally spent.

*****

In the remaining hours Marta and Anna were together, it was difficult to fully grasp the inevitable parting of the two. There is only so much grief and sadness a human being can withstand and any previous limitations to their endurance had long since been surpassed. Anna had gradually become much more coherent. It was her survival instinct reawakening within her; hence there was no time to be wasted reminiscing about the countless fond memories of their time spent together.

As she sharpened her focus, Anna's determination enabled them to address only those immediate decisions within their mutual control. Difficult as it was, they would deal with whatever the future held with the knowledge that both Pietra and Dietrich would be safe. Amazingly, Anna fought through the demons that surrounded her, and she was no longer helplessly disoriented. Her weapons were her formidable character and strong will. As this metamorphosis unfolded, so too did her strong conviction that her ultimate reunion with her family was not in question. It would just be a matter of when.

"I want you to contact Pietra and tell her what has happened. You have her aunt's contact information, but I want you to handle this personally, Marta. She will be devastated about her father, and oh my...she has barely recovered from her grandmother and grandfather's passing, and now...my goodness what do we say about me?"

"Let us agree now the details would only be counter-productive, as they will only exacerbate her pain. This is just too much for anyone to reconcile, but just like her mother, she will." As Marta said this, she squeezed Anna's hands in hers to reinforce her confidence. "Once travel permits are once again available and passage is safely assured, I will visit her again in New York...and take Dietrich with me! I promise you Anna."

"Thank you, Marta. I know you will do the necessary things. Until I learn what I may or may not do, or what freedoms I will be permitted, I would be frantic without knowing Pietra and Emilie are safe, and you and Dietrich are together with Manny and Klaus. I cannot thank you enough."

Anna paused for a moment, as there was so much to think about, and so very little within her control. She continued to adapt, focusing her mind to keep her emotions in check. As she began to become more coherent, she started to prioritize other related issues that began to surface. "It does not concern me about this home that was once ours. No one can take my memories from me. Our possessions mean little to me, if we have our health to enable us to survive for whatever time is required…However, there is something very dear to me I will always treasure. Please wait here for a moment."

Anna left the room only briefly. Marta was totally unprepared for what would follow.

When Anna returned, she held in her hand an exquisite silver case, engraved with the initials *MJL*, Marissa Johanna Landesburg. Marta knew what the case contained and was immediately brought to tears. Anna opened it facing Marta, as her father had once presented it to her mother. "Marta, I want you to have this in memory of me, to keep it safe, to one day give to Pietra on my behalf, if I am…if I…" Anna struggled to continue, "…if I am unable to do so."

"Oh Anna! Please do not speak of such things! I could not even bear the thought of you…if …if anything ever happened to you…you know that I will! This is a cherished family heirloom. I will keep this in safe custody, and I promise to accompany you when you present it to Pietra yourself, agreed?"

The friends both collapsed in each other's emotional embrace and held tightly to prolong the moment, and to defer their imminent parting, albeit for just another instant.

Once they regained their composure, Marta strenuously reassured Anna, "I will do everything you ask of me, you always know I will. It is so difficult to speak of such things, but I fear we must. I will find a way for us to communicate with each other. I could not bear to be unable to speak with you. I need you in my life in ways I cannot describe Anna, but please understand I must make certain not to compromise Klaus or his father. It may take me some time, so you must be patient. Promise me you will never give up hope! Do you understand me, Anna?"

As the afternoon was winding down, the telephone suddenly rang and broke the somber conversation between them. It was none other than the general, offering his heartfelt condolences to Anna as best he could. It was a very difficult and almost terse conversation, during which time he asked for her trust in him to also provide for the safety and security of Emilie and her daughter Gertrude as well.

The general was not a sentimentalist and needed to confirm Anna's total cooperation. After reassuring him she would do what he asked of her, Anna expressed her grateful appreciation for all he was doing for her family and turned the telephone back to Marta.

"I have stayed with her as long as time permitted, and I promise you I will be gone before those pigs arrive. I am trusting she will not be harmed or threatened in any way. Are we agreed?" The general acquiesced and then Marta insisted, "You will call me when she is in your custody, correct?"

"Yes, yes. You have my word!"

It was time for Marta to leave. There was not much left to say. They were both emotionally drained and in deep dread at their sad circumstances. When Marta closed the door behind her, Anna was alone but felt as prepared as she could be. The logistics of her predicament had forced her to confront her situation and prepare for the next hurdle, whatever it might prove to be. She would steady herself over time and focus on what must be done to keep her family and herself safe from further harm.

For Marta, it was not dissimilar. She was fully prepared to take some time away from the symphony to focus on assisting Walther in the processing of Dietrich's adoption process. It was critical to her that she used every means at her disposal to explain this life changing sequence of events in such a manner that respected Dietrich's own personal feelings on the matter.

He was now almost fourteen years old but at such a tender young age, he had already experienced more tragedy than most people would endure in the course of a lifetime. It was of paramount importance that Dietrich be given the time and support he needed to psychologically reconcile his profound losses, not to mention yet another significant twist of fate on the road of life he would be forced to follow. It was, in fact, the loss of his grandparents, both parents, and his home—all that was familiar and dear to him in one fell swoop. Marta was determined to care for him and nurture him as her own, and to never allow her faith and belief in Anna's safe return to falter.

Within the hour, two military cars bearing Nazi swastikas parked conspicuously in front of the house. Normally the evictors would arrive with trucks and significantly more support personnel to carry out their forceful denigration and intimidation tactics. This was not the case on this intervention. General von Brauchitsch's influence and his promised consideration for Anna remained apparent. Anna answered her doorbell promptly, without fear or reluctance, and unhesitatingly invited the three officers to enter the premises.

"Good day, Madame Anna. I am Major Hirsch of the 1st Command office." They had not been given Anna's family name. It was none of their business to know it, and no further questions were asked of her.

"I see you have been expecting our visit today. On direct orders from General von Brauchitsch, we are here to escort you to a more secure location befitting the special capacity of your service to the Reich. May we help with your bags?"

With acceptance, Anna calmly left her home without looking back, never to return. Throughout the process, she was never threatened, nor disrespected, nor harmed in any way.

Despite the scars of her numerous ordeals forever burned into her very soul, it was as if she was now being spared from additional suffering. As a significant gesture of respect, she was being accorded every possible courtesy. She knew nothing would erase her pain and the depth of her anguish, but she immediately vowed to separate herself from these apparent courtesies to achieve what she must to keep her remaining family safe from further harm. The day would surely come when she would have to reconcile the inevitable internal conflicts of protecting her family, and at the same time serving this vile enemy that had almost eradicated it.

During the ninety-minute drive she remained calm and silent, watching pensively while the escort left the city behind as it headed north. She was at the officers' mercy but was not disturbed in the least. Her grieving process had begun shockingly and ended tragically, transforming the life she knew, and replacing it with one of which she knew very little. Her faith was entirely based upon her undying trust in dear Marta and her powerful military family. Anna vowed to do whatever was expected of her.

As they arrived at the front gates, she had no way of knowing her father had passed through this same fortified entrance several years ago, when he was ordered to appear before then-Field Marshal von Brauchitsch. Today, that same man was now a general in the service of the Fuhrer. As she was processed through security, Anna was only starting to grasp the magnitude of power this man must command to grant her such consideration. It had to be more than her deep friendship with his daughter-in-law. She could not help but ponder how significant the extent of his debt to her father must have been, and what Sigmund must have done to deserve such respect.

Within an hour, she was taken to the general's personal adjutant and greeted hospitably, though not surprisingly absent any reference to her personal loss. Clearly whatever decision may have been made to arrest her dear Jacob, it was apparent it had no connection to General von Brauchitsch. This revelation only heightened the profoundness of the love and respect Anna felt for her father—evidence of the fact that even after death, his influence lived on for the safety of his beloved family.

"The general will see you now, madame. Please follow me." said the officer respectfully.

The general was already standing in front of his desk and approached Anna graciously, though not in any way subserviently. They had met years before but only briefly, at Marta's wedding—very different circumstances to be certain. Following expressions of his own sympathies, and devoid of any apologies on behalf of harsh military actions, he ushered Anna to a chair and sat adjacent to her. The door had been closed behind her.

"Anna I am told you are a woman of numerous talents, which can prove to be most useful. My achievements within the military have been significant. I am optimistic, and most insistent, that your loyal contributions will ensure my greatest achievements are yet to come. I know the quality of your character through my son and his dear wife Marta. I also know what pain and suffering you must have endured to this point in your life, and I humbly regret I could not protect you and your family from them. However, from this point forward, as Klaus has already explained to you, my staff and I most certainly intend to do everything within our power to keep you and your children safe."

Anna was intrigued. She only had a cursory expectation her multilingual talents would be required in some unique capacity. Clarifying further, the general referenced her demonstrable intelligence, her character, and the trust she had earned from his own family. This, when combined with her obligation to him personally, made her unquestioningly reliable in handling heavy workloads of confidential document translations, much as she had anticipated. In addition, her talents would also assist in frequent interrogations, often obtained under potentially harrowing circumstances, all of which would be highly secretive.

"In the past year, Abwehr has become the Central Agency of Military Intelligence under Vice-Admiral Wilhelm Canaris, head-quartered in Berlin. It is to him I report directly. Within a few days, once your debriefing is concluded here at the base, you will be escorted to your new accommodations at the heavily secured office complex of Abwehr. Going forward, you will live in a dignified and comfortable manner within the military base, with all personal needs being provided. Tight personal security will be assured, twenty-four hours a day.

You and your family will always remain safe, the only proviso being your absolute focus and dedication of purpose—that purpose being to serve the Reich. Espionage is a vital aspect of war, Anna, and any action or intent inconsistent with the Fuhrer's mandate would be considered treasonous and punished accordingly.

To be clear with you, we do not believe for a moment any such harshness will ever become necessary, but until such time as you have proven your merits beyond a doubt, these are the conditions within which we must function. Do you understand and acknowledge your acceptance of this arrangement?"

Before Anna could respond, an expected tap on the door inter-rupted the general's interview. Klaus was announced and he was ushered into the office.

"Hello Anna." Klaus only offered his extended hand to her. There would be no indication of personal affection inside or about her working place. That became clear. "I trust you are as well as could be expected under the circumstances."

The general continued, "Klaus will be your direct liaison between Abwehr and myself. You will be reporting directly to him. For the time being, no one other than Klaus and myself will know of your ancestry and our personal relationship. Although this has been a long day for you, it is imperative we cover a few significant details before you can properly rest for the day."

Klaus continued to address her under the watchful eyes of his father. "It is essential you be given a new identity. As you can appreciate, your Jewish heritage could never be accepted, tolerated, or understood. You must have expected as much." He opened a large manila envelope from which he withdrew several official documents for her to review.

"These documents have been prepared for you and will certifiably confirm you are Anna Christina Pavlova, born Roman Catholic in Koblenz in 1901. You graduated in mathematics and languages at the University of Bonn, etc., etc. You will find them to be in perfect order and believe me when I say they will withstand the closest scrutiny, although I personally guarantee none will be necessary.

Tomorrow you will be given a routine medical examination and will be taken to your private quarters here on the base, where suitable clothing will be provided along with any personal items you may require. In the following days we will verify final security checks and rudimentary documentation pertinent to your special posting, all of which will remain sealed and classified. We want to be certain you are deemed fit for your new assignment prior to your permanent relocation to the Abwehr HQ in Berlin. Please review these legal documents and apprise me of any possible issues or questions you may have when we meet again tomorrow. Any questions at this time, Anna?"

"No, not at this time. I prefer to defer my questions for the moment. Thank you," Anna acknowledged.

"Very well. Understand you will be strictly monitored, day and night, without access to any telephones, secured or unsecured. Anna, you are strictly forbidden to contact anyone outside your business-related responsibilities, including Dietrich and Marta. I cannot emphasize this point any more clearly."

"I will not disappoint either of you. I will always remain loyal and do precisely as I am instructed, by you, General, and you Klaus, and to anyone or anybody of authority you may instruct me to obey. However, may I be permitted to speak freely to you both?"

"Forgive us both Anna. We interrupted you before you could respond to one of my previous questions. Do you have a question for me now?" the general asked.

"Not a question, as much as a clarification."

The general nodded and gestured for her to continue.

"I will not speak of this again, but I believe I must address this matter now, if you will bear with me. I swear my loyalty to you both, and it will never be in question. I am humbled by what you have done for us and I understand you have done so personally, not militarily. By so doing, you have no doubt placed yourselves in harm's way. For this I am forever grateful...I will give my life to you both, but I cannot ever promise to become loyal to the Fuhrer, despite the threat of potential harm to my family and myself. It is simply more than I will ever be willing to do."

Klaus and his father were taken aback by Anna's forthright confession, and remained speechless for a moment, saying nothing to her, or each other, sharing only exchanged glances.

"You realize you are not in a position to bargain for anything, do you not? You are correct about the risk we have accepted to secure your safety, as you are also correct about the peril in which your children could be placed. Yet you emphatically express the unbending limitations of your loyalty." The general paused reflectively and walked slowly to reposition himself behind his desk.

Klaus knew better than to interrupt his father's thoughts. The general would ask for Klaus' thoughts when he needed to hear them. This was not one of those times. Several silent minutes passed.

"You have *chutzpah* Anna. I respect that!"

"I sincerely apologize if I have offended you, General. It was never my intention, I assure you."

"No Anna, I am not offended. I am impressed by your strength of conviction...and your confidence to express them, just like your father. You are also correct about your point—this will never be spoken among us again. We accept your pledge to the Reich, and we encourage you to learn all you can, as quickly as you can. Now, please go with Klaus and get some well-deserved rest Anna. We will speak again when the time is appropriate."

Anna ate very little of her dinner that night, even though she could not help but notice the fine quality of the meal she was offered. Her complete exhaustion had numbed her hunger to be satisfied another day. Sleep was what she needed most, and that was an order she followed without hesitation.

CHAPTER TWENTY-FIVE

IT WAS MID-SPRING 1939, AND ANNA WAS ONLY BEGIN-
ning to realize the general had not been exaggerating about her
workload. The translation of official documents seemed endless, but
Anna embraced her task. It kept her mind stimulated and was instrumental in taking her focus away from her morbid reality. She needed
the demand her work required without which she would surely have
become irreversibly despondent.

She discerned most of the documents she received were of foreign
jurisdiction, primarily Czech, Slovak, and Austrian, which was
logical since the recent German annexation of the Slovak Republic
and Sudetenland. Although it was never explained to her, the content
was mostly administrative in nature and though it was tedious at
times, she was regaining her competence and speed with the technical aspects of the material. Nothing contained a hint of intrigue.

She kept mostly to herself for obvious reasons and made no
conscious effort to assimilate into the group of a dozen or so other
administrative translators, assuming they were assigned similar tasks
as herself. Other than brief courtesies each morning, there were no
other attempts at verbal exchanges from any among them toward
Anna. She became somehow aloof, perhaps with good purpose.

After several months of the same tedium, Klaus contacted Anna
early one day to advise her she was about to be summoned to the
office of Major General Hans Oster. This general apparently worked
closely with Klaus and his father and they supported his interaction
with Anna. Although Oster's name was unfamiliar to her, Anna soon
learned he was the commander of the Central Division, reporting

directly to Vice Admiral Canaris, the most senior officer in charge at Abwehr. That was a name she recognized.

By mid-morning, Anna was directed to General Oster's private office by his personal assistant and was offered tea upon her entry. The general was a man of slight build and although revered as a man of position and high ranking, he had the manner of a gentleman; methodical, precise, but very approachable and not at all overbearing as one might have expected.

"Welcome Anna. I am General Hans Oster. Please be seated and make yourself comfortable. I assume you are settled into your daily routines by this point?"

"Yes, General. You are all so kind. Thank you for asking."

"You come to us from very credible sources. General von Brauchitsch spoke highly of you and I hold him in the utmost respect. As you might expect, we have been closely scrutinizing your work here, and I am pleased to say your work ethic and the precise manner you complete it, are exemplary. My heartiest congratulations to you."

"Thank you, sir. It is the only way I know to do it."

The general laughed and added, "Would that others in my department had a similar attitude. I imagine the material and documentation you have completed for us to date must appear somewhat mundane to someone of your obvious intellect. Would that be safe to say?"

Anna couldn't help but show signs of curiosity and simply stated, "I work with what I am given, sir, but yes, on occasion it does become, shall I say, monotonous from time to time. That is not for me to judge. I simply do as I am instructed."

"So it would appear, Anna, which is something I wish to discuss with you this morning. I have had numerous consultations with General von Brauchitsch about many matters, and some concern your outstanding progress. We have agreed your talents are wasted doing…monotonous tasks, as you put it. Although scrutiny of your work will continue, of course, the security level of your assignments will be upgraded from this day forward. Your linguistic skills are always precise, but more than that, you have the unique ability to detect appropriate nuances of conversation that are imperative, particularly for what we have in mind for you. I presume you are aware more than most that human conversation conveys more by inflection, body language, facial expression, and other non-verbal cues than the spoken word."

Anna nodded affirmatively as the general continued. "In our line of work, this is a vital advantage to an interpreter. In my opinion, your mastery of these skills helps you to 'read between the lines', so to speak. As the importance of your responsibilities increases, do you have the confidence that you would be capable of what I require of you, Anna?"

"At the risk of appearing impudent, I certainly do not see why I would not be sir. I welcome the challenge."

"Excellent! That is precisely what I wanted to hear! He shouted to his assistant, "Elisabeth!" and then asked Anna, "I believe you have already met Elisabeth?"

When his assistant came in, he said, "Elisabeth, please escort Ms. Pavlova to her new workstation and provide the necessary introductions. The general is expecting her." Returning to address Anna, he stated, "I am confident you will find your accommodations most suitable, Anna. I look forward to speaking with you again soon."

*****

Once again, an armed guard escorted Anna to another section of this massive facility, this time with Elisabeth. Anna couldn't help but be intrigued by the level of security that was customary whenever her duties took her to other sections within these headquarters. Was it for her protection, or to prevent her attempt at escape? Neither reason was tenable as she was under no threat of imminent harm, and escape from Abwehr was impractical, even perhaps impossible. Furthermore, if she did escape, she had no viable means to support herself, and nowhere to go. She did wonder, though, if perhaps the tight security was because her work was yielding results that were becoming increasingly valuable. It was evident her intrinsic value appeared to be growing since her detainment here.

Following the maze of hallways, and several heavily secured double-doorways, they arrived at the office of yet another striking-looking officer, who summarily broke away from his conversation with a very prim and professionally attired woman of some degree of importance herself, no doubt.

"Good afternoon Anna. Thank you, Elisabeth. I will take Ms. Pavlova from here."

"Yes, thank you Elisabeth. I hope to see you again soon." Anna respectfully acknowledged.

"I was informed you would be transferring to us sometime today. Let me introduce myself. I am Major Helmuth Groscurth." He snapped his heels and lowered his head slightly.

The major guided Anna to his office and stated, "You have been a subject of some discussion among us for the past few weeks. I have been quite anxious to meet you personally. Please be seated, Anna." They both entered his warm, wood paneled yet functional office. "You have outstanding credentials, Anna, and your performance here has exceeded our high expectations of you.

From now on, based upon the recommendations of General von Brauchitsch, you will be working within our department." He withdrew a silver cigarette case, removed a cigarette, and tapped the exposed tip familiarly on the now-closed case. "There are those among us who have determined you have the appropriate skill set we are seeking. Succinctly put, Anna, you are extremely capable technically, you keep your mind focused on your tasks, you ask few questions, and you have powerful superior officers who have confidence in you. I believe I will be among them in very short order...Forgive my manners...may I offer you some coffee or tea perhaps? I can assure you our discussion today will not be brief."

"Yes, that would be lovely, you are most kind, Major Groscurth."

"We serve at the pleasure of the Fuhrer and I work directly under the command of Colonel von Lahousen. I believe you know of Admiral Canaris, who heads all aspects of Abwehr functions?"

Anna nodded affirmatively. "Not personally to be sure, but yes, I am aware we are under his command."

"This division of Abwehr has been tasked to co-ordinate, develop, and monitor logistical strategies for oversight of all sabotage and counter-intelligence, with intent to weed out and contain potential internal and external threats to the Reich. There are now more than one thousand employees actively employed by Abwehr since Admiral Canaris took command. You were specifically selected to work in this division, based upon your standards of excellence and trustworthiness of character. I have been instructed your background has been well vetted and is therefore not for me to question. I follow my orders,

Anna, as you apparently do as well. I must be clear with you that we will get along just fine in our service to the Fuhrer, so long as we do what is asked of us, without question."

Anna confirmed her clear understanding and as she had been previously instructed, she did not utter a word about the circumstances leading her on this path, nor her previous confidential discussions with General von Brauchitsch. The major explained Anna would be entrusted with access to top-secret documents and intelligence information crucial to the success of various clandestine operations.

This spoke volumes about what Anna had started to understand about her potential value to Abwehr specifically, and the war effort in general. She deduced there was more to her special treatment and her unique skill set that had gone unspoken.

In the next two hours, the major outlined in greater detail the various aspects of her new work environment, which was more in the capacity of assisting him with implementing orders he received. It was clear she would no longer operate in a strictly administrative capacity. In fact, she would become his personal technical assistant, while any customary administrative duties would continue to be Elisabeth's responsibilities.

"Anna, I am eager to see you in action, so to speak. Gather what you need. I want you to join a group of us in the boardroom…no time like the present, wouldn't you agree?"

Throughout the balance of the day, Major Groscurth and a small group of highly trained associates working in different areas of specialization continued to brief each other in Anna's presence. She was not introduced to any of the attendees, nor were they to her. The major as her personal escort, spoke volumes about her instant credibility.

It was a fascinating series of discussions demanding intense, undivided attention. They spoke mostly Polish and Silesian, and it was apparent some of these associates were not German military. Rather, this was a selection of loyal Nazi supporters, specially trained by the military for carrying out operations behind enemy lines, hence the need for Anna's expertise.

They were part of a group of special forces referred to as Battalion Ebbinghaus; extremely adept in martial arts, hand-to-hand combat, technical engineering, armaments, sniper and marksmanship, amongst many other talents. The battalion was led by Alfred Naujocks, a German SS grunt with a colorful past in amateur boxing.

He was often required to exploit his gift of physicality to commit ruthless sabotage and when necessary, executions.

These highly trained forces knew full well that once deployed behind enemy lines they would be unsupported by German forces and if captured, the military would deny having any knowledge or relationship with them that would connect them to Germany. They were regarded as being Polish private militia for hire, presumably working for private interests. As such, they would pose as Polish laborers and dress accordingly, in civilian clothing prior to crossing the border onto Polish soil.

It was their mission to seize and secure strategic points within Poland that had been predetermined by Nazi leadership to be essential, prior to the scheduled invasion of Poland on August 26th, 1939! Anna was aghast but dared not demonstrate any visible concern. She simply and steadfastly continued to interpret when required and took notes when told to do so.

The cigarette smoke in the closed room was almost unbearable for Anna, to the extent that even the smokers must have strained to view the large, detailed maps splayed across the boardroom table.

There was a tap on the door and none other than Klaus von Brauchitsch entered the room. Anna was delighted to see him but only exchanged brief eye contact with him upon his entry. She was encouraged just to see him again, this being the first time seeing each other since almost eight months ago.

Several rounds of information were exchanged, mostly between two of the unnamed special-forces men, Major Groscurth, and Klaus. The logistics and timing of the operation, dubbed *Plan White*, were critical to their success in facilitating little to no resistance to the subsequent invasion from a largely unprepared Poland. Entry was to be swift, unrelenting, and punitive toward what was expected to be only minor resistance against the battalion and the armed forces that would follow.

Several hours later when the briefing was finally concluded, Major Groscurth gave Anna a few rudimentary tasks to complete before her work for the day was completed. As she was standing alone, organizing her paperwork at the expansive table, Klaus approached her after departing the major's office. He took her quite by surprise as her back was turned toward the door.

"Anna! It is wonderful to see you looking so well!" He spoke hurriedly and in hushed tones. "I am not permitted to linger with you now, but I wanted you to know Marta and Dietrich send their love. Dietrich is thriving at school and speaks of you often. He and Manny have become brothers and he is adjusting very well. He misses you terribly though, but he understands there is nothing more we can do about seeing you at this point in time. He always remains hopeful, as do we all."

Anna was deeply touched by Klaus' kindness and became understandably misty eyed. "Thank you, Klaus! Thank you! Please give everyone my love and assure them I am doing well. You and the general have been so kind to us in a manner I shall never forget! Now please go, as we must not draw undue attention."

With that said, the two friends parted as Anna resumed her work, having been recharged with conviction she was here for a much greater purpose. This realization left her more determined than ever to see her family again, no matter how long or by what manner it took to be reunited.

In her quiet hours of that night, she continued her self-introspection and realized it wasn't just talent and trust making her best suited for this service. It was also the stark reality that she was the only person in her department who lived entirely within this military base. She had no other life, and what may have remained of it outside these walls was tenuous at best and could always be threatened if her total compliance to her duties ever wavered.

Essentially, she was permanently held in this high-security prison, forced to be complicit in her captors' deceitful actions against humanity. Holding her son as a surety bond was nothing less than extortion.

Even after the war, whether Germany became the victor or the vanquished, she assessed that her life would be at tremendous risk. What secrets she would know would be of incredible value to the enemy. The employer she served most certainly knew this and would have no hesitation to have her killed when she no longer served their purpose. This was a prison like no other, and her incarceration was most likely for the duration of her remaining lifetime.

In the months ahead, numerous high-level meetings became routine. Anna tried her utmost to familiarize herself with the main characters intent on reshaping the world, redefining almost indiscriminately where new borders would be allocated to co-operative alliances. In return for those alliances, it would be possible for under-manned and unprepared countries to completely avert the gruesome havoc of war. Other regions of Western Europe would be divided up among them, as if bartering for territorial concessions was likened to a game, each player with his own limited number of chess pieces.

For Hitler, this proved to be a highly cost-effective method of annexing regions of Europe, both for Germany and for the van-quished that would otherwise have been decimated by the German military juggernaut. Bribery and deceit were also commonly used to provide effective incentives to expedite Germany's plans for global domination. It was a tactic Hitler had already masterfully utilized with numerous of those under his command.

As the months passed, most of the meetings concerned the co-ordination and strategic command of the complicated logistics of the attack on Poland. This major invasion would incorporate each divi-sion of the German military. The Oberkommando der Wehrmacht (OKW) was the high command of the armed forces, comprised of three major divisions: The Heer (Army), the Kriegsmarine (Navy) and the Luftwaffe (Air Force). Oversight of the OKW was minimal and more administrative in nature, and each division exerted its own command authority, often found to conflict with the other.

Anna's strong opinion of this system was that it was inefficient and not at all cohesive. However, it was so by Hitler's own design. In the close confidence of his personal mentors such as von Ribbentrop, Bormann, Goebbels, and Canaris, he confessed his preference to appoint leadership positions to people of limited intelligence, as they would be less likely to someday oppose him.

Based upon similar reasoning, his penchant for divisiveness was expressed in his constant insistence on preventing any singu-lar command from being a predominant factor in major military decisions, choosing instead to leave such decisions to his own supreme control.

These most powerful advisors represented the upper echelons of the government and the military. They brought with them their own distinctive personalities, arrogance, and obstinate behaviors and were often unwilling to bend or accede to the control of the other. These were modern-day bullies who had grown accustomed to the total subservience of others. Compromise was frequently attainable only through a constant battle of wills, neither side conceding to the other, often necessitating intervention by the supreme commander.

Hitler visited the Abwehr offices only rarely, preferring instead to assume his leadership responsibilities from his mobile field office, a heavily armored private train named the *Fuhrersonderzug*, which continually crisscrossed most of Western Europe. In his absence, he was kept apprised of every decision demanding his attention in order to remedy conflicting viewpoints on appropriate strategy by his various chiefs of staff.

This staff included Martin Bormann, Hitler's private secretary. Bormann's responsibility was to control all access to the Fuhrer. Joachim von Ribbentrop was also a very close and personal confidant of Hitler's, serving capably as his ultimate authority on world affairs.

Others of note adding to the list of henchmen were Erich Raeder, admiral and commander in chief of the entire armed forces; Joseph Goebbels, propaganda and public media; Hermann Göring, the founder of the Gestapo and commander in chief of the Luftwaffe; and, of course, Heinrich Himmler, who was next in line as supreme commander of the Third Reich. It was a gallery of brilliant but increasingly deranged characters.

Anna noticed the ebb and flow of the very powerful egos within Hitler's inner circle, and the almost total disregard they had for each other to establish a workable co-operative spirit. High rank combined with ruthless and cunning manipulation followed its natural course to create a barely functional chain of command.

It was not always military rank that decided the issues, but often the fear of punishing and deceitful reprisals from those who were obsessive about ingratiating themselves to the ultimate recognition of the Fuhrer. Scattered throughout these prima donnas, however, remained those very few who maintained their steady resolve, apart from the company of misfits. These few distinguished themselves in Anna's eyes by way of demonstrating gallant professionalism and genuine respect for those they commanded.

Significant among these gentlemen were Admiral Canaris, General Oster, Major Groscurth, and General von Brauchitsch. In Anna's estimation, the bond of mutual respect between and among this group of outstanding individuals was palpable, but she suspected there was much more to their professional relationship, judging by the apparent depth of their personal commitment to each other.

They were unlike the rest of Hitler's henchmen. There was no backstabbing and no apparent denigration or fear of possible reprisals from each other. There were disagreements, for certain, but there was no timidity, or disingenuous platitudes spoken. The friendship and co-operation among them were somehow different, she thought… it was genuine.

Anna had a quick mind and had proven to be highly capable in coding and decoding high security messages. Her contributions to Abwehr were becoming more remarkable during her tenure there, especially as the pressure on her was continuously escalating. Acquiring her talents had become a great source of pride for General von Brauchitsch and as a result, it became apparent he had curried favor with the Fuhrer.

In view of her exceptional contributions and commitment within Abwehr, von Brauchitsch felt it advisable to confide Anna's circumstances only to General Oster and Admiral Canaris. After he did so, it was evident to both gentlemen that in addition to her dedication and professional capabilities, the leverage that existed upon Anna would assure she could be trusted with matters of even greater importance.

Through her secret and highly sensitive translations, which on the surface were her primary responsibility, Anna's keen talent for logic and reasoning were always apparent and as such were fully exploited by the few who commanded her. The trust and confidence General von Brauchitsch felt toward Anna was well deserved and consistent with General Oster's learned opinion.

Both were influential men who believed strongly in her natural affinity for mathematics. It was a gift enabling her to code and decipher voluminous amounts of particularly sensitive information for the Counterintelligence Unit. Few, if any, existing staff had either the necessary security clearance or the trust from the generals to handle these highly secretive communications.

It was decided Anna was the perfect fit for a responsibility to which only she was uniquely qualified.

*****

When Anna was requested to attend a private audience with General von Brauchitsch, it was a meeting she had anticipated for months. Her keen expectation was that it would concern news of Dietrich's welfare. Other than the whispered word from Klaus some months ago, there had been nothing by way of news of her family. She ached to hear anything the general could provide.

When she was graciously received by the general, his personal assistant was conspicuously absent, and the door was closed behind Anna. Surely this was the meeting she had been eagerly awaiting, and her heart raced excitedly.

After a few words of the usual but brief banter, the general gave her what he knew she wanted to hear. "Anna you have been most patient with me. I know Klaus spoke reassuringly to you some time ago, but only briefly. Dietrich has been broken-hearted to not be permitted to speak with you since that terrible day. His love for you has never diminished. Please always know that."

They sat adjacent to each other, sipping hot peppermint tea in an uneasy, momentary silence that made Anna think there was another shoe certain to fall.

"He has been thriving at school and adjusting well to life with Marta and Manfred. The knowledge that you are also thriving seems to rest his soul. He trusts Marta absolutely in that regard. She always sends her deepest love to you and, I might add, she never forgives me for keeping you from her. I think by now you can appreciate the secrecy of your work here, and my continued insistence it must never be compromised."

"Yes General, I am well aware of that but…"

"Forgive me, but I suspect I know what it is you are about to ask. Let me address the point directly, Anna, but regrettably not at this time. On a related matter, there is much more I must discuss with you now. I assure you, the matter of you and Marta is a priority for me, one of several I'm afraid to say, but know this—I commit to make certain accommodations to you very shortly along those very lines. I promise to you, on my honor as a military officer."

Anna was visibly relieved, and she placed her hands together in a prayerful position on her lap and slightly lowered her head as if offering a silent prayer of thanks to heaven above.

The general went on a short time with well-deserved compliments about her work. They were not only genuine but served to acknowledge the confidence he and his command staff had in her role in Abwehr. The ability and sureness she always exuded were perfectly suited for her unique role in matters pertaining to espionage and counterespionage.

The general shifted his chair to be closer to her and began to describe his endless struggle for maintaining the often-delicate balance between effective commands in service of the Fatherland, as well as an often-conflicting adherence to fundamental consciousness of morality and humanity. In times of war, it was near impossible to do both. He went on to clarify. "Certain officers among high command remain to this day, silently opposed to the persecution and maltreatment of people, whether they be Poles, Serbs…or Jews."

Anna's eyes were riveted on the general's as they conveyed to her the magnitude of this confession.

"Do you understand the gravity of what I am telling you, Anna?"

Without uttering a word, as she was in astonishment and rendered speechless, Anna simply nodded affirmatively. She never broke eye contact with him.

"We need you to continue doing what we instruct you to do, without question, without compromise. Certain matters will soon come to your attention that we will be in a stronger position to affect, and potentially influence for the better. However, many… I repeat… *many*, we simply cannot affect without exposure to undue risk…risk that could potentially kill us all. If we give you a command to carry out, whether you are supportive of its content, or otherwise, you must be unwavering, without question, and without compromise."

The general took a deliberate pause and maintained his steady gaze, as if trying to read her very soul. "Anna, will you work with us in this secretive collaboration of the best long-term interests of the service of Germany?"

She was mindful of his specific omission of *the best interests of the Fuhrer*. "I can only imagine the risk you and the others are taking, General, to confide in me to solicit my support. You must already know I will serve you honorably in whatever capacity you ask of me."

A smile creased his face, but only fleetingly as he placed his hand on her still folded hands. It was a fatherly demonstration of his deep affection for her.

In the days ahead, news of Anna's elevated status was confidentially disclosed to the few very select officers she had already served with such distinction, only now it was a markedly different relationship than before. Among this selective ensemble were none other than Admiral Canaris, Major Groscurth, General Oster and of course, General von Brauchitsch. There was unanimous acceptance of Anna's clandestine appointment into this inner sanctum.

Although they were all pleased with this affirmation, there would be no apparent celebration among them outside of the boardroom doors. Business was to be conducted as usual and there was no time for any an ill-advised distraction.

Upon Anna returning to her office, no reference was made to anyone on her own private administrative staff as to the nature of her afternoon meeting. This was not uncommon between them, as her personal assistant Brigitte was already accustomed to simply respond and react to whatever Anna directed. Anna confided in no one outside of her immediate superiors.

As the frequency of strategic military decisions increased, sentiments among high command ranged from giddy enthusiasm and daring bravado, to nervous and anxious trepidation.

Anna's new perspective provided a fascinating look into the mechanism of war involving the life and death decisions emanating from this very command center; a command center in which a widowed Jew would play a crucial and pivotal role, potentially affecting the reshaping of Eastern Europe and the millions of lives within it.

ACKNOWLEDGEMENTS

WHILE ON A FAMILY VACATION IN A QUIET RESORT IN Playa Del Carmen, Mexico in 2010, my young grandson Ben, found an auspicious ring lying at the edge of a garden not far from the beach. To young Ben, it was like finding buried treasure. I played along with the excitement and celebrated his discovery, despite my first thought that it was just a very old piece of costume jewelry that had been weathered by years of wind, sand and rain.

Months after returning home to Toronto, we had it with us on a visit to our jeweler regarding other matters, and to indulge my grandson's fantasy, I asked him to determine if it was worth anything of significant value. Much to our astonishment, he called back within a few days and very excitedly informed us that the small stones we suspected were just cut glass, were indeed eighteen hand cut desert diamonds dating back to about 1865! The diamonds surrounded a scruffy, worn out synthetic stone, which seemed extremely odd since the ring mantle itself was eighteen karat gold. Why would someone of apparent wealth at that time in history have a beautifully crafted ring to feature such a worthless centerpiece? It seemed so inconsistent.

My mind raced with thoughts of what stories this ring could tell throughout the history of its travels. I decided to learn more and upon further investigation, discovered that the small, private Mexican resort at which we found the ring was owned by a German family. Surprisingly, the entire management and staff spoke German fluently. I learned this resort promoted their hotel to European niche markets, and enticed visitors primarily in Germany and Switzerland to the Mexican Riviera with a reassurance that they would encounter no language barriers with the hotel staff.

I suddenly realized the possibility that this antique ring may have inadvertently slipped off the finger of an elderly German woman, perhaps of Jewish descent. Did her family have to sell the original precious stone to buy her or her family freedom to escape from Nazi Germany? It must have had tremendous sentimental value and the owner must have felt heartbroken to have lost it, quite likely because it was a reminder of precious events in her memory. Equally irretrievable, was the chronicling of the woman's memories.

Surely, it must have represented the joy and love passed on from one generation to the next, as well as the heartbreak and devastation that inevitably occurred. To celebrate the depth of history wrapped around this once beautiful ring, I had it refashioned to build up the frail shank and replaced the weathered synthetic centerpiece with a stunning blue sapphire. The diamond surround was kept in its original settings to more fittingly represent the endless circle of lives touched by the stunningly magnificent ring.

This amazing ring became the genesis of the Trilogy, Tracks of Our Tears. The timeline of the story thoughtfully describes the commissioning of the ring, and later, its presentation from Sigmund to his beloved wife Marissa. The imaginary story of joy and heartbreak that follows the ring ensues through successive generations up to the day Benjamin found it. Together, Ben and our family presented it to his grandmother, my loving wife Regina, shortly before her death in 2017.

It is with deep respect and thankfulness that I acknowledge the fortunate safe passage of the ring to my family, from another family we will never come to know. In so doing we will strive to enable the ring to continue touching the many lives of those who will surely follow.

My sincere thanks to my family and the many friends who patiently supported my efforts to research and recreate unique perspectives of historical events through which our ancestors prevailed; that we as their descendants, once read about in high school. May today's generation learn about those times before the personal stories of our parents and grandparents are forever forgotten.

To my son Stephen, who committed so much time editing the manuscript from the beautiful shorelines of Thailand, far from any shore his loving father could share; to the shining light in my life, my wonderful daughter Jennifer and her dedicated and loving husband Mark, for their unwavering loyalty and unconditional love and most of all, for giving me our three wonderful grandchildren Benjamin, Brandon and our little princess, Miss Gracie; to my dear daughter Kristen and her wonderful husband Liad; to Liz Morris, who is not just a dear family friend, but one who has truly become another daughter to me; to my lovely sweetheart, Edith, who steadfastly reinforces in me the confidence and thriving desire to stay the course before me, and causes me to strive every day to be a better person for having met her; to my dear friend Stephen Freedman for always keeping our friendship alive and becoming my confidant and publication advisor in the process; to the professional and supportive publication staff at Friesen Press, and especially to Diane Cameron, who was infinitely patient with me as I learned to be a first-time novelist, and for introducing me to Rhonda, my extraordinary editor who taught me more about writing a great story than I ever thought possible; and finally to Regina, who has been the love of my life since we first met, when we were just seventeen years old, and who was sadly taken from us after more than fifty wonderful years together. Without her silent inspiration guiding me day by day, the journey to tell this story would never have been taken.

On every page Regina guided my fingers across the keyboard as surely as if she were standing at my shoulder, nudging me on when I had little understanding or knowledge of exactly where I was heading. I am forever grateful to her.

About the Author

James was born in Toronto and graduated from York University in 1978. Over the next thirty years he was a successful Chartered Life Underwriter and financial advisor. Shortly after his beloved wife Regina passed away, after almost fifty years together, James retired to begin his career as a novelist. *From Promise to Peril* is the first of three books in a trilogy, in which he brings his amazing fictional characters to life by creatively weaving them throughout actual historical events. He now resides in Milton, Ontario close to his daughter and her husband and their three young children.

Source Notes

Diamond Mining in Namibia – Past and Present
All Diamond by Ehud Arye Laniado

History of Diamond Cutting
Erstwhilejewelry.com

The Industrial Revolution of Germany
Searchinginhistory.blogspot

Berlin 1914: A city of ambition and self-doubt
BBC News, Berlin by Stephen Evans January 8, 2014

The Paris Peace Conference and the Treaty of Versailles, U.S.
Department of State: Office of the Historian

Berlin in the 1914-1918 War
Arnulf Scriba

Capital Cities at War. Paris, London, Berlin 1914-1919,
J. Winter and J. L. Robert, Cambridge, 1997

Wilhelm 11, German Emperor
Wikipedia, the free encyclopedia

Otto von Bismarck Biography
History.com

Otto von Bismarck Family Tree
Geneanet.org

Humboldt Universität zu Berlin
Berlin University Alliance – Short History

Tiergarten Park 1900's Berlin
Wikipedia, the free encyclopedia

Jewellery Makers of the 1920's
Fahrner (Germany, 1855-1979)
Trufauxjewels.com

Pforzheim
Wikipedia, the free encyclopedia

Preeclampsia After Birth
Healthline Parenthood by Ann Pietrangelo, Feb.14, 2019

Neue Synagogue (Berlin)
Insiders Berlin.com

Anton Drexler
Wikipedia, the free encyclopedia

Communist Party of Germany
Britannica

Joseph Goebbels Biography
German Propagandist by Helmut Heiber

Germany in the 1920's: The shadowy figures that look out at us from
the tarnished mirror of history are – in the final analysis – ourselves.
Detlev J. K. Peukert

1920's Berlin
Wikipedia, the free encyclopedia

Sex and the Weimar Republic: German Homosexual Emancipation
Laurie Marhoefer - 2015

Gabrielle "Coco" Chanel (1883-1971) and the House of Chanel
Metmuseum.org Citation Jessa Krick

15 Things You Didn't Know about Coco Chanel
Mentalfloss.com

NeuroTribes: The Legacy of Autism and the Future of Neurodiversity
By Steve Silberman
Science Friday /Writer Adam Wernick September 20, 2015

Abdication of Wilhelm 11
Wikipedia, the free encyclopedia

Adolf Hitler; Dictator of Germany
John Lukacs Professor of history, Chestnut Hill College,
Philadelphia, Pennsylvania

Hermann Göring German minister
Heinrich Fraenkel, freelance writer.

My Jewish Learning 1933-1939
Early Stages of Persecution / How Hitler Laid the Groundwork
for Genocide

Germany Recalls Hitler's Rise to Power
The Irish Times/ Derek Scally

SS Leviathan
Wikipedia, the free encyclopedia

SS Bremen 1928
Wikipedia, the free encyclopedia

Calvin Coolidge Speech to American Doctors: Praising Medicine
and Venerating Reason
May 17, 2017 by Jared Rhoads

Henry Souttar and Surgery of Mitral Valve
Richard H. Ellis, London U.K.

The Impact of Nazi Racial Decrees on University of Heidelberg
by Arye Carmon Yadvashem.org

Tracks of Our Tears Trilogy I

Germany 1933: From Democracy to Dictatorship
Anne Frank House

Beer Hall Putsch (Munich Putsch)
Holocaust Encyclopedia

Rudolf Hess
Wikipedia, the free encyclopedia

Josef Goebbels
Wikipedia, the free encyclopedia

The Nazi Terror Begins
Holocaust Encyclopedia

'Hitler's Pawn' Review: Who was Herschel Grynszpan?
The Wall Street Journal, by Ian Brunskill (Feb. 8, 2019)

Nazi Germany and the Jews 1933-1939 Yad Vashem
The World Holocaust Remembrance Center

Walther von Brauchitsch
Jewish Virtual Library – A Project of AICE

Fast Times: The Life, Death, and Rebirth of Amphetamine
Science History Institute

Night of the Long Knives
Wikipedia, the free encyclopedia

Berlin Diary: The Journal of a Foreign Correspondent 1934-1941
By William L. Shirer

The History Place: World War 11 /1934 Timeline
Wikipedia, the free encyclopedia

Gordon Alles
Wikipedia, the free encyclopedia

Fast Times: The Life, Death, and Rebirth of Amphetamine
By Jesse Hicks April 14, 2012

Holocaust Trains
Wikipedia, the free encyclopedia

Oberkommando der Wehrmacht
Wikipedia, the free encyclopedia

Sachsenhausen Concentration Camp
Wikipedia, the free encyclopedia

Christian Wirth
Wikipedia, the free encyclopedia

1936 Summer Olympics
Wikipedia, the free encyclopedia

What Happened When Hitler Hosted the Olympics 80 Years Ago
By Emma Ockerman

The Nazi Olympics Berlin 1936
The Holocaust Encyclopedia

Berlin 1937, Berlin 1987
The New York Times
by Frederic V. Grunfeld May 10, 1987

The November Pogram
The New Republic, Adam Kirsch November 12, 2009.

Death & Mourning in Judaism
Chabad.org

1938 – "The Fateful Year" Yadvashem.org
Holocaust Survivors and Victims Database
Ushmm.org

Tracks of Our Tears Trilogy I

Twenty Key Quotes by Adolf Hitler About World War 2
Simon Parkin Historyhit.com

Abwehr – Espionage
Wikipedia, the free encyclopedia

Bribery of Senior Wehrmacht Officers
Wikipedia, the free encyclopedia

The Oster Conspiracy of 1938: The Unknown Story of the Military
Plot to Kill Hitler and Avert World War 11
By Terry Parssinen

1939: Key Dates
Holocaust Encyclopedia

Brandenburgers
Wikipedia, the free encyclopedia

Helmuth Groscurth
Wikipedia, the free encyclopedia

How Hitler Staged a False-Flag Operation to Justify the Invasion of
Poland, by Matt Fratus

Alfred Naujocks
Wikipedia, the free encyclopedia

20 July Plot
Military.wikia.org

Hitler's Inner Circle: The 10 Most Powerful Men in Nazi Germany
Historyhit, by Tina Gayle

Gleiwitz Incident
Wikipedia, the free encyclopedia

Countdown to WW2 August 22 – September 1, 1939
Tropagander.tripod.com

Bloody Sunday (1939)
Wikipedia, the free encyclopedia

The Berliner Philharmoniker in the National Socialist Era
The Reichsorchester by Misha Aster

The Era of Wilhelm Furtwängler
Berliner-Philharmoniker.de/en

International Mercantile Marine Company
Wikipedia, the free encyclopedia

J.P. Morgan & Co.
Wikipedia, the free encyclopedia

December 25, 1937: Arturo Toscanini's NBC Debut – Old Radio
www.oldradio.org

Manuel Rosenthal
Wikipedia, the free encyclopedia

Printed in Canada